STABS

RAW RECRUITS

by

PETE MC HOUGH

ISBN: 979-867-055-5012

First published in 2013 by PublishNation

www.publishnation.co.uk

This 2nd edition published in 2020

This is a work of fiction. Names and characters are the product of the author's imagination and any resemblance to actual persons, living or dead, is entirely incidental.

In memory of Tom and Zeb, two larger than life lads who died tragically young.

Originally written in 2003 as part of a trilogy, this is volume one of STABs.

I was involved in a Road Traffic Accident in 2009, and now due to my injuries have difficulty walking and using my hands. I am disabled. So in light of this I must express many thanks to my family and friends who spurred me on to edit and publish, and also my children & Grandchildren, who in between caring for me have re-typed it up.

Many thanks to Freddy Hall and Mark Gilmore for proofreading and feedback.

Introduction

When the Royal Air Force flight from Afghanistan touched down at RAF Brize Norton on July 26th 2010 there had been 16,000 incidents of Improvised Explosive Devices recorded. It took just one to finish the TA career of Thomas Tucker. CQMS Tucker was one of the funniest, life-affirming and professionally diligent men you could ever have had the privilege to meet. As I helped wheel my best friend's coffin off the tailgate and out onto the tarmacked runway, a summer breeze lifted the Union flag above where his head rested, and for a brief moment it looked as if Tucker had sat up for a peep at his own homecoming. There was no logic for him being in that wooden box, as the unit's Quartermaster Sergeant his role was in the rear with the gear and did not entail going out on patrols in the sandpit. Corporals customarily head a platoon but Tucker liked to get involved, especially since this was his last posting before retirement. When I last saw this bloke alive he was suppressing the enemy with covering fire while his platoon maneuvered out of immediate danger. He didn't go down without putting up a fight; it was probably the adrenaline that made him laugh as he chased his lads away to safety prior to the bomb blast.

Chapter 1

Thirty years earlier. The sky hung low and oppressive, the colour and shades of a badly bruised eye. Artificial light from blazing headlights in the railway car park pierced the gloom of the frost cold dawn, silhouetting the small ticket office building and railings bordering the shoe scuffed concrete platform. Monotonous metallic ding-ding-dinging disrupted the rural peace of the sleepy hamlet encompassing Liss railway station. Fervent activity exploded as the motionless first train down the line from London opened its doors and disgorged its baggage laden human cargo. Doors slammed shut noisily and the guard blew his whistle and waved his tiny flag. Released from the clamour of discarded travellers the metal slug whirred electrically and slipped unrestricted through the blinking red lights of the level crossing and disappeared mechanically into the gloom, wheels clinking over the gaps in the tracks, pting pting, pting pting, pting pting, pting pting, south bound to Portsmouth harbour. The alarm ceased. The electric barriers swished upright and silence returned. It was the briefest of intermissions. Having found some bearings the travellers surged like a herd of sheep and shuffled through the ticket collectors barrier into the carpark to board the waiting vehicles. Tucker managed to break free from amidst the scuffling of the jostling throng and athletically clamber up into the back of a rickety green truck, which was now mostly laden with suitcases and other personal kit loaded onto it. There hadn't been enough room on the fleet of ancient khaki coloured army buses parked up in the drop off zone for us all to sit in comfort, so six or seven others besides myself had drawn the short straw and were deftly directed to the truck which Tucker had already boarded of his own choice. He shrugged his shoulders at our dilemma and grinned as he reached down and gave me a hand up. No sooner was the tailgate slammed shut, the convoy of military vehicles awoke jarringly, surged forward and clattered across the tracks of the level crossing like guilt ridden marauders. The luggage barely remained upright as the truck changed gears and speeded forcefully away from the village, passing possibly the last pub we would see for the next fortnight, but before we had barely contemplated this anguished notion we were heading down narrow country roads as if driven by a vampire trying to stay one step ahead of the sunrise. The vehicles following us strained to keep up. Tucker checked his watch again; I checked mine, 7:20 am. With every minute that passed we felt relief at getting away from the traffic congested streets of northern England, and the stark ugliness of the oil terminals and miasmal stench of chemical industry festooning the Mersey estuary.

'What's the rush?' Tucker protested peevishly as the crazy chauffeur flung the truck precariously through a series of bends which skirted the fringes of frost rutted fields. 'This can't be a proper Royal Corps of Transport driver?'

'No mate, it'll be an undesignated one. Saturday morning, he's probably been press-ganged into doing it!' answered a fellow traveller who splayed his legs awkwardly across three bulky suitcases, his knees tightly clenched in order to stabilise himself. 'He doesn't give a shit does he?'

Negotiating the meandering course which now cut through a lush pine forest, the driver threw the vehicle from side to side causing everything on the back of the truck to sway precariously with the threat of toppling over completely. For some stability I nestled my back against the truck's headboard. Tucker clung tightly to the cold metal framework supporting the coarse canvass roof in order to keep *his* balance. The truck stopped throwing us about as it eventually hit a straight bit of road and zoomed up to full speed, causing the icy slipstream to roar in through gaps in the canvas sides to bite my ears and sting Tucker's numb fingers. Whilst clinging on for dear life Tucker studied the features of the vehicle intently; it was a formidable aging army truck, the same model as seen in old newsreel films. Noticing his bemusement, one of the other lads, oddly dressed in a long black leather coat and Joe 90 spectacles, yelled over the noise of the engine in an unmistakeable Birmingham accent. 'It's a Bedford RL 3 tonner is this!'

The T.A. were known as the TA&VR in the nineteen seventies, and this class of HGV was standard issue kit to the Territorial Army & Volunteer Reserve during that period. Such vehicles are rarely seen nowadays unless the fire brigade goes on strike and the Home-office has to pull the famous Green Goddesses out of mothballs. The cab had the same rounded front and split windscreen, and was fitted with a petrol engine which I considered unusual for an all terrain vehicle of such size, for it seemed to lack horsepower. What it lacked in horsepower it certainly made up for in noise. It was fast beginning to dawn on us that the traditions, values and importance bestowed upon the TA were principally neglected during the 1970s and as a consequence the TA seemed to be surviving on hand me downs and second hand equipment – nothing new to Tucker of course; with being the youngest nonidentical twin of five brothers and an older sister he had survived on hand-me-downs for most of his childhood - not his sister's of course!

'No doubt during the next two weeks we'll get real familiar with this piece of crap?' Tucker consoled himself and anyone else who could hear him above the din of the engine and icy wind billowing the canvas covering. I couldn't discern the make of the other vehicles which closely followed ours but suspected that my father during national service, and my grandfather during WW2 had undoubtedly been ferried around in the very same modes of transport. We began to think that we'd gone through some sort of time warp when arriving at Martinique Barracks. Tucker just about managed to keep his balance as the small convoy of Dad's Army vehicles squealed to a halt outside an old-fashioned wooden guard room complete with regulation red and white striped barrier pole that barred the way. At the side of the barrier a metal "A" board informed visitors that the vicinity was at "Security State - Bikini Black Alpha!" whatever that meant?

A smartly dressed soldier, armed with a rifle, approached the drivers cab door. He tapped dictatorially on the window indicating that he wanted to check the driver's identification. Another two efficient soldiers walked amongst the vehicles, probing underneath with mirrors attached to long shafts at an angle, searching for explosive devices. Eventually the barber's pole was swung up out of the way by another competent squaddie dressed in combats with a rifle slung over his shoulder. He waved the convoy of vehicles through hastily, and once admitted, the gates were secured and once again manned by the armed guard. Our procession approached a large frost covered Parade square and veered left, avoiding a line of large blocks of gleaming whitewashed stones spaced three feet apart bordering the square. To one side of the square a wild and scary mature Monkey puzzle tree towered above the camp. The evergreen looked Jurassic; it was the first of this species I had ever seen! The trunk was five feet in diameter, if not prehistoric it was certainly a hundred odd years old so the camp may very well have been built around it. More wooden huts were tightly huddled together on the left and far end of this giant tetragonal spread of Tarmac; they each had solid green wooden doors interleaved at the gable ends. The ancient wooden Nissan huts looked tired and worn-out beyond repair, and as if to offset the ravages of weather the decrepit wooden cladding had been treated with uninspiring burnt brown creosote particular to military installations the whole world over. Such a vast amount of wood and inevitable flammable creosote fumes obviously posed an immense fire hazard, and unreassuringly to my mind at least, a solitary red fire bucket filled with sand and sundry discarded dog-ends had been plonked outside the doorway of each building.

The aerial view of these austere structures resembled the shape of a letter H with three legs jutting off to the left and right. The centre span had pipes protruding from the panelling and consisted of showers and ablutions; bog standard nothing fancy. The legs on either side were no doubt dormitories, just as clinical and bleak! All the accommodation huts on this base were laid out in identical formation. They were simply referred to as “The spiders”.

I clocked Tucker surveying our surroundings comparable to a potential property developer, the look on his face said it all, I conferred with a Gallic shrug of my shoulders, joining the T.A. was beginning to look like a major mistake. The exoticness that the name Martinique had conjured up in our minds was a million miles away from the reality, not at all what we had anticipated on the way down to London in the luxury of a British Rail Inter-City 125 Pullman express; we’d bunked into First Class as soon as the ticket guard had knocked off, as you do! The old Cheshire town of Runcorn we had left behind had imprudently sold its soul to the devil on a promise of improved housing and assured employment, but the grip of recession had guaranteed an explosion of dreariness for our community. Compared to Martinique barracks though, Runcorn was a veritable Shangri-La!

‘Fucking hell mate, it’s like a prison camp,’ grimaced a bloke with spiky hair and bloodshot eyes sat next to Tucker. Spiky-head had obviously not slept well on the train down from Carlisle; he looked as if he was suffering from conjunctivitis. He hacked a cough, producing a slimy green glob of phlegm which he hoiked up and spat out of the back of the truck. ‘Is that barbed wire meant to keep people out or stop us escaping?’

On the approach to the barracks the road had been lined with small red berried Rowan trees to ward off evil, but sure enough once inside the perimeter this rudimental defence was augmented by sturdy razor wire and an armed guard to ward off terrorism. What with the sub zero temperature, galvanised barbed wire, plus an armed guard at the gate, me, Tucker and our snotty spiky-headed chum from Carlisle could have been forgiven for thinking we’d been taken into custody at a Russian Gulag. The reality was distressing. Security across the UK had been heightened due to the December bombing campaign carried out by the IRA in Southampton and Bristol. On the 17th January 1979 a gasholder in Greenwich along with an oil depot on Canvey Island had been targeted; and as if Coventry had not been bombed enough during the Second World War, the IRA hit that city too. Tucker and I were more than aware of the Irish Republican Army and its bombing campaign on the British mainland, the IRA seemed to dominate the news throughout the 70's. It all started with the Kilburn Battalion of the IRA detonating a bomb in the London Post Office Tower on October 31st 1971, luckily no one was injured. But on February the 22nd 1973 the IRA killed seven civilians in the Aldershot bombing. In that same year a car bomb exploded outside the Old Bailey in London and on September the 10th the IRA detonated bombs at Kings Cross Station and Euston Station in London, injuring twenty one people. In 1974 Terrorism really took off and military personnel became the target; eight soldiers and four civilians were killed by a bomb on a coach driving along the M62; the Houses of Parliament were targeted injuring eleven people; the Guilford pub bombing killed four off-duty soldiers and a civilian and injured forty four others; an IRA bomb exploded in London injuring 3 people; the Birmingham pub bombings killed twenty one and injured one hundred and eighty two other people; and in one of Bristol's most popular shopping districts, during the run up to Christmas, an IRA bomb exploded injuring seventeen people.

The reek of burning brake shoes fouled the air as the truck we were on squealed to a halt outside a very unusual building at the far end of the Drill Square. Like the others, it too was made of creosoted wood, but there the resemblance faded. If I had to describe this architectural oddity I would have struggled, I still do, it was single story with a sort of balcony at the front with white rails outlined on each side. Tucker commented that it looked like one of those old shacks you see in Hollywood films about the Mississippi in the Deep South of the USA. To me it almost resembled a cricket pavilion of sorts while rather bizarrely managing to look warlike. Its window frames and doors were painted armed forces red, and the steps to the veranda were worn from utilization. A prominent plaque hung from the door frame displaying a motif of a Lion and crossed swords above a golden crown, announcing in bold lettering underneath that this construction was the Military Training Wing. The surreal picture we were building in our mind promptly disappeared when a tough looking Sergeant

Major type exploded out of the front doors and leaped onto the porch; he was sporting a shiny peaked hat, a neatly pressed green jumper, razor sharp creased trousers and shiny black boots. The larger than life Alpha-Male stared at the passengers of the vehicles harshly. The glossy peak of his cap came down flush with his nose, under which a military moustache bristled like a road sweepers brush.

'What are you horrible lot gawping at?' He screeched and marched noisily across the wooden stage before jumping athletically to the tar macadam road. He continued to bawl his head off at a hundred decibels while charging menacingly over to the vehicles. 'Get your miserable arses down here now in front of me, you aint got all bleedin' day, do you hear me, double up you shagging donkeys, move it, move it.'

As the mass of bodies bailed out of the vehicles he never stopped for breath; he was the epitome of a training instructor. 'I can see that I'm going to have my work cut out with you lot. One line in front of me, go.'

We shuffled into an extended line. 'Right let's have a look at ya. Bloody Nora, they've sent us a right selection of mongs this time. Where did they round you lot up from?'

We didn't have time to feel affronted at his callousness.

'Leave that bleeding bag alone,' he screamed into the face of a struggling skinny bloke by my side. 'Did I tell you to bring your handbag? No! So why did you bring it?'

'What the fuck are you looking at?' He bellowed at me, poking a shiny wooden stick with a polished brass tip into my face. I was completely taken off guard at this supersonic encroachment on my space; my heart skipped a few beats and then speeded up, I didn't know what to say so I took a deep breath to control my nerves and muttered, 'Fucking hell that's shiny.'

Tucker was standing next to me grinning. The instructor noticed this and laid the stick on Tucker's chest, then went ballistic. 'What are you smiling at numb nuts?

'Nothing Sir.' replied Tucker. His hands had instinctively clenched into fists, but as he relaxed and uncoiled his fingers he must have realised that he *was* actually smiling. 'It's nerves Sir. I'm just happy to be here.'

Like a little schoolgirl the instructor mocked him, 'Sir… Sir, nothing sir, just happy to be here sir.' Then growled, 'You must be fucking retarded, do you know much about the Army?'

'A little bit captain,' assured Tucker.

The instructor exploded once more, right in Tucker's face, enabling Tucker to smell the shouty mans Typhoo-tea reeking breath. 'Do you see those two stripes lovingly stitched to my shagging arm mister?'

The angry man stepped back smartly, smashed his shiny black boots into the ground and shoved his right arm in front of Tucker's face. Large as life, there were two neat chevrons firmly stitched onto it.

'Sorry Corporal, how the frigging hell I missed them I'll never know!' mused Tucker aloud. 'I thought you were a Sergeant Major or something?'

'Shut up!' bawled the corporal, snarling and gnashing his teeth. 'Sergeant Major, hey, you're taking the piss now you maggot?'

'Sorry corporal,' apologised Tucker, sheepishly.

'You will be you scrote bag, face the front!' The NCO's eyes narrowed and the swollen veins at his temples throbbed. 'I'll tell you this for nothing, when you do meet the Sergeant Major you'll know about it Mister! You will positively shit yourself, cos he's an animal, what is he?'

'An animal Corporal!' lamely replied Tucker.

'I can't hear you ya miserable faffing fairy!'

I was willing Tucker to say. 'An arsehole corporal!'

Tucker's powers of telepathy failed him, instead he found himself shouting out more assertively. 'An animal corporal.'

'That's correct, and just you remember *that* over the next few weeks you bag of scum,' the screaming skull curled his lip up and cursed. 'I'm watching you bollocks!'

'Bleeding hell knob-head give us a rest and go pick on somebody else', I sighed to myself. The corporal must have been clairvoyant because the next second he'd gone in a flash. Five paces down from Tucker, he started ripping into a scruffy chubby bloke who was dressed in a brown leather bomber jacket and faded flared jeans. Tucker unclenched his fists fully, splayed his fingers wide and relaxed, we both felt like we'd been let off the hook for now. I felt like laughing at this load of old bullshit but managed to restrain myself, Tucker winked.

'What's your excuse?' The corporal enquired of the scruffy chubby bloke.

'Excuse for what, Corporal?' the scruffy chubby bloke gulped away nervously.

'Shut up you cheeky man, I ask the questions around here.'

'Sorry?'

'You will be,' he was really laying on his authority. 'What's your name?'

'Todd, corporal.'

'You sure about that, you look more like a Humpty fucking Dumpty to me. Go on, get down and give me ten press ups now!'

He then turned on some other unfortunate and sneered. 'What you looking at fuck features? Do you wanna join'im? No? I didn't think so, face the front!'

Once the chubby lad had completed his press-ups, the corporal started to calm down a bit. You could see that he wasn't used to being this nasty first thing in the morning; it was taking a strain on him.

'Come on you, on your feet and get fell in. I don't want you going sleep down there. Right, my name's Corporal Bastard, because I am one, got it, but you ladies can call me Corporal Hazel, it's got a more affectionate tone to it, hasn't it?' he paused menacingly. 'Mess with me and I think you'll all agree your feet won't touch the fucking ground. Now listen in all of you, I'm not in the habit of repeating myself, so when I say go, I want you all to change places with one another, tallest on your right and shortest on your left. Go!'

A hundred odd lads shuffled around in confusion. 'Come on ladies, this isn't bleedin rocket science, move it. That man there,' he pointed his shiny stick at the spiky-haired bloke with bloodshot eyes who'd sat next to us on the back of the truck. 'Yes you bollox, stop faffing around and swap places with him, that's right, are you getting the hang of it now? Right ladies, settle down!'

He lurched forward and gently rested the brass tip of his shiny baton on the chest of a ginger headed lad dressed in a black Harrington bomber jacket, blue & white checked Ben Sherman shirt, turned up jeans and shiny red Doc-Martin boots. 'Fuck me I seem to have a piece of snot on the end of my stick.'

The lad was a cockney and confidently answered back with a chuckle. 'Well it aint on this bleeding end china!'

'You hard faced little bastard, press up position now and give me twenty!' ranted the NCO. When the London lad had finished activating his arms and had gotten back up, the corporal continued bawling in his ear. 'Listen in when I tell you to and none of your fucking wide boy lip got it!'

The Cockney lad acquiesced and the corporal flexed his chin. 'Right Gentlemen, now we're getting somewhere. When I say turn to the right, you turn to the right, got it? By the way, does anyone not know his left from his flaming right?'

Silence, it seemed a rudimentary question unworthy of response. 'Good. Turn to the right, that's fucking awesome gentlemen, keep it up!'

Utilising an evil glare Cpl Hazel wordlessly corrected two lads who had turned to the left, then he about turned and strode off with his pace-stick hoisted in the air like a London Tour Guide. 'Follow me!'

He marched to the side of the square as if he had a scaffolding pole wedged up his backside, whereupon he came to a halt and the ninety foot long conga-snake of raw recruits following him instinctively stopped in its track. He spun around smartly, and then called the queue forward one at a time and marshalled each man into three ranks, pointing with his shiny stick, praising or admonishing. 'One two three, one two three, one two three. Get a move on lad or I'll stick my dick in your ear and make you look like a petrol pump. That's it, well done, keep still!'

He picked up the pace and in no time at all, all the new arrivals had formed up in three ranks and the military process begun. 'Parade,' he screeched. His voice reverted back to a growl. 'As you were, stand still. Parade, come on brace up when you hear that word, head up, stomach in, chest out, shoulders back with the body erect and square to the front.'

The NCO screeched once again 'Parade, that's more like it. Parade shun! Standat ease.'

Like a host of holy statues arranged across a carpet of glittering frost, the new recruits struggled to stand motionless in the dull morning sunshine. A perceptible raw Siberian breeze blew across the open Hampshire heath-land, rustling the spiky branches of the Monkey puzzle tree and causing the congregation to shiver involuntarily. The cold numbness ate away at fingers and toes, and every single man clenched his teeth determinedly. A Botticelli halo of candyfloss breath momentarily formed an arctic circle suspended at head height, before fleeing unrestricted on the breeze like a sprite. Cold and hungry, our minds started to wander. I looked around me inquisitively. Tucker was in the same rank as me, fidgeting by my side, struggling to keep still. Saturday normally broke the curse of the humdrum for him; its liberation began with a bit of a lie-in before traipsing up to the pub at dinner time to meet up with pals for a few shandies. It was a lazy day normally, I usually met up with him later on. Saturday night was Saturday night, enough said; more often than not it typically finished with him getting his girlfriend to drop her knickers for a quick knee-trembler down a dark alley before kissing her goodnight on her doorstep, provided he'd managed to avoid a fight with some knuckle head down at the pub that is. With a romantic box of chocolates, proper bonking was reserved for when parents were absent and their double bed vacated!

As Tucker turned his head in my direction I clocked the look on his face. I knew him so well and could see he fleetingly wished he was back at home snuggled up to his Sarah in a warm double bed under a soft thick quilt. But I also knew that he was struggling to console himself that *that* was the boring alternative. Runcorn was in sad decline and Tucker was bored with the place; genuinely mind boggling bored, bored silly like a gutsy spider trying to scuttle out of a bath tub inevitably slipping back towards the plug hole frustrated and more determined. I had a different temperament, I was laid back and never let things bother me one way or the other, but Tucker knew in his belly that it wouldn't be like that for him forever, he hated any delay.

That's how it was back in the 1970's, the nation was in procrastination; Great Britain seemed to be going through some sort of menopause and Tucker was not going to let that drag him down; staying one step ahead of the game was all part of his simple creed. It was the age of mass strikes, redundancies and Giro's, when if you wanted a personal loan you had to make an appointment to see your bank manager, then attend an interview, dressed in your best suit and shiniest shoes, with your hair neatly parted and a jolly good reason why you should be granted a loan in the first place and proof that you could afford to pay it all back with interest because money was tight. Occasionally due to the dreaded Power-cuts, families had to sit around reluctantly twiddling their thumbs in the dark with only candles for light - tremendous fun if you lived in Norfolk, or so we and some of our scallywag mates had mused over a frothy beer while trying to locate a worn out dartboard in the candlelit duskiness of the Grapes public house! It was not all doom and gloom though; in reality it was a period when Great Britain was on the cusp of change, and Tucker like so many others was more than ready for some of that; he was brimming with optimism. Mobile phones, personal computers and satellite TV had not yet stamped their indelible mark on everyday living, and senior citizens by and large were still respected for putting their life on the line during two world wars to shield the British nation from a lifetime of tyranny under a potential Nazi occupation. Industrial strength lager had not yet been invented either, so generally most kids were off the street and in bed by nine o'clock, and once news at ten had finished most responsible parents would put the cat out for the night along with the empty milk bottles, lock up and turn in themselves; anyone walking the streets after mid-night were generally up to no good!

It was about this time that Elvis Presley kicked the bucket and Punk Rock exploded onto the scene, heralding yet another dawn of anarchy against the mighty establishment. Tucker was as pissed off as any other young man who'd tolerated the boom-shangalanging of the Bay City Rollers or had passed up the chance of staying alive with the Heebegebees, or fortuitously declined the offer of joining Gary Glitter's dodgy gang. He was too mature to get involved in this new punk craze though, he thought that Punk was for nutters. It didn't appeal to him, he didn't understand the irony and anyway there was too much spitting and jostling, and like most fads akin to Skinheads and Teddy Boys it would soon pass, or so it seemed to him, a prisoner of empty time. His dad believed in the heuristic approach to life and had given youngest son Tucker a very long lead with little counselling, hoping that one way or another he would discover things for himself and eventually be his own man. Whenever I messed up though I got a clout around the head with a dictionary to knock some sense into me and was then made me read from it for an hour. During these periods of penance my mind was filled with all sorts of trivia to benefit me in later life. Grandparents had a wealth of knowledge to pass on down the generations in the good old bad old days, amongst much supplementary advice grandfathers conveyed such wisdom as marry in haste and repent at leisure. Being a little head strong Tucker had been sagely warned that he should never make a decision when he was upset or drunk and so far he had diligently heeded that perceptive guidance! Even so he frequently sensed that he was swimming against a tide of sad disillusionment and the one thing he was certain of as he splashed his way through disappointments was that there were no longer any guarantees in life, just opportunities. With few viable alternatives he reached out and clutched at the horns of life when serendipity did eventually throw him a lifebuoy. A foreman at work had mentioned that the Territorial Army was recruiting, and to shake off its Dad's army image the TA had begun to implement a much needed revamp. Tucker decided to give it a good kick in the Jacobs to see where it would take him. Being as close as we two lads were at that time I got dragged along too, it was like enlisting into one of Lord Kitchener's First World War Pals-Battalions. On attending that initial interview with a retired infantry Colonel up at the British Legion in Halton village, the officer had been taken with Tucker's optimism and managed to convince us both that we were about to change our existence forever, we were typical recruit material and ticked all the boxes necessary to instigate the TA's modification. We were seductively assured that as uncorrupted mature twenty one year olds eager for challenges and hungry for adventure the TA would satisfy our Cre-de-Coeur. So that was that then, adventure time, it would be like bunking off school for a short period, Tucker naively imagined, I was more pessimistic but didn't want to burst his bubble. Tucker had confidently packed a bag, put on a suit and dragged me down south with him to have a crack at being a part time British soldier; after all, what could we possibly have to lose? He'd wanted something different and here it was, just like the rest of us in that freezing hell hole, he would have to be pragmatic about his new circumstance and not let a massive dose of reality piss him off.

The corporal slinked past us and his tone of voice became affectionate. 'You lovely, lovely Bar-Stewards, I can see that you're going to take to this very, very quickly. I'm immensely impressed gentlemen; some of you have done this before haven't you? Right seeing how you're enjoying yourselves and it's all still fresh in your tiny little minds, we'll crack on and do some more shall we? The temperature today is minus six degrees, taking into account the wind-chill factor of course, so I'm gonna do you all a ginormous favour and get ya nice and warmed up. Say thank you Corporal!'

'Thank you Corporal!'

Tucker, me and our new companions practiced coming to attention and standing at ease for five minutes and then the corporal marched us around the square for fifteen minutes more shouting "Left wheel" at the corners before marching us back towards the strange looking timber shack where we'd had our first encounter with this nightmare of a man.

'Halt! Turn to the right in threes, right turn. Stand at ease stand easy.'

He strolled back and forth through the ranks clocking our faces. 'What's your name?'

'Whittling sir,' responded a shy lad.

'Whittlingsir, what sort of a name is that, are you royalty or something?' Tucker and a few others sniggered at the NCO's humour. The NCO leaned forward and stared into the shy lads face. 'Are you breaking those teeth in for someone?'

Whittling shook his head uncertainly.

The NCO mellowed. 'All right gentleman relax, what's going to happen now is, we're going to do a roll call so as to establish who has turned up and who has ducked out?'

The NCO heaved himself up onto the stout veranda, stepped back a few paces and picked up a clipboard. His boots bashed the wooden stage, clunking rhythmically on the planking like a big bass drum. The pantomime giant paced back and forth across the veranda calling out a list of names to this beat. 'Adams?'

'Sir!'

'Baxter?'

'Sir!'

'Benson?' No reply.

'Benson? Do we have a Benson? Come on squeak up. Oh dear his Budgerigar must have had a fit or his Granny's been involved in a serious knitting accident. Sod him, he won't be missed!' The NCO crossed off the name from his list with a red Biro pen.

'Boiler?' No reply, 'Boiler, what's up with you lot, got cloth ears?'

'It's Boileiu Corporal!' corrected a tidy looking lad with a black Zapata moustache and a two piece Worsted wool suit worn over an open neck purple penny round collar shirt. He looked like an extra from the film *Saturday night fever*!

'Whatever! Carlisle?'

'Sir!'

'Are you wearing an ear ring Carlisle? Get rid of it before I rip it from your head.'

'Sir.'

'Only girls wear jewellery. Right, where am I, Churchill?'

'Sir!'

'Corbett? Is your nickname "Sooty" by any chance? No? Well it is now! Sooty Corbett? Well answer your bleeding name sunshine.'

'Sir.'

'Cruikshank? Dawson? Dumbervand? Emerson?' he rattled names off like a machine gun.

'Sir.' Sir.' Sir…' the roll call was interspersed with replies as he hastily turned the pages on his clip board.

'Jennings?

'Sir.'

The NCO stared incredulously, then leapt from the veranda and strolled up to Jennings. 'Good god, what have we got here then?'

Jennings wore a three quarter length black leather overcoat and National Health spectacles which magnified his eyes so much that they took on the appearance of bloated fish floating around in small bowls. 'I think you've come to join the wrong bunch mate, this is the T A not the national bloody front, you look like Gestapo officer material!'

Jennings looked demeaned but said nothing in response. The corporal continued the roll call from a stationary position like a town crier. 'Jones A? Jones P?'

The two answered in unison, 'Yes Corporal!'

'Right, from now until the day you die, which is currently being arranged, Jones A will be known as Jones one, and Jones P will be known as Jones two. Have you got that you Jones's?'

The two responded in unison, 'Yes Corporal!'

'Right, face the front. The rest of you will be given your numbers later!'

The corporal returned to the veranda to continue the roll call. 'Kelly? MacAndrews? Manson? Murray? Nansen? Come on wake up! Saunders? Seddon? Smith, is that one "F" or two "Fs" Smudge? I can never work that one out!'

'Not sure corporal?'

'Humpty fucking Dumpty? Come on Todd, answer your name!'

'Sir.'

He carried on, in due course reaching, 'Yarwood?'

'Sir.'

The NCO dropped from the veranda like a jungle cat and moved powerfully along the formation, then as if remembering something, marched stiffly back to the veranda like a Cold-stream-guard and casually dropped the clipboard through an open window.

'Listen in! This is the itinerary this morning. At ten thirty hours you will report for admin, followed by a trip to the stores at eleven hundred hours where you will be issued with all your lovely, lovely kit,' he paused for effect. 'Dinner is at twelve hundred hours and at thirteen hundred hours you will meet up back here dressed in combats, whereupon the barber will gladly issue you with a decent hair cut at the knock down bargain price of fifty pence each.'

The NCO concluded by tugging his sharply creased green jumper down through his Stable belt teasing it taught, then tweaking the peak of his cap further down his nose before stepping across the veranda to the door of the shack, knocking politely and poking his head through. 'They're ready and waiting sir!'

Eventually a stocky Regimental-Sergeant-Major appeared on the veranda of the wooden shack, he was followed by a bunch of highly polished NCOs clutching shiny Pace-sticks under their left arms, undoubtedly his squad. The Corporal, who had greeted the new arrivals looked less significant in comparison to these big guns; right mean bastards the lot of them. There was a whiff of starch as they filed down the steps in procession, approaching the recruits and eyeing them up and down like birds of prey locked onto vulnerable quarry.

The leader of the pack cleared his throat and addressed the gathering in a voice that could crumble granite. 'Right gentlemen, without further ado, let me introduce myself. I am RSM Daniels and this is my team from the Military-Training-Wing. They will assist me in the formidable task of turning you men from mere civilians into fighting fit soldiers.' He paused while his vultures gave their victims the once over, vetting for undesirables.

John Daniels' uniform was pristine and its creases razor sharp, a silver French Foreign Legion parachute medallion proudly gleamed on his left breast pocket like a sheriff's badge. He wore it like a badge of office. He had escaped the monotonous ugliness of Industrial Birmingham, and over the course of time had even lost the midlands twang that initially held him back from promotion; he had overcome a great many other things in his life too, including seven tours of northern Ireland and an acrimonious divorce. 'We have just two weeks in which to carry out this task and we rely on you to give us one hundred per cent in effort, we will manage the rest. We will teach you all you need to know. How to dress, how to march, and how to correctly wipe your arse. When you have convinced us that you have competently mastered these basic requirements of soldiering, we will then turn you into ruthless killing machines and more importantly, teach you how to avoid being killed yourselves.'

The weightless ease in which the RSM moved his body conveyed a lot about his station in life, *he* was the man in charge and no one should dare defy him. He came across as intuitive, instinctive and aggressive. His frame filled the space in front of the assembly like a superstar on stage, his body solid from years of military training and his eyes brimming with discipline. I sensed that this man had no time for tossers, and as if to emphasise that observation, the RSM concurred. 'You don't need the brains of an Archbishop to successfully complete this course, just commitment, bags of the stuff. Anyone caught not pulling their weight will answer to me personally. If you are unfortunate enough to land in my in-tray I don't have a shed full of options, I will bin you for wasting my staff's valuable time. Let's not beat about the bush, if any of you want to leave, go now, we cannot afford to carry time wasters. I'm not out to fail you, only you can do that, so gentlemen I repeat, if you can't keep up with us, it's Foxtrot Romeo Oscar, Fuck Right Off!'

It appeared to me and Tucker that the Warrant Officer had glared at us personally for added emphasis, but in fact all the recruits experienced the same phenomenon, such was the breadth of the RSM's glare. At this point Tucker, me and a few of the others began to feel hesitant and had to question ourselves - before becoming too institutionalised, were we really up to this unfamiliar ordeal? What had Tucker dragged me into? I flippantly dismissed the thought and sighed. 'Sod it I'm here now aren't I?'

'The Commanding Officer will arrive shortly to address you, and when he speaks to you, you *will* show him courtesy.' The RSM's bone crunching voice rose by an octave at this juncture. 'And if I find anyone being discourteous to the commanding officer, I will personally cut their balls off and use them for maracas' got it!'

Fleetingly his minions turned their heads towards him in a gesture of support, then back to the recruits, implying that they would collectively hold down any miscreant while the RSM tore off the genitals.

'Now I believe that Corporal Hazel has already taught you how to come to attention and stand at ease. Right, let's have a quick recap before Major Einstein arrives.'

'Listen in,' his eyes challenged anyone to disregard him. 'Parade. Parade shun.'

Thud responded 119 raw recruits stomping to attention. 'That's impressive Corporal Hazel! Stannat hees.' There followed another thud, then silence, not a word.

A raven cawed fore-warningly from its perch upon the nearby Monkey puzzle tree. Five eerie craws from the death bird echoed thickly across the stillness of the camp, stirring a recollection of a poem by William Canton which I had once heard Mr Starkey reading aloud at St Edwards school during History, or was it during English-Lit: "With rakish eye and plenished crop, oblivious of the farmer's gun, upon the naked ash-tree top, the crow sits basking in the sun!".

But there was no basking sun on that freezing day in Hampshire. The egg-yolk star offered up no thermal energy as it hung low in the sapphire sky. I desperately wanted to reach out and bang it on the top to give it a kick start. The bleak wooden buildings skulking in its paltry light, cast short grey shadows barely reaching the edge of the frosty drill square. Was it sheer coincidence that the RSM seemed as merciless as the meagre weather? 'Stand still in the ranks!'

Eventually a lovingly restored two tone Silver & Green 3 litre Rover Coupe drove around the corner. It pulled up short of the Mil-Trg-Wing shack and out stepped a shiny shoed officer of the rank Major, closely followed by a slobbering hound. The tall and gangly officer walked lithely towards the RSM expelling short trails of moist warm breath from his nostrils; the stout mutt sniffed at the air as it padded loyally in his footsteps - the dog was some sort of Mastiff.

The RSM, being the most senior soldier on parade, stiffly saluted the mousy haired clipped moustached officer, and the officer reciprocated as if casually waving to an acquaintance. They briefly chatted in an informal Saturday morning sort of way as the RSM stooped and patted the dog's head affectionately. Very cosy, I thought!

The RSM braced up, excused himself, saluted, and then took a few smart steps forward to menace the recruits. 'Listen in! Paarrayyde shunn.'

Undisciplined as we yet were, me, Tucker and our new cohorts re-enacted our only practiced manoeuvre.

'Pin your ears back; Major Einstein will now address you!' Then turning to his mate, the RSM stiffly saluted. 'You have the parade sir!'

A cockney voice in the ranks muttered. 'Fucking pantomime this is!'

I smiled. Tucker nodded agreement. The RSM glared.

‘Thank you Sergeant Major,’ the officer, insentient to the remark, responded in a church-side Edinburgh accent. Having a Penicuick High-School diploma and a Heriot-Watt university degree in his back pocket, the Major had climbed the greasy pole rapidly from the rank of Second Lieutenant, and though destined for the rank of Colonel, had momentarily hit a glass ceiling. Consequently he wasn’t senior enough to appear pompous, so came across as a bit of a lad who seemed to know his onions.

‘I must congratulate you on arriving safely,’ he announced in a stentorian voice as if he had all the time in the world at his disposal. His face was reminiscent of a Gaelic clan chieftain; hard intelligent blue eyes blazed earnestly either side of a pointy nose which separated the Celtic creases nestling between brow and cheekbone. ‘This wintry weather has not enabled easy travelling for you I know, and the long-range forecast predicts a fluttering of snow. Still, that should sort out the men from the boys, don’t you agree?’

The instructors’ nodded agreement, none of the recruits did.

‘Training will proceed as normal throughout the next two weeks, so I want you to be alert at all times.’ He paused and casually looked around the assembly, noting our neophyte faces for future reference.

‘Now that you’re here I am optimistic that you’ll all enjoy yourselves. Look upon it, if you will, as an adventure, and please endeavour to have some fun.’

He would not have been out of place wearing a Billy Butlin’s Red-Coat, delivering a line like that, and though his sincerity was doubtful, his humour was warm! He gestured to his fidgeting dog to sit at his heel. ‘Do not lose your sense of humour gentlemen; it may be the only thing that can win you through the next two weeks. Now I gather that you come from all walks of life and various occupations no doubt. You should make some interesting and excellent friends whilst here at Martinique barracks, so please, don’t be afraid to mingle.’

Like a married couple conferring, the Major and RSM briefly exchanged glances. ‘During your second week, towards the end of your training, you will go on exercise. This exercise is seen as the culminating point of your training programme, whereby you as soldiers can affirm the knowledge and skills which we are about to impart. It offers the ideal opportunity to show qualities of leadership, team spirit, resolve and a competitive attitude; all essential ingredients to an efficient, effective fighting unit in today’s Territorial Army. Just bear that in mind during week one of your training and give us bags of effort,’ he punched the empty air in front of him with his brown leather gloved fist. 'And to make life more interesting we have organised a competition. You will each be given points for your turn out and amass further points as a platoon for tasks well done. The winners are to be awarded the coveted Platoon Trophy at the end of the course.' He paused very casually for his words to be digested.

'I'm in charge of your welfare throughout the next two weeks and should you experience any problems, any at all, please report them to a member of staff…' he glanced sideways in the direction of his intimidating team and collectively they over-sincerely nodded back. '…and they will redirect such matters to me.'

The training Major lifted his gaze to the melancholy cerulean sky and concluded his fustian chitchat. 'Remember, he who hesitates is last. I cannot do much about the great British weather I'm afraid, but everything else is within my remit. Anything I may have forgotten, which you feel important, please do not hesitate. That will be all, carry on Sergeant Major!'

'Paarrayyde,' bawled the RSM. 'Parade shunn.'

The Major and his dog ambled back to the warmth of the car, leaving his henchman in charge to direct the parade. 'Stand at ease, stand easy.'

The two-tone 3 litre Rover coupe droned off towards the guardhouse, past the Monkey puzzle tree, leaving plumes of white exhaust vapour swirling dejected in the freezing air. The armed-guard on the gate saluted ceremoniously as the car purred past the erect red and white stripy barrier pole to mooch out of the camp to the real world beyond the barbed wire fence. The barrier was lowered securely, hemming in the raw recruits like disregarded POWs.

'Listen in!' bawled the RSM, dragging all the recruits back to harsh reality. 'Parade. Come on, brace up, parade shun. That's better! Parrraaade stanna hees. Stand easy.'

He mellowed slightly and became more businesslike. 'You're in the army now so switch on and be alert. We have a lot to get through today and I need you to be bright eyed and bushy tailed from the start! Let me introduce you to the Training staff. Company-Sergeant-Major Parker here is in charge of administration, more on that in a moment.'

The RSM introduced each member of staff and they each in turn took a step forward so that we could put a face to a name. 'Staff Sergeant Mackintosh is in command of one platoon…' S/Sgt Mackintosh like the RSM also wore a silver French parachute medallion on his left breast pocket, he stepped back smartly once he had been introduced.

'… and Sergeant McBride is responsible for Two platoon. Corporal Hazel, who you have all ready met, is in charge of three and Sergeant Royce will be platoon fours' instructor.'

Mackintosh, McBride and Royce, were Celts; the entire population of Scotland number five million inhabitants give or take, the remaining ten million seem to be in the British Army. And then a younger soldier, who looked less sure of himself than the others, hesitated forward prematurely.

'And finally, assisting the CSM and in charge of stores and equipment, Lance Corporal Hughes.' A euphemism for a lackey I correctly surmised. Tucker gave me a sideways knowing glance and I grinned back at him.

'You will give my staff full cooperation at all times. If one of my staff gives you a task, it will not be unreasonable, you will do it, no questions asked.'

The RSM introduced the CSM properly, and he stepped forward on cue. 'As I have mentioned, the CSM here is in charge of admin.'

The CSM seemed a nice enough sort of bloke, a bit like your favourite uncle. 'Each day I will post your orders up on the company notice board, which is situated at the entrance to the spiders. These orders are called part one orders and contain all you need to know as pertaining the next day's events, a schedule if you like. It is each mans duty to read part one orders so that he is fully aware of and thereby fully understands the next day's procedure, so be alert.'

The RSM waved his highly polished baton from left to right across the assembled recruits as if he was casting a spell on us with a magic wand. 'Do not rely on your mate to tell you what is going on around here, because if you miss something of importance and are not where you are supposed to be at the correct time and appropriately dressed, you will have some explaining to do! Carry on CSM.'

'Right chaps as you were, listen in for your allocated platoon. When you hear your name, fall out and fall in on your platoon commander. The faster we do this, the quicker you will get away to the warmth of the spiders. I will do the remainder of administration from there, and then you can get yourselves over to the stores and draw your kit. Listen in!'

The portly CSM read out a list of names, thirty at a time, in no particular order. Each man got fell in on his platoon commander and made himself familiar with his new comrades. Tucker and I were in 3platoon, Corporal Hazel's platoon, along with a range of blokes who had fleetingly made eye contact with us earlier, including a giant of a bloke who drew nervous glances from some of the more insecure recruits. On first impressions our new companions seemed like a decent bunch. Amongst them was Whittling, the lad with prominent teeth who Cpl Hazel had ridiculed on arrival, and Jennings, a know-all Brummy who liked to dress like a Gestapo officer. There was also Todd, who everyone now referred to as Humpty Dumpty. Our hold-all's and suitcases had been dumped from the old Bedford RL truck into a neat line at the perimeter of the frosty parade ground.

Corporal Hazel addressed us in a low conspiring growl. 'Close in, close in. We do not leave items of kit lying around all willy-nilly. The reason being is that it contravenes the rules on security, so when I say go, get away and grab your personal kit at the double then fall in on me. We are number three platoon but will be number one at everything we do for the next two weeks so be alert, got that! To your kitbags, go! Come on lads before the other scum wake up to what you're doing, Move it, move it!'

We raced away, grabbed our belongings, and returned burdened and faintly panting.

'Right, follow me to your new abode in single file and keep the noise down.'

Chapter 2

Leaving the frozen Tundra of Hampshire outside, 3Platoon filed through the green doorway into the warmth of the spiders' entrance and shuffled down the corridor, each step made a noise like a locomotive. Thud thud, thud thud, thud thud, thud.

We tried to squeeze through the second door on the right but the lad in front of Tucker, who Cpl Hazel had ribbed on arrival for having big teeth, immediately stopped stock still with his hands in his pockets; we ploughed in to him like a pile up on a motorway. While we wondered what the hold-up was, the gormless twerp at the front of the logjam surveyed the room in a leisurely manner as if it was all a figment of his imagination.

'Move you morons.' The corporal pushed past us and jostled Tucker and Whittling out of the way. 'Stop gawping and pick a bed you shagging donkey. The rest of you get in here now and stop chinfing.'

One by one we entered a polished barrack room. The light in the room was dim and artificial, rows of empty green bed frames stood on either side like church pews interspersed by grey metal lockers. The floor surface down the centre was as shiny as brown glass, not so much as a footprint marred the virginal turf, well not up until the corporal's shiny boots squeaked along the lustrous surface. I could now see the NCO's reflection in the glaze, it was totally daunting!

'Don't look so surprised gentlemen.' The NCO removed his peak cap and placed it adroitly in the cleft of his elbow under his left arm. Unusual for a 30 year old male, his head seemed prematurely bald and as shiny as the floor, accentuating his responsible comportment.

'There's about forty years of hard graft and loving care gone into this floor and during the next fortnight you lot are charged with its upkeep.'

Cpl Hazel delighted in the look of incredulity on our faces. 'I don't care how you do it, but from now on you lads are to maintain this sheen all hours of the day. Look upon this task as a reflection of your very own personal standards!'

The NCO's facial features were handsome in a roguish sort of way. His piercing blue eyes were intense and appeared lit up with inner energy. He jabbed his index finger indicatively at the glazed surface. 'That is the level of attainment I will expect from all of you, as individuals *and* as a team, in everything you do here at Martinique Barracks, got it!'

He walked tentatively to a tall green two door metal locker which smelt of cleaning agents. Carefully he placed his hat on top of it and then with both his hands retrieved an unusual antiquated device. It looked fairly heavy, approximately 25-30lbs. Attached to it by a swivel device was a six feet long wooden handle. The metal block measured 18inches by 10inches and the surface underneath was covered in bristles.

'This is the means by which you will care for this beloved floor gentlemen, it's what is known in army jargon as, a Metal-Bumper one of! You will treat it as your Saviour. The only thing preventing a humungous bollocking when I enter this room is *this* magic instrument.'

He returned the contraption to the locker and retrieved his peak cap and planted it squarely on his hairless head, pulling the peak down tight over his nose.

'These are your beds, fifteen per side,' he marched up the centre of the room, and our eyes followed him. I noticed a layer of dust and morsels of unfettered fluff under each empty bed frame, redolent of graves settling in a mass burial. 'To prevent the spread of germs and nasty ailments you are responsible for the cleanliness of your bed space. In a few moments you will return from the stores and pack away your civilian clothing into your baggage, then deposit said baggage at the Platoon storeroom situated at the end of the block, and for your information, the door is securely locked at all times, as I have the only key and access is via me. Any questions? Good!'

He gave nobody time to answer. 'Right listen in…'

Cutting him short the young L/Cpl assistant from the welcoming committee entered the room and whispered in his ear. Cpl Hazel nodded and cleared his throat. 'Right men change of plan. We're running late and we've got shed loads to do, so the CSM says he will now carry out admin at the Company Head Quarters. You will make your way neatly over to Company H.Q. and each man shall take with him the documentation he recently received courtesy of her Majesty's royal mail. Does any man not have his joining instructions? Excellent, file out and form up outside on the road in three ranks, go!'

We pushed and jostled each other out onto the road and formed up into two ranks.

'What are you dense imbeciles doing?' Cpl Hazel got a bit upset as he bounded out robustly behind us. 'Three ranks not two.'

He pointed animatedly like Lord Kitchener. 'Right bollocks, you what's your name?'

'Tucker Sir.'

'Right Tucker, get down in the press up position. Good, now stand up and jump with your legs and arms stretched out like a letter X. Come on, don't take all bleeding day. Again only faster this time, that's it. Listen in, that is called a "Starburst" and every time you fuck up I expect you limp dicks to perform ten of them. Press ups and jumps like a star, got it? Well now, you've just fucked up you maggots so let's have a little practice shall we? Ten Starbursts GO!'

Tiring and humiliating the Starbursts were completed to the NCOs satisfaction. Since we didn't have a pot to piss in, our fortunes were the corporals and he wanted us to know it, and just to emphasise the fact he started to rag us about silly. Fifty metres away stood the solitary Monkey puzzle tree.

'Do you see that tree over there? Run to that tree and back, GO!'

Tucker sighed, 'Shit!'

I laughed. The Corporal screamed at us. 'Don't bimble. Start switching on you thick sods, we can do this the easy way or the hard way, you choose. Come on move it…'

We legged it to the tree and Tucker called out to me, 'Frigging heck I hope it's not going to be all like this for the next two weeks!'

The NCO calmed down a bit when we returned puffing and panting. 'One line in front of me close up, come on stay alert, tallest on the right and shortest on the left, yes good, eyes front. Now we're getting somewhere, number off from the right.'

We did, thirty numbers were called out consecutively.

'Now you divvy fuckers, form up over there by the company H.Q. in three ranks like I taught you before, go!'

We charged over to the Mil-Training-Wing panting even more and formed up in three ranks. 'Now you're switching on ladies, start using that tiny blob of grey matter between your fucking ears.'

The NCO followed grandly with his pace stick clamped under his left arm and as he approached he bawled out. 'Listen in, who can ride a Bike?'

Keen to impress, twenty hands shot up in the air. Cpl Hazel smiled cunningly and pointed to the most enthusiastic looking bloke in the centre of the front rank. 'You'll do, what's your name?'

'Wilson, corporal!' answered a lad who was wearing a black Barafia blazer, grey trousers, and a pair of horn rimmed National Health glasses which made him look like an owl.

'Ahhh, lovely. Tug Wilson!'

'Tug, corporal?' Wilson was distracted by the NCOs apparent delight.

'Your nickname mister! It's traditional in the forces. There's always been a Tug Wilson in the ranks and now I've got one of my very own - thank you god, yes!'

He looked at Wilson affectionately, as if he was gawping at a pet dog. 'Listen in Tug; from now on you are Platoon-senior. You're responsible for making sure everything is ship shape and Bristol fashion around here. You will make sure that three platoon are where they should be, when they should be, properly kitted out and formed up. Got it?'

'Yes sir, erm corporal!' Wilson furrowed his brow nervously at being chosen to assist.

'Good man. You lot will help him in his endeavour by being punctual and smart. He's not in charge of wiping your smelly hairy arses; you will pull your own shagging weight around here, got it?'

'Yes corporal,' shouted the entire platoon.

Due to his initial eagerness Tug had been stitched up with the burden of responsibility, no lengthy election process had elevated him, no procrastination, just his own over enthusiasm. Tug Wilson was it, end of. He smirked, he'd been duped, he shook his head and sniggered retrospectively. Lesson learnt, I thought to myself, don't get spammed (involuntarily volunteered) for anything! I noticed that some of the others around me seemed niggled that they had not been chosen, but the last thing we needed with so many competing alpha males in the ranks was a little Hitler to get our backs up. Cpl Hazel was more than enough of a task master to contend with, so gullible Tug Wilson was prudently the preferential choice!

'Right, from now until you leave here, all members of the Military Training Wing will simply be referred to as Staff! The exceptions being: the CSM, the RSM and the O/C - Major Bert Einstein, comprendez?'

'Yes Staff!' we comprehended.

"*BERT?"*- Tucker snorted aloud. I gave him a dig in the back in warning. We were both reading from the same page but it was too early to be singled out for special attention. The NCO's manner was hardly protocol but it was endearing and revealed that he had a dry sense of humour, nice one corporal. A few of the others in our ranks guardedly chortled at the wittiness too, we were learning to read between the lines and differentiate the crack from all the bullshit!

'We don't want to fill your tiny heads with too much bumph, there's a lot to cram in, so just for the gormless twerps amongst you, we're gonna will keep it super duper easy. There's an acronym we use in the military called KISS – Keep It Simple Stupid!'

KISS? I had just worked out what an acronym was, most of us had never come across the word before but it now seemed self-explanatory and we would encounter more such acronyms to digest during the next two weeks!

'Number three platoon, come on you're not children, brace up, be alert.'

We emerged from our thoughts.

'Three platoon shun, good, stanna ease, not bad, it's coming along. Tug… Fucking hell Wilson, come on wake up, don't be a biscuit!'

'Sorry corporal sir, Staff,' he mumbled shyly. Despite the keenness Tug had displayed a moment earlier, he now seemed at odds at being delegated course senior, a little paranoid even!

'Wilson, did you just call me a cunt?'

Shocked into action, Tug shouted defensively. 'No staff, no way, honest!'

'Well stop fucking muttering, you're supposed to be the platoon numero-uno? Right Tug, get away to the CSM and ask him very politely, whether he's ready to do three Platoon's admin yet? Don't bimble, double up, go!'

While our platoon waited for Tug Wilson to return, the peaceful barracks exploded with frenetic energy. One of the other platoons was marched across the parade square by a bawling NCO and the members of another platoon were double-marched to the stores to be issued with kit. Considering how the other recruits were being pilloried by the NCOs, I surmised that admin must also be conducted in double quick time too, but we experienced the strange phenomenon which materialises whenever you walk into an office environment – that sedate pace of life detached from the real world. Shiny arse clerks and office workers are meticulous and patient in their activities, they don't always look industrious to the uninitiated, but beneath that calm exterior they are often performing mental gymnastics. Each man had his identity checked by date of birth and national insurance number, then issued with a service number, an ID card and a set of Dog Tags unique to each individual. As soon as the information inscribed on the Dog Tags was confirmed as being correct, the medallions were retrieved and replaced in a strong brown envelope to be securely filed away. Me and Tucker and our newly acquired colleagues were steadfastly assured that the only time this item of kit would be issued would be during a national emergency; since I was only joining the Territorial Army for a bit of a laugh such a stipulation was very reassuring!

Portly CSM Parker was refreshingly laid back and mellow, which seemed at odds with the rest of the Mil Training Staff. At the age of seventeen, Ronny Parker had experienced a tide of events which had changed the world forever. 1953 was the year the teenager was born. Bill Haley and the Comets were banging out *Rock around the clock*, and Elvis Presley was recording the first of many of *his* hits too. Mount Everest was conquered that year, and colour Television and the Hydrogen bomb were invented. The mapping of the double helix of DNA was also discovered and a vaccine against Polio created. CSM Parker had joined the Para's initially and had seen action all over the globe: Korea, Suez, Oman and Malaya, and took every opportunity he could to tell us about it whilst puffing on a pipe full of tobacco and administrating the day away.

'When I was in Malaya… blah blah blah… local Head hunters… Bollocks dangling from trees… Close Target Recce's…Worst thing was the humidity… Japanese Encephalitis, tropical impetigo, trench foot, and a bad back, I'd had enough by then of course!'

He called each of 3Platoon forward one at a time, necessitating him to raise his voice. 'Next! Don't get me started on Africa… United Nations… the white man's grave… Kenya was bloody harsh lads; the Mow-Mow… no more than babies some of them. Then the Middle East, sand got into everything, parched your throat and scratched your eyes out. Next! Before too long back to fuckin' Borneo, I'd known nothing like it; fungus, insects, snakes… feet completely fucked… barely a mile up river, coconut hit me on the head and I had to be airlifted out. Next!'

A soldier's soldier, touched by life from every country he had ever been stationed in. Now he was stuck in this backwater on the outskirts of Aldershot giving the benefit of his vast experience to STABs (Stupid T.A. Bastards); well you have to be stupid to volunteer for what *he* and the rest of the Mil Training Wing were about to put us all through, the rigours of winter promised to enhance the hardship even more!

The CSM must have been topping up his pension fund; he had the spiel of a Market stallholder. 'If any of you lads want T.A. Sweat shirts, military badges, mugs or key rings as a memento of your stay with us, come and see me next pay-day and I'll sort you out with a bloody good deal! I've got top of the range perfumes and some lovely silk Kimonos too. Nice treat for your wife or fancy piece back home, yeh?'

Puffing away like billy-o on his pipe, he completed the task of checking joining instructions against the company strength documentation, and then individually passed each man on to an Army-Pay-Corps Sergeant who meticulously extracted a signature for a £30 advance of pay; an unexpected bonus for us two Runcorn lads and our new mates. The Pay-Corp man looked like any other bank teller, except that he wore a black beret and starched green uniform in place of a pin striped suit. The sumptuary moneyman counted out the notes as if they were his very own personal expenditure. He appeared reluctant to part with any of them. All encounters with Pay Clerks are the exact same M.O. They can't call you back once you've left the building, so bearing that in mind, they never unwittingly overpay anyone! Because Pay-Parade is in fact just that, a parade, we had been advised to salute the clerk and say "thank you sir!"

He dismissed us with a disapproving look as if we were going to squander his cash imprudently. 'Next!'

All the members of 3Platoon were each dismissed and unceremoniously shunted back into the frozen hell out side. One by one we gradually formed up into three ranks, a lot happier for having thirty quid tucked away in our back pocket. Tug Wilson had already spent a pound of his, he had bought a TA Regimental badge from the CSM to sew onto his blazer; he was really buying into the whole TA deal! Cpl Hazel eventually took command and brought us all to attention. 'All done and dusted, right then, off to the blanket stackers.'

The pace was furious, making us all half shuffle/half run like cold and bewildered refugees. Tucker struggled as we romped around the corner of the wooden stores-building with Cpl Hazel following at the rear calling out the step as if cracking a lion tamers whip.

'Eft ight, eft ight, eft ight, eft, come on pick up the step, right wheel, platoon halt. Turn to the right in threes, rigghhht turn. Stanna ease, stand easy.'

The Corporal slinked past his body of men like a prize fighter. He approached the steps leading up to the main door and stretched his right arm forward to retrieve a white enamel mug of steaming hot tea which had been placed on the top tread in anticipation of his arrival. He sipped, burned his lips and winced. Replacing the brew on the steps he dabbed a finger at his scorched mouth and muttered an injured hello. 'Bore da Taffy.'

'Wela i chi Corporal Hazel,' greeted the sniggering Store man jokily. Taff rebelliously blew a lungful of cigarette smoke in the direction of the wounded corporal. 'Sut dych chi heddiw?'

Tetchily Cpl Hazel tried to elbow L/Cpl Hughes out of his way, but the Welshman sidestepped the instructor to give him a respectable wide birth. Cpl Hazel jutted his chin out condescendingly. 'Dim yn ddrwg, Arfon, a chithau?'

'Fine diolch, sut mae eich te?' The Welshman spoke in a rich tenor voice.

'Fel lafa folcanig chi anghyfreithlon!'

It was all double Dutch to the likes of me and Tucker, and confusingly I thought we were about to be whisked away to be taught fluent Russian and brought up to speed on the communist anxiety or something, after all it was the height of the cold war?

'Your Welsh is improving!' congratulated the Lance-Corporal hesitantly.

Having grown up in the Welsh border town of Oswestry, Cpl Hazel knew a smattering of the lingo. He snorted petulantly and spoke some Spanish. 'Basta ya de tonterias (Shut it!). Usted hace una taz de te horribles!'

'So is your Diego!'

Linguistics must have been an agreeable pursuit at Martinique Barracks? The wiry Welsh man drew on his cigarette again and shrugged. 'Si, pero el camarero es muy guapo!'

'Besame el culo. Carry on then Arfon, bore da and that, all yours!' Cpl Hazel disposed of his charge and wandered off tentatively cupping the scolding hot mug of tea between his cold hands.

'Bollocks I chi i,' gruffly sighed Taff, then turning away from the parting corporal, he brightened up and welcomed us. 'Konnichi wa, croeso!'

A West-country lad behind me responded cheekily in his pirate drawl. 'Iach y dda Taff!'

Taff was broody, athletic and multi-lingual. He sported a number two haircut and had severe acne. Normally he'd have had intelligent eyes too, but today they were misty and hung over. He would later divulge to us that he believed his liver was diseased in some way; it wasn't hypochondria he genuinely suspected this condition existed, but none the less he could not leave the drink alone despite this nagging feeling.

He seemed very sure of himself, once intimidating Cpl Hazel had gone for his tea break, and nonchalantly he flicked his cigarette butt into a nearby storm drain. Red sparks splashed into the air as the abandoned dimp bounced and sank through the iron grating where it snagged on a frozen mass off leaves bound up in a spider's cobweb, sending up a lazy ribbon of blue smoke to drift and dance in the cruel morning breeze.

Taffy was anxiously awaiting promotion to Full Screw. He had been promised his second stripe as reward for jacking up the hardware, issuing kit and being general dog's body to the CSM for the following two weeks; a small price to pay for a leg up the ladder!

He sauntered into the stores and the lads of 3Platoon followed him, ready for action. That's precisely what we encountered from his team, plenty of action. Down the right of the store building was a wooden counter, 40ft in length from beginning to end. On the business side stood five reluctant volunteers drafted in from C Company, one of the regular army units on the base; they had been dicked into handing out clobber to STAB's. The impromptu store-men were warmed up and ready to have some fun. Behind them was an Aladdin's cave of military clothing awaiting issue. Stacks of green trousers, jumpers, socks and shirts sprouted up from the floor like an array of shrubs at a garden centre. Haversacks and webbing were formed up in tidy little queues wanting to be dispatched, while hanging stiffly from a wooden pole on the ceiling, pairs of black boots tied together at the heels with parcel string resembled braces of rabbits in a butchers shop. At the other end of the counter Pillows lounged about insecurely on top of grey serge bedding, some were fluffed up and others squashed together with the ends cutely pouting like frogs lips. Taff cleared his throat and in a Welsh Tenor voice took charge of we dishevelled looking refugees.

'Listen in, start by heure with yewer Mattresses right and make sewer there is no stains on'em; cos yewer to sign for everything yewer issued with see. Tis yewer responsibility to return'em in the same condition mind, no piss stains or cigarette burns even. OK then, make yewer way down the line and my boys'll load yews up with the rest of yewer kit,' he almost sang the words to us.

Our mob made its way along the line of store men, stopping at each station to be deftly questioned and issued with army clobber: Boots Directly Moulded Sole (DMS) two pairs of. Tea cup White China, one. Knife Fork and Spoon (KFS) metal, one set. One Combat Smock Disruptive Pattern Material (DPM) and one pair of Combat Trousers DPM, and then one DPM Combat Hat. A quilted green Body-Warmer, two pairs of full length green socks and one standard issue black beret came next, and all work in the stores momentarily ceased as Tish Hewitt, the giant in front of Tucker, was issued with his headwear.

Tish Hewitt tried on ten hats before one eventually fitted, then a Geordie store man stood back admiringly and grandly announced. 'Howay man, ya could carry spuds in that. Your head is a Sniper's fuckin' dream!'

A set of 58 Pattern webbing came next already assembled, so the giant simply fed his arms through the straps and dangled it from his back, and once we had seen this done the rest of us lads of 3Platoon followed suit. Next up, a green sleeping-bag (Maggot) and a sleeping bag liner (to prevent muddy boots from soiling it), then a pair of brown puttees and green woollen gloves, then a red P.T vest and blue shorts.

One pair of black plimsolls were lobbed at Tucker in the same instance as another store-man was handing him two white cotton single sheets, a mattress protector and a white cotton pillow case. Tucker dropped the plimsolls but managed to trap them against the counter with his right knee. One feather pillow and two pairs of green under pant's (Shreddies), and a large green woollen jumper were placed on top of his pile while he bent to retrieve the gym shoes, then two best dress brown cotton shirts and two crude green woollen shirts were placed on top of his teetering pile when he stood back up. He shook his head in disbelief!

Tish Hewitt had size 15 feet and took a size 22inch collar! Taffy was incredulous.

'Hey now, look at the size of you bach. Twenty two-inch neck it is see and feet like flippers. A megapod! Ewes could use those boots for coal barges isnit. There you go butty, ewes might as well take the boxes they came in and use them for slippers whiles ewes are here see!'

Next came 2 pairs of green leg warmers. 'Akchewly yous'll be glad of these during the next two weeks by here, them's fabewless, them'ill keep yews warm as toast they will see. Them're a God send boyos, believe me, oh yes!'

We piled all of this kit onto the mattresses and moved to a pile of blankets at the end of the wooden counter where we were issued with two each.

'Sign here please, underneath where it says last item. Always, whenever yewers signing for kit, whether big or small or anythink, make sure the words "Last Item" follow the itinery you's have been issued with. Otherwise some unscrupulous baztard can just add a few things he can sell down the pub when yewer gone see, it happens I'm afraid, it's human kneechewer isnit! Any items nadged, mislaid or not returned in full working order will be one-two-sixed against your pay account and the money deducted at source, fankewe and bloody good luck. Yews is gonna need it isn't it'

Twelve minutes from beginning to end, the sadistic grinning store team had deftly and professionally piled kit on to our mattresses. They had moved like an army of soldier-ants loading me and my beleaguered mates up to the gunnels before prompting us on toward the double doors at the end of the counter, and then hurriedly ushering us out onto the skating rink outside.

Using a bit of nouse, Tucker had joined forces with Tish Hewitt and between them balanced their two piles of kit awkwardly together; good job Tish was a big bloke. It seemed like a bloody good idea so I followed suit and roped in the lad behind me and we did likewise.

Corporal Hazel was nowhere to be seen by the time we had completed drawing kit, he was probably only half way down his scolding cup of tea such was the swiftness of the store men, which was a great relief. None of us needed an NCO breathing down our necks as we crabbed sideways trying desperately not to drop anything. Tish was absolutely one of the most massive blokes that I had ever met, he must have had a big appetite too because I heard the Yorkshire lad's stomach rumble. Big Tish introduced himself and I heard him tell Tucker that he passed his spare time as a rugby prop forward, playing for an Amateur Rugby League Football Club in Leeds. While imparting this information, big Tish suddenly lost his footing and his legs started to go ten-to-the-dozen in all directions. I couldn't help laughing, as you do at someone else's misfortune. Fortunately Tucker managed to stay firmly rooted to the spot like an anchor man on a tug-o-war team.

'Fuck me; this place is a death trap!' Tish Hewitt hissed through barred teeth.

Tucker burst out laughing, trying not to be toppled as he did so. 'Nice leg work Tish!'

They both held on grimly to the mattresses until Tish brought his feet under control. Recapturing some composure the big man announced. 'Ballroom dancing Tucker – never thought it would save my fooking life though.'

As big and tough as Tish Hewitt appeared, now that his guard was down he seemed to have a softer side to match his slight speech impediment; he spoke as if his teeth were marginally too big for his mouth. He confided in those of us within earshot that he was a champion ballroom dancer. Tish was six foot ten inches tall and built like a brick shit house, so Tucker just shrugged at the unbelievable disclosure and I assumed that the giant was merely taking the piss? We couldn't really envisage the huge Yorkshire man fox-trotting around a dancehall swishing about in Top hat & Tails; it stretched the imagination to incredible limits!

'Do you know what Tish?' Tucker was on the verge of hysteria as he sucked ice cold air deep into his lungs. 'If someone could see us now they'd die laughing.'

Unbeknown to us, that was exactly what was happening on the other side of the parade square in the spiders of 'C' Company. The occupants were in pleats of laughter watching 3Platoon slip and slide their perilous way between the spiders. Some of the Mil Training Staff, while drinking morning coffee, were also peeping through the windows of the Mil Training Wing shack, I noticed the blinds moving. Apparently, once every six months, on a Saturday between the hours of eleven and twelve, the new intake of STAB recruits could be relied upon to provide priceless entertainment for those on the army-base unfortunate enough not to be away on leave. Tish and Tucker were in safe reach of the spider's entrance and me and the lad I was two'd up with were right behind them when we caught sight of the line of stragglers behind us. Items of kit lay strewn all over the place as the rest of 3platoon struggled like dung beetles with the heaps of kit.

Red faced Jennings from Birmingham cried out in distress. 'Fuck it Sooty, we'll come back for it later!'

Somebody else pleaded. 'Drop your end down will ya, I've got all the bleeding weight!'

Without stopping, Tucker and big Tish barged down the corridor of the spider and into the shiny room, dumping the entire pile of bedding, combats and sundry kit, into the first available space they could find. Me and my new mucker traipsed in behind them.

'I'm having this one here,' claimed Tish, collapsing on to the first bed frame on the left of the door. His massive arms and legs dangled Octopus style to the polished floor while the bedsprings strained under the weight of his huge bulk. Tucker collapsed onto another cot, centre right away from the door. I claimed a bunk on the left across from Tucker and my oppo plonked his self down on the bedsprings next to me. Our arms felt like they'd been ripped from out from their sockets under the immense burden of kit.

Two by two the rest of 3Platoon scrambled in, exhausted like beasts of burden entering Noah's Ark. They dropped what was left of their bundles beside the nearest available bed-space before collapsing insensible onto the bare mattress springs.

No sooner had we relaxed we were immediately startled back into life by Cpl Hazel's thundering voice. 'Stand by your beds!'

We scuttled to attention like a gang of Mere-cats.

'You ain't got time for a siesta you lazy lot, so listen in.' Cpl Hazel was keeping his platoon on their toes from the outset. 'Get all this kit squared away, and then change into your lightweight green trousers, woollen shirt, jersey, boots and Combat-Smock. Come on Tug, stay alert, get a fucking grip or you'll miss lunch. I want your personal belongings stored away securely in the room at the end of the corridor, then your kit laid out for inspection as per this detailed diagram.'

He circulated a bundle of cards depicting a kit lay out. 'This ladies is how I want you to lay out your kit each morning for inspection, got it?'

Some of the lads looked bewildered.

'And when a member of staff walks into the room you're to stand to attention, not loll around in your pits like limp dicks. First person to sight a member of staff will warn the platoon, "Corporal present/Sergeant present", is that understood three platoon?'

We replied obediently. 'Yes staff!'

The corporal made himself scarce as we snatched at the piles of kit on the floor and packed it all away neatly. Once completed, we quickly changed out of civilian clothing and into army clobber. Pity nothing fitted properly; in the Army there are only two sizes of clothing, too big and too small!

Chapter 3

Tucker's mind was alert; it was constantly on the go. All those officers and NCOs banging on about being attentive were wasting their breath on a bloke like him. He was always revved up and needing to challenge himself at every opportunity. When he was younger he had harboured boyish dreams of becoming a rally-car driver or climbing a mountain taller than Everest, or even piloting a rocket to Saturn, but realistically didn't have a clue what he wanted to do in life. Unless you are privileged or profoundly unlucky, nothing out of the ordinary ever seems to happen in verve-less towns like Runcorn, and sadly this innocence had not prepared Tucker for his future. As a result he had grown up with very few rich life experiences locked away in his psychology; I hadn't fared much better myself!

Our initial sentiment on arriving at Martinique Barracks was disappointment; it was hard to believe we were in the middle of Hampshire; it was more akin to being assigned to an outpost of the British Empire in the Nineteenth Century. Tucker had been excited by the prospect of joining the TA, whereas I tended to take things in my stride; we kept each other in check like that, he rubbed off on me and I rubbed off on him. But the stark reality of sleeping for two weeks in an uninsulated wooden hut during the depths of winter had dimmed his expectations. Mind you, he was not a defeatist, our surroundings might not have been state of the art but they certainly had character. I could see that he was weighing up his options and was hoping that I'd buckle first and say "Fuck it let's go home!" but I loved to see him squirm. I shrugged; he understood this gesture from me. He steeled himself to make the most of it and once resolved he regained that look in his eyes, the one that said this could turn out to be a great little adventure if he ditched his preconceptions and changed his outlook. His granddad was very fond of imbuing Tucker with positive viewpoints; I know because the old sod cherished getting on my case too, his favourite advice was - "When life gives you lemons, make lemonade!"

In the space of a few hours the recruit course had gone from 1st gear to 2nd gear, and now Cpl Hazel was about to dip the clutch and ram the whole show into 3rd gear. At this rate we would not have a moment to think straight. The thirty minutes the assertive NCO had allotted us to sort ourselves out had flown by.

'Corporal in the room.' Bossy boots hovered over us like a hawk.

'As you were, haven't you finished yet?' Cpl Hazel browsed over our efforts of displaying kit for inspection, and while frowning solicitously, prodded and lifted bits and pieces of kit with his shiny pace stick as if checking the consistency of dog turds.

'It's coming along boys, but look what you're doing to this beautiful floor! Tug, delegate someone to polish up occasionally and change the detail three times a day so that each man gets a shot at it, including you, got that?'

'Yes corporal, sorry sir, I mean Staff, corporal.'

'Listen in. When you're not detailed to carry out a task by Tug here, you will be working on your second pair of boots. These boots are your sacred boots. Your sacred boots will be your best boots and only be used for special parades, is that clear? Working on your best boots takes a lot of graft and will occupy every spare moment you spend in the spider, even when revising any of the bumph we're throwing at you. Consequently you will not be chinfing off to the pub in the evening for a shandy and packet of crisps, no you will not, you'll be too busy boning up and bulling! What will you be?'

'Boning up and bulling boots Staff!' reiterated the platoon spontaneously.

Confined to barracks? It looked as if we were on the wagon for the next two weeks, and with no sex either, those measures were bound to make events very intense!

Cpl Hazel beckoned the lad called Corbett with his index finger. 'Sooty, bring your best boots here and I'll demonstrate the method we employ to attain a high gloss to the caps and heels!'

The 6ft 3inch, broken nosed, blond haired Nordic giant lurched forward and accompanied the corporal to a table at the far end of the room, upon which was laid out an electric iron, a tin of shoe polish and a yellow cleaning rag. The instructor plugged the electric iron in to a socket and summoned the rest of us. 'Gather round and observe, come on ball-bags close in. This electric high-on has cost me precisely seven pounds and fifty pence. My name is not corporal Oxfam, so this is not a charitable act on my part. There are thirty men in this room who will each donate fifty pence to Tug, who in turn will recompense me for my unstinting generosity, got it!'

The instructor paused while the iron heated up. 'At the end of this recruit course this state-of-the-heart electric-high-on will be raffled free of charge. Look, it even de-scales itself, what a bargain!'

The thermostat clicked and the red light in the handle extinguished, prompting the corporal to continue. 'Now before you even think of applying a speck of polish to the surface of your lovely boots, you'll have to make them smooth so as to provide an even surface to work on, does that make sense to you?'

'Yes Staff.' Tug Wilson responded while everybody nodded.

'In fact, by the time you pass out in two weeks' time, your boots will have become as smooth and polished as you, I promise. Now in order to do this, we bring the electric-high-on up to a moderate heat, not too hot. Then we carefully smooth out the dimples on the toes and heels like this!' Cpl Hazel demonstrated his talent for ironing army boots and bizarrely it worked.

'We then procure a generous dollop of shoe polish onto our cleaning cloth and work it into the leather in minute circular motions like this!' Tucker was fast becoming bored with the demonstration; the prospect of polishing shoes for hours and hours on end was daunting, he just wanted to splash about in mud shooting a rifle.

'Now for the challenging part gentlemen,' the instructor presaged. 'The graft!'

Cpl Hazel sensed that he was losing the attentiveness of his platoon, but there was no way of making this mundane task seem more interesting. He gathered Tucker's wavering attention by throwing the boot to him. Tucker caught it uneasily, he was startled. With a stern look the corporal gestured to Tucker to pass the boot back so that he could resume the demonstration. 'Alas, the leather will only absorb so much polish, so what we have to do is methodically build up the polish layer by layer onto the surface.'

Tucker tried to look captivated but Cpl Hazel knew from experience that Tucker and one or two others were simply feigning interest. 'It takes a life time for a hundred odd bumble bees to knock up enough earwax to compliment the ingredients required to fill one of these little flat tins; in the scale of things you've got the easy bit. By spitting on your boots you provide moisture, use that moisture to manipulate the polish and by repeatedly working the polish in tiny-tiny-tiny-tiny-tiny circles you will build up a sheen, just like our beloved floor here!'

The corporal raised an eyebrow to signal a response from his audience and a lad with a West Country accent obliged him, a little too enthusiastically. 'Ooh, yes Staff.'

We all sniggered while Cpl Hazel gave an imploring look. 'Don't be a smart arse!'

'Ok, now that you have an electric high-on, I expect your turn out to be immaculate at all hours, all items of uniform to have razor sharp creases pressed into them, no excuses right?'

'Right Staff.' The instructor was assured.

'That's right, so crack on with the dimples on your boots and get this floor sorted out. Lunch is at twelve thirty hours, when all of you are to get away to the cookhouse for a hot bacon butty and a slice of tonsil varnish. You can stand a spoon up in army tea, its lovely stuff! After which you will be stood down until thirteen twenty hours for personal admin. Make the most of your personal admin breaks as they are far and few between. Write to your wife, your girlfriend, your boyfriend, whoever I don't care. I want you outside Company HQ at thirteen thirty hours with the fifteen quid what you're all generously donating to Tug for the electric high-on, plus another fifty pence in your possession ready to go for haircuts. As you can see I don't need one because all my lovely hair fell out when I was sixteen - that was a scary game of cards I can tell you!'

'Can we smoke Staff.' asked a recruit?

'Burst into flames for all I care!'

Cpl Hazel left 3Platoon to buckle down with their chores. Bulling boots and ironing kit was all part of the agenda; it put everybody on a level playing field, focusing the mind and helping to build up comradeship. There are set parameters in military life and by instilling self-discipline and personal pride right at the beginning, an individual can ascertain his strengths and weaknesses and work towards balancing them out. Tucker and I were learning this lesson fast. Paying attention to little details had never been Tucker's forte, which fundamentally had been the reason why he had not managed to nail down an apprenticeship when leaving school. School had bored him silly, consequently he could never adhere himself to any extra-curriculum challenge. Lamentably Tucker and I had attended the same school, which all of our family, father and six uncles a generation before had graced with their presence; both of us were grudgingly taught by the very same teachers that had edified that previous generation. On the practical side Tucker was ok at Woodwork and Metalwork, and a little better at Technical Drawing. He'd muddled through the 3 R's as best he could, then left the establishment at fifteen years of age having attained five average grade GCE's and a good attendance record; hardly the qualifications of a Rocket-surgeon. At fifteen years of age you're a bit screwed up aren't you, not sure what's happened, what's happening, or what's going to happen, and lacking any positive direction from a life coach, you're prone to drift along unencumbered for a while.

Tucker had loathed the thought of being indentured for three years in a job that only paid £7 per week while his mates were getting £11 to £15 per week labouring for a living. The principal employment in Runcorn at that time was process work for the Imperial Chemical Industry (ICI) or loading and unloading cargo ships on the Docks at Percival Lane, or if you were extremely lucky, dragging container vessels by Tugboat between Eastham Locks and Salford Quays for the Manchester Ship Canal Company. Alternatively, if you had family working at the big oil refinery at Stanlow or could get an apprenticeship with the Gas-Board, you were set up for life, if you didn't, you were pretty much knackered. Luckily for Tucker, one of his uncles had got him a job in Quality control at a car manufacturing plant along route seven, and so long as money jingled in his pocket he was reasonably happy. He had wanted freedom from academia, craving to get his hands dirty and earn a proper wage so that he could hang out with the lads down the pub at night.

Being a steady Eddie I got trained up as a Gas Fitter with the Gas Board. Some of our school mates who had gone to technical college on day release were now reaping their reward too and earning vast sums of money since completing apprenticeships. Being considered by the lasses as being a good catch, most of these lads were married with kids by the age of twenty and were now settling down to a future of domestic bliss in their own house; however Tucker preferred to chance his arm without a millstone mortgage around his neck. Although he secretly envyied his buddies their earning potential he shuddered at the thought of being locked into that domestic lifestyle, too restrictive, they were only allowed out with the lads once a week. Tucker wouldn't treat a dog like that, he cherished his emancipation!

Dinner time could not have come sooner. The other ranks mess smelt of school dinners, it was warm and inviting and a welcome change from the freezing cold weather outside. A mound of thick white china plates were precariously stacked on a plate warmer next to trays of hot food laid out buffet fashion on the hot-plate. A teetering tower of sliced white bread snuggled up to the food seductively. Behind the grub stood three of Andy Capp's Commandos (Army Catering Corps) ready to serve us. One of the cooks was a lumpy jumper (female soldier), dressed in pristine chef's whites she looked totally unconcerned. In contrast one of her male colleagues standing by her side seemed to be the more industrious, he had splashes of gravy and dinner gongs (food stains that looked like medals) adorning his garment, and the other cabbage commando must have been the section commander, he had two silver chevrons gleaming on the arm of his white chef's jacket.

The full screw cordially announced. 'Come on lads, you must be starving, grubs up. The Tea-urn is over there, help yourself to sugar and bring your plate back when you're finished, we don't have a waitress service!'

He did not repeat himself, no need to, the food was free and copious, and the line of new arrivals was famished! Another cook who looked as if he was taking a well-deserved break wore a chef's hat set at a jaunty angle and a tea towel slung over his shoulder. This cook stood silhouetted against the doorway of the kitchen with his arms folded like Odd-Job in the 007 films, he had three gleaming silver chevrons displayed on his arm and a sardonic grin on his face. 'Stop that pushing or you can go outside and start again! Oy do you hear me? Stop that pushing.'

With the onset of cold and hunger, niceties had evaporated and the behaviour of the recruits had now descended into that of savages. Within an hour of arrival we had been screamed at and beasted around a sub-zero parade square, then force fed through the sausage machine to be administered and clothed, and we were now impolitely pushing and jostling each other for protein, carbohydrates and a hot cup of cha.

'Sorry mate!' apologised the cheeky press-up performing cockney from earlier.

'I am not your bleedin' mate!' yelled Odd-Job.

The recruits instantly stopped pushing - this bloke meant business. Rubbing his hands with the tea towel he stepped forward to the servery and started lecturing us about dining etiquette. We tried to ignore him and nevertheless shuffled on more slowly still loading up our plates with boiled potatoes, bacon and baked beans as we passed. We didn't want to upset the cookery sergeant any more than we had for fear he might wreck our feeding frenzy.

'When you come into my mess, you will leave all of that military crap outside and act like civilised human beings, displaying a modicum of courtesy and exercising your best manners at all times gentlemen…'

Tucker kept his head down and made a beeline for the safety of the dining area.

'…we spend all day cooking this delicious cuisine so that you…' the sergeant droned on as Tucker sat himself down at a table and ruthlessly set about devouring the chef's hard work.

'…are you men listening? So that you can share half an hour relaxing in a calm warm convivial environment. Got it!'

'Fucking hell, who rattled his cage?' laughed a ginger headed Geordie bloke standing next to me, and as I moved off with my laden plate a Welsh lad conspiratorially muttered, 'He'd make somebody a lovely mum he would!'

Odd-Job gave up the ghost. 'Why am I even bothering?'

Most of the recruits had travelled down by train overnight like me and Tucker, and as such had not eaten properly since the evening before, we were so hungry that we sat munching away in near silence.

I sat off at a table next to Tucker; the one he was sitting at had filled up while I was still in the queue being served. We weren't joined at the hip so it was of no consequence. It was hard for Tucker not to choke as he stuffed his face, a piece of dry white bread he'd been nibbling on had lodged itself to the roof of his mouth, so he slurped half a mouthful of tangy sweet tea and squelched it around his chops to displace the dough. Once he had settled down he piled boiled potatoes and a meagre strip of bacon onto a round of bread and clamped it all together much like an improvised pasty. Mopping up bean juice to moisten the bread so as to prevent him choking again he continued filling his face. He was not lacking in table manners, he simply preferred finger food; he would not look out of place sat amongst third world natives at a feast. You'd have thought someone was going to rob his food as he alternated between the butty and scoops of baked beans, shovelling legumes into his mouth with a fork that had a Crows foot stamped onto the shaft; the Crows foot is the emblem of Government Property as seen on convicts clothing in cartoon strips.

Once nourished we leisurely surveyed our new surroundings, piping faces for characters as you do when you're a stranger in town, there's always one or two lads that stand out in a crowd. This was not your usual crowd though; these lads were hungry for adventure or just seeking an escape. Some were unmarried and bored with the routine of tedious work, the rest were probably wedded before they had achieved all what they were capable of doing during the short period between puberty and marriage, and now like chained convicts found themselves on a short leash, sitting at home domiciled with tormented pangs of regret; not all of them of course, some were loved up and happy with their lot. A few hard cases tried to look impassive in a restrained fashion, they gave off the Alpha male vibe. Tish Hewitt, the giant of a man who had helped Tucker carry his kit from the stores, stood head and shoulders above the rest of us and with being six feet ten inches tall he was imperturbably confident. Judging by body language quite a few of thc lads found Hewitt's size intimidating and although he was built like a brick outhouse I and one or two others, Tucker included, remained undaunted. Absurd as it seemed Tucker had mentioned to me that he felt somehow that he knew big Tish from somewhere; he told me that he could not place him and asked me if I knew him from wherever? I didn't have a clue; maybe it was de-ja vu, perhaps it was down to the sheer size of the colossus, he seemed a bit like a permanent fixture!

Nervous first day chatter started to buzz around the room, there was the odd outburst of ironic laughter as people found they had similar things in common. It was comparable to arriving at a party when the host has not turned up yet and everybody smiles politely because no one has been introduced. As the groups became less self-conscious the noise from conversations slowly escalated and I took a moment to take in all the faces around me. These guys were strangers for now but at the end of the next two weeks they would undoubtedly be like brothers to me. I caught the eye of others who were on the same level as me and nodded in acknowledgement; we would no doubt gravitate towards each other once the party got underway.

The dining hall was sparse and pleasant, nothing to write home about. The tables were basic, made from Formica with moulded metal legs for easy stacking. They had plastic red & white chequered table-cloths draped in a diamond arrangement across them and sat four people comfortably, some tables were pushed together to seat more. To the far end of the dining hall dominating the south wall was a large mural; it was a scene from a Tropical Island depicting palm trees and sandy coves bordered by aquamarine sea and blue azure sky, heart-warming on a cold winter day. To the north was a mural of conflicting contrast; ranged across it were glacial Alpine Mountains with Fir-tree meadows covered in snow. I made a mental note to strive to be first in line so as to eat in the tropics for the remainder of this recruit course, no doubt Tucker thought the same. One of his new companions, the Birmingham lad from the back of the truck, was a bit of a shoulder clapper; you know the sort, they pat you on the back and rub your shoulders, effecting familiarity as if they're your long lost buddy or something.

I winked at Tucker and mouthed to him. "Who's your new mate?"

Tucker's new pal enquired with his Brummy twang. 'All right dad, are you thinking what I think you're thinking? I can see you've got this place sussed out already, Scouser ain't yer?'

'No Cheshire, well Merseyside I suppose. Runcorn, heard of it?' replied Tucker.

'Right, that's where that big bridge with all them boats tied up beneath it is when you go into Liverpool isn't it?' continued the chubby Birmingham lad.

'Yep, those boats are part of the Runcorn Whaling-Fleet.' Tucker dryly pulled the chubby lads leg about the Tugs which moored up along the Old-Quay promenade.

'Learn something new every day!' Chubby did not get the joke, he held out his tactile sweaty paw for a handshake. 'Took the wife there once I did and her says "Us ain't gonna drive over the top of that bridge are we love? I don't think me stomach can take it you know, looks bloody high does that!" don't be daft I said, that's the arch span, the bloody road goes underneath it not over it!' the Brummy gestured with his podgy hands. 'Dopey cow wouldn't have it though, not until we got a bit closer you know, anyway, should of seen her face dad. Liverpool was depressing though, yes, very tense you know!'

'Yeh, hard times,' feebly agreed Tucker.

'Oh yes. Don't get me wrong dad, the people were lovely, but it looked like a bomb had hit the place…'

Tucker's eyes glazed over. I felt his pain. Jesus this bloke could waffle for England, not so much a conversation, more a whine. If he'd gone back to Liverpool in 1981 after the Toxteth riots, he'd have really had something to tut about. He was the sort of bloke who liked the sound of his own Black-country twang and my spine shuddered apprehensively causing my bum to clam up tight as he continued. 'Still, what they did with the docks is marvellous aint it? That Maritime Museum, been there tons of times me and me misses has, us go everywhere together us do, should of gone to see Nick Drake last week but…'

I surreptitiously glanced around the mess hall looking for his wife, then before the Brummy had a chance to adoptively put his arm around Tucker's shoulders and drain him of the will to live I interrupted him, then me and Tucker quickly picked up our empty plates and fled.

'We're just going to see if we can get some more scoff pal, won't be a minute.'

The Brummy called after us and half waved. 'Yeh all right then, tarrah for a bit.'

At the stainless steel servery Tucker nervously helped himself to left over potatoes and more bread which he slid around in the serving trays mopping up the bacon juices, not daring to turn back in the Brummy's direction for fear of encouraging this tenacious character. I kept my head down too, slitting our wrists was becoming a tempting alternative in speedily terminating this fledgling acquaintance. Suddenly an avalanche erupted in the room as chairs were pushed away from tables. Within seconds half of the other diners were lining up behind us, ready to polish off the remains of the grub; it seemed that no one had wanted to be first up for extras in case Odd-Job started crying again.

Tucker was nudged in the arm with an elbow by a green eyed athletically built lad who was in the same platoon as us. The lad grinned cheekily, his impish eyes flitted around the room similar to a look out on a bank robbery and when he spoke he spoke with a sort of mischievous west country accent, but wasn't yokel, in fact he sounded more like a pirate.

'Here then, was that there bloke giving you ear ache were he?'

'Just a bit mate, just a bit!' Tucker laughed, rapt by the other lad's cordiality.

'He were like that on the train all the way down here,' chuckled the pirate as Tucker sized him up and down. The pirate had a wide flat forehead beneath a shock of blond hair, and an almost Pixie like nose; he was built like a Devon dry stone wall. 'He don't ever shut the fuck up. Thinks he knows everything does that one, drones on and on and on and on and on and on.'

'Bit of a Head Wrecker?' Tucker dismissively joked. I straining to decipher some of the pirate's sentences - there seemed to be more regional accents in that dining room than could be mustered by a United Nations international security forum.

The pirate was very mercurial. 'It's not funny boy, he's right off his noggin, the sort of bloke who makes you wanna rip your eyeballs out and stick'em in your ears. Hope I don't get lumbered with the same platoon as him in, know what I mean!'

'Too late mate,' Tucker dubiously replied. 'We already are!'

‘I’m putting in for a transfer then; don’t wanna share the same billet!’

‘Think you can do that do you?’

‘Compassionate grounds I might!’

‘He could be amusing, I’ve met worse!’

‘Yeh not much though, we don’t like him.’

‘Oh yeh, and who are *we* then?’ I asked. In my experience, little cliques were more trouble than they were worth, me and Tucker tended to avoid them!

‘You’ll learn!’ He nudged Tucker’s arm. ‘Look boy, me and a couple of other fella’s reckon we’ve got this recruit thing boxed off. That Corporal was laying in to you a bit thick before weren’t he, you piss taking bastard? Bloody good wind up were that, “Yes Captain, No Captain”. Reckon he taken a shine to you already.’

‘Bollocks he’s a right nasty piece of work that one; he needs to go on an anger management course!’

‘Yeh I’ve met meself some hard sods in me time, but that corporal is a new breed, right in your face.’

‘You’re not wrong there mate.’ agreed Tucker.

‘Mind you, ya don’t wanna jump ship just yet; we ain’t got to know any of the other NCOs have we. Were you in cadets?’

‘Air cadets, why?’ This pirate bloke was perceptive too.

‘It shows boy; I was in Sea Cadets. Listen matey, act keen but a bit naïve, that way they’ll think that they’re actually teaching you somet. If you act like you know it all they’ll give you a hard time boy, and let’s face it, you’ve already made a talented impression on that shag nasty corporal this morning. You see that Birmingham bloke Jennings who were bending your ear just then, he’s arse mate, watch his gig and you’ll see how not to do it. I say he don’t make it through week one, I’m Martin by the way!’

‘Glad to meet you Martin, I’m Tucker!’

‘Allright Tucker, see that big table over there by the Palm trees, that’s Tom on the left and Robby on the right - there’s a few seats going spare if you want one and a radiator too. Made that table ours we have!’

‘Sound Martin, I’ll have some of that.’

Tucker had a knack of attracting people to him, he was more talkative than me but I was more observant. He liked talking to people, getting to know them, while I preferred watching and listening, sussing out the surroundings. He wasn't the sort to get stuck in a rut that early in the game, like me he was more into loose associations than competing egos. He wasn't a Nancy or granny or anything, just unsophisticatedly independent, whereas I was more the circumspect type, analytical and a bit reserved at first until I get to know people. But what the hell, we were trying to change our routine and this pirate saviour was offering the ideal opportunity to sit at the top table; in at the deep end, sink or swim, we didn't want to be aloof. To tell the truth I could see that it was the radiator that won Tucker over, pure and simple, so grabbing a fresh cup of tea to wash down his extra bacon sandwich Tucker wandered over to meet his new dinner partners. I followed on uninvited; by the time I got there the pirate was already making the introductions.

'Allright lads?' nodded Tucker cheerily.

'Oy oy Tucker,' Robby nodded enthusiastically. His ginger hair was cropped to a number two setting and he sported long thin sideburns like a scooter-boy. I remembered him, the whole recruit course remembered him; he was the gobby cockney geyser who had answered the corporal back when prodded with the shiny stick outside the Military Training Wing. Robby was very dynamic and when he talked he used lots of different facial expressions. 'How's it hanging mate?'

'Fine Rob, sound!' Tucker huffed deferentially.

'Watcha Tucker, who's your Oppo?' winked Tom intuitively, he looked like a right tough nut.

'Frank!' Tucker introduced me.

Tom had a mischievous grin. His eyes were as brown and shiny as conkers, set above a nose that had been smashed flat and spread across his even flatter face like a boxer, which rather affected his speech. As if to compensate for the lack of nasal intonation, Tom's voice was solemn and husky and came from the throat. He sported a mature bushy moustache as thick and wiry as his eyebrows, with broad brown sideburns to match which did little to take attention away from his broken nose. His auburn hair was neat and collar length and bore the guise of the Jason King TV Detective character popular with the ladies at that time, but he would soon resemble a troglodyte when his crowning glory was shorn off. Not for the first time, I ingenuously mused how angry do you have to be to want to punch someone's face in?

'All right Tom! Where are you lads from then?' asked Tucker; most southerners sounded like cockneys to me and him.

'Plymouth,' replied Martin, helping to pin down the pirate accent.

'London,' Tom rubbed his broken nose sniffily, confirming Tucker's initial inkling.

'Dagenham,' idly replied Robby. 'But originally from the East-End like Tom here, well me family was anyway, Poplar!'

Robby and Tom had obviously bonded in the short time they had known one another.

'Fucking hell, the Cray's!' Tucker feigned disbelief. I grinned; he had a way with words.

'Ere, I likes that Tom,' chuckled Robby. 'Ronny and Reggie, this geyser's awl right!'

Leaning forward enquiringly, Tom asked, 'Where's you from china?'

'Do I look Chinese?'

'No no, not China you smart arse!'

'Runcorn.'

'Where the bleeding hell's that then?'

'Up North fella's, the wild Northwest'.

'Me too.' I added.

'Up north hey, well we can forgive ya for that just this once,' smiled Robby, warming to me and Tucker instantly. 'Take a seat boys, we were just ripping this lot to pieces, you gotta have a laugh when you're loafing.'

'Shoot down the weaker animals,' recommended Tom. 'It gives ya the edge see?'

'You look like a bit of a mad bastard yaself mate,' observed Robby to Tucker. 'Been around the block have ya?'

'Yeh, taken a few knocks!' Tucker replied dismissively.

'Modest too Martin. I reckon we're gonna have some fun down here in the Cuds!'

Martin was a Lagger by profession in a Plymouth dock yard, Tom a Geophysicist who assisted in mapping out building sites and such like, and Robby worked for Matchbox-Lesney manufacturing model cars. The five of us together made a very diverse working-class amalgam!

'Put that smelly cigarette out!' Odd Job bawled from the sterile recesses of the steamy white tiled kitchen. 'I can smell it from here!'

Tucker and his new acquaintances looked past me across the room at five blokes who were stubbing out cigarettes, and when I turned around the smokers were wafting the air to dispel the evidence.

Odd Job charged over like a Rhinoceros in musk. 'You filthy bastards! You had to spoil the ambience. Who's the smelly turd stinking my refectory up?'

He was shouting at no one in particular but wagged his index finger towards the Alps accusingly. The commotion quickly turned into a pantomime as everyone in that vicinity twisted their heads animatedly to look at the Alpine scenery, purposely ignoring the blue-grey smog hovering around the north face of the Eiger. Odd-job stabbed his finger at the haze above their heads but the Alpine dwellers shrugged their shoulders curiously and stared back at the head Chef as if he was hallucinating.

'I will not have smoking anywhere in this building gentlemen. Understood?'

'Yes Sergeant!' lamely chorused the entire recruit course.

'Does that go for burnt toast as well?' Martin joked to anyone in earshot.

'Who's this we got here then?' Tom sneered cynically at the sergeant.

'You met Odd-Job when we queued up!' Tucker jested.

Rob & Tom started giggling uncontrollably. 'Odd-Job? You mad fucker, Tucker!'

'Oooh, dear me,' mocked Martin, tartly. 'That man's in the wrong profession, the poor love's so stressed out. Must think he's dishing up his nosh in the Savoy or the Ritz or something; totally incompatible for our little circle!'

'Oh, I say ducky, he's chosen the wrong vocation entirely,' minced Robby. 'With his social dexterity he'd make an absolutely charming padre darling. He'd be in his element giving out sermons in a frock to his flock!'

'You lot can shut it too!' Odd-job turned on his tormentors.

'More Tea Vicar!'

I laughed at these mad sods pissing around like a bunch of Queens at a mad hatter's tea party. Odd-job retreated to his sanitary kitchen, clearing away empty dishes from the servery as he passed. Once he had departed, Tom then outrageously started ripping into the chubby lad that Cpl Hazel had picked on outside the Mil Training shack on arrival. Unfortunately Todd was sat merely two tables away.

'Oy, Sweeny Todd,' Tom growled throatily like a gangster. 'Who ate all the pies then?'

A hush fell on the dining room, silently supporting the provocation, expectantly awaiting developments.

'You better belong to a loss of good looks club,' countered the tormented young man as he continued chomping on the last of his bacon sandwich, 'cos you're gonna need one mush!'

'Don't bite your hand off lard arse,' taunted Tom antagonistically, playing up to his captive audience. 'Tell you what Humpty-Dumpty, you'd make a smashing murderer you would, you'd never get yourself caught cos your big fat hairy arse would rub all your footprints away as you wobbled from the crime scene, wouldn't it hey?'

Todd shoved the table away from him roughly, attempting to get up to make a lunge but checked his temper and sat back down again. Hewitt the giant who everybody seemed to be wary of sat back nonchalantly sipping a cup of tea, looking amused. Tucker was surprised by this harassment and tried to defend the chubby lad. 'I thought you Cockney's stuck together!'

'You're making a humungous generalisation there ain't ya? That minty git ain't got no Cockney in him,' clarified Tom. 'He's a mushy!'

'Got no bleeding sense of humour either,' added Robby.

'What's a Mushy then?' I asked naively.

'Fuck me don't get awkward Frank; I thought you two were switched on! Your Mushy is deplored by you Mickey Mousers.'

'We're not technically Scouser's Tom,' Tucker tried to correct him, 'but bollocks, go on, what are you on about?'

'Don't you know nothink? Mush's are from Southampton and you Scouser's are from Liverpool!'

'Ah, football,' misinterpreted Tucker.

I suspected that we were being wound up so as to join in on the conflict and show some solidarity. 'But we support the Linnets!'

'No, not bleedin' football, ships. It's all about ships init. Don't worry son, us Londoners can't abide'em either. It all goes back to the Navy day's dunnit, when "Good Old Blighty" ruled the waves. Your Merchant Navy, right, would pick up a crew from its next port of call:

London, Liverpool, Glasgow, wherever yeh and they'd all mix together good as gold, same sort of background and all that. But your Southampton lot wouldn't mix with the likes of us, gawd knows why! S'pose it was cos they had the Queen Mary and QE2 and all that palaver. Leave'em to it mate, that's what I say!'

'Yeh, well something like that,' chipped in his mate Robby. 'I was told it was all about the Titanic, you know, maiden voyage from Southampton or something. Couple of years ago I was havin' a pint with me older brother's father-in-law, he's been in the merchant navy, and he said summit about how the White Star Line used to run all its services to Australia and America from Liverpool, did it for Donkeys years they did! Then in nineteen o seven they started operating from Southampton and by nineteen eleven they were sending three ships a week from Southampton to New-York. Well what can I tell ya, losing all that work meant Liverpool was left with just the Canada run, it caused humungous animosity?'

'But that's all in the past now surely?' Tucker was sceptical. I had to agree it all sounded like bollocks and not worth starting a fight over. Were the Cockney lads geeing us up to get us on side?

'Past my aunt Aida, he's still an ugly fat get!' provoked Tom, Loudly.

'Hey nonce,' challenged Southampton holding up a clenched fist like a school bully; besides being greedy he was compulsive and easily rattled too. 'Do you want some of this do ya?'

'Give it a rest fatty, I've just eaten ain't I,' jeered the Cockney.

'Any more from you and you'll be sucking your food through a straw.'

Tom laughed incredulously. 'Wind your neck in or I'll sort you out in three hits. Me hitting you, you hitting the floor and the ambulance hitting seventy miles an hour!'

'Right that's it, you two, pack it in now!' demanded Odd Job, surging through the forest of Formica tables and plastic chairs to get to the Tropics. 'What's all the brouhaha? Do you two want to go on a Fizza? It's your first day here you bunch of bleedin' animals! I'll put you both on a charge big time if you don't stop winding each other up, got that?'

'All right Sarge, no need for an eppy, they're just having a laugh!' insisted Robby, trying to take the heat out of the situation. 'Honest, you're over reacting china, it's just a bit of banter, they're best mates really, ain'tcha boys?'

Both lads gazed around the canteen at the staring faces and laughed apathetically. No one was in any doubt that Tom could've wiped the floor with Todd; he was just flexing his muscles and setting out his stall, the sort of behaviour you see between rivals in a pub after a football match.

Tucker glanced at me and raised an eyebrow. I read his thought, "This is a bloody good start isn't it?"

Just the sort of thing me and Tucker normally avoided, we didn't want to sit on the side lines, but then again we didn't want to sit on the fence either. That's the problem with being sensible, it's incompatible with passion. Who should we choose as our mates, blokes who we had instantly clicked with, or blokes who by default we had ended up being in the same platoon as? Tucker's maturity surfaced and we decided to be diplomatic and sit this one out for now. We could casually give this lot a wide birth next mealtime and sit at another table, we didn't want to be marked down as being trouble makers; it was early days yet!

'It ain't funny,' solemnly persisted the head chef in a standoff, but although his authority was being undermined he seemed reluctant to be too heavy handed.

'Allright, calm down Mush!' No need to tell you who said that.

'Mush, mush? I am not you're bleeding dog…' seethed Odd Job towards the chubby lad from Southampton.

'All right Sarge, Jesus you're over reacting!' Tom intervened, barely hiding a smile.

'…I'm watching you lot,' cautioned Sgt Ernie Lee, 'drink your tea and bugger off!'

We hurried back with our platoon mates to be fleeced by the Barbers; even those who didn't need a haircut went through the motions and parted with a fifty pence piece. It's funny how a short-back-and-sides can alter someone's appearance isn't it. Haircuts can transform persona too, some people lose a lot of their confidence when they lose their crowning glory while others seem to bristle like little hard knocks. It perked me up, it was very therapeutic. The barbers shuffled through the growing mass of hair clippings developing on the wooden floor and one of them set about trimming up the hair on the lad who had big teeth. Once Whittling had got his head exposed, it transpired that he had big ears too.

Tucker was cropped next and as he brushed the hair trimmings from his shoulders I began to wonder how much Cpl Hazel was making out of all this; surely there must have been a pint or two in it for him, he'd already collected £15 from us for a £7.50 electric iron!

Having left the warmth of the barbers we joined all the other new recruits and ambled back up the slope towards the Military Training Wing to once more get the run-around from the corporal who had met us at the onset of this ordeal. One hundred and nineteen civilians full of bacon, beans, spuds and hot army tea silently formed up into the three ranks the junior NCO had sorted us into on arrival. We seemed to wait for an eternity. The back of my neck began to feel the cold as I looked around at my new mates who were loosely stood in three ranks. I knew from their expressions that like me their minds were simultaneously screaming, "Come on you buggers we're freezing out here, what happened to military precision?"

In their own time the instructors appeared and then double marched us recruits across the parade square to a lecture room. "EFT, IGHT, EFT, IGHT, EFT IGHT, LEFFFT."

Two men from HQ 7 Intelligence Company of the Army-Intelligence-Corp greeted us on arrival, one a lanky fair-haired Staff Sergeant with a barrel chest, the other a balding Captain with the beginnings of a paunch whose belt seemed to hold him together in the middle.

The NCOs from the Mil Training Wing promptly disappeared; they had an innate mistrust of Spooks - or the Green Slime, as servicemen of the British Army commonly refer to them. The ice was broken with a few nervous jokes about the intelligence-corps' role in military life, then the two men launched into their specialist subject and talked at length about espionage, terrorism, subversion and a soldiers responsibilities regarding security. The sneaky beaks taught the recruits a condensed edition of the Do's-and-Don'ts, covering documents, equipment, arms & ammunition, then swiftly on through to blackmail, loose talk, researchers & investigators, and unsolicited questionnaires received from publishers of directories through the mail. To drive the point home the spooks gave an example whereby Soviet intelligence had gleaned a list of Territorial Army Reservists names and addresses, then systematically written bogus love letters in female hand writing to their home address, doused in perfume and very explicit: -

Darling I miss you, when are you coming back again?

Life isn't much fun without your little visits, and the odd weekend here, and a fortnights leave there is not nearly enough time for us to spend together! Little Ben misses you too; he's growing up quickly and asks about you all the time, it's difficult to explain your absence to him. He needs a man in his life, and quite frankly I do too. I tell him that you are a very important soldier in the Army darling, and that one day you will come home and settle down and he will have a happy family life like his friends.

While you've been gone I've been able to find some part-time work, the money you send each month isn't enough to support us both and you did promise us more. I wish you would be as generous with your money as you are with your love making you horny sod. Oh, I'm sorry to go on like this, it must be difficult for you too while your away, but I miss you so much, my body aches for you and you're always in my dreams my love. Phone me. I want to hear your voice again. My nipples are tingling at the thought of you.

All my Love… Felicity xxxxx

You can imagine the response from a suspicious wife after steaming open something like that! How do you explain it away? "It's ok love; the Secret Squirrels said something like this might happen one day, honest!"

No more fortnights away for this bloke! It had now become apparent that hostile Intelligence Organisations operate in all walks of life, and apparently, from now on, mine and Tucker's job was to play the game and defeat them! As with everything else the Army teaches to its trainees, the talks on security are ingrained and suspicions are quickly roused when something out of the ordinary occurs - Eyes & Ears.

It had been comforting to relax in the sedate warmth of a classroom but once the secret squirrels had sufficiently spooked us out, the platoons were formed up outside in the freezing cold and marched back to the spiders at quick time and ordered to change into red PT vests and baggy blue shorts. We were then jogged down to the perimeter fence at the back of the base and funnelled through a steel security gate in single file. Once outside the boundary, we ran for fifteen minutes through farmland to warm us up, stopping occasionally to perform push-ups on the frozen track. Daylight was fading as we neared a sandy embankment. Cpl Hazel brought 3Platoon to a halt to get our breath back, or so we thought. After two minutes the stragglers caught up and the entire recruit course was ordered to climb the steep sandy slope as fast as we could. Pandemonium set in as one hundred and nineteen recruits jostled each other to reach the top of a thirty foot high sand bank, only to be forced down the other side at double speed and around once more to start the ascent again. With seven instructors barking at us continuously, there was no holding back. I congratulated myself for all those extra hours me and Tucker had put in, pounding the streets and canal paths back home in an endeavour to improve our fitness, but nothing had prepared us for this. We forced ourselves up the bank a second and third time, but like countless others, my whole body screamed with pain. My lungs were burning and my heart thumped like a trip hammer as I struggled up the incline for the fourth and last time, Tucker had a stream of snot hanging from his nostrils. Back on the path at the bottom of the sand bank, the platoons were reorganised and formed up into three ranks, legs buckling like jelly and sweat streaming from their foreheads in bucket loads; I could feel my heart beating in my teeth. Tucker wiped his snotty face against the back of his sweaty forearm. Todd, the lad they now called Humpty-Dumpty, pushed past Tucker gasping for air. Todd's eyes were rolling around in the sockets of his bright red contorted face. No time for him to rest though, once he was fell in with the rest of us the platoons set off back towards the perimeter fence in a brisk jog. Each and every man sucked air deep into their lungs while once more stopping along the way to perform press-ups on the frost covered dirt track; it was both knackering and exhilarating. Back at the spider there was no congratulations from the staff, just an informal dismissal.

'Every man get a shower, changed back into uniform and get away for your evening meal, GO!' barked a Scottish Staff Sergeant.

The spider was a hive of frenzied activity as fights for the steaming shower cubicles erupted. There was no standing on ceremony. As one bloke stepped out of a shower another dived in. The smells of toothpaste, soap, shampoo, antiperspirant and testosterone fuelled the air as we ran around frantically drying ourselves with green army issue towels barely big enough to wrap around the waist. Wet footprints littered the building creating yet another task to attend to before meal time, but no one seemed to care.

As soon as Tucker and some of our new chums were showered and clothed, they bolted out into the cold air and ran down to Odd job's chow house for some welcome scran and a mug of hot sweet tea. I needed to get my head together, all this dashing around was no good for me; I liked to wind down a bit at the end of the day. When I caught up with the others queuing to enter the dining room it was pitch black outside, save for the light streaming from the cookhouse windows. The temperature outside was plummeting fast.

Tucker was already sat in the Tropics at the table by the radiator, along with Martin Flowers, Tom Lloyd and Robby Watson - Tish Hewitt and a few others from 3Platoon had grabbed some of the spare seats, I was relegated to the table next to them by the time I was served. The dining room buzzed noisily with conversations recounting the day's events; the din was amplified by the sound of rattling plates being slid from the warmed stack on the stainless steel servery while metal serving utensils smashed down on the china plates to dislodge stodgy food.

'This is triffic, could get used to having a meal ready on the table when I get home after knocking off!' Tom Lloyd lived alone in a flat; his no-nonsense diet was mainly micro-waved chicken ding meals, boil-in-the-bag concoctions, or something lacklustre from the local chippy on the way home.

'Did you see Humpty Dumpty's chubby face when we were running up that sand dune? Beetroot he was!' giggled Robby Watson.

'Yeh, that fat git needs to shift some weight mate.' speculated Tom Lloyd.

'Haven't you heard,' interrupted Sooty Corbett. 'Todd's been taken away by the medics in an ambulance, suspected heart attack or something!'

'You're having a bubble ain't cha?' exclaimed Tom with genuine surprise.

It wasn't long before the jungle drums were out and the grim news was buzzing around the mess hall. We all finished our meal in subdued silence; nobody likes to hear bad news at mealtime.

Chapter 4

Martinique Barracks was located far enough away from civilisation to offer a sense of sanctuary; it appeared very calm by night. The wooden buildings absorbed any noise produced by localised activity, which in turn created the sort of muffled hush you often experience when camping out. The quiet of the wooden Spider was occasionally interrupted by the hissing of the steam iron as it pressed two trouser legs together, or the intermittent thud of boots wandering along the corridor up to the entrance, followed by the front door squeaking open and thumping shut as the wearer of the boots stepped outside.

The mood remained a bit sombre after we had returned from our evening meal. We sat on the ends of our beds bulling up best boots whilst quietly speculating on how the chubby Southampton lad was getting on? Other than the hissing of the steam iron, the only sound in the room emanated from Whittling who swiftly manhandled the bumper from side to side across the floor in an endeavour to eradicate recent boot marks and restore a sheen. He momentarily stopped bumpering and mused. 'There must be an easier way to keep this bloody thing shiny?'

'There is dad!' offered Brummy Jennings matter-of-factly. He was counting up a stack of ten pence pieces which he had collected in order to phone up his wife from the public telephone box down at the NAFFI. 'We need to get hold of a spare blanket right, and cut it into squares to walk on don't we, that way right, while we're shuffling around we'll be keeping the flower polished, won't we hey?'

'That's champion Jennings,' acknowledged Tish Hewitt.

'Yeh I thought so, bosting aynt it.' Jennings enjoyed compliments.

'Only one problem,' criticised Sooty. 'Where are we going to get a spare blanket in a shit hole like this?'

'Stand by your beds!' Cpl Hazel bawled as he barged down the corridor and in to our billet; he sounded well pissed off. The peak of his hat was pulled down menacingly over his eyes and nose so that his moustache and chin were the only discernible features on his face. He pointed his shiny parade stick commandingly in the direction of Todd's bed space.

'Tug, get someone to help you gather up Humpty-Dumpty's belongings and move them over to the stores, chop chop, he won't be needing them now. Lance Corporal Hughes will meet you there in five minutes. Hand all his kit in, and any loot or personal effects that you find, pass them on to me. The rest of you crack on with your boots.'

Tug recruited Sooty and Tish to help him. Jennings stared at the blankets on Todd's bed-space and nodded suggestively while making polishing motions with his hands. Tucker winked at me craftily and we volunteered too, between the five of us it wouldn't be such a burden as it had been transferring the bundle of kit from the stores to the spider earlier on in the day.

L/Cpl Hughes was ready and waiting when we arrived. The Welshman was wrapped up in a non-regulation green Parker. The fur-lined hood and his foggy breath obscured his spotty face. He must have been practicing for the eisteddfod because he was singing Land of my Fathers or something, '… ac ar y fferm roedd ganddo wartheg, E I E I Oh…. right listen now boys, where has yewer been? Stood by heure five minutes I bloddy have see and it's colder than a Penguin's bolocks, isn't it!'

The kit was bundled away into the allotted places. Boots with boots, socks with socks, 58 Pattern Webbing with Webbing etc., and the mattress and one blanket stashed away in the bedding department - the Store-man never noticed one missing!

'Right that's it, off yewer go then,' Taffy hastily dismissed the removal men. 'Got some serious drinking to do I have see, haven't I. Welwn ni chi wedyn.'

On the way back to the spider we bumped into Brummy Jennings returning from the NAFFI after phoning his dear wife. He told us that he liked to keep a check on her on account that she had suffered a prolapsed disc in her spine which had gone on to rupture. Consequently the disc had been surgically removed and she now suffered from a lot of pain because of it. His wife would have had to rely on pain management alone if it wasn't for Jennings' fussy inventive nature; he was always thinking up ways to make her plight more bearable. Holding down a fulltime job and caring for his wife's needs put a strain on Jennings too. So he had signed up for the T.A. as an escape from his burgeoning responsibilities. No matter how much he loved his wife, he realised that he needed a safety valve to let off a bit of steam from time to time and likewise she needed to rid him from under her feet. They were both hoping that the TA would provide this catharsis. Most of the lads thought he was a buffoon, but I thought he was more a boffin and maybe should have volunteered to help out the National trust or Greenpeace or something less demanding, somewhere he could relax amongst likeminded people. He seemed too passive and a tinge apprehensive in nature for all of this army lark. When he did become animated he couldn't contain himself, he bordered on the neurotic where intellectual challenges and originality of thought were concerned. He explained to us a brainwave that he'd had whilst returning from the telephone box and we had to admit that it sounded feasible, well at least it would be fun trying it out!

Back at the billet, Jennings put an arm around Whittling's shoulder and coaxed him into sitting in the centre of the blanket which had just been purloined; the rest of us took turns at sliding Whittling up and down the floor, it was immense fun! When we had finished buffing the floor, Jennings measured and cut the pilfered bedspread into squares to be divided up amongst the platoon to use as slippers. We all practiced sliding around on Brummy Jennings novel creation and congratulated him with thumbs up gestures.

Tug Wilson slid around the room on his squares of blanket switching on everyone's bed-space light to check that all the bulbs were working satisfactorily, and when content that all were in working order he switched off the main lights and slumped onto his bed. He casually explained that having once been rescued from his blazing bedroom after being electrocuted so badly that he'd laid in a coma, he now had a healthy phobia of all things electrical. Once Tug's mind was reassured of his personal safety he then started to sew onto his blazer the TA Regimental badge he had bought from the CSM during admin. The position of authority that Cpl Hazel had bestowed upon Tug seemed to have its perks, none of *us* were allowed access to our clothing but Tug had been able to retrieve his black Barafia jacket.

With a flourish, Whittling gracefully sashayed to his bed space at the other end of the room, displaying an elegance which Lionel Blair would have been proud of! This exhibition caused one or two raised eyebrows, and Tish Hewitt softly wolf whistled?

When Whittling reached his bed space he then flopped onto his mattress and gingerly switched on a transistor radio, which was tuned to a talk show. Wrapped up in himself he then lolled back against his pillow as if the external world around him only existed insofar as to serve his self-centred purposes, well that's how his detached solipsist behaviour appeared to the rest of us in the platoon!

An older lad, a heavily tattooed biker from Northampton, calling himself Spike, who had been listening to Led Zeppelin on his Sony Walkman, lifted one of his headphones aside, lit a cigarette and casually asked the lads. 'Did you hear about the bloke what got put inside for mugging a granny, got three years he did, fucking bastard. Anyway, first night in the slammer he got banged up in a cell with this mad Hells-Angel from Winchester called Beelzebub Gardner. "Let's play Mummy's and Daddy's" suggested Beelzebub, "who does you wants to be?" Well the mugger shit himself, he didn't want to be the bitch so he suggested, "The Daddy," and Beelzebub growled at him, "Right Daddy, get over here now and suck Mummy's cock!"

The lads laughed good heartedly at this anecdote, it was a helpful icebreaker. Spike noisily snorted back some mucus from his nose and swallowed it.

'Do you think that Corporal Hughes is gay?' asked Tish Hewitt, trying to act blasé, but the remark sounded comical coming from the gruff Yorkshire-man because when he spoke he sounded as if he was wearing his granddad's false teeth!

'Why, do you fancy him then?' Spike feigned surprise while coughing some phlegm up from his lungs with a harsh yocking noise, gargled the sticky residue from his throat with a mouthful of spit and gulped the resulting slime as if it was a delicious oyster. It made me feel queasy.

Big Tish's belly rumbled audibly as he squeezed out some gas. 'No mate, it's just that he walks like he's got his knees tied together, that's all.'

No doubt Tish Hewitt's unsubtle invective was intended to be provocative, it certainly worked. A Cockney lad called Stan, who had claimed the bed next to Tucker, idly took the bait. 'A mincer, nah, hardly Oscar Wilde is he?'

'Nope, can't see it,' joined in Sooty Corbett as he Blue-tacked a page 3 girl onto the inside of his locker door. 'A sheep shagger maybe but not a bender, not in this man's army surely. He's just a bit dramatic, you know passionate; the Welsh are like that mate.'

Stan agreed, 'I ain't never met a pillow biting sheep shagger yet! I don't think they exist do they?'

Sooty Corbett then took out a photograph of his wife from his wallet and Blue-tacked that next to the page 3 model. With a boastful wink he announced "Hello beautiful."

Spike chuckled "You should see my wife!"

Sooty replied "Why is she a stunner?"

"No, she's an optician mate!" Spike chuckled.

The joke seemed to go right over Sooty's Head, but it made some of us grin with a grimace, ouch!

Martin Flowers had the bed the other side of Tucker. He was unusually quiet and acting a bit standoffish. To my mind he was prone to be a bit of an attention seeking joker in a crowd, always laughing like a mischievous scallywag, but he seemed to be unsettled and introspective now that he was back in the wooden hut, as if he'd sooner be somewhere else. I'd heard him telling Tucker earlier that he and his wife had split up; maybe his recent divorce had unnerved him a little too. He wore his heart on his sleeve; I sensed that he would've been better placed with Robby & Tom his cockney friends in 2platoon where he was better ranked socially. Tish Hewitt and Spike had gravitated towards each other like two planets and drew people into their orbit with their uncouth banter; Tish was a bit of a meat head and Spike was as smoky and smooth as a single malt whiskey. There were a lot of strong characters in 3platoon to contend with and Martin seemed a bit depressed at having to adopt a subordinate position. He had tried to hide it, but I could sense that he didn't particularly like Cpl Hazel either (who did?) and didn't relish being in his platoon. Fortunately these trials have a knack of sorting themselves out in a competitive environment; Martin's sullenness would be short lived and there would be no loss of aspiration!

Tucker was on the ball, he noticed me studying his neighbour and raised an eyebrow. He grinned and then turned to Martin Flowers enquiringly, 'What's up?'

Breaking his broody silence the pirate shrugged his shoulders and pulled a face dismissively. He then joined in on the smutty banter instigated by Spike and Tish Hewitt. 'Whores piss, Taffy's as gay as a row of cottages. I bet he likes his bread toasted on three sides.'

'You don't know that.' Disagreed Tucker, latching onto the curious insinuation floating around the barrack room, no doubt it was inadvertently directed at skinny Whittling.

I latched on to it myself; was there a slight whiff of bullying? It felt like they were trying to brand Whittling the whipping boy. Mind you, he had brought it on himself by prancing around like a fairy, that sort of behaviour always gets your back up doesn't it, and if you disregarded Whittling's graveyard teeth and his sticky out ears, he was reasonably pretty too? I naturally assumed that Whittling had inherited those diverse features from his mother and a bad dentist.

I shook my head to displace these thoughts, the banter was humorous and too light for victimisation, the lads were merely being macho, clashing their wits, establishing their manliness, talking the talk, adapting to a new dominance hierarchy by humorously intimating at how hard they each were. Big Tish resembled a Silverback Gorilla, so had no need to beat his chest, but even so he farted a lot to emphasise his manliness. I was familiar with the chest beating, Tucker was too; our older brothers had often invited us to a game of chance and uncertainty with their card playing mates, weighing one another up and flexing muscle by throwing disrespectful jibes at each other was all part of the game. Interacting in this way was a tonic for the recruits too; they were gaining affiliation rather than just coexisting.

Being the baby of his family, Tucker had learned to fight his own corner or put on a poker face in such situations and not yield to anyone rattling him; I'd seen him in intimidating positions similar to this, and like me he was particularly good at playing his cards close to his chest. I had discovered that it was much more effective to act like a nice guy and be reasonable; it was easier than a double bluff. Instead of wasting my energy bigging it up and being offensive, I could more effectively concentrate on the cards which life had dealt me. I found out by trial and error that I can afford to be compassionate, lax, and courteous because once in a while, when least expected but completely justified, I will savage someone who has crossed me, an enemy, just to show that I can walk the walk.

Tucker was more forbearing than most and could not condone mob rule, especially against someone who was a bit different, even if they did make you feel slightly apprehensive. He would have to check himself because his tolerance rather rubbed against the grain now that he had gotten himself involved with a militia. Like a majority of men he was not aroused by homosexuality and considered it to be perverse, but so long as it was kept out of his face, he was quite tolerant about it. My attitude too!

To my mind Whittling appeared more fey than gay and could be forgiven for being a bit of an introspective knobhead. To deflect the attention away from Whittling I steered the conversation back towards the Welsh store-man. 'Taffy's just visiting,' I shrugged irrelevantly. 'He'll be back in the valleys in a couple of weeks' time.'

'Yeh suppose so,' Tish Hewitt eyed me and Tucker sternly, weighing us up and down. Once the assessment was over, he stared long and hard in Whittling's direction and then farted. 'There's nowt as funny as folk except thee and me and thar's a bit queer!'

Whittling turned off his transistor radio. His eyes were turbulent as he slowly rose to his feet in an attempt at asserting his own masculinity. The room fell silent. If you're going to do it, do it right now! I thought supportively.

Whittling's quavering voice was angst ridden. 'What are you getting at Tish?'

'I was just saying; watch your backs, just healthy homophobia!' Tish Hewitt smirked, pleased with himself that he'd struck a raw nerve.

Brummy Jennings rebuked the lame insinuations, whether deliberately levelled at the Taffy Store-man across the way or sarcastically poking fun at Whittling. 'You can make out that any body's a ring jabber if you try hard enough, am I right everybody? Your average sheep shagger probably discovers incest before any homosexual tendencies surface; the Welsh are too busy gathering slates and stealing coal dust, ain't they.'

'Yeh, sex with miners' ain't a crime in Wales,' joked Sooty, gesturing to Whittling to sit back down and not cause a scene by drawing any more attention to himself.

'Taffy's probably led a sheltered life,' added Spike, winking at Whittling supportively. 'Give him another year and he'll be just as big a bastard as those fucking NCO Instructors sipping tea across the road there. I'm telling you lads, it's a hard life in the army; no one gets pampered!'

'I were only asking opinion that's all, you know, didn't mean nowt by it.' Apologised Tish, back-pedalling defensively now that his remark had backfired!

'You do fancy him, don't you big man?' teased Sooty, ruthlessly pinning the Yorkshire-man against the ropes. 'I bet you want to polish his rusty sheriff's badge and give him a chocolate starfish! Anyway, how's that boy?'

‘What boy?’

‘That boy you sleep with!’

Tish threw the boot he’d been polishing at Corbett’s head and grunted. ‘Fook right off, ya lanky streak of piss.’

Sooty jumped off his bed, and holding Tish Hewitt’s discarded boot by the toe hammer like, slid on his squares of blanket across the floor reminiscent of a stealthy ninja. Tish tensed up expecting Sooty to lay into him with the boot, but Sooty simply advised. ‘Keep still big man!’

Crawling from the light fitting above Hewitt’s bed-space was a spider-monster going on a walkabout. As Corbett approached, the arachnid stopped dead in its tracks, vainly hoping that it had not been noticed.

Tug Wilson jumped up to examine the spider. ‘Corr, look at size of that bastard, must have come over on a Banana boat.’

However, before Corbett could strike, the spider decided that its best course of action was a swift retreat. So, keeping one eye on the direction of travel, five of its other eyes searched for alternative routes of escape. It scuttled back towards the sanctuary of the light installation, fixing a seventh beady eye on Corbett’s looming shadow; its eighth eye scanned the hasty approach of Whittling gliding across the room clutching a teacup. Anticipating that the game was up, the eight legged creature danced despairingly on the spot then stopped once more, hoping to blend into its surroundings, but taking consideration of the interest it had attracted, it judiciously changed its mind and furtively inched its hairy way up towards the ceiling.

The commotion aroused Jennings from his bed. ‘Blimey, that’s a belter ain’t it dad?’

‘Don’t kill it,’ pleaded Whittling, placing the cup against the wall to trap the beast. The spider retreated into the drinking vessel as Whittling placed a bony hand over it. Satisfied that the dextrous organism was captive, Whittling majestically skated across the shiny floor to the fire exit by his bed space, opened the door and launched the spider, sling fashion into the chilly night air, he then did a pirouette. ‘It was probably cold; they come inside for a warm you know?’

‘Sod off you divvy fucker, it won’t get any warmth in here boy,’ Martin Flowers joked.’

‘You should have mashed its brains in and put it out of its fuckin misery.’

‘Someone ought to put you out of your misery you morbid sod,’ replied Whittling, his lips spreading across his prominent buckled teeth in a satisfied smile.

‘Shut the door!’ sorely insisted the others; he was letting all the precious heat out.

‘There are thirty two thousand species of spiders in the world,’ Jennings drearily informed us in his Black-country whine. ‘Bet you didn’t know that then did you hey?’

Stan interjected. ‘Do you know that the word gullible ain’t even in the Oxford English dictionary?’

‘It is isn’t it, surely it is? Jennings frowned. ‘Have to look that one up when I get home!’

Stan picked up a newspaper dismissively in an attempt at ignoring the bore of Birmingham, the rest of us returned to quietly polishing our boots and other stuff.

‘Plus, two thirds of all insects are Beetles,’ the Brummy continued mind-numbing the lads of 3Platoon. ‘There are twelve million species of beetles you know, and the humble bumble bee is responsible for keeping the planet habitable. If it weren’t for them pollinating the flowers and trees and stuff, there wouldn’t be any oxygen produced and we would all die from air pollution within a year we would, so next time you want to kill one….!’

‘Boring, I knobbed my cousin at a party once,’ confided Spike, stumping out his cigarette and exhaling a stream of smoke from his nostrils. ‘I was fifteen and she’d just turned fourteen, gagging for it we were, pissed as farts, couldn’t help ourselves. She’d been for a piss and when she came out of the loo she had the back of her dress caught up in her knickers. I copped an eyeful, couldn’t help myself could I, just peeled them down and grabbed hold of her snatch. I know what you’re thinking lads, dirty bastard alert! Before you knew it we were at it good style, know warra mean? Don’t get me wrong fellas, it was mutual attraction and it was all over in a jiffy. As soon as the dirty deed was done, we felt embarrassed. No harm in it hey, only a bit of fun, animal magnetism and all that. Fucking hell, come on, you never fancy your cousin or what?’

‘Close family are you?’ Sooty, scoffed nonchalantly.

Jennings piped up supportively. ‘Sure we have Spike, it’s only human nature ain’t it. You’d be a hypocrite if ya said ya never had lusty thoughts, just gotta cattail your feelings is all dad. Hypocrisy is the homage that vice pays to virtue you know!’

Spike’s lude intimacy produced embarrassed awkward sniggers amongst the rest of the lads. His frank revelation was a bit disconcerting, too profound to be aired in a room full of strangers; it was such a thing as uncle bob's suicide, or aunty Flo's extramarital affair with the insurance-man, something which is vaguely hinted at during a family get together and best forgotten.

Boys will be boys I thought. I'd never been sexually attracted to any of my cousins, although Tucker once told me he considered his aunty Grace to be a bit of a stunner, and admittedly I thought so too. I didn't dwell on the subject for very long though; we had far too much to be getting on with so I returned to industriously bulling up my boots, more in the way of a distraction. The steam iron and ironing board became vacant so Tucker had a turn at meticulously pressing creases into his green light-weight trousers. The rest of the lads quietly attended to their personal admin too.

Brummy Jennings had now abandoned his boot polishing to write a brief letter to his wife, his fishbowl glasses were perched on top of his forehead like a Hollywood superstar as he composed; he obviously didn't need them for reading and writing. I couldn't help noticing that Jennings seemed to be reading the brief few lines he had written over and over again and would then stare off into space absorbed in thought. Intrigued by this, it dawned on me that the writer was in actual fact composing poetry; the silly sod was in love!

Tucker noticed this too; intrigued, he momentarily stopped ironing one leg of his trousers and a hiss of steam issued into the cold air as he stood the iron upright on the end of the ironing board. There was a slight magnetism about Jennings, trivial but fascinating; a seductive energy which cancelled out all of the Birmingham master-bore's annoying know-it-all character traits, nevertheless you wouldn't want Jennings pitching up a tent in your back garden. As meditative as he was inclined to be on occasion, sure as night follows day Jennings was unable to keep silent longer than five minutes. He looked up between sentences to tell any of his new companions who was listening that he was from Edgbaston and that he worked for security at Coventry Airport, he just blurted it out. He said that his wife had a twin, and when Spike the biker asked him how he was able to tell them apart, Jennings replied that one of them had a baldhead and a moustache.

The lads of 3Platoon each in turn then followed suit; occupation, marital-status, interests and age; Spike seemed to be the oldest, he was approaching middle age. There were a lot of thrill seekers in the room, a couple of chaps with a degree in fun and a few masters of mayhem thrown in for good measure too. There was a joiner, a heating engineer, a clerk, a grave digger, a driving instructor, a few fruit machine players with lots of pens in their top pockets (computer whiz-kids), several mechanics and assorted drivers, and a sundry clutch of fascinating factory workers. Ronny Churchill was a builder from Chepstow, and Rodger Boileiu, from Towyn in North Wales, said that he didn't really have a job as such because his dad was a successful Scrap-metal Merchant who provided Rodger with an allowance to live off - what a lucky sod? Tish Hewitt was a roofer, Tug Wilson an undertaker's assistant from Norwich, Sooty Corbett was training to be a Lab-Rat for Kodak in a film laboratory, and the bloke in the next bed down from Tucker, called Stan, was a Cabby from Walthamstow in London, which promptly earned him the nickname Stan-the-Cab.

Jennings asked why they had each wanted to join the T.A. and answers ranged from: "For a laugh and the sheer hell of it!" to, "Got to get away from the wife and kids!", and finally, Skinny Whittling's whimsical reply. 'I want to be in a gang!'

Tish Hewitt scoffed at this last rejoinder. 'Billy no mates!'

Whittling was the victim of sarcastic bullying in his home town, like a bad smell it seemed to follow him around. He was different and that disparity attracted widespread condemnation amongst his peers, Martinique barracks was no safe haven either. He proceeded cautiously; as his diffidence melted though it became clear that he was a bit of an attention seeker. His confidence grew sufficient enough to tell his new gang that he was into genealogy, and that he'd once traced his family descendants back to King Edward III, making him a Plantagenet. Tish Hewitt pointed out that Edward the 2nd was reputed to be bisexual; which made me think to myself, here we go again, more queer bating?

Ironically, Tucker recalled the earlier conversation he'd had with Tish Hewitt regarding his penchant for Ballroom dancing, so he pushed the Yorkshire lad for more information.

'Here Tish, were you serious about being a champion dancer or was you having a giggle?'

'No it's straight up is that, I've won cups and medals from allova't place; Scarborough, Blackpool, Brighton, allover.'

'Bleeding hell Tish, you don't look like a fairy!' scoffed Spike the Biker, lighting up another cigarette.

'Walked right into that one didn't ah?' he mused then confided in a man-to-man tone. 'No right, me Gran got me into it as bit of a lark to try and keep us out of trouble. I were a tear-arse heading for Borstal me, a reet flipping mad Aleck.'

'Recklessness!' Jennings peered over his glasses at Tish Hewitt reproachfully. 'Subject to a failure of will power and reasoning by a childish and unparalleled heedlessness at the very instant when prudence and vigilance are most essential, hey dad?'

Tish Hewitt paid no attention to the insightful remark, he simply did not comprehend it. 'Gran brought me up on todd cause of me mam clearing off and leaving us when ahr were two; me mam were seduced as lass by an older man. She were only fourteen at time, and he was in fifties!'

'Yeh well that would do it that would!' Jennings exonerated Tish Hewitt.

'A Paedophile,' realised Spike aloud, 'your Dad?'

'S'pose so, but happen that don't matter. Gran brought me up by herself as best the lass could on pension.'

'She's done a good job of it too by the looks of ya. I'd sooner keep you for a week than a fortnight, you must've eaten her out of house and home China!' imagined Stan-the-Cab.

'Yeh, reckon so!' reflected the huge Roofer.

Stan-the-Cab was in his thirties, laid back and a bit of a daddy; he was the salt of the earth. His head was full of the knowledge, which somehow leant him a very forthright approach to things. Crow's feet prematurely lined his eyes with just a hint of grey at the temples of his thick black hair; he had a bit of a Groucho Marx moustache growing too. His physique was amazing, like a Victorian human cannon ball; the anatomical man which you see in medical books, perfectly toned, not an ounce of fat, chiselled to within an inch of Leonardo de Vinci's Vitruvian man; the only thing marring his chiselled looks was an angry scar stretching from the back of his neck and downwards across his right shoulder blade, a wound inflicted by a mugger who had demanded Stan's takings at knife point from the rear of his cab. Stan retaliated and the offender had fled empty handed, but robustly Stan, aided by his fellow Cabbies, had managed to hunt him down! Stan-the-Cab and big Tish complemented each other.

You got what you saw with Tish, his own personal creed was simple – to appreciate the best in life, you have to have suffered the worst. He had no sides, just a straight up front take it or leave it attitude, a typical Yorkshire-man. He had no regard for compassionate analysis. 'Growing up were hard lads, but no harder than for others in Leeds, especially Christmas time when you got what you needed and knelt of what you really wanted, but luckily for me I were a grafter and always had job ont side. I did newspaper round in week before school and delivered meat for Co-op on estate of a Satday. Gran luffed bones off of me and never gave up on us. When she first got me going Ballroom I thought it were proper soppy, till I started meeting lasses like. I were a proper boy, into usual, you know, rugby and robbing cars and burning them out on estate of a night, till I met Gina.'

'Love of your life is she? Sooty Corbett hinted with a knowing grin.

'She's nearly as tall as ya sen fellah. She'd just moved down from Donny, didn't have a boyfriend yet. I lost it lads, made her me dancing partner, fell head'ova'heels in love we did. I remember first time I met lass, some youths were jostling her about outside dancehall, trying rob her dancing shoes for a laugh, but…'

Stan-the-Cab congratulated him, '…and you intervened, good lad!'

'Dead reet ahr did. Took one look at me and didn't want a piece…'

'…too right mate,' nodded Stan, 'suicidal to mess with you, I'd have scarpered too!'

'It's man's natural instinct is that dad,' appreciated Jennings, 'protecting a female! I used to do some boxing meself you know, oh yes; I'm no stranger to the ring!'

'Oh aye yeh,' guffawed Spike the Biker. 'A ring doughnut?'

'I keep myself in shape dad.'

'Yeh balloon shape!'

Nothing could get to a bloke like Tish Hewitt, he was solid. 'Married with three babbies now and other ont way, things have habit of working out in't end if ya ler'em!'

'Ah now, don't know much about that boy, my maid is a proper little house keeper,' proclaimed Martin Flowers, recently divorced. 'Yeh, when I got bin-bagged she kept the bleeding house and all the sodding furniture too she did!'

'I'm still living at home with my ninety five years old mother.' Said Sooty Corbet. 'I pick her up out of her bed every morning and carry her down stairs to make my breakfast. There ain't many sons considerate enough who'd do that for their poor old mother these days is there!'

The lads all laughed at that, then a small bloke known as Diddy Baxter, a cheerful grave digger from Derbyshire, told an amusing tale. He came from a small town in the High Peaks, you know the sort of place, rural, curtains twitching, where everybody knows everybody else's private business; not much to do socially other than catch up on all the gossip at the local pub. Diddy Baxter reminisced about the time he had split up with his girlfriend. He'd gone to the pub to drown his sorrows following their separation, but a few pints later, decided he wanted to be alone with his thoughts.

He went for a walk and headed towards the river to sort his head out, and while crossing the eighty foot high bridge, he chose to climb upon the parapet and walk along it with a devil-may-care sort of attitude. Unfortunately he lost his balance and slipped, and with nothing to grab hold of, plunged over the side and dropped like a sack of spuds. Purely by chance he managed to bounce off the branches of a tree on the riverbank, which fortunately broke his fall; otherwise he would have ended up like so many suicide victims who had favoured that particular spot, a pile of splattered meat and broken bones on the rocks below. He picked himself up, caught his breath and dusted off his bruised and battered body, then staggered home for a wash and change of clothing. His brush with death on lover's leap had sobered him up no end, so in hind sight he decided to try and patch things up with his fiancé and have a bash at giving their relationship another go. Once he had showered and changed into fresh clothes he headed back to the pub, situated on the far side of the bridge. Whilst returning he couldn't help noticing that a crowd had gathered mid-way across it. He asked a policeman what was going on, and the copper told him that some poor sod had committed suicide.

"Who was it?" asked Diddy Baxter.

"A bloke called Diddy Baxter, do you know him?" replied the trauma-weary officer "We're dredging the river for his body now!"

On informing the police officer that he was Diddy Baxter, the policeman went berserk and arrested him for attempting suicide, but had to drop charges once Baxter had convincingly pleaded his innocence and established that his fall was not intentional. Diddy Baxter *was* cautioned for wasting police-time though!

The lads of 3Platoon shook their heads in wonderment at Baxter's near death extravaganza. That anecdote was the last sentence any of us heard the taciturn individual utter for the next few days, it was as if Baxter had finally gotten something off his chest, and now that he was purged of it, had nothing more to disclose, not even an opinion, just yes sir no sir; mind you he giggled a lot.

No one appeared to know who should follow Baxter. Sooty Corbett looked like he was about to say something but thought better of it, so the lads simply carried on polishing boots and other stuff. Jennings went back to writing his love letter, no doubt filling it with sweet nothings and telling his wife how much he was missing her. Only he wasn't. As Tucker strode over to me with his immaculately pressed trousers to see how I was getting on with polishing up my boots he couldn't help peeping at Jennings's attempt at romantic scripture.

Jennings did not conceal his journalism from prying eyes, in fact he was not bashful at all as he boasted that it was not his wife but his girlfriend he was pouring out his feelings to. He told us about the girl he sloped off to for a good time and the all-important sexual congress. Her name was Cathy, she was the one person who kept him sane and admitted that he only stayed with his wife out of a sense of duty!

Oddly I didn't feel disgust, but I didn't feel envy either. Watching Shakespeare at work was enough to make Tucker reflective too; he whispered confidentially in my ear but it was so hushed, crude and garbled; I got the gist of it though. Tucker coveted Jennings knack of keeping two women on the go, and empathised with his being separated from the two women in his life, however misconstrued Jennings had made it all appear. Tucker was going through a bad patch in *his* personal life and no doubt felt a pang in his groin and a sense of loss at having recently finished with his girlfriend.

To be truthful I knew that Tucker was not having an epiphany; he just wanted his nuts, as you do at that young age! Owing to his lack of commitment though, Sarah had reluctantly called it a day on their long suffering relationship, well for that reason and a suspicion that he was having an affair behind her back, which he wasn't.

He really wasn't, it was just some bird he knew who fancied him rotten, she was spreading malicious gossip in the vain hope that Tucker's girlfriend would see her arse and ditch him. It succeeded, she had. For all his pleas of innocence his defence merely dug him deeper into a hole. Typical of girls squabbling over a man; if a tart like Jenny Menstrual couldn't win a bloke with a flutter of the eyelids, a wriggle of the bum and a flash of the boobs, then no other woman was going to have him either. If Tucker hadn't been such a sensible lad his head would have swollen!

For his part he couldn't be bothered tapping off with a new one down at the Friday night Disco in the Cherry-tree hotel, not until it had all blown over and the dust had settled at any rate. Inevitably he still felt something for Sarah and simply wanted things to go back to the way they were, besides, none of the other local girls seemed good enough to take her place;

in fact the last girl he'd kissed was under mistletoe at Christmas, and to be honest if he'd been sober he wouldn't have kissed her under anaesthetic. Having grown up in a small town, Tucker assumed that the local gossiping talent knew him too intimately, which in his mind, made courting them almost incestuous. Dating-agencies and Speed-dating venues were none existent, and public transport took an eternity to get anywhere to experience pastures new. Tucker's options were limited with the lack of a night bus; he had occasionally ventured as far as Wigan Casino for a few night-outs, but the place was full of pill poppers and pie eaters. The only substitute to seeking exotic alternatives in foreign parts was late night boozing down at the Blue Lagoon and mixing with whores & foreign sailors or chatting to Bomber Lancaster and his bouncers. The first two weeks when he and Sarah had finished were the worst, they hadn't talked or seen each other at all and by the end of the fortnight Tucker had accepted the situation, they were through for good. It would have come to a head anyway now that he'd joined the TA; both of Sarah's parents were of Irish descent and he'd already upset them some years previous by contemplating joining the Parachute regiment on leaving school. As Catholics they considered the Para's to be murderers, they had lost a nephew in the troubles during Bloody Sunday and Tucker sensed that they envisaged he was betraying them!

So that was that, he had got on with it and began piecing his life back together. Oddly enough that's when Sarah had relented and wanted to patch things up, but Tucker felt offended at not getting an apology for something he hadn't even done. Tucker's granddad commented that it often happened that way; in his experience a boy suffers all the emotional turmoil and doubts in the first two weeks of a separation while the girl is generally wallowing in self-righteousness and a misconception that the boy will come running back to her with his tail between his legs, begging forgiveness; but when he doesn't she gets all moody and self-reproachful, worried that he hasn't called, yearning to reinstate the status quo; all the birds and bees stuff!

It had been some time since breaking up and Tucker was now wondering if things had changed irreparably between them, now that he was away from the situation. I knew that he had thought about the circumstances and contemplated patching things up with Sarah when he returned home; well if he did try he might at least get his leg over if he was lucky. I advised him that the alternative was to just keep moving on until he found someone new. It was a classic dilemma, he hadn't had much luck in Runcorn and needed something more than just the odd casual bonk now and again.

Jennings coughed and pointed his biro at Spike, indicating that the biker should pipe up and have a say. 'Come on dad, what's your story? You look like a bit of a mad sod you do!'

The Biker snorted back some mucus from his nostrils, annoying Stan-the-Cab in the process, and gave an interesting reply. 'I joined the T.A. to get away from the bleedin' family init! Bit too old for this lark really, but I'm in a jam, my son's doin' me head in, thinks he knows everything don't he hey, know watta mean?'

Apparently Jennings was knowledgeable in regards of Spike's predicament. 'He's at that age dad, I was a bit like that back then you know.'

'You still are!' laughed Martin Flowers.

'Shut it you.' Jennings heaved a dismissive sigh. 'When I was seventeen right, I thought my father was a total waste of space, a complete wazuck, but by the time I'd reached twenty-one, I was amazed at how much my old man had learnt in the space of four short years - we get on like a house on fire now!'

'On a rainy day?' laughed Martin Flowers.

'Yeh, but you weren't doing drugs were ya?' Spike ignored Martin's interruption and proceeded to snort back more mucus.

Stan-the-Cab chucked a packet of pocket sized tissues over to Spike. 'Here, blow your nose with one o them before I bounce over there and break it for ya, ya filthy greasy git.'

'I did try some pot once,' continued Jennings. 'It just made me dizzy though; sick as a dog I was. I think people who use drugs only end up losing it you know, the ability to stand on their own two feet, drugs as a crutch to get through life, no need for it dad, no need at all, more substitution than dependency. Here, your lad's not a space cadet is he?'

'Not really, just a phase he's going through.' Spike cleared his sinuses and held up the handkerchief to display the deplorable deposit to Stan. 'Poor sod's not been the same since he went to see that Ziggy Stardust concert in nineteen seventy three!'

Stan shook his head lamentably. 'Oh yeh, David Bowie, now he's a real space cadet he is - Major Tom to ground control?'

Spike reminisced. 'When I was a kid right, it was hard as Dickens to get hold of anything exotic, a bit of home grown grass maybe, a few uppers or downers, but none of this Cannabis resin they're all chonging on nowadays; that was for rock stars that stuff!'

The lads sat on the ends of their beds in the stark wooden hut on a freezing winter's night, sparking up their kit and listening to Spike gem them up about drug culture. Spike admitted that his son didn't believe in the ethics of earning a living anymore, so he'd dropped out of the rat race completely! His son bought enough Cannabis to split into thirds, selling two thirds to cover his costs, and then smoking the other one himself. Other people's dependencies paid for his own, so there was no incentive to give up a self-sustained habit. His poor wife still worked however, paying all the bills and keeping him in clover to the familiar radical tune of Tune in and drop out!

'More fool her,' said Ronny Churchill, indifferently, 'what a mug!'

'Exactly,' whined Jennings, he was appalled and started pontificating. 'Imagine if we all did that, absolute anarchy. Here dad, I thought you said it was just a phase he was going through....'

Tug Wilson sat on the end of his bed playing about with a nasty looking hunting knife in a leather sheath, attempting to attach it to his webbing.

Stan the Cab asked him. 'What you faffing around with a rubber dagger for china?'

'Just seeing what it looks like. You never know when you might need one out in the wild!'

'Dream on. You don't ever wanna get that close mate I'm telling ya; get yourself a big gun, the biggest one you can frigging find!'

Tug shrugged uninterestedly and slunk back against his pillow as Spike went on to explain how his son was eventually made to see what damage he was doing to himself. At first he would just get a bit mellow or silly, then as time went by he became withdrawn and gradually started to go around the bend. He would come home from hanging out with other pot heads and start talking nonsense and get the giggles. He was convinced at one point that cats were far superior in intellect to any other species on earth, and that they had once ruled the planet.

The others in the room pissed themselves at his son's plight, but Spike just snorted back some snot and smiled at their naivety. 'He even tried to convince us that there was a tunnel under the Atlantic Ocean linking Great Britain to the U.S.A. and that you could travel to New York in forty minutes. He reckoned American scientists had developed a way of overcoming the effects of G-force and they used trains powered by huge magnets to glide through the tunnel, he was away with the fucking fairies!'

Jennings removed his glasses and pointed out the fact that you would have to be travelling at Mach 7 which is more than 5,000miles per hour, and if you built one of those tunnels to Australia, you could be in Sydney in 2 hours, cutting 20 hours off of the slog!

The lads howled with mirth and Stan-the-Cab fell off his bed in hysterics. 'He's a laugh aint he, fucking no brainer. What else china, come on what else?'

'He would sit in his bedroom listening to that fucking mind bending Pink Deep Floyd Purple music and write gibberish all over his walls with a Felt-tip-Pen. The next day, embarrassed by what he'd scrawled, he would paint over it all to hide it. Why he couldn't use pen and paper was beyond his wife, he said he wrote on the walls because he was inspired by a voice in his head and it was important not to forget any of it - complete basket case.'

'I like a bit of Pink Floyd,' admitted Sooty Corbett approvingly.

'Me too rocker,' agreed Tish, farting while applying more spit and polish to his boot cap.

'Yeh but it hardly gets your feet tapping does it twinkle toes?' teased Spike.

'Here, is this yours?' Tish fumbled about in his shirt pocket, as if looking for something, then withdrew his hand with his middle finger erect. 'Up yours Spike.'

Spike casually returned a two-finger salute and lit up another cigarette. 'He used to get the munchies and eat everything in the house, but if that wasn't bad enough, he started getting schizophrenic, only mild, but the schizophrenia was something else. We had to get him to stop smoking the weed long enough for him to see what it was doing to his life, because he couldn't see anything wrong with his behaviour, one minute normal, next totally deranged. He'd have these memory lapses too, simple things like forgetting where he had put his house keys.'

'Pity he didn't forget where he lived while he were at it!' suggested Big Tish.

'Sounds like pre-senile dementia does that dad!' said Jennings.

'Yeh, well, sometimes he completely forgot to take his keys with him when he left home and would think nothing of shimmying up a drain pipe, or smashing a window in the front door to break back into the house to retrieve them.'

‘Why didn’t his wife just move house while he was out with his mates; that would have messed around with his head wouldn’t it?’ giggled Martin Flowers uncontrollably. Diddy Baxter and Stan-the-Cab creased up with laughter too.

‘Suppose so. When he finally got straight he could see how pathetic he had been, and admitted that when he was stoned out of his head his thought processes were impaired; every little thing he thought of magnified itself and seemed like a good idea to him at the time?’

‘Some people just can’t handle being cabbaged!’ reasoned Tug Wilson.

‘Yeh but *you’re* doing a bloody good job of it!’ giggled Martin Flowers.

Tug Wilson finished attaching his Sheaf-knife to his webbing. ‘It’s like a disease isn’t it?’

Jennings agreed. ‘Any type of drug abuse eclipses reason doesn’t it like, you know like a failure of willpower attacking the brain, like a sin I suppose. Then the withdrawal kicks in dunt it hey, the need to get stoned again, gradually developing and reaching its fever point just before the sin is committed, and then continued with the same neglect at the moment of getting stoned and for a short time later, depending on an individual’s craving, and then passed off inconsequentially like any other criminal activity rampant these days.’

We all gawped at Jennings. There was nothing superficial about his views on life; he had very profound depths to his character.

Tish Hewitt didn’t like to be outwitted by some intellectual waffle he couldn’t fully grasp; he said that if any of his kids wanted to be cabbaged, he would take a Baseball bat and knock some sense into their head.

Noting big Tish’s inability to comprehend what he’d just divulged about his own personal take on drug addiction, Jennings responded. ‘Yeh, well I suppose it saves tying yourself up in ideological knots does that dad!’

Sooty judiciously changed the subject; he imagined Spike to be a bit anti-establishment and asked the biker the real reason why he had chosen an interest in the TA. The biker puffed on a roll-up and replied. ‘Truth is right, I fancy razzing the bollocks out of one of those army jobs. I bet those Can-Am motor cross’s can’t half take some punishment, know warra mean?

‘Fucking hell, get Steve McQueen over there!’ laughed Tucker sarcastically.

‘Fuck off you faggot. I’m not subversive or bohemian if that’s what you’re thinking, I just like adventure. I’m at one with me bike and go wherever me bike takes me.’

‘Yeh, you’re at one with your bike until you lose it doing a Ton-twenty on a bad bend you daft bugger, and then you’re at one with a tree!’ Big Tish hammered home the discrepancy. ‘I see you’re into leather then, you must be into older women too!’

‘Wanker!’ Spike pulled on his cigarette and shrugged as he replaced his headphones; he was very laid back and not the type to let Tish Hewitt wind him up. The other lads liked the bikers attitude.

Jennings looked bored; he had finished writing to his wife. ‘Be missing Coronation Street just now we will!’

‘Bloody Coronation Street?’ said Martin Flowers acerbically.

‘Oh yes dad, love us soaps me and the misses does. Never miss an episode; she’ll be videoing it for us!’

‘I can’t afford a video recorder, not until they come down in price!’ Spike was only half listening as he blew a smoke ring into the air above his bed.

‘Bet you could do if you didn’t drink and smoke so much!’ advised Jennings.

‘Sooner go out for me entertainment, hate being stuck in the house,’ he sighed. ‘What someone should do right, is invent something that will let you watch whatever you wanna watch whenever you wanna watch it!’

‘What not like a video recorder then, how do you mean dad?’ Jennings was intrigued with the inventiveness of Spike’s imagination.

Spike took another pull on his cigarette, switched his Sony Walkman off completely, and while blowing a stream of smoke from his nostrils elaborated. ‘You know, instead of recording things, just being able to look at a menu for the days’ viewing and watch what you wanna watch, when you wanna watch it; that way you could get on with your life!’

‘Sorry to disappoint you Logi Baird,’ Stan-the-Cab interjected. ‘But it wouldn’t work would it? Some Muppet would doubtless tell you what’s happened before you’ve even had a chance to see it for yourself mate. No anticipation, no excitement, where would you be then sunshine?’

‘Yeh, look away now if you don’t want to know the scores.’ added Tucker.

‘Good point!’ agreed Sooty Corbett who’d also been listening intently. ‘Gotta have some suspense in your life, even if it means watching all the other junk what’s on before it.’

'Talking about junk!' Tucker told them about a foreman at work who was nicknamed "Junky" because he was always saying, "When you've finished doing that, come and see me and I'll have some more for ya!"

'Very clever Tucker,' chuckled Stan-the-Cab, who was now busy checking out the day's racing as he flicked through the sporting pages of the Sun. 'Morphia, yeh nice one, I likes that! Gonna have to give the missus a bell to see how these nags have done.'

'You into horses then?' asked Tucker.

'Not nags so much, dogs mate, I likes me wolf I do. I live right by a Dog-Track and all. You a betting man then are ya?'

'Who isn't? Just horses though, prefer going to races than seeing it on TV when I can!'

'Yeh, the glass nipple ain't the same is it. I love watchin'em run too, they're so graceful.'

'When they gallop they are.' Jennings interrupted. 'There's a point when all four feet are up off the ground, as if they're flying!'

'You got a point there china, that's how I am with me dogs' as well, passionate!'

'Yeh dogs are faithful but horses are noble!' Tucker wrestled the conversation back from Jennings.

'Yeh fair play!' conceded Stan-the-Cab.

Sooty Corbett considered his self to be a kung-Fu expert and made claim to have been a pen friend of Bruce Lee. Sooty said he could perform a hundred press-ups on his knuckles. The lads were not taken in by any of this, Sooty was clearly a bull-shitter who couldn't help but out-bragg anybody who had done something unusual and the lads were getting wise to this. I couldn't help laughing as they started winding Sooty up for amusement by having him prove to them that he could indeed do one hundred press-ups using his knuckles!

While the Nordic Ninja pumped his body up and down on the floor, Egg-head Jennings idly caught a moth which had been flitting around his bedside lamp. He was still trying to impress anybody who'd listen to him by disgorging entomological facts and figures.

'Did you know right, that moths don't eat because they don't have a mouth or stomach!'

Martin Flowers was tired of Jennings now. Dismissively he switched off the lamp above his bed space and climbed in. 'They only fly around light bulbs for a light snack then do they? Do us all a favour Jennings, shut the fuck up.'

'Ahr now, that's something else is that dad…'

Martin Flowers slid between his crisp starched sheets and pulled up his coarse woollen blankets over his head in a vain attempt to block out the stark reality of the cold military Nissan hut. The conversation of the past few hours had made it fundamentally more endurable and many more evenings such as this would follow, but the real test would be sleeping on a thin foam mattress on a hard sprung bedstead in dormitory conditions. Within moments Martin Flowers was asleep. One by one the rest of us called it a day and turned in, but I couldn't sleep at first, I was a bit restless with being in strange surroundings. It didn't bother Tucker, he was out like a light too; he could curl up on a dustbin lid.

The musky room smelt of stale cigarette smoke, floor polish, farts and sweaty feet, and to cap it all somebody at the far end of the room started snoring irritably, like a rumbling volcano. Jennings must have bored me to death in the end though, because the next thing I knew it was 0500hrs Sunday morning and Cpl Hazel was strutting around the billet screaming his head off and prodding everybody with his shiny pace stick!

Chapter 5

'GOOD MORNING LADIES, THE SUN IS SHINING FIT TO BURN YOUR SODDING EYES OUT. STOP CHINFING YOU SHAGGING DONKEYS, WHERE DO YOU THINK YOU ARE, THE PARIS HILTON? MOVE YOUR HAIRY ARSES NOW. IF I'M UP, YOU'RE UP!'

This was not at all like being roused by Terry Wogan's dulcet tones! Startled into life, I jumped out of bed while Tucker recoiled against his pillow clutching a blanket to his chest. I grinned as the momentum spilled Tucker out of bed into a snotty heap on the floor. He picked himself up and aimlessly scuttled around like a frantic mouse not knowing what to do?

Considerate to a fault, Cpl Hazel gave him an effective suggestion. 'Stand still!'

In our green army underpants the platoon stood rooted to attention on the shiny brown floor whilst the cold of a fresh crisp day crept unwanted into our new-fangled lives.

'Right gentlemen, this is what we call a sparrows fart; you might know it as an early start. You'll be having lots of sparrow's farts, so get used to them. Get your P.T vests-shorts-and-boots on, now, then form up outside on the road and don't take all bloody day about it, go!'

We got going double quick. The sound of the convulsive hectoring corporal's booming voice reverberated inside our skulls; he barked insults until we had formed up with the other platoons outside.

The temperature was minus 8° centigrade. I yawned uncontrollably through chattering teeth. Like me, Tucker and our new chums were not in the mood for running three miles at

5.15 in the morning; unless you're contemplating entry into the Olympics you're not that dedicated are you? During the night hoarfrost had enveloped the Mil-Training-Wing shack creating a Christmas card nativity scene, more enchanted with the monkey puzzle tree glistening in the background, but somehow I didn't think baby Jesus was going to materialise and help us out with one of his marvels. The icy air bit into our shivering exposed flesh, prompting us to slap our arms against our bodies and do spurts of running on the spot for warmth. It seemed like the middle of the night, the dormant sun would not show up for at least another two hours.

'I was in the middle of a dream just then,' Sooty Corbett yawned. 'My wife was in bed with a lesbian. Ooh I was annoyed; they had the heating on full blast!'

A bulky Sergeant Physical Training Instructor, assisted by a PTI Corporal, brought the platoons to attention and stood us at ease again. The menacing Mil-Training-Staff hovered around in the background dressed in designer Tracksuits, gloves and woolly hats; they had the appearance of armed robbers.

'Right, let's get you all warmed up then shall we. We'll start off with jumping by numbers. When I yell one, jump in the air, and when I yell two return to the standing position. Right, listen in, one!'

We sprung into the air like kangaroos.

'Why have you all come back down, have I counted to two yet? OK then relax, just my little joke. Each and every morning you will begin your training with a three mile run. This is not designed to bugger you about; we need you to be at a level of fitness necessary to carry out your duties at all times. We won't be there to drag you out of bed when you go home, so this is where you learn the standard required of you. Each year, as a qualifying assessment towards your Bounty, you will have to pass a Battle Fitness Test. It's not hard; you will be graded by age on your performance. Today for the first mile and a half of your BFT, you will run as a squad at a nice steady even pace and no racing. After that it's Yo-yo. You're on your own!'

'Staff, my mouth is cold!' moaned a deep frozen recruit.

'You'll have to grit your teeth then won't you, ha ha ha!' The PTI had a harsh comedic rejoinder for every grumble.

Tucker was not impressed. 'He's hilarious isn't he!'

The platoons turned to their left in three's and moved off into the cold black emptiness. After five minutes of easy cadenced jogging, we all started to warm up a bit. Every now and then the PT buster slowed us down into a quick march so that we didn't run ahead of our schedule. The course wound its way around the frosty inner perimeter road which almost bordered the barbed wire fence, eventually it brought all the runners back to where we had started fifteen minutes earlier and from that moment on we were on our own. The fitter runners eagerly broke away and the rest of us pursued in a dogtrot. Tucker paced himself because he said his legs felt a bit stiff from the previous day's exertion of labouring up and down the sand bank at the back of the base; I fell back with him because we both had the added contention of breaking in new boots too.

As we plodded around the road I mused, what a way to spend a Sunday bloody morning. The army base was as dead as a dodo; mind you it was early yet and any normal person would still snuggled up in a warm bed until mid-day. Prior to 1994 there wasn't any Sunday shopping other than the corner news-agent which closed at noon, so most people had a long lethargic lie in, making Sunday mornings an ideal time for driving lessons if you weren't that much of a church goer. I wasn't much of a god botherer, neither was Tucker. I'd sometimes make the effort out of respect for my parent's religious views but Tucker, now that he was old enough to make his own decisions, staunchly shunned praying on the Sabbath, he was an agnostic bordering on atheism. Once his batteries were recharged after a big night out on Saturday he would typically hang out with his mates on Big-Park, kitted out in his togger boots, ready to kick the stuffing out of an old leather Casey on a lumpy football pitch refereed by Albert Dixon. Albert's German wife Emmy administered the magic sponge to the injured and dished out half-time oranges to the thirsty. Citrus juice being a meagre thirst quencher, Tucker and his team mates normally retired to a pub where they met up with me and one or two other dinnertime boozers for proper refreshments. This Sunday pint was the only religious thing any of us really did in our lives. Granddad had instilled in me as a kid that god would provide for me, I only wished that god *would* provide for me until he eventually decided it *was indeed* time to provide for me! Tucker was not a big drinker, once he had got a whiff of the barmaids apron it was generally time for all of us to totter home for our Sunday roast, and as very few people could afford microwave ovens, dinner would often be dried up from being kept warm on a low heat in a gas oven; but to us, after a few pints, that meal with the gravy baked to the sides of the plate had a taste all of its own! Then before we knew it, it was Monday morning again with inflation running at 14% and bank-lending rates teetering at thirteen and a half per cent, plus the sad reality that industry in the Northwest was in fast decline; small wonder that the weekend was generally one big pub-crawl!

My toes felt cramped in my new boots, the stiff hide chafed my Achilles tendon. I could see that Tucker was enduring this torment too; as fit as he was from playing football, like me he was beginning to struggle. The Mil-Training-Staff didn't let up; they heaved praise onto the cream of the crop. It somehow spurred Tucker on to catch the others up; I traipsed after him on his shirt tails while rotten abuse was hurled at the stragglers.

'You're a waste of rations laddy!' roared a red headed Scot's Staff Sergeant at Jennings who developed a wobbly bottom lip which tripped him up dead in his tracks.

'What's the matter with you lard arse? You're like a fat fucking fairy, swinging daintily atop a shagging Christmas tree. Move yourself now.'

No one was allowed to drop out of the early morning run, no excuses. The training team pounced on Jennings like a pack of Hyenas and after a few seconds of concerted persuasion he saw the error of his ways and started running for his life. At the finish outside the Mil-Training-Wing the recruits stood braying like sweaty horses following completion of the Grand-National. I sucked lungful after lungful of crisp frosty air to steady my racing pulse.

On the whole the PTI's were happy with us, a bit of praise went a long way at that time of the morning. 'Good effort lads, keep it up!'

'Listen in,' the RSM brought his recruits to order. 'There will be a room inspection by Platoon Commanders at o-eight-hundred hours. All your lovely kit will be laid out as detailed yesterday and your quarters cleaned from top to bottom. If you pass inspection you will march smartly to the cookhouse for breakfast, if not, you will be held back until my staff are satisfied. Take note that reporting for breakfast is a parade in itself gentlemen and that it's a Court Martial offence to miss one. It's a long day here at Martinique Barracks when you haven't eaten, so get on top of your presentation right from the start. Mind you, one or two of you fat lazy bastards could skip the odd meal and still keep a Biafran village sustained for a month!'

Jennings self-consciously sucked in his belly as the RSM continued. 'Gentlemen, we had our first fatality yesterday, a touch of angina. Mr Todd is now recovering at the Cambridge military hospital, it's nothing critical. If you want to send him flowers it's tough titty, we don't go in for that sort of thing around here. The Major was quite specific, any problems, notify a member of staff. Chest pains fall into that category you dipsticks, got it?'

The RSM didn't look unduly concerned, there was a pitiless grin playing at the corners of his thin cruel mouth. 'Now get away and have yourselves a shit, a shave and a shower, and don't forget to clean behind your ears, foreskin, armpits and crack of your arse. I don't like smelly soldiers, a smelly soldier is a polluted soldier; do I make myself clear on that? Right listen in; Falllll out.'

The showers and washbasins were beyond my reach at that precise moment in time because the queue stretched way down both corridors of the spider. I could see a pecking order developing, one that could only be resolved by fisticuffs. In between getting a shower and changing into our army clobber, dusting, wiping, brushing and polishing, was carried out in a competitive spirit. Once those chores were completed, we got to grips with the instruction card for making Bed-Blocks.

Tug Wilson studied the card and glimpsed at his blankets. He read the directions out aloud like Mary Poppins, as if by doing so, Bipadee Bopadee Boo, his bedding would magically transform itself into the diagram on the piece of paper. In reality it was simpler than assembling Ikea furniture but took several attempts to perfect the knack and pass it on. Straightforward really: fold one blanket in half, fold the two sides evenly to the centre, then fold over in half again; this to be repeated with the other blanket. It was identical with the two sheets, which were then sandwiched between the blankets to make a symmetrical bail, utilising the counterpane as a cummerbund to hold it together. This ensured that the bedding was aired daily and made presentable for inspection. The Bed-block was then placed at the head of the mattress with a pillow crowning it. The remaining kit was displayed in the centre of the mattress for inspection purposes and best boots placed toes front at the base. All the Bed-blocks were identical in size and shape with no variation, thanks in large part to Jennings passing around a tape measure he had constructed out of a spare boot lace; he must have been a *Blue Peter* fan or Girl Guide or something!

To do this each morning was going to be a pain in the arse but Jennings thought he had a solution. 'How about if we don't use our bedding for sleeping in at all, but keep it folded up in a square and just use the counterpane and pillow?'

'Doh,' chided Sooty Corbett, slapping his forehead with the palm of his hand. 'You must have brain rot.'

'There's no need to be belligerent,' whinged the Brummy mastermind. 'Aint no call for it.'

'Don't spit your dummy out Jennings. I'm just saying it's too bloody cold in here at night for any of that lark!' rebuked Sooty.

'We'll just have to make them up each morning then,' conceded Tug Wilson. 'Even if it means getting up earlier!'

'Whores piss, if we're going to get into the ablutions for a shit and shave, we'll have to get up early anyway,' complained Martin Flowers. 'I don't know about you lads but once I've made up this here bed block it's staying made up and not getting used. I'm gonna sleep in my sleeping bag from now on.'

'Bleeding hell, nice one Martin, I'll have some a that,' Stan-the-Cab commended him. 'At this rate we'll have to have our shit and shave before we do our three mile run anyway.'

'Stand by your bed,' interrupted Cpl Hazel from the doorway. He was a very crafty fox; we just never knew when he was creeping around in the shadows.

'Corporal in the room,' shouted Tug, bringing everybody to attention.

'Fuck me, who's farted? Smells like a skunk has crawled up a tramps arse and died. Open that window!' the corporal instructed Martin Flowers.

'It aint me corporal,' Martin protested. 'Smells like a Runcorn fart does that, full of chemicals!'

'Piss off shitty arse!' Tucker objected.

The NCO loudly deliberated. 'You're taking too long with this cleaning fella's! First at everything I said, which includes the ablutions, and don't forget to keep an eye on part one orders, because you'll be in charge of cleaning the bogs from time to time. The RSM's a stickler for hygiene and checks them daily in person!'

Hearts were sinking fast at all this bad news, we were rapidly becoming the domesticated "New man" which was all the rage in the late 1970's; where was all the fun?

‘Right you scumbags. I’m happy with your effort up until now, good work, keep it up. You’ve got exactly twenty minutes to get your breakfast and return here, and then your arses are mine. So eat it now and taste it later. Go on out of my sight, toodaloo!’

I suspected that some of the others besides me normally grabbed a bowl of cereal or a couple of slices of marmalade on toast in the morning. Spike the Biker was the sort of guy who started the day with a cup of coffee and a cigarette, so the novelty of having a full English breakfast was a luxurious treat to most of us. Tucker had the perk of a works canteen so was used to it; mores the pity there wasn’t time to savour this culinary treat. Stan-the-Cab had muesli and yoghurt, whereas fickle impatient Whittling spooned a few segments of grapefruit into a bowl and grabbed a round of marmalade on toast to nibble at. Martin Flowers helped himself to two boiled eggs on toast, and like the joker he was, couldn’t resist taking a couple of raw eggs from the carton next to the frying plate and placing them alongside the boiled eggs, switching them for two boiled eggs which he placed back in the carton with the raw ones to be fried.

‘That’s a cheap laugh!’ scorned Tug Wilson at seeing what the clown had just done.

‘Fucking imbecile, grow up!’ Sooty Corbett swapped the eggs back around, then filled a bowl with a variety of cereals, topping it off with muesli until it was near full.

‘By heck, twigs and leaves!’ derided Big Tish. ‘What are you, a bleeding hamster?

Me and the others weren’t so fussy, we scoffed down our eggs, bacon, sausage, beans, tomatoes and fried bread, then slurped it all down with tonsil varnish. We rushed it all down in fifteen minutes and then rushed back to the spiders to get crammed onto the back of one of the ancient Bedford RL trucks parked up by the parade square.

The engines coughed and spluttered as they warmed up, then the trucks lurched forward and transported our platoon out of camp to a neighbouring barracks about a mile away. The vehicles coughed and farted a sombre greeting to the cold grey dawn as the wagons dropped down a gear to tackle a gradient. One of the trucks was pulling a green trailer, a sort of windowless armoured box on four wheels which had a door built into the rear with retractable steps for easy access; it was called a Binner.

A mile down the road the armed guard on the gate of the neighbouring barracks scrutinized Cpl Hazel’s ID before permitting the small convoy to snake its way through the camp to the armoury. The building was a concrete fortification with thick anti-bomb-blast steel doors.

Once 3Platoon had debussed and entered the confines of the armoury, the green steel doors were slammed shut and a gate of iron bars was secured into place as an added precaution. Me and my platoon mates were each handed a rifle, and then Cpl Hazel moved among us adjusting the butt of the weapon to fit individual requirements - unlike most things in the Army one size does not fit all. We were also issued with two empty magazines, a sling and a green tin like a tobacco tin, which contained a cleaning kit and a tube of barrel oil. Once we had checked that the tin contained all the implements vital for maintaining the weapon, the pernickety armourer made a note of a serial number on the weapon's breach block, and then made each trainee sign a document for the whole caboodle. Tucker told me that he felt a bit like James Bond being kitted out by 'Q' and could not resist joking in an English boffin sort of voice, 'Pay attention 007!'

Not wanting be outdone, Martin Flowers tagged onto the end of Tucker's impromptu send-up by donating a faultless Sean Connery impersonation. 'I'm shitting on my bed polishing my gun mish money penny, oops it shims to have gone off!'

We all fought it was funny but the armourer raised an eyebrow and Cpl Hazel sniggered.

'Hello, we've got a couple of wise guys!'

Cpl Hazel roughly shoved a roll of white cleaning cloth at Tucker and advised him to guard it with his life. It was the size of one of those toilet rolls that are placed in toilet dispensers in public lavatories. It had thin red stripes woven across it at intervals and was simply known as "Four-by-two".

Rodger Boileiu, the rich scrap merchant's son was handed a long rod with a metal wire brush screw attachment on the end of it, and lamely asked. 'Where shall I stick this corporal?'

Without batting an eyelid, the instructor promptly replied. 'Bend over!'

Armed but not yet very dangerous, we shuffled out of the armoury and bundled the arsenal into the back of the green Binner alongside boxes of blank ammunition. With all the weapons securely locked away, the Armourer returned to his hidden stash of pornography and our vehicles trundled back to the main gate, where some of the older guard gawped reminiscently at the vintage Bedford RL trucks. The vehicles tentatively edged out onto the main road and then rolled along the tar macadam lane back to Martinique Barracks, coughing and farting like the Trotters 3 wheeler Robin Reliant van.

Chapter 6

‘Listen in. Don’t wave these weapons around at anyone,’ instructed the corporal during the skill at arms period, ‘and don’t walk around with them pointing in the air either. We only carry them like that for security purposes in Northern Ireland; it gives us the benefit of having one hand free to enable a stop and search of suspects.’

Cpl Hazel had ditched his peaked hat in favour of a Beret, the mean bastard looked as if he had stopped and searched many suspected individuals during his military career. ‘You point your weapon at the ground at all times, unless you’re on the ranges, where you point them down at the targets on the Butts. Have you all got that?’

As soon as we’d assured him that we had, we were formerly introduced to the weapon. The FN. FAL Battle Rifle had replaced the Lee Enfield as the personal issue weapon of the British Tom. It was developed in Belgium by Fabrique Nationalle (FN) and was classed as a *Fusil Automatique Leger* (FAL) – (***Light Automatic Rifle)*** or as the British simply referred to it – Self Loading Rifle (SLR) or “Slur”. It had been evaluated in Malaya during the early 1950s and having proved worthy, replaced the Lee Enfield 303 soon after. In fact it was such a popular weapon that ninety two other armies around the world employed it at that time. It fired a 7.62mm round, known as a tumbler round. On impact, the round was designed to tumble through flesh, thus ripping a large hole at its point of exit, and if it didn't kill you out right, it would severely maim you. Modern rounds pierce the body and cavitate, sucking in dirt and debris so that when the wound closes up, the foreign particles cause infection which will have to be removed surgically or you die; equally debilitating.

While the other platoons were engaged in map reading, first aid or drill, Cpl Hazel's platoon were shown how to strip and assemble the SLR and how to clean it. Next up was Standard Operating Procedures (SOP's), followed by NSP's (Normal Safety Procedures). Being unfamiliar with weaponry, we were given a run through of military Gun-speak to make us more articulate: Zeroing, velocity, recoil, stoppages and Immediate Action (IA) drills etc. We were then given practical demonstrations of firing positions, breathing techniques and the correct way to hold the weapon to offset the effects of recoil while still maintaining our aim. Having digested this, we were taught what was involved in the annual training tests for the SLR. Test 1: Safety. Test 2: Stripping, cleaning and assembling. Test 3: loading magazines with 20 rounds (Timed). Test 4: loading the weapon in the standing position (Timed). Test 5: immediate action and Gas stoppages (Cock, Lock and Look). Test 6: Unloading in the lying down position (Timed).

Feeling a bit Gung-Ho, the lads of 3Platoon returned the SLR's to the Binner and secured them in gun racks, then had a smoke break, after which we made our way to the Parade Square for some drill with the DI (Drill Instructor) Sergeant McBride. The DI was a short stocky, swarthy skinned, no nonsense bloke whose broad northern Irish accent was as thick as Ulster slice and whose oratory could quite literally reduce a grown man to a gibbering mess! McBride was the product of a mixed marriage, his Spanish mother, before she died in the troubles, had been a catholic, and his elderly father who had met her while fighting with the Socialists in the Spanish civil war against General Franco's regime, was a protestant, which had caused his son Enrique heaps of trouble growing up in Belfast. Enrique McBride, his father called him Henry, got the job done without any quibbles because he was the sort of bloke who'd resort to an unpleasant physical beasting if you fouled up; he didn't have a sentimental bone in his body.

The Drill-Pig strutted across the Square in front of us with an inverted V shape contraption rotating at his side. The twirly thing was his pace stick, hinged at the top and opened out at an angle like a set of compasses, the points of which measured his gait as they connected with the parade ground. He looked as if he might take off like an American baton twirler, and if this display was meant to make an impact on recruits, we were suitably impressed.

'Listen in,' he screamed at us glacially. 'This is a regulation military pace-stick. Pin your ears back otherwise I will shove this pace-stick through your ear holes and ride you around this parade square like a motorbike! There are two paces yay need to learn - Quick time and Double time. Quick time is the pace for marching on parade and Double time is the rate yay maggots should be travelling at in a smart uniform and military fashion between lessons, have yay all got that?'

This wasn't a question it was more a command, but nevertheless Tug Wilson as platoon senior felt obliged to answer the drill instructor on our behalf. 'Yes sarge.'

'Sarge? Don't yay call me that princess; there are only two feckin types of sarge's in this mob, passarges and sausarges! My god yay are an ugly feckin man, how can ye be so ugly with only one head?'

From beneath the peak of his cap, he surveyed the rag tag motley crew assembled before him and winced. Our appearance in our newly acquired uniforms was awkward, none of our head dress fitted properly which gave us the appearance of at best, the artist Rembrandt, at worst, Benny Hill's comedic character Fred Scuttle! We were raw but he knew from experience that we were as malleable as fresh clay, all recruits are, and his job was to mould us into an interrelated corps by reformation, a task he could patiently achieve without breaking us completely. At Sandhurst he had trained Officer Cadets to lead parades and also put Guardsmen at Pirbright through their paces too (sometimes by whacking them across the backside to gain their full attention when they fouled up); if he was skilful enough to make Rupert's and wooden tops march like tick-tock then a hundred odd Territorial Army novices would present no problem; he'd soon have us licked into shape.

Sgt McBride sprang into action like a clockwork toy, pacing back and forth giving it the business in front of the ranks. 'Look this way for a complete demonstration. Does anyone not understand this movement? The step in quick time is thirty inches specifically, and at double time the distance is lengthened to thirty-six inches specifically. I say specifically because some of yay people will have to drag ya short fat sorry arses considerably further than that monstrosity over there emulating a human being!' he curtly jerked a thumb over his shoulder in the direction of big Tish Hewitt.

'A pace is a length measured from the point at which the heel of one foot is raised, to the point at which it is set down again after an intervening step by the other foot; that's five feet in plain English. Two steps equal one pace, thirty inches per step multiplied by two, equals sixty inches, which all said and done, converts to five feet specifically. All yay have to do is listen to me calling out the timing to achieve the rate of speed at which the activity of marching emanates and get your arms shoulder high. Noi gentlemen, yay are to banish all other thoughts from ya tiny minds for the remainder of this drill period and solely concentrate on my commands so ye are – have yay all got that?'

'Yes Staff,' we recruits confirmed a trifle unconvincingly.

'I'VE HAD MORE MEANINGFULL CONVERSATIONS WITH A SHOP FULL OF CUDDLY TOYS. I CAN'T HEAR YAY!'

'YES STAFF,' we bellowed more persuasively.

'That's right ye have, and in a moment yez'll prove it to me. Listen in. The Romans were able to achieve the vast distances they travelled in one day by setting a marching pace of one point five metres, which conveniently for us Brit's converts to almost five feet. Coincidently, the fact that one thousand of their tidy paces equates to one of our standard British miles is bloody convenient too, and because the Romans liked nothing better to do all day than march along lovely straight roads, they were subsequently able to measure distance and thus calculate the extent of their vast expanding empire. You're impressed aren't yay?'

'Yes staff,' bellowed his audience, none of whom dared make any form of eye contact with him. Sgt McBride was not a social animal, consequently he had few friends and plenty of enemies, and furthermore he must have had some history since even the Mil Training staff seemed wary of him. For a full two hours, the DI quick marched 3platoon over every inch of *His Square*, resting us up with just one ten minute smoke-break. On completion of the Drill period the DI marched us over to a lecture room at the far end of the square at double time for a lesson on Map reading and Navigation.

Map reading was complete gobbledegook to most of the recruits on the course, Tucker and myself included. I felt my brain cease up when silver haired Staff Sergeant Mackintosh from

1pltn explained the differences between True North, Grid North and Magnetic North, which was something to do with Grid Magnetic Angle or magnetic variation and depended on two factors; time and place. It was explained that as the position of the Magnetic North Pole moves slightly eastwards, so the Grid Magnetic Angle changes too. This is known as Annual Magnetic Change and must be accounted for when converting magnetic bearings to Grid Bearings and vice versa. The Grid Magnetic Angle varies from one part of the country to another. After this baffling explanation, me and my new mates were given further perplexing details describing Magnetic-Declination, Grid-convergence and Elevations, with something involving four and six figure map references thrown in for good measure too.

'Don't worry too much for now if it doesn't all sink in,' enthused the instructor. 'It will all become clear to you this afternoon during your orienteering tasks. Just remember, grid to mag add, mag to grid get rid!'

Contours and Grid lines were easier to digest but just when we recruits thought we were beginning to grasp it all, the map was divided up into Easting's and Northing's, and degrees on a compass were converted into mils. Although Tucker had done some map reading in Air Cadets he looked perplexed and scratched his head in bewilderment when an introduction to individual compass error was levelled at us. I was dizzy from it all too; I wondered how anybody managed to get from A-to-B with this entire bumph sloshing around in their head. It was a lot to take in but by the end of the lesson the majority of us were beginning to make *some* sense of it.

Back at the Spider, Cpl Hazel gave us an improvised demonstration on how to mould a Beret into a half decent shape to fit our heads. He led his protégés into the ablutions and arranged us into a semi-circle around the white ceramic washbasins.

'Listen in, we don't want you toss pots chinfing around looking like "ooh Betty" Frank Spencer, do we? For fucks sake lads, look at some of you, all you're short of is a bike and a string of smelly onions and you'd easily pass for a dozy Garlic muncher!'

He carefully cut away at the plastic square that was sewn into the inside of Diddy Baxter's hat and removed it, then immersed the beret for a few minutes into a sink full of steaming hot water. Aided by a pencil, he deftly scooped the beret up and plopped it into the next sink containing cold water. He repeated this hot-cold process three more times before gently wringing the Beret out.

'Kneel down numb nuts,' ironically Diddy Baxter obliged, as if he wasn't already short enough for the corporal to mould the beret to his head. 'We'll have to stop meeting like this Baxter, people are beginning to talk. While you're down there sunshine, give us a spit and polish, there's a good lad!'

'Fuck off!' tersely replied the stunted conscript as he shuffled backwards on his knees to distance himself from the NCO's unsolicited sexual advances.

'Fuck off Corporal!' corrected the instructor. 'OK, that is how you will personalise your headdress, and then maybe you'll stop showing me up by bimbling around like a crowd of Muppets. Do it this evening and wear it while you're bulling up your boots and it should start to take shape by bedtime, then tomorrow when it's completely dried out, it will naturally encompass your skull so you look like proper squaddies. Right, skid-addle and get your meals, and make sure you're back here in thirty minutes.'

After a lunch of Cornish pasty and chips, we re-assembled on the square along with the other platoons, ready for the recruit navigation exercise. It was an orienteering task specifically designed to acquaint us with the features on an ordnance survey map. Orienteering does exactly what it says on the tin, it is a sport which crosses hills, forests and rivers, like a car rally on foot; ideal for testing the entire bumph learnt in the map-reading lesson earlier. For this next phase of training, we were starkly dressed in boots, combat trousers and flimsy red PT vests, despite the temperature loitering around minus 2°C all day. Sgt McBride, from 2pltn, divided us all up into squads of five. Tucker and I was teamed up with, Tish, Tug, and Martin Flowers, then handed a compass and topographical map of the local area, together with sheets of foolscap paper containing instructions to be abided by. I looked over his shoulder as Tucker studied the information which included a list of map references, called control points. On arrival at a control point, the orienteer's task was to locate a large fluorescent red diamond shaped indicator which had a Swedish marker attached to it. Swedish markers are a sort of punch, similar in shape to a small stapler or large cloths peg, designed to mark a corresponding space adjacent to the grid reference on the instruction sheet. To discourage cheating, each Swedish marker impresses its own particular imprint to establish which specific control point has been discovered. Over the following few hours, the indicators proved difficult to find and could often only be seen from a close distance, usually less than 30 metres, which in a wooded area proved to be a challenging mission, especially when a pair of snide bastards like Tish Hewitt and Martin Flowers concealed the markers away from the other teams who followed. Fortunately matriarchal Tug Wilson was on hand to conscientiously traipse back and rectify the mischief.

Each squad set off at ten minute staggered intervals, tackling the course in alternating directions to minimise cheating, our crew was one of the first. Tucker surprised me, he had already plotted a route to the initial control point, so our team raced off like hares, passing beneath the dominant Monkey puzzle tree and ducking under the red & white barrier pole at the Guardroom. We then raced away towards the wood on the left of the approach road leading down to Martinique Barracks. We veered left through the pine trees and picked up a trodden path leading to a clearing, then trotted between the undergrowth towards a wooden fence which dipped down to a partially frozen stream. Big Tish Hewitt crossed first and helpfully reached down and hauled the other four of us up, playfully letting go of Martin Flowers who slipped broadside into the icy water for a brief moment. Tish grabbed again and dragged him out in one big heave but after that the pair continually tripped each other up and shoved each other into trees at every opportunity. Despite this, we were a good team and made a good start by stumbling across the first control point more by chance than skill. Tucker perforated the team's instruction sheet with the Swedish marker, while Martin Flowers reset the compass to a new bearing. We then headed off in the direction of the next control point, not quite sure of what we were doing but progressively growing in confidence.

At the edge of the woods the route traversed a main road before carrying on across gorse covered heath-land. It was much easier to navigate across this patch of land but very difficult to traipse through. Tug Wilson started to moan, not because it was hard going but because he thought we should have reached our next marker by now, we were perplexed too. Martin Flowers showed us where he thought we were on the map; he had only been holding the map sideways. Big Tish was incredulous. 'You bell-end, over here is over there and over there is over here!'

Tucker nominated Tug Wilson to get us back on track and we agreed, Tug seemed to have the most confidence with the map, but even so we kept an eye on him and got him to explain exactly what he was doing to assure us. For the next half hour Big Tish was put on point to trample down the frost covered flora and forge ahead enabling the rest of us to quickly hit two more control points. But our luck did not hold out for long, for when we reached a bend at a chest deep gurgling river there seemed no obvious means of crossing it. Tug Wilson spotted a marker enticingly suspended from a branch on a solitary tree on the opposite bank, and after pointing it out to the rest of us, didn't relish the idea of wading through the icy tributary to reach it. The peacefully soothing flow of water lapped briskly at the steep riverbank and Tug acknowledged that the strong current might easily carry him away. Tucker checked the map for a bridge in the vicinity while the rest of us caught our breath; unfortunately the nearest crossing was two kilometres downstream. While Martin Flowers playfully shoved big Tish about, Tucker helped to box the obstacle off by resetting the compass. Martin ran at big Tish and banged into his legs. Startled Tish toppled off balance over the riverbank but Martin snatched hold of the giant's red PT top and pulled him back to safety. Tish Hewitt's heart was in his mouth, he turned on Martin, grabbed him in a bear-hug and shuffled towards the riverbank and suspended the squirming captive over the edge. Tug Wilson flexed his authority and scolded them like a distraught parent reprimanding naughty children; this caused the imbeciles to burst out laughing. Their clowning around managed to disturb a heron which was standing elegantly on one leg a little way up on the opposite riverbank. It had been minding its own business, silently surveying the bubbling water for the shimmering giveaway movements of fish, but the pranksters had disturbed the bird's meditation so it vaulted into the air, briefly flapped its giant propulsive wings and then effortlessly glided away like an ancient pterodactyl. I was momentarily mesmerised by the birds' evolutionary freedom in empty space, it suddenly occurred to me that we had escaped the claustrophobic constraints of Martinique Barracks and the controlled mayhem which army regulations had fostered upon us. Tucker stared at the fleeing bird; he confided that he felt like an absconding prisoner. I chuckled at this and conceded his point. Joking aside we fleetingly considered running continuously to the nearest railway station and jumping on the first train home but on reflection thought better of it. It was a mad thought, what would it achieve, surely Tucker was trying to escape from Runcorn, or was he? One town is much like another when you're running away from yourself; it was time he met his demons head on, put them to rest and tried to go with the flow for a change, after all he'd found space to develop now and was among kindred spirits too!

Tug Wilson had not been distracted by all the larking about; his mind was focussed on the task at hand. He'd decided to trample a course through the dense undergrowth to a fording place downstream; no doubt a more experienced map reader would have retraced the route away from the watercourse and headed off across more lenient terrain, but being new to this game we simply traipsed after the leader through the ferns and bracken regardless. A young couple with three children playfully walked their Doberman-Pinscher along a path on the opposite bank, teasing it noisily as they threw sticks for it to retrieve. The dog was a strange looking mutt with a long curly tail, strange because I had only ever seen this breed with its tail docked and the image embedded itself in my mind. The ford we headed for was located at a sparsely populated spot, where traffic seemed sporadic and sensible people feared to tread. Tug Wilson was pioneering as he safely forded the bubbling knee deep river, encouraged by whelps and cries from the rest of us as we attentively followed suit, but army issue boots are not waterproof and subsequently water seeped through the lace holes to soak our green multi-fibre socks.

Cold and glum, we squelched like cross-country runners back to our previously intended co-ordinates to resume the orienteering task, but barely a kilometre along the way, Martin Flowers exclaimed excitedly. 'Bloody hell, isn't that Jennings!'

'Where, where?' none of us could see him!

'In the water lads,' tittered Martin elatedly. His darting eyes proved on a par with any radar system currently on the market. 'Look, down there you blind bats!'

'Oh yeh,' Tucker chuckled naughtily - well you would wouldn't you?

'Jesus, he must have fallen in,' raucously chortled Tish Hewitt, doubled up in pleats.

I tried to stifle a laugh as Jennings frantically thrashed about trying to reach the riverbank. He seemed magnetically drawn to the middle of the watercourse, where, tumbling and twisting out of control he was getting vulnerably swept away. On the opposite riverbank, Spike, Stan-the-Cab and other team mates struggled desperately along the edge, vainly throwing branches for the unfortunate Jennings to cling onto. Jennings gasped, spluttered and splashed as he kicked his legs trying to reach for the bank, but the force of the water was twice as strong as him and his wet clothes were weighing him down so much that his arms went limp with the effort.

Between bouts of exhilarating laughter Tucker pointed cooperatively down river. 'There's a ford around that bend, he'll be all right once he reaches that; it's only about two feet deep down there.'

'He might have drowned by then,' yelled Ronny Churchill, another of Jennings frenzied panting squad mates. This set the laughter off again.

'He'll be champion honest, anyway where's his butterfly net?' hollered big Tish, guffawing uncontrollably. The force of the water drove Jennings downstream, pressing him to safety. 'I'm not jumping in there to freeze me fooking knackers off, are thee? Besides, the big Jessie in't shouting for help, just cussing a lot!'

Begrudgingly, Tucker dived in fully clothed and swam across to Jennings in a burst of energy. It was all getting a bit fantastical. Efficiently reading maps and now saving lives, our Tucker was revealing hidden talents. There was no time to ponder on this as we ran back along the riverbank only to be set upon by the curly long tailed Doberman-Pinscher we'd seen earlier, it must have thought we were threatening the children who were playing nearby. The owners tried to call the dog off, but the sound of Jennings awkward screams and frantic splashing must have psyched the pooch out. Tish Hewitt and Tug Wilson froze as the dog bounded over snarling and yapping through protruding fangs. The dog freaked me and Martin Flowers out so we exited the vicinity in different directions. The dog took a particular liking to big Tish who tried to dodge it like a rugby winger; trouble is you can't outrun a Doberman gnashing away at your heels, no matter how agile you think you are, but big Tish gave it a bloody good go and proved that he did possess enough skill to dodge the beast sufficient enough to stop it pinning him against an oak tree. Before the hound of the Baskervilles could do any lasting damage Tish reached for a branch and hauled himself up out of harm's way. The pooch went ape shit, barking and growling, and bouncing up and down like Tigger out of Whinny the Poo. The intense situation had the others on the opposite bank laughing insanely, especially when Tish Hewitt pointed towards Tug Wilson and encouraged the dog to chase after him.

'Fetch, go on get him, that's a good boy; fetch!' he appealed to the black and tan beast; it took the hint and lurched off in search of new quarry, its long curly tail trailing awkwardly behind it like some sort of antenna. Just as the dog pounced for the kill, Tug leapt sideways into the river hitting the water with a splash. Shocked first by the cold and then by the stony bottom, the impact knocked the wind out of him. He gasped at the iciness and started yelling at Tish Hewitt, calling him all the bastards under the sun. The water only came up to Tug's waist at this point. He was lucky that the dog didn't fancy getting wet too, choosing to simply bark and growl antagonistically. Relieved at the dog's benevolence, Tug waded to safety and snatched hold of the belt on Jennings' combat trousers as he and Tucker passed by. Tucker and Tug tried to haul Jennings to his feet, but Jennings' wet clothes sagged around him substantially; his limp legs were too heavy from exhaustion to assist. By now the water was losing momentum as it spread out and widened into a pool. Once Tug and Tucker had reached shallower water, Jennings summoned up a final surge of energy and tried to stand on his own two feet, but the rocky bottom was slimy with algae so his legs slipped and wobbled. He shivered uncontrollably and sagged into a sitting position, teeth chattering and lips turning blue; he was finally sapped of strength. Me, Martin Flowers and Jennings team-mates splashed in and trawled the slippery fish to safety.

'You fucking divvy,' screamed one of Jennings' upset colleagues above the noise of the barking dog. 'What were you trying to do? I told you the current was too bloody strong didn't I, didn't I hey!'

'Calm down pal he's in safe hands now,' Tucker laughed, trying to soothe the situation. The trouble was Jennings was far from unharmed; the poor sod didn't even have the strength to sit up, never mind stand. He was ashen and trembling uncontrollably.

Tug Wilson snapped commandingly 'Someone flag a car down so we can get him back to barracks,' and all laughter ebbed away. 'Listen lads, he's in shit state, shape your selves come on!'

The Doberman sensed distress and stopped barking, then remembering that Big Tish was still stuck up a tree, rushed back playfully to tackle him but Tish had used the diversion to make a break for it. Waving hysterically, he ran for dear life in front of a passing GPO delivery van and used the vehicle to shield himself from the dog. Fortunately the beast was called off before it could do any lasting harm. Tish banged like crazy on the side of the red Comma van, yanked the passenger door open and jumped in beside the postman. He guided the driver over towards where the lifeguards were squatted over the victim, explaining the state of affairs on the way. By the time they reached us, Jennings was shivering feverishly and his pulse was feeble. Tug didn't know what to do; none of us actually knew what to do, so we pleaded with Jennings to tell us what to do? If anyone knew what we should be doing it was bound to have been him but he was out of it! Luckily the big red Comma van had pulled over in the nick of time. The driver jumped out as Jennings drifted off to sleep.

'Quick!' urged the incisive Royal Mail man assuming control of the situation. 'Get him in the back; come on hurry!'

When Tish Hewitt caught up with the postman he dropped to his knees and started thumping poor Jennings rhythmically in the chest to revive him. 'He's stopped breathing, look he's turning blue.'

'You'll break his fucking ribs doing that you doughnut!' Stan-the-Cab shoved the clumsy giant off the hapless wet casualty. The Postman intervened and resuscitated Jennings with mouth to mouth and proper heart massage. The blubbery walrus responded by spewing up a torrent of frothy river water. 'Get him in the back of my van and hug him, quick, there's no time to piss about, he needs your body heat, come on, before he croaks it!'

He wasn't joking; old Jennings looked like death warmed up. We shoved parcels and postbags up towards the front of the van and propped Jennings against them, then we all bailed into the vehicle and set about hugging Jennings back to life, soaking the parcels and bags of mail in the process.

'You lad's from Martinique Barracks,' shouted the Postman needing a destination?

'Unfortunately!' simultaneously muttered Tucker and Stan-the-cab.

'Good god, they're not still doing recruit courses down there are they? That bloody place was condemned years ago!'

The red GPO van lurched away and sprinted down the country lane to the main road with postman Pat frenziedly parping on the horn. It skidded to a brief halt at the junction, sending ten wet passengers colliding into one another and squashing Jennings and all the parcels in the process. Unhesitant the vehicle turned right and raced on towards the army base. When the red ambulance arrived at the guardroom tooting its horn like crazy, the sentry on the gate came to life, skipping all formalities. He took one look at Jennings's crumpled wet body in the back and quickly directed the postman to the medical centre, then phoned ahead warning the Medical Officer that a T-1 (immediate attention) was on its way. By the time the post office van arrived, a warm bath was running. We slid Jennings wet torso towards the rear doors. Big Tish hauled him out of the vehicle and then holding Jennings like a lifeless puppy dog in his arms, lugged the limp body into the reception area. The duty scab lifter (medic) guided us through to a sterile treatment room and broke out a silver space blanket to wrap around Jennings shivering body. Tucker cupped Jennings head and I held the patients' feet out straight while Tish lowered the body onto the examination bed. The medic turned the blue man onto his side, peeled down his pants to reveal his soggy bottom and inserted a rectal thermometer up his back passage.

Martin Flowers, cringed, "Ooh!"

CSM Parker hastily arrived on the scene dragging Cpl Hazel in tow. Both had been notified of the situation by the Guardhouse and were full of praise for the conduct displayed.

'What happened?' enquired the Sergeant Major.

'Dunno sir, the last thing we heard him say was "Ah, phylum chordata!" whatever one of them is? Then he jumped in and was swimming with the fishes!'

'Are you sure you never pushed him in?' enquired the CSM suspiciously.

'No sir, absolutely, I promise!' assured Ronny Churchill.

'Anyway, whatever, quick thinking lads,' congratulated the avuncular CSM. 'Similar thing happened to me in Norway in sixty nine, any longer he'd have been a lollipop. Well done, splendid!'

Daylight had faded by the time we returned to the Spider. The ubiquitous junior NCO unceremoniously scratched cryogenic Jennings from ration strength, he was not overjoyed by the news that another recruit from his platoon had been issued with a P7R (unfit for front-line duty) and sternly warned us, 'First Todd gets a biff chit, now Jennings, don't any more of you blokes go spazz on me!'

Cpl Hazel organised a removal team to shift the lockers and beds which the Brummy mastermind and cardiac-arrested Todd had so deftly vacated. Whittling threw open the fire escape door allowing a shaft of light to flee from the hut into the gloomy twilight world of Narnia, along with most of the heat too. With barely an inch to spare the bedroom furniture was squeezed through the fire exit and prised out the other side.

Once we had deposited the beds and lockers at the Quarter-Masters stores, 3Platoon were stood down to get replenished with Italian grub in Odd job's pizzeria. Being first in the queue we were able to bask in the warmth of the radiator and contemplatively twist overcooked spaghetti around our army issue forks, a cheeky Chianti would have washed the wormlike pasta down a treat. None of us particularly relished leaving the warmth of the cookhouse to spend the next two hours in the formal environment of a wooden classroom engrossed in a session on voice procedure utilising a clansman radio, however, once we were stuffed full of pasta, garlic bread and Chinese wedding cake (Rice pudding with raisins in it) we all seemed to buck up a bit.

With his usual shiny eyed enthusiasm, Tug Wilson warmed to the idea at playing radio ham on the Army network, his fervour sparked a smouldering degree of interest from the rest of us. Each of the lads got a go at operating a radio set, which after the energy draining cold afternoon we'd spent running around the sticks searching for orange fluorescent markers, was stimulating in a fun relaxed sort of way. So much so that Martin Flowers did not feel too embarrassed at getting brain dribble and fluffing the whole thing up. Sgt Royce was a gentleman; he spoke with that soft Scottish accent which sounds like a man who smokes a hundred cigarettes a day, because that's precisely what he was, a heavy smoker with the onset of emphysema. He patiently helped the radio announcers relax so that each was able to get the broadcasting procedures right. Whittling was particularly good at all this; admittedly his style was reminiscent of a cheesy Radio One DJ, but it made us smile; ten four rubber duck!

Sgt Royce then issued more paperwork to add to the ever growing bumph that we were accumulating. The printout was written in signalese, it contained the phonetic alphabet to be learnt by rote in our spare time? Alpha, Bravo, Charlie, Delta, Echo, Foxtrot, Golf, Hotel, India, Juliet, Kilo, Lima, Mike, November, Oscar, Papa, Quebec, Romeo, Sierra, Tango, Uniform, Victor, Whiskey, X-ray, Yankee, Zulu.

When eventually we returned to the Spiders, we conversed in radio-speak for the remainder of the evening. We did this whilst bulling up our best boots and ironing all our kit ready for an inspection by the RSM the next day. News of this inspection had been posted in the foyer on part-one orders while we had been out at the classrooms. Besides a BFT at 5.30am and a show inspection for the RSM at 1000hrs, 3Platoon were also detailed to attend a lecture at 11.00hrs on the history of the TA, and surprise-surprise, another two hour bash on the drill square in the afternoon with the beloved Sgt McBride. Part-One orders also detailed 3Platoon to clean the ablutions at the centre of the complex. The long day had taken its toll on us all, and so, smelling of garlic and Parmesan cheese, we said our prayers at ten o'clock and crashed out reasonably knackered!

Chapter 7

"Space; the final frontier. These are the voyages of the Star ship Enterprise. Its five year mission; to explore new worlds; to seek out life and new civilisations; to boldly go where no man has gone before. Captain's log supplemental: just beamed down for a shit and left beaming!"

Besides mildew in the showers to contend with, some nitwit had scrawled graffiti onto a wall in one of the crappers. Whittling said it was almost certainly the work of one of the meat-head tosser's from 4 platoon, probably the Cray-Twins (Robby or Tom), but Martin Flowers thought it was too intellectual for them and was doubtless written by one of the Startreck anoraks from One platoon. Underneath the spaceman's journal another wit had scrawled "Be alert. The army needs more lerts!"

Whittling, Tucker, Martin Flowers and me had been unceremoniously promoted to the rank of Acting Bog Cleaner Second Class, and in taking up our new status we were detailed to clean out the ablutions. Whilst Tucker and Martin flossed behind the U-bends with cleaning rags I mopped the floor, Whittling on the other hand busied himself huffing onto one of the mirrors above the basins and rubbing specks of toothpaste and shaving suds from it. Martin nudged me; he'd caught Whittling admiring his own image. I threw a damp rag at Tucker to gain his attention, nodded in the direction of Whittling and then shrugged. Whittling had been observed several times clocking himself in the mirror whenever he passed one, he couldn't resist it. He thought that he looked good in a uniform despite being all skin and bones and having teeth like a row of bombed out houses and skin complexion as pale as a bottle of semi-skimmed milk. Despite his love affair with himself he was devoid of any embryonic attraction; we were not being prejudiced, he was obviously a bit of a poseur who no doubt wanted to large it up in front of his mates back home in Aylesbury! I shook my head in disbelief!

'Reckon he be a clothes dobbin!' Martin's pirate accent was scornful but amusing.

'Yep, loves himself!' Tucker exaggerated a cough, which abruptly stopped Whittling from poncing around like a male model. Tucker nudged me. 'Come on Frank, grab his arm. You too Martin, cop a hold of his scrawny fucking legs!'

With devious laughter Tucker guided us out of the ablutions, down the corridor and out of the main door. Once we had man-handled struggling Whittling out of the building, we steered towards a window which looked in on our dormitory. Tucker lifted Whittling's head to the window, pressed his nose up to it and asked him. 'What do you see in there?'

Whittling replied in grumpy puzzlement. 'The lads cleaning up our room?'

Tucker nodded to me and Martin Flowers. 'Right, back inside!'

We frogmarched Whittling back into the ablutions and stopped in front of the mirror where we had abducted him from. Tucker motioned to us to let go. 'What do you see in there?'

Whittling replied perplexed, bordering on superciliousness. 'Me looking at me?'

Tucker said no more. He just folded his arms and smiled triumphantly. For a second or so Whittling looked puzzled, until the penny dropped. Humiliated at his vanity he pushed past us and contrived to get the ablutions spick and span in his own inimitable style.

'He'll get there eventually!' Tucker beamed.

As soon as all of the dirty graft was completed we set about mucking in with the others to get the accommodation room ready for inspection. Tug Wilson had delegated Sooty Corbett to make sure that the contents of the lockers were laid out in identical order, bed blocks squared off perfectly and kit arranged on beds to the specifications on the instruction card. While he was sliding around on his squares of blanket, Sooty tried to blag Spike the Bike's head that he had once smuggled gold ingots into the country hidden in the heels of his shoes when returning from China. Spike the Bike and a few others were finding this latest tale hard to swallow, after all Sooty Corbett had up to now claimed that he was a computer hacker and that he had three degrees in electronics. Me and Tucker had reasoned that if Sooty did in fact possess three degrees in electronics then why hadn't he applied for a commission as an officer in the Royal Electrical and Mechanical Engineers? Tug Wilson seemed to hang on Sooty's every word though, he was easily impressed. He listened intently while checking every man over to ensure that they were all cleanly shaven, uniforms immaculately pressed and that the floor of the dorm was gleaming. Tug Wilson was very optimistic that Cpl Hazel would be full of pride with his platoon when the RSM scrutinized our labours.

'Stand by your beds!' hastily commanded the instructor, completely psyching everybody out as the sound of hobnail boots stormed along the corridor. Contrary to procedure, the RSM had decided to start snooping at the opposite end of the building first and work anti-clockwise, throwing the whole Spider into disarray to create extra trepidation. Being a bit of a mean bastard the RSM didn't enter our room straight away, choosing instead to search the washroom for stray pubic hairs, scum and detritus. Cpl Hazel brought us to attention, we stood rigid not daring even to blink when RSM John Daniels did eventually stroll in.

Comparable to a conductor in a military brass band the RSM wore a red sash draped diagonally across his uniform jacket together with a pair of white gloves. His eyes assiduously analysed the room, seeking out microscopic germs and miniscule dust particles ill guided enough to dance in the feeble rays of sunlight bleeding through the windows. His lug holes worked in synchronisation as if eavesdropping for the crackle of unfettered micro-organisms.

'The ablutions pass muster, just! Stand your men at ease Corporal.'

Gleaming hobnail boots squeaked robustly across the floor, gouging imprints into its lustrous surface like fossilized dinosaur tracks. The Sergeant Major ran his pristine white gloves meticulously over all exposed surfaces and examined his finger tips for the merest indication of filth; he then directed his forensic curiosity onto each occupant. Starting at the row of beds on the left, the RSM systematically scrutinised Tish Hewitt from head to foot, then drifted leisurely like a bumblebee, as if collecting nectar from the petals of kit displayed upon the Yorkshire man's bed space. The RSM kept the suspense going by running his eye over Tish Hewitt a second time, hopeful that a button might have come undone under interrogation or that a shirt collar may have curled up at the corner in surrender, neither had. RSM Daniels backed off unobtrusively, making no comment as he drifted along the line of beds. The whole kit and caboodle appeared in order as each man snapped to attention, calling out his name and number apprehensively.

'Have you shaved this morning?' the inquisitor demanded of Wilson.

'Yes Sir!' stalwartly confirmed Tug.

'Stand a bit closer to the blade next time!'

The RSM approached Corbett, whose knife, fork and spoon were analysed with objective scrutiny. The fork was tersely held up to Sooty's face. 'Dirty, yes?'

Sooty Corbett said nothing as the item of cutlery flew through the air and clattered dejectedly onto the floor, he was too afraid of the consequence; it was obvious the RSM was not going to let the issue go unremarked and Sooty knew it.

The RSM stared at Sooty as if he had just caught sight of maggots wriggling from every orifice on Corbett's shamefaced head. 'Disgusting, isn't that how we get nasty diseases?'

Sooty Corbett blanched and gulped remorsefully. 'Yes sir, sorry sir!'

'You will be if I see that sort of shit again mister, personal hygiene is each and every man's individual responsibility. It's no fun when a unit goes down with dysentery, which is why manky bogging utensils are not tolerated in the British Army!'

The Sergeant Major rifled through Sooty's kit, looking for more discrepancies but none were found. Dissatisfaction lined the RSM's face as he proceeded determinedly to the next bloke, then onto the next, checking every fork for food particles and every razor for tell-tale soap stains, but Cpl Hazel had warned his lads that this was another of the RSM's bug-bears, rendering it a mission for us to polish the razors daily after use.

The Warrant Officer grunted disapprovingly at Spike, correcting the position of the biker's white tea cup before admonishing him. 'Work on those boots!'

Tucker realised that his own cup was out of place too, and while the RSM had his back turned towards him, Tucker gingerly twisted ninety degrees and corrected its position. Cpl Hazel was incredulous at Tucker's rectification and shot him a panicked expression, his eyes popping out of their sockets beseeching "WHAT THE FUCK ARE YOU UP TO?"

The RSM stared at me glacially as he checked me over, then moved down to the end of our row of beds and started on the opposite side. On reaching Tucker, the RSM stared at the white cup suspiciously and then adjusted the position of the cap badge on Tucker's beret with a fussy minute tweak and grumbled. 'Over your left eye!'

"Nit picking bastard!" I thought, and then I grimaced as Tucker spoke. 'Thank you sir.'

'You're welcome!' The RSM passed Stan-the-Cab's bed space and mumbled approvingly at the cabdriver's kit layout. The white China teacup was ornamental and meant for display purposes only, but Rodger Boileiu, the daft bugger two beds up from Stan-the-Cab, must have been using *his* cup to drink from. RSM Daniels hooked his pace stick through the handle of Boileiu's tannin stained cup as if lifting a flea bitten dead sewer rat, and elevated it an inch from the offenders petrified face. 'WHAT IS THIS GERM INFESTED ITEM OF SHIT?'

'It's my cup Sir,' Rodger Boileiu spluttered ineffectually.

'IT'S MINGING!' the RSM flew into a rage and threw the cup crashing to the floor, but it didn't break, it just bounced and clattered down the length of the room, closely followed by an angry man distraughtly stamping on it with an hobnail boot. The cup seemed indestructible as it lurched unscathed from each unsuccessful attempt, bouncing and wobbling more and more out of control along the shiny wooden dormitory. John Daniels got so incensed by its refusal to rupture, that he swung his parade stick at it, raining swipes until the damned thing exploded into tiny pieces across the polished floor. The RSM stormed out of the room and fumed under his breath at 3platoon. 'Get a grip of your shit!'

Cpl Hazel shook his head in disgust and called out retrospectively. 'PERMISSION TO CARRY ON SIR?'

But the request went unanswered as the enraged hygienist stomped down the corridor breathing brimstone and fire. The next three minutes were strained, up until the silence was broken by the clang of lockers crashing to the floor. The RSM went ballistic giving 4platoon a collective almighty rollicking as the clatter of upended beds reverberated through the Spider.

'YOU DIRTY LAZY BASTARDS! WHAT ARE YOU DOING HERE?' Crash-Bang-Wallop. 'WHAT THE FUCK IS THIS? WHAT THE FUCK IS IT?'

The conflict went on for ten whole minutes, but it seemed like an hour. He threw boots out of windows, scattering them willy-nilly so that no one could distinguish one from another. Fighting broke out later over claims of ownership - come on, if you found a pair of boots that fitted and were shinier than yours, you'd hang on to them wouldn't you? The RSM then moved on to the next platoon and an eerie silence descended, they must have got it right! It didn't last, this momentary stillness was eventually broken by more intermittent shouts and the occasional crash or clatter as the remaining platoon was inspected.

After forty minutes of clinical scrutiny, Cpl Hazel gave 3Platoon the all clear. 'Well done lads, not too bad a turn out. Bare this in mind though; no combat ready unit has ever passed inspection, and no inspection ready unit has ever passed combat! Sooty you minger, you heard the man, don't get caught out like that again, and you Balloo…'

'It's Boileiu, Corporal!'

'…don't you fucking interrupt me Balloo, you should be bloody well ashamed of yourself. What the fuck have you been doing with that cup? DISPLAY PURPOSES ONLY!' he roared. 'Did you have to have an almighty afternoon shit innit?'

Boileiu could not placate the NCO. 'Tug, this man's volunteered for extra cleaning duties - from now on, anything needing cleaning Balloo does it, he's been pinged! OK, Mr Balloo, or Boilerwho, or whoever the fuck you are, GET YOUR SELF SORTED OUT MAN!'

After packing away their stuff, 3Platoon filed outside ready to be shunted to another lecture, and on the way out we surveyed the damage which "Hurricane Daniels" had inflicted upon 4platoons' dorm. It looked like an explosion in a custard factory; there were piles of kit and bedding strewn all over the gaff inside and out. Ravaged mattresses were draped across upturned beds and bits of clothing swung from rafters like vampire bats, whilst overturned lockers formed steeple chase hurdles which restricted escape. With a full days training to yet get through, the lads of 4pltn busied themselves salvaging some of the wreckage. And just to add insult to injury, once the evening meal had been eaten they were going to have to blitz the room and complete a show parade all over again! Consequently as the days rolled by, each and every man absolutely dreaded kit inspections.

All the platoons were eventually formed up and marched to the wooden classrooms where Major Einstein warmly introduced us to a couple of training Majors: Major John Hobbis-Harris, and Major C.J.M. Wood T.D. from the Yorkshire Volunteers TA.
Bert's huge Mastiff was there too, settled in a slobbering heap at his feet.

Silver haired ruddy faced Major Hobbis Harris, who was due for retirement, tapped out his mundungus brier pipe against the heel of his shiny brogue shoe, then stood up to address the assemblage.

'Let's get down to brass tacks shall we,' he launched straight into his topic. 'On passing out at the end of this course you will become members of the Territorial and Army Volunteer Reserves. As a volunteer soldier you will be a part of the British armed forces, and believe me, because the volunteer reserves have a fundamental role to play in our nation's defence, you are joining an army that is admired and respected throughout the world. The reserve forces are fully integrated with the Regular Forces in this country's operational plans, and they are a particularly efficient way of using manpower and financial resources. The Territorial and Army Voluntary Reserve number some sixty thousand men and women, and in an emergency, would make a major contribution to the reinforcement of BAOR, as well as to security within the United Kingdom.'

I reacted like most people do when enduring claustrophobic classroom conditions, after about ten minutes I found myself fighting to stay awake. Church gatherings have much the same effect, my eyes glaze over and my head lolls to my chest like a lump of lead. Tucker sat next to me, he was just the same. Only he slipped down in his seat like a hibernating tortoise and floated away somewhere for a winter break!

'Pay attention there, yes you, Tucker isn't it?' snapped Major Einstein coarsely. His dog must have thought that his master was snapping at him because it stood up and began pining for the door. 'Sit Rex!'

'Sorry Sir,' replied Tucker, sitting up into a sterner posture. 'The lights are on but there's no one at home!'

'Tell me about it!' retorted the officer. The rest of us tittered, but truth be known, we were all verging on forty winks due to sleep deprivation and oxygen starvation.

Once Major Einstein had reeled Tucker back from fluffy slumber-land he strived to retain our wavering attention. 'You'll have to fight through the fatigue young man, it comes with the uniform I'm afraid. Next week,' he predicted, 'when we're putting you through your paces out on the exercise area, you'll come to know what real exhaustion is all about!'

Major Hobbis Harris patiently waited for Major Einstein to finish his interruption then smiled politely and continued. 'I am particularly pleased to announce that as from today the traditional and well understood name of Territorial Army is back to stay. The Shapland Committee has made a number of recommendations to Francis Pym, the Secretary of State for Defence. The present title of Territorial and Army Volunteer Reserve was introduced in nineteen sixty seven and never really caught on, well it's a bit of a mouthful I think you'll all agree. So although you chaps have signed up for the T and AVR, you will now simply be known as the Territorial Army or TA for short.'

The major's voice was monotonous. 'This decision implies no change in the role of the force and no return to the concept of a part-time citizen's army. The Territorial Army will continue to be a trained volunteer reserve, fully integrated into the country's defence plans. You can be proud in the knowledge that a large part of the Territorial Army has a history which can be traced back through all major conflicts to its formation in 1908, and even before that during Anglo Saxon times in the eleventh century, when civilians were embodied with their own weapons.'

Most of the recruits started to fidget out of boredom. 'Many of you will be proud to relate that your forefathers fought in famous campaigns or took part in specific events. Their gallantry and examples of leadership will always be remembered as part of the traditions of their Regiments or Corps. Territorial Units suffered over five-hundred-and-seventy-seven casualties during the First World War, and won no less than seventy-one Victoria Crosses. And during fighting in North-Africa, Sicily, Burma, Singapore and North-West Europe in the Nineteen-Forty campaign, Territorial's again won a further seventeen Victoria Crosses. The same traditions will be true of the units to which you will be posted on completion of this course. Your Officers will no doubt tell you about the history and traditions of your particular regiment or corps, once you arrive there.'

I was bored. I looked at Tucker, he was finding it hard to concentrate too, his eyes were glazed, his mind had started to wander again; his Granddad had been involved in the two World Wars, finishing his service career as a Warrant Officer class three, a Staff Sergeant by modern equivalence. Granddad had joined the Territorial Army in 1910 for a bit of extra pocket money. Most of the lads he had grown up with in Runcorn had joined up too; it was a bit of a laugh, like Army Cadets for grownups. He didn't laugh for very long though, he was called up to serve in the Cheshire Regiment on 11th August 1914.

After the First Balkan War of 1912-1913 the Ottoman (Turkish) Empire had lost lands north of Greece which then became Albania and southern Serbia. The Serbians - supported by Russia - strived to expand their territory by endeavouring to establish a sea port on the coastline of the Adriatic Sea to ensure that their country was not completely landlocked.

The neighbouring European nations, namely Germany, Austria-Hungry and Italy felt threatened by the speed of expansion attained by the Serbs, so to contain this new development they clubbed together to form an alliance. Great Britain, France and Russia countered this move by forming an alliance in support of Serbia.

On the 5th July 1914 this scenario got a bit tricky; Arch Duke Ferdinand, heir to the throne of the Austro-Hungarian Empire was assassinated by a member of a Serbian secret society - the Black Hand - whilst visiting the province of Bosnia-Herzegovina. The whole world is aware of what happened next!

With an assurance of unconditional support from the Germans, the Austrian-Hungarian Empire retaliated by declaring war on Serbia on the 28th July and mounted an attack a day later. This got the Russians jittery, so on the 30th of July they began mobilizing their troops in support of Serbia. Madness ensued, and on the 1st of August, Germany then declared war on Russia. France got a bit jittery and mobilized troops the very same day, and on August the 2nd Germany entered Luxemburg, declaring war on France.

The British were disinclined to be drawn into a European land war but in the end they sent out an Expeditionary force of four divisions and one Cavalry division, a very inconsiderable army such was their hesitancy. But if everything went tits up, there were a further fourteen Territorial divisions of volunteer reservists to call upon wasn't there!

Enter Tucker's Granddad; at the beginning of the conflict, amidst artillery bombardment, he fought in the waterlogged trenches alongside thousands of others, defending the sappers with rifle fire as they dug tunnels out into no-man's land enabling them to undermine the enemy trenches and plant explosives to blow the Bosh to kingdom come. Mind you, the Germans were at it too, so in effect it was tit for tat mutual destruction stuff! Sixteen million people died during that war and a further twenty one million were injured; ten per cent of these figures were civilians.

Except for shrapnel wounds, Granddad managed to stay pretty much in one piece throughout the First World War, right up to his demob on 31st March 1920. Like so many others of the time, granddad assumed that since the war had ended, the struggle was now over too, after all, they had just endured the greatest war of all time and by rights everything should have returned to normal. But there was no work for him when he returned home; in the nineteen twenties there was a great economical depression and the economies of many European countries sank into chaos. Germany, which had been a thriving military and industrial power before the war, now owed large sums of money in reparation to Britain and France for starting the war, which led to its own economy collapsing. It was a knock on effect; other nations suffered too as they in turn paid back money borrowed from the United States to finance their own war effort. Unemployment was high and work was scarce, so by the 31stDecember 1920, Tucker's grandfather bit the bullet and headed back to the ranks of the Cheshire Regt and signed up as a regular soldier, serving right through until 30th December 1924 when things had picked up sufficient enough to be able to find a job. After leaving the army he re-joined the T.A as a hobby.

Great Britain was not out of the woods yet though. Many people in the USA had invested money in stocks and shares, which unduly pushed share prices up beyond any real value. In 1929 share prices reached a peak, and then dipped, so investors started to panic and sell them off recklessly. The price of shares tumbled and thousands of people lost all their money, which caused yet another financial crisis as the US called in loans from economies around the world. By this time Britain and Germany were really feeling the pinch, unemployment had gone through the roof as exports of raw materials fell by more than seventy per cent, which also ruined the economies of many colonies who depended on exporting raw materials and food for their income. However, Runcornians' were luckier than most, explicably due to the towns' location alongside the industrious river Mersey, and straddling the Bridgewater canal and Manchester ship canal.

Waterways had been considered the Motorways of Britain during the Industrial Revolution, they were the arteries of commerce before the railways and road transport were properly developed, and this helped Runcornians make a concerted effort to succeed and struggle free from means tested hand-outs. A plethora of commerce was established in the town offering ample employment based around the Chemical Industry, the Sandstone Quarries, soap production, and the manufacture of leather from raw hide at the Tanneries. On the back of all this Runcorn thrived and Tucker's grandfather prospered and settled down in marriage to raise a family.

But in spite of this serendipity, in 1938 at the onset of the Second World War, he was called up to train new troops. The British Army establishment was only 250,000 strong at that time and totally unfit to fight a first class war on the continent of Europe. Tucker's granddad considered himself too old, but he had survived the first world war in which so many people had lost their lives in a five year period, and as a survivor, his vast field experience was precisely what the Army needed in motivating a new generation, a generation who had previously thought that the "Great War" was the one that had ended all wars.

Unfortunately, Adolph Hitler held different sentiments. Hitler was hell bent on re-armament and forming a German empire that would pale into insignificance anything that Frederick the Great during the seventeen hundreds, or even Bismarck in the 1870s had achieved. Where the previous first and second Reich had been thwarted in maintaining a united Germany, Hitler's National Party had plans for a Third Reich which included in its manifesto, German unity and the pursuit of world domination; The Roman Empire and no doubt Charlemagne's Kingdom of the Franks were partly inspiration for this.

In 1933, having united many right-wing groups behind him under the banner of the National Socialist German Workers Party, Adolf Hitler manipulated President Hindenburg and became Reich Chancellor of the German nation. In the beginning he was very pioneering and perversely the introduction of motorways (autobahns) and affordable personal transportation (Volkswagen) to the masses was innovative, but the majority of his ideas were extreme. Hitler's belief in Darwin's evolution of species, led to attempts at developing a Super-Race through genetics, consequently demonising Jews, gypsies and others he deemed undesirable and advocating the ethnic cleansing of Europe. He got to grips with the economy by calling upon a financial Wizard, Hjalmar Schacht, to affect an economical miracle and reduce unemployment from around six million to a few hundred thousand. This was mainly achieved by heavy financial borrowing from Germany's successful chemical industries and the banning of Jews and other foreigners from being employed, then aryanising the nation's workforce by creating a programme of public labour to create employment to build up munitions and the armed forces. This *success* allowed Hitler to accelerate the re-armament of

Germany, which contemptuously broke treaties brought into effect at the conclusion of the First World War to dissolve the mighty German Empire and establish the Weimar republic.

The Nazis corrupted German politics and then imposed total control on the people by banning all opposing political parties and introducing a secret police, which allowed the brown-shirted Sturmabteilung to create a moral vacuum. In 1939 with the working classes behind him, the dictator invaded Poland, initiating World War Two, and wasted no time in occupying Denmark, Norway, Holland, Belgium, and Luxembourg shortly after. The following year his forces rumbled into France, enabling him to build a huge naval base along its north-west coastline to house Germany's deadly U-Boat fleet. This location allowed unhindered access to the shipping lanes of the North Atlantic, so that the U-Boats of his navy could hunt down and destroy British convoys carrying vital food and medicine to the United Kingdom, and subsequently cut the nation off from the rest of the world and starve its people into hopeless submission.

In 1941 Hitler invaded Yugoslavia and Greece to complete a stranglehold on mainland Europe, but the felonious Third Reich feared the gutsy British. After the First World War, Max Hoffmann's opinion that the British were a realm of lions led by donkeys was a profound assessment of the British nation, and no doubt Adolph Hitler bore this in mind when he tried to seduce King Edward the 8th, who was himself of German ascent, into condoning the expansion of German territory. By all accounts the king gave Hitler's plan the nod but fortunately for the UK, the king abdicated, otherwise the British might have been disenfranchised and its democratic government overthrown and freedom consequently jeopardised forever, leaving Great Britain open to absorption by Germany! Well that's what granddad lead me to believe, and he should know because he was around when it was all kicking off?

On the 6th April 1938, Tucker's granddad and many like him in the Territorial Army were mobilised to join the Royal Artillery to train men in the Heavy Artillery section to fight campaigns in France, Germany, North Africa and Italy.

We were once told a tale of granddad coming home on leave displaying a pair of Spurs worn on his boots, and granddad drunkenly clicking his heels together so that the spurs locked into one another causing him to fall over! The spurs were largely ceremonial by the 1940s but at one time, probably during the First World War and certainly during the Boer

War, had actually been used to dig into a horse's flanks to drive it forward whilst heaving the great Guns of the Heavy Artillery across battlefields; real grizzly blood and sweat stuff.

Tucker told me that he had once got a glimpse of granddad's medals, which the old boy was reluctant to exhibit. Besides Pip, Squeak and Wilfred, awarded for WW1, he had also received the Africa Star, the Italy Star, the France and Germany Star, and the War Medal 1939-45 Oak leaf.

Granddad once told us that shrapnel had wounded him in his right leg, and while unconscious he'd woken up on a surgeons operating table just as they were about to amputate. With no penicillin in those days, Gangrene was a major problem, especially Gas Gangrene - so the surgeons would simply cut the infected limb off to save a life and hope for the best!

"Cut that leg off and I'll kill you!" granddad had threatened the Surgeon.

The medical team left it alone and he recovered at his own pace. Apart from what had lead up to both wars and the story about the surgeons trying to cut off his leg, granddad never talked about his part in either of the conflicts; he'd seen too much horror to be able to make any of it sound rational!

Tucker's thoughts drifted back from his daydreaming with a loud yawn and I fought with my own oscitance to the blah blah blah of Major Hobbis-Harris drivelling on about the modern day TA.

I whispered to Tucker, 'Blimey, this bloke can waffle for Britain; he's an Olympic gold medallist!'

'It is sometimes said,' the Major concluded, 'perhaps mischievously, that the Regular Army of this century has really only been there until the Territorial's could be mobilised. Certainly a modern war on the scale of those "wars to end wars" cannot be fought without a general mobilisation of the whole population. Therefore the role for what you have volunteered is a very important one, one with considerable responsibility and trust, for that reason you should ensure that you are worthy of upholding the traditions of this service and maintaining the respect of the nation.'

I massaged my temples and rubbed some life back into my eyes, then looked around at the fidgeting rows of fellow recruits each of whom had glazed expressions on their faces too. The Major stoked his pipe with tobacco, tamped it down with his thumb, lit it up and puffed like billy-o; he had not yet finished with us. Pacing back and forth, he delved into a brief history of the TA and conveyed his knowledge as unexcitingly as he could.

'The Territorial Army and Reserve Forces Act of 1907 had created for the first time in British military history an organisation specifically designed for war, before that there had only been a citizen army of militias or auxiliaries. Auxiliary forces at one time or another have played their part in defending the kingdom since the time of King Alfred, who organised the Fyrd or General Levy which fought the Danes at Maldon. This force engaged in the Battle of the Standard in 1138, and also at Bannockburn in 1314. Incidentally, none of these troops could be used to fight wars overseas because they were not obliged to serve outside their own shire except in extraordinary circumstances, and since they were paid for out of money raised by their own counties it was illegal to send these troops to fight in foreign wars.'

Major Hobbis-Harris would have made a strong contender for Mastermind. He told us that in 1782 the first of the Volunteer Acts was passed, and in 1793 the declaration of war with France caused a further strengthening of the Volunteer force. In 1794 and again in 1798, Volunteer Corps were given statute, and by 1803 they numbered 380,000 men. Also in 1794 a force very distinct from the Volunteers was formed, this was the Yeomanry. Originally the Yeomanry were drawn from the efficient farmer class and were well disciplined. In 1808 the Local Militias Act was intended to bring in compulsory service by means of the ballot; Volunteers could only escape this by paying a fine. To further entice Volunteer forces to increase the numbers of the Militia ranks, a bounty was paid, an enticement still in force today. Subsequently in the course of these cut backs the Volunteer Forces dwindled in existence, and by 1814 the majority were disbanded. Only the Honourable Artillery Corps was to have a continuous existence, surviving up until the Great War in 1914.

The Major relit his pipe and concluded by telling us 'In 1881 the Secretary for State, Mr Cardwell, had territorialized the Regular Army, and at the same time grouped Volunteer Corps under their respective regimental districts. Regular officers of the Territorialized Army began assisting the Volunteers for training purposes ten years later. Large numbers of Volunteers and Yeomanry served during the South African War alongside the Territorialized Army as non-professionals, and provided excellent value. But up until 1914 there had never been an organisation for war, so the War Minister, Mr Haldane, transformed the Volunteers, the Yeomanry and the Territorialized Army into an army so far advanced in training that it stood the test of the Great War, making it an Army to be truly reckoned with!'

'Which brings us on to the subject of the Oath of Allegiance!' interrupted Major C.J.M. Wood, positively bristling with his segue. He was an odd looking man, his captivating eyebrows met in the middle giving the impression that they were just one very large one, and rather amusingly the eyebrow performed a Mexican wave whenever he changed his expression. It certainly got my attention.

'In many countries the armed forces are seen as, and often used for a political end. In this country however, a soldier makes his Oath of Allegiance, not to the countries' political leaders but to the Monarch, Her Majesty Queen Elizabeth the second. In the world we live in today there are many ways of considering the Oath of Allegiance, and irrespective of your reasons for becoming a Volunteer Soldier it is occasionally worthwhile reflecting on the meaning of the Oath.'

The Major turned to an overhead viewer, switched it on and projected a copy of the oath from a view foil onto the wall behind him. The words were a little distorted at first, but with a twiddle of a knob they quickly loomed into focus.

Major Woods' solitary eyebrow danced in synchronicity to his voice. 'Righto chaps, I know you pledged your allegiance individually at your investiture on completion of your interviews last year, but would you now recite the oath once more with your platoon comrades to reiterate its special significance!'

We all cleared our throats and sat up straight, it was reminiscent of being back at school during morning assembly, chanting prayers and singing hymns projected from similar apparatus. It read: "I swear by almighty God, that I will be faithful and bear true allegiance to Her Majesty Queen Elizabeth the Second, her heirs and successors, and that I will, as in duty bound, honestly and faithfully defend Her Majesty, her heirs and successors, in person, crown and dignity against all enemies, and will observe and obey all orders of Her Majesty, her heirs and successors, and of the generals and officers set over me."

In his soft Edinburgh brogue, Major 'Bert' Einstein reflected on the oath. 'It puts things into perspective don't you think, and should give you all a common reason for being what you are – Volunteer Soldiers! Your task it is to retain our freedom and defend our country, and the society we live in from aggression, either from within or from without the United

Kingdom. Serving here in Britain or as part of NATO, or indeed anywhere else for that matter, makes no difference. Many of our predecessors have measured up to this serious commitment and it's now your responsibility to do likewise!'

"Serious stuff!" I thought as the class was dismissed for a welcome breath of fresh air.

After dining on Spanish Omelette, salad and chips at Odd-job's Taverna, we were issued with SLRs and reassembled on the parade square in front of Sergeant McBride who warned the rank and file not to drop them. Despite the freezing cold we held on to the rifles as if they had been smeared with super-glue. Without further preamble, Sgt McBride made the formation bash *His Square*, holding the weapons in the marching order position, swinging our free arm back and to. The weight of the weapon was 9lb 9ozs (almost 5 bags of Sugar) and the strain from the stress and position which we held onto them took a while to get used to. Tish Hewitt was appointed Right-hand-marker while the Drill-Pig mercilessly put us through all Drill movements. Left wheels, right wheels, left turns, right turns and about turns. When we were eventually given a rest, it was merely to get some circulation going in our numb fingers and toes.

'You'll get used to the weight so you will,' vowed the DI. 'When yay's got some feeling back, we must press on, we have got a lot to cover so we have, so practice these manoeuvres using a broom in the comfort of your warm billet during your spare time.'

"What bloody spare time, what bloody warm billet?" I thought.

Sgt McBride demonstrated how to Port Arms, Shoulder Arms, Order Arms and Present Arms, but would not let us marchers massage our stiff-arms. All of this drill was done to numbers, 123–123–123–1.

If you ever see a military parade like the changing of the Guard at Buckingham Palace and wonder how they achieve all that precision timing, it's all down to the 123 system taught on basic training. Off we all went again crossing the square like languished clockwork penguins, round and round, back and forth, bish bash bosh.

'Left right, left right, left right, leffft.'

I was beginning to hate Sgt McBride so much that I wanted to stick the rifle right up the Drill Instructors jacksy, not caring to see the bloody thing ever again. The feeling was mutual, Tucker felt exactly the same.

By the time we were eventually knocked off for the day it was getting dark and even colder; a hearty hot meal was more than welcome, it allowed the lads to socialise and compare horror stories while bathing in moderate warmth, but it was over far too soon for us to really enjoy the full benefit. The remaining few hours was taken up ironing kit and revising.

Plagued by nervous energy, Tug Wilson found it difficult to unwind, he claimed that he hardly ever slept, but Tucker said he thought Tug was too much of a dreamer for that to be true. Tug proved Tucker right by imagining himself as a Coldstream-Guard as he marched around the spider complex calling out orders while clutching hold of a broom. 'Shoulder arms two three, port arms two three.'

Spike was jaded by all this bullshit so he showed us a neat key bending trick he'd picked up while watching Uri Geller performing pshycokinesis on the TV; me and the lads laughed in amazement. Whittling wasn't too amused; it was his key that Spike had twisted out of shape.

Martin Flowers quietly confided to me and Tucker that he thought Whittling had the biggest ears he'd ever seen on a human being! Tish Hewitt must have had big ears too because he hollered like a football hooligan. 'Wingnut, Wingnut.'

'Well at least they don't look like cauliflowers, you friggin great ape!' snapped Whittling defensively.

'Leave it out fellah's,' petitioned Stan-the-Cab. 'He must be sensitive about this or whatever…'

'I give as good as I get!' assured Whittling, abruptly.

'It's all right China; I'm on your side, fuck *this* lot off, allright?'

'Hold your foot up Stan,' intervened Tucker, tongue in cheek. 'We're supposed to be a team aren't we? Nothing was meant by it, was it Martin?'

'No boy. I simply said they're the biggest fucking ears I ever seen. What the hell's the marrer with *you*?' - He pronounced the word "matter" like a pirate.

'Persecution complex,' Stan jabbed a finger at Martin accusingly. 'Turn it in, right?'

'Whores piss!'

Tug Wilson completed parading around the Spider and returned the broom to the locker which contained the cleaning paraphernalia, and then tactfully intervened. 'Could murder a pint right now!'

'I think we all could, hey Stan?' I winked exasperatedly at the London Cabby.

Tug was right, a few pints and a game of pool would've eased the tension and gone someway at impeding Stan's zeal for protecting Whittling; it was only banter after all.

Cooked up in a stuffy room with a bunch of farting sweaty bodies was repressive and there was definitely a bit of rivalry emerging between Tish Hewitt and Stan-the-Cab. When either of them spoke, the others in the platoon would hush up and defer to them, the Alpha-Beta male thing! Stan and Tish were weighing each other up and there was nothing coy about their brazen aggression. I was indifferent to all this and I knew that Tucker was familiar with such situations; the two of us had grown up with older brothers and a good dollop of sibling rivalry. We felt no peer pressure from either big Tish or Stan-the-Cab, and found the whole macho rivalry for group authority amusing. After all, we would only be at Martinique Barracks for a fortnight so it wasn't worth getting our knickers in a twist, besides, Cpl Hazel was running the show and wouldn't let personal animosity interfere with training, and just to prove the point, the corporal casually strolled into the room, and we all stood to attention.

'Stand easy.' We all went back to looking industrious as the instructor strutted from bed to bed like a Bantam Cock, checking the progress on best boots. 'Right settle down and get an early night, you're on the ranges tomorrow.'

'Are you going to tuck us in and read us a bedtime story corporal?' asked Corbett.

'Fuck right off Sooty.'

'You really know how to hurt a bloke's feelings corporal.'

'Fuck off you faggot, I'm trying to turn you into trained killers. The only feelings you should possess are instinct and intuition, not emotional. You will have a swinging brick for a heart by the time you leave here, I promise!'

The corporal seemed happy with his platoon. 'Those boots are gleaming Wingnut, Good man!'

The instructor must have heard Tish Hewitt hollering "Wingnut" earlier and put 2+2 together, and fully endorsed the nickname. Whittling was to be known as "Wingnut" for the rest of his TA days, providentially deflecting attention from his self-absorbed narcissistic character traits.

By 2200hrs the corporal had withdrawn so most of us decided to call it a day and turn in for a kip. That's when the snores started again. I had imagined that getting away from Runcorn for two weeks would be unmitigated bliss, seeing how the town lies beneath the approach path of Liverpool Airport and the noise from commercial jets droning over the town every five minutes was unavoidable, but this nauseating snoring was torture.

'Stuff a sock in his mouth,' impishly murmured big Tish.

'You can't do that, he might be asthmatic,' whispered Tug Wilson objectively.

Tish was incredulous. 'You're a bleeding-heart you are cocker.'

'Here, I'll do it, go back to sleep Tug.' volunteered sniggering Sooty Corbett.

Tug called out comically. 'Nurse, he's out of bed again!'

There was a fit of choking as Wingnut turned blue and twisted onto his side gasping for air.

With peace restored, everybody drifted off to sleep dreaming about the ranges the next day and the excitement of firing live rounds – like little kids on Christmas Eve.

'Snorrrr.. Snorrrrrrr.. Snarrrohhrrrr. Snorkuharrr kharrrr hrhmm.' The peace lasted until about 2am. It was maddening; Wingnut was giving it shed loads. One by one we were reawakened by him, how the hell were we supposed to crack any zeds at this rate?

Martin Flowers was a conniving character. He skated across to Wingnut's bed space on his squares of blanket and picked up the snorer's alarm clock and reset it to go off in five minutes time, then whispering, covertly organised the rest of us into a plan of action. Giggling like naughty schoolboys, we made our beds look as if we had all got up for the early morning run, then leaving the main lights on, we sneaked out and hid in the ablutions. Martin and Tucker lingered by the doorway to witness Wingnut waking up; I inched back and peeped over their shoulders. The alarm went off and vacuous Mr Whittling dragged himself to his feet and sat looking around the deserted billet wondering where everybody had gone? Thinking he'd been left behind while we were running around on a BFT, he made a mad scramble for his PT vest and trousers, hurriedly laced up his boots, then combed his hair and checked his appearance in his locker mirror. By this time we had been joined by Big Tish and Stan-the-Cab, who pushed their heads over our shoulders to get a peep through the crack in the door; this had to be seen to be appreciated, it was both devious and delicious. When Wingnut made his move to leave the dorm, Tucker and Martin cautiously pushed us back into the washroom where we melted into the darkness of the hidey-hole, just in time as the sound of Wingnut's solitary boots bashed up the corridor and out into the freezing cold night.

Once the Spider door had slammed shut, everybody creased up laughing, even Tug Wilson rejoiced. 'Martin Flowers, you devious fucker.'

Howling uncontrollably, we made our way back to our beds, turned the lights off and drifted good humouredly into the arms of sleep, the silence occasionally broken by the odd chuckle. Meanwhile outside in the darkness, young Wingnut raced around the 3 mile circuit trying desperately to catch somebody up. Thirty minutes later he staggered exhausted back to the Spider and collapsed on his bed fully dressed. He hadn't realised something was amiss until he had finished the course and the DS staff were not there to shout at him for taking so long. Now his ardent snoring was replaced by exasperated mutterings. 'You bastards, you puerile fucking bastards!

Chapter 8

The Snorasaurus had it all to do again at 0600hrs and to make matters worse, the PTI's were breathing down his skinny neck. 'Hello, sometime today Wingnut, if you can manage it that is; have you lost the will to live yet?'

Wingnut gasped 'I can't breathe corporal!'

The PT Buster replied sardonically 'I can't play the fucking piano, but you don't hear me moaning about it do you!'

The other PTI joined in. 'My fucking eighty year old granny can run faster than you and she's only got one leg. What's all this waving your hands from side to side business, you run like a little school girl trying to dry her nail varnish!'

'He waves his hands around like his fingers are on fire.'

'It doesn't bear thinking about does it, Wingnut spontaneously combusting!'

'Oh I don't know, I think I'd like to see that!' the first PTI laughed.

After breakfast, Cpl Hazel gave his platoon a trouble-free room inspection, after which we clambered aboard the Bedford RLs to be ferried to the ranges situated five miles away.

Firing on an outdoor range was all new to me, as indeed it was for most of the other men on the recruit course. However Tucker did have the advantage of shooting a .22 calibre rifle on an indoor range when he was a kid with the Air Training Corps, and he'd once discharged a Lee Enfield .303 during summer camp at RAF Leaming in Yorkshire too. Me, well I'd only ever shot an Air-Rifle on a fairground attraction.

On arrival at the ranges we were issued with waxed cardboard boxes containing 20 rounds of ammunition; we were given three and a half boxes each. Tucker fed 3 lots of 20 bullets into 3 of his 4 magazines like a professional, feeding the remaining ten rounds into a fourth magazine. I watched and copied him. Mine were a little bit fumbled but loading the rounds into my magazines actually gave me a feeling of potency and served to focus my mind on the task at hand. The Mil Training Staff were far more focussed and potent, as regular soldiers they were very much at home strutting about on the ranges handling weaponry; it was very much their forte!

The RSM barked "Listen in!" and ordered us to get down, then test and adjust. I got as comfortable as I could in the prone position and supported the SLR in the firing position.

The Razzman then called out. 'Ten rounds in your own time,' then roared, 'Go on!'

We fired the first magazine of ten rounds at a target to check that our grouping was tight. The weapons didn't go off with a bang as I expected, it was more of a very loud snap, like a whip due to the rounds being supersonic in speed. The SLR had a powerful kick. Tucker commented that the SLR being a 7.62 calibre easily matched the Lee Enfield .303 for recoil. Once everybody had fired their first ten rounds and unloaded, we were ordered to advance to the "Butts" where the targets are displayed. Tucker's ten rounds were off to the right and spaced within a hand span of the little white centre patch glued to the outline of a man printed on the target; 306 Squadron of the Air Training Corps had taught him well. My grouping how ether were a little higher and wider, but not a bad grouping for a first attempt though.

Cpl Hazel zeroed Tucker's rifle by minutely adjusting the sights with a small tool. 'Bravo Zulu, well done. You've fired before Tucker, ain't yer lad, I can tell?'

'Yeh, I had a Johnny Seven Tommy-Gun when I were a kid!'

'A Johnny Seven, hey? I bet you had the helmet and walkie-talkie too!'

'And a Raleigh Chopper bike.' I chortled. He hadn't had either; neither of us had, we'd never been that well off because there were too many mouths to feed when we were kids. Chopper bikes and Johnny Seven one-man-army machine-guns were the sort of playthings owned by boys whose families could afford to go to Billy Butlin's for a holiday; the likes of me and Tucker were lucky if we ventured any further than Ourgate or Windowview for our summer Hols.

The corporal had put Tucker on the spot; Tucker didn't want to be singled out like a performing seal, but he couldn't just put his skill down to pot luck. 'Air cadets, staff. I was in the ATC in my youth.'

'Ah now, that's very interesting Tucker,' Cpl Hazel cocked the working parts of the weapon three times - all part of the SOP's he'd taught us in the classroom - and once Tucker had checked and confirmed that the rifle was clear, the corporal passed the improved SLR back to him so that he could decimate more targets. 'I was a blue job (RAF personnel) before transferring to this mob!'

The corporal twiddled with *my* rifle sights to lower my aim and gave me a pat on the back to dismiss me. As we returned to the firing line Cpl Hazel caught us up, and being intrigued about the revelation of him initially being in the air force Tucker prompted the instructor to elaborate. The corporal was not coy, in a few words he brusquely revealed his passion for hill walking and mountaineering. He'd been part of the RAF's mountain rescue team, and having caught the bug for the great outdoors, had gone on to scale the 3 peaks: Scarfell Pike, Ben Nevis and Mount Snowdon, and a great many of the Munroe's in Scotland. He had walked Wainwright's Coast to Coast and conquered the challenging Pennine way, and had once helped raise £10,000 in cash for the Duke of Edinburgh Award scheme by completing the arduous trek from John'O'Groats to Lands-End with a team of fellow Airmen. Cpl Hazel had run out of things to conquer in the UK and after discussing his dilemma with another accomplished climber, had been invited to join a British Army Expedition in Alaska. The only trouble that existed was that he was in the wrong arm of the services and was therefore asked if he wouldn't mind swapping over to the Army if they jacked it all up for him. Blue for Khaki was not an obstacle in his mind, so he had summarily exchanged services.

Prior to being drafted onto this recruit course as a short term posting while awaiting his departure to the Denali National Park in the spring, this iron man had just completed a stint of patrolling the streets of Belfast. I was surprised that the instructor confided in us so heartily, it was a brief but very interesting conversation. But I couldn't help thinking, what does a career-soldier living in a shrinking world attempt after accomplishing a trek across the wilds of Alaska; maybe Everest, but then what? We knew nothing of the SAS back then, very few people did. The surgical procedure of Operation Nimrod a year later during the events of the Iranian Embassy siege on the 5th May 1980 would soon change all that!

Back at the 300 metre firing point, we took up the prone position. Tish Hewitt who was positioned to my right called over to Tucker on my left. 'Hey Clint Eastwood what were all that about with corpral Hazel?'

'Rules and reg's mate, rules and reg's.' Dirty Harry replied. We didn't have time for a girly half hour, so Tucker promised to spill the beans to Hewitt later on back at the ranch.

"WITH A MAGAZINE OF TWENTY ROUNDS, LOAD," sternly ordered the range commander. I adopted the loading position, ensured the safety catch was set to safe, unfastened one of the ammo pouches on my webbing and took out a magazine of 20 rounds. A quick examination told me that the magazine was correctly loaded, so I slotted it onto the rifle, guaranteeing it was secure, before firmly re-fastening my ammo pouch. Tucker gave me a wink. Finally we pulled our ear defenders into place and awaited the next word of command.

"READY."

Tucker set his sights to 300 and cocked the weapon. I followed suit and aimed off at the target area, and then tested and adjusted my position until I was satisfied with my sights.

"WATCH AND SHOOT, WATCH AND SHOOT!" We were in business.

The marksmanship skills taught to us in the classroom kicked in; breathing, trigger operation and follow through. I released my safety catch and waited for the targets to appear down the range. At a silent order the targets using a pulley system were raised on trestles by hand. There were two figures in my eye line, I chose the right hand one and having identified the target, took two deep breaths, breathed out half way and then held it. I squeezed the trigger until I felt the first pressure, then squeezed a little more and the rifle cracked with a punch, then spat out an empty shell case and reloaded automatically; the sound of Chinese-fire-crackers erupted all around me as the rest of the rifles banged out a tattoo.

Tucker was focussed on his shot, he kept the target in view the whole time, following through with his aim, and I did exactly the same and imagined that I saw a hit on the wooden shape in front. I fired more or less when he fired and still had time to put another round down the range at the twin figure on the left before it vanished from sight.

Once again two deep breaths, hold half way out and crack! Yep, I liked the SLR; its accuracy was very impressive! The targets popped up and down another nine times until we completed the shoot, and then we were ordered to "UNLOAD!"

We had practiced this manoeuvre over and over in the classrooms, it was of paramount safety on the ranges, and once unloaded and the weapons had been made safe, the range staff checked that each rifle was indeed harmless, then individually patted each recruit on the back and confirmed, "CLEAR, EASE SPRINGS!"

When we stood up I smiled with elation, Tucker thumped me playfully in the arm and grinned. 'You soft bugger, think you're Rambo do you?'

The shooting party moved forward to the targets for an appraisal. All of Tucker's twenty rounds had found their spot; some of mine had gone astray. Cpl Hazel was full of praise for Tucker. 'Now you're cooking, nice tight grouping that. You're a natural lad, keep it up!'

Stan-the-Cab and Big Tish had matched Tucker shot for shot but like me most had scored ten to fifteen. Some of the other blokes had not been so lucky. Jocularly, Cpl Hazel called the rest of the DS Staff over to have a butcher's at some of the targets. 'Fuckin'ell Churchill, you shagging Donkey, you couldn't hit a cows arse with a spade. While you Wingnut, fuck me, you've managed to excel yourself by scoring twenty eight!'

It was not quite so amazing; by aiming at the wrong target, Ronny Churchill had increased Whittling's possible score by eight. But what was amazing was that each target was clearly marked with a giant number from one to thirty above it.

The RSM looked mildly surprised and gave a dubious groan. 'Twenty-eight, hardly born killers are they hey?'

'Mark them down for fourteen each…' advised Sgt McBride disbelievingly.

'…and get them a Goldfish?' suggested Cpl Hazel.

'Bollocks, fourteen each and a swift kick up the jacksy!' suggested Staff Sgt Mackintosh.

'Wingnut, Churchill, that was abysmal,' insisted the RSM, hiding a smile. 'Ten Star Bursts, GO!'

The recruits spent the rest of the morning firing from differing distances, in different positions: sitting, standing and lying down. We were shown how to judge distances by utilising Ranging Fire, which involved using a correctly zeroed weapon and estimating the distance to an object, setting that distance on the sights, and then firing tracer ammunition at it. After observing where the tracer was striking, the sights were adjusted until the object was struck accurately. This sight setting was the distance to the object and the rest of the section was notified of it, enabling us to rain hell on the object!

After completing each shoot we were ordered to "Unload", and the empty magazine was removed from the rifle and the weapon cocked three times, then the trigger was squeezed to make sure the chamber was empty - the DS (Directing Staff) were taking no chances with a lethal cocktail of raw recruits and live ammunition. It wasn't enough to just clear the weapon; the prudent DS had to physically verify that each rifle was safe and sound.

"FOR INSPECTION, PORT ARMS!" ordered the burly RSM.

3Platoon remained lying down. We cocked our rifles and locked the working parts, then leaned the weapons to the left slightly so that the DS could see into the chamber. When the instructors were satisfied, they tapped us individually on our shoulder and ordered "CLEAR, EASE SPRINGS!"

Discipline was tight; no one was allowed to stand up until this procedure had been carried out, as Rodger Boileiu found out to his detriment. His weapon jammed at one point during the shoot, but instead of holding up his hand and signalling for help like any normal person would, he stood up to show a member of staff the problem. It was a recipe for disaster, two DS Sergeants grounded him in a rugby tackle and hollered like crazy, "CEASE FIRE, CEASE FIRE!"

The DS went ape shit and hauled Boileiu up in front of the furious RSM for castigation, he seethed. 'Do not under any circumstance, when on a live firing range; point your weapon anywhere other than at the targets!'

Cpl Hazel looked as if he wanted to punch the miscreant to the ground, but refrained, choosing instead to bawl into Rodger Boileiu's ear hole instead. 'TEN STAR BURSTS MISTER BALLOO, GO!'

The recruits were rotated at the end of each shoot. When not firing, we either sat around cleaning our weapons or took a turn in the Butts, supervised by L/Cpl Hughes, to patch up the targets. This involved tearing off perforated black or brown paper squares from a booklet similar to cloakroom tickets, and pasting the squares onto the targets with range glue which had the consistency of male semen, to repair the damage caused by the rounds being fired. On a spoken command from the lance jack, the figure eleven targets were then hoisted up on a rattling trestle contraption to be fired at again. Taffy would blow his whistle like an exigent school teacher and the contraptions got pulled down again. This was boring and tedious after the excitement of shooting the boards to pieces, but necessary. The biggest dilemma of doing the "Butts" was that cold metal, frosty concrete and damp sandbags surrounded the recruits repairing the damage; it was a challenge to keep warm. It was minus five degrees as supersonic bullets whizzed overhead.

When the all-in-Stew arrived in Hay-boxes on the back of a Land Rover at noon it was more than welcome. Everyone loaded up their Mess tins with the stodgy Meat & Veg concoction and scooped one slice of dry white bread each, plus a mug full of tonsil varnish. I mused, as I inevitably did at picnics and barbeques, how peculiar it was that food always tasted better out in the open air and how eating it en-mass was a great social equaliser. As the hot hale-and-hearty stew slipped down our oesophagus it started to hit the spot. Our surroundings were cold and bleak but the lads winked at each other between mouthfuls and grinned like comrades-in-arms. The hot meal perked us all up no end, even the Range Warden decided to join us for a bite to eat.

Mick Crosset was a rosy cheeked genial Civvy, who wore a green corduroy flat cap, silver rimmed spectacles and an old scruffy army jumper underneath Tatty regulation brown overalls. He'd brought with him a giant bottle of Brown Sauce, which he passed around us to spice up the meal. Mick chatted away to the recruits about Civvy things; football, politics, that kind of stuff - a refreshing respite after days on end of military bumph. Conversely, the Mil Training staff sat off to one side having a bit of a conflab, engrossed in military chatter.

Staff Sgt Mackintosh, who had served six years in the French Foreign Legion as a younger man was in some sort of discussion with the RSM, who himself had once enjoyed secondment to that elite Corps. The other NCOs were grouped together like a flange of gorillas discussing bananas. Between knowing laughter, such place names as Grantham, Pirbright, Deep-cut and Bisley, were mentioned. The instructors were all boys together and very institutionalised. Each one of them had completed at least two tours of Northern Ireland, and having acquired such experiences only encountered by observing dodgy situations through the telescopic sights of a rifle, their very other-worldly confidence appeared extreme to the likes of us. Their razor sharp professional manner permeated their whole body as did their military ambition, a quality difficult to shake off even when relaxing; each looked like they could hold their nerve in difficult situations.

I sensed that I was being observed, assessments and comparisons were being made and on the spot mental notes were being filed away for future reference. After the meal had been consumed the DS Staff continued chatting amongst themselves, nodding and disagreeing as if they were up to something? The RSM raised himself to his full six feet two inches and grandly announced. 'OK then, we will settle this right now!'

Cpl Hazel sauntered over to us and beckoned Sooty Corbett and Stan-the-Cab. 'Over here you two!'

Both boys were led off to one side, where they were joined by similar pairs of recruits selected from each of the other platoons. It became very quiet for a moment as the eight "volunteers" glanced at each other uncertainly. The RSM stepped forward and matched one chosen pair off against another. Stan-the-Cab and Sooty were contested against a mean looking pair. One of their rivals, known as Pin-head, had the remnants of a fading black-eye and the physique of a bulldog, and the other contender, a tough stocky Geordie lad by the name of Jobling, looked like he could handle himself too. They were told to pick an opponent each and then the four of them went about grappling and wrestling each other to the ground.

Sooty took on Bobby Jobling, while Stan-the-Cab, once he'd dodged a few body blows, lifted Pin-head up off the ground and turned him onto his back, planting all his weight across Pin-head's squirming shoulders. Sooty and Jobling were evenly matched as they pushed and pulled, but Sooty just about managed to get the upper-hand with a Judo throw. The Cray-brothers (Robby and Tom) grunted and huffed as they took on a couple of lads from One Platoon, called, Maddox and Stoddard. There was much applause from the other platoon members as Maddox and Stoddard put up a brave fight, before capitulating to the Cray twins who fought like wild animals, and then it was all down to a face off.

Tom took on Sooty, it was very scrappy, and although Sooty had had a chance to rest, he was outmatched by the meanness of Tom who thought like a gypsy. Robby put on a good show against Stan-the-Cab, but Stan got the better and swept Robby off his feet with his right leg and pushed him back off balance, then dropped full spread on top of him.

Now you might think that by process of elimination, Stan-the-Cab and Tom Lloyd would be in the final bout, but the cunning DS Staff had a twist up their sleeve. The RSM called forward big Tish Hewitt, who removed his combat jacket provocatively, then ran full pelt at the two remaining combatants in anticipation. It was a good move as he sent each of them sprawling to the ground, but Stan and Tom weren't down for long. The two Cockneys quickly helped each other up, dusted themselves off and nodded to each other resolutely before setting about Tish Hewitt like a pair of Pit-bull-terriers. The rest of the lads rallied them on, choosing no side in particular as it was a good scrap all round. Tom grabbed hold of the giants' legs and held on grimly while Stan jumped up and hooked his whole body around Hewitt's neck. The monster crumpled to his knees, thrashing out at Stan-the-Cab and dislodging him. He then peeled Tom from off his legs. But before Tish could get upright, Tom and Stan-the-Cab were back at him, turning him on to his back and pinning him down. The onlookers cheered like crazy as the leviathan roared and arched his back, raising his legs into the air while Tom and Stan-the-Cab hampered his intended manoeuvre. He almost struggled free, but the RSM signalled to Pin-head, Bobby Jobling, Robby, Sooty, Maddox and Stoddard from One Platoon, to pile on top of Tish and finish the job off. Unfortunately for the DS Staff, that was the point when events went out of control! Tucker turned to his platoon mates and motioned to us, 'Come on lads, let's help Tish. Chaaarrrge!'

After much shoving and pulling, order was eventually restored and the RSM hastily concluded the lunch break. We were then introduced to the Small Machine Gun (SMG), the Light Machine Gun (LMG), and the General Purpose Machine Gun (GPMG). The LMG replaced the Bren gun, which had been used between the years 1939-1945. This weapon had almost identical specifications to the Bren, but differed in calibre. The Bren took the same .303 calibre round as the old Lee Enfield rifle, being as it was of the same generation of firearms. The .303 gauge converts to 7.7mil, slightly larger than the then up-to-the-minute NATO round of 7.62mil, so principally to keep the gun in service only the breach and barrel needed modifying. It weighed in at 10.5kg (ten and a half bags of sugar) and on single shot had a rate of fire of 40 rounds per minute and could knock out bursts of 650 rounds per min on automatic. It had a heavy recoil necessitating the gun to be steadied by placing your left hand on top of the butt, and had a 30 round magazine (reduced to 28 for a practical load), which was carried in a canvass carrier which had room for 4 magazines all told. The spare ammunition case had a 12-mag capacity and because of the weight, was lugged around in vehicles.

Handling the LMG was a schoolboy fantasy; all young lads imagine firing a machine gun at some stage in their lives, but the novelty paled significantly once we were introduced to the GPMG or as it was more affectionately known, the Gimpy (with a soft g as in jimpy).

'Listen in,' demanded Sgt Royce. 'The Gimpy has a range of eighteen hundred metres, and its firepower is awesome!'

'Six hundred and twenty five, to seven hundred and fifty rounds per minute,' extolled the RSM equally animated.

'That's right and with that rate of firepower gentlemen,' continued Sgt Royce, 'it has to be belt fed. Each round is connected to the next via a small metal clip which makes up a belt of ammunition; the clip is discarded once the round has been loaded into the breach. You often see African rebels on the nine o'clock news wearing bandoleers criss-crossing their torso, macho fashion like they mean business. That's one way of carrying your ammo I suppose, but we British carry the belts in the boxes kindly provided by the Armoury - as you do!'

Sgt Royce's delivery made everybody chuckle.

'These boxes hold a belt of fifty rounds and the weapon itself weighs ten point nine kilograms, that's twenty four pounds in old money. Now the strange thing about the Gimpy is it has a tendency to pull you forward, so to counteract this, dig your toes into the ground and hold on tight.'

Having splayed his feet, Sgt Royce jabbed the toes of his boots into the sandy ground and gave the recruits a practical demonstration of the weapon by loosing off short bursts down the range. Bursts of no more than five or six rounds at a time zinged towards a metal plate which was suspended across a target. The ferocity of the controlled bursts of ammunition ripped the metal in two and the bottom half fell to the floor impressively.

At the end of the shoot we all had to fan out and scour the ranges for discarded empty ammunition cases. We placed the cases inside our berets, and once full then tipped the contents out into empty wooden ammo boxes to be taken back to camp. Rodger Boileiu, the scrap metal Merchant's son, was astonished at the amount of leftover brass that was found; the Army manage to get through thousands of tons of ammo each year!

Later, all the recruits were formed up by platoon into three ranks and each platoon loosely marched over to the Small-Arms range for a demonstration of the SMG by Staff Sgt Mackintosh. The clued-up Scotsman informed our platoon. 'In nineteen-forty-four, a hundred Stirling Small Machine Guns were made for troop trials. The sixth Airborne Division used them in Arnhem and Normandy with great success, but it wasn't'til nineteen-fifty-three that the Stirling Small Machine Gun replaced the Sten-gun as the general issue to Airborne Troops. The Army still use the SMG to this day for close quarter battle purposes, such is its reliability.'

Staff Sgt Mackintosh then stripped the weapon down to expose the uncomplicated working parts, and then reassembled it. It was hardly a Rubik's Cube; it merely consisted of three parts: a cocking pin, a grooved metal shaft connected to a large spring, and the barrel which housed a folding stock & trigger grip. The whole procedure took less than a minute as Staff Sgt Mackintosh exclaimed. 'Simplicity itself!'

He checked the safety catch, clipped on a full magazine, and cocked it. 'This weapon takes the same nine millimetre Parabellum round as the Browning High Power side arm.'

At this point the RSM stepped forward, removed a Browning from a Holster on his Webbing, cocked it and fired at the figure eight range in front of him. When he had emptied the magazine, he removed the clip and made safe the weapon.

'Listen in, a pistol round will not blow a man off his feet. Reactions to being blatted with a pistol vary from being hit and falling over, to just getting very angry and more determined to kill you. The trouble with nine mill military ammo, is that it's fully jacketed and doesn't expand; if it doesn't hit bone or something it will simply pass through the body with little damage - believe me, it can take a full clip of thirteen rounds to put a man down!'

Staff Sgt Mackintosh then stepped forward raising the SMG into his shoulder, strafed the target with a hail of bullets, and announced. 'No ones gonna get up from that wee lot, hey lads!'

He was talking from experience because he had actually killed someone with an SMG which secretly haunted him daily.

When all four platoons had been subjected to this final display of weaponry, the RSM called it a day and led the audience back to the service road which ran down the length of the

Ranges. We squatted down and stripped and cleaned our rifles, and once the DS staff was content with our efforts, they then had us reassemble the weapons.

The RSM looked impatient. 'Listen in Gentlemen, one straight line in front of me, GO! Come on, the sooner we do this, the sooner we can get away.'

Before leaving, everyone had to empty the pouches on their webbing and hold the empty magazines in one hand and the cleaning kit in the other then make an individual declaration to the RSM. 'I have no live rounds, pyrotechnics or empty cases in my possession Sir!'

The RSM made a physical check of the pouches on all the webbing, just in case any recruit had forgotten something. When the boss was thoroughly satisfied, he concluded the parade by advising. 'If for any reason you later find any rounds about your person, hand them directly to a member of staff and no further action will be taken. That's it, thank you gentlemen, the fun is over, well done.'

The range detail was wound up and we novice riflemen formed up into platoons to be compacted back into the trucks. After crawling down the service road the trucks exited the ranges and recklessly jostled us along dusky forest lanes back to the bleakness of Martinique Bks. The rears of the Lorries were exposed, creating a vortex which sucked in a mixture of cold twilight air, exhaust fumes and varied swirling dead leaves thrown up in the vehicles wake. The canvass roof and side panels offered little insulation from the elements as the wagon's slipstream whistled unsolicited into the back of the vehicle. The lads of 3Platoon were packed together like hapless sheep on market day, some sitting, some standing shoulder to shoulder, flaccidly hanging for dear life from overhead supports like mutton in a butchers shop. Torpor took hold of our cramped and listless limbs, until finally the enforced restrictiveness wilted our crucified bodies. My knees gave way, plunging me gawkily into dissenting passengers below. Tucker was one of them. He complained to me that sitting on the hard wooden bench seats was bum numbing, there was little more for him to do than stare at the buttons on his combat jacket. I was jealous, at least he had a seat. The syrupy whine from the thick knobbly rubber tyres thrumming on smooth tarmac, combined with the Doppler effect of trees whizzing past outside seemed to impact on Tucker's body, soothing him and folding him up into a crumpled beaten mess. Even the sporadic nerve jarring clangs of the metal securing chains hanging lazily from the tailgate could not interrupt his languor.

He awkwardly shifted his position, endeavouring to stare out of the rear, hoping to stimulate a spark of life into his somnolent brain. The winter light was dim but I still had a clear view of the receding road, perversely this helped little. The long straight road disappeared uninterestingly into obscurity, and when the convoy momentarily slowed on the approach of a series of bends, fleeing branches lit up and danced spectacularly in the mesmerizing halo of strobe effect red brake-light, hypnotising me all the more. Squashed as he was, Tucker inevitably lost the fight to stay awake, his head sagged forward onto his chest and his hands slipped from his rifle which momentarily startled him, but he could not fight it, his drowsy mind slipped serenely into the morphed embrace of that warm temptress sleep and the mad fleeting dreams which accompany her. I glazed over too.

'RIGHT LADS, ON YOUR FEET, YOU'RE NOT ON YOUR DADDY'S YACHT NOW YOU KNOW!' Cpl Hazel wrenched open the tailgate and startled us from our stupefied slumbers.

'Your weapons are to be stripped, cleaned, oiled and reassembled. Quick as you like, it's your time you're wasting, chop chop! The sooner you hand them back to Sergeant McBride at the Binner, the sooner you get away for a hot meal.'

My head felt like cotton-wool as I jumped from the back of the truck and made contact with the road jarring my whole body. I hunkered down next to Tish Hewitt and dismantled my rifle; by now we'd got used to stripping and reassembling the SLR, so it wasn't too taxing to take the weapon apart, give the components a protective smear of gun oil and fit the mechanism back together again. The tricky bit was slotting the working parts back onto the slide in the breach; they had to be guided in, like an aircraft landing on a runway.

Tish Hewitt was sandwiched between me and Tucker like an Atlas between bookends. Despite the cold, Tucker vied with Tish Hewitt to complete the task but was just a few seconds slower at reassembling the weapon, I plodded along at an unremarkable pace. Once the working parts had been cocked three times and the trigger mechanism depressed to release the firing pin, the impeccable weapons were passed along the line of recruits and handed to Sgt McBride at the back of the Binner who stacked the rifles efficiently into the gun racks inside.

"BANG!"

Everyone instinctively hunched up into a ball; the familiar acrid cordite smell of the ranges now polluted the clean icy air of the barracks.

'WHICH ONE OF YAY STUPID BASTARDS HAS NOT CLEARED HIS RIFLE?' Sgt McBride demanded. He jumped lividly from the Binner with the smoking gun in his hand. Steam poured from his ears and nostrils as he strutted back-and-forth, head switching from side to side like an aggravated Rottweiler mauling a traffic cone. 'COME ON, OWN UP, WHO WAS IT?'

Our silence was a denial of the crime. Shocked and devoid of responsibility, we instantly apprehended the gravity of the situation. We collectively felt guilt ridden as we uncoiled from the foetal position. The Ulsterman took umbrage at our reticence and seethed. 'Right yay lot, dinners off, yeezer all for the fecking high jump sose ye are!'

The other Mil Training Instructors raced from their different locations and started to push and jostle people about. We were shitting our pants because the DS Staff were truly aggravated. If Sgt McBride had appeared intimidating out on the parade square during the drill sessions, he was positively hostile now; he was so upset you would think that someone had just driven over his foot with a Land-Rover. 'GET INTO YAY PLATOONS, FORM UP INTO YAY FECKING PLATOONS NOW!'

The perturbed RSM appeared and hastily took control of the situation before somebody got hurt. He laconically announced. 'That was an "ND" gentleman, a negligent discharge, punishable by Court Martial!'

He sounded more disappointed than furious. 'Even for you men, an "ND" is a mortal sin! From day one you've been taught the importance of SOP's, you have had it drummed into you. These weapons were individually cleared for inspection on the ranges, then cleaned and reassembled, and each of you swore an oath that you had no live rounds, pyrotechnics or empty cases in your possession. These weapons have since been stripped again, oiled and reassembled. Unless by a million to one shot someone has slipped through the net and neglected to carry out these fundamental tasks, I can only conclude,' deduced the RSM, 'that there is a homicidal maniac amongst us?'

Sgt McBride was the only man present who appeared manically homicidal!

'Take a look around you, who could it possibly be, you know it wasn't you. However, one of you is guilty of gross negligence or premeditated mischief, something which could quite easily have resulted in death or serious injury. I don't take misconduct lying down, not in these circumstances, so while I waste my precious time making a report for Major Einstein's consideration, you can bloody well contemplate the consequence of an "ND" whilst climbing the Sand hills, and I promise you, you'll remember it for the rest of your natural. Get them out of my sight Sergeant McBride.'

The entire recruit course were doubled away to be beasted up and down the Sand Hills at the rear of the base until we were on all on our chinstraps (knackered). The rest of the day was thrown out of sync after that; we missed out on the evening meal and had to sustain ourselves until morning on growlers (NAFFI pies), crisps and Mars-bars. Every time we received or returned our weapons at the Binner, we snatched a retrospective glance at the ceiling and searched for the hole that the 7.62 round had made!

Chapter 9

After an early morning 3 mile BFT and some much needed breakfast, we poor subdued recruits were put through our paces out on the frozen Parade Square by being relentlessly drilled by numbers, 123–123–123–1. To make matters worse Sgt McBride was not on speaking terms, after all, someone had tried to kill him the day before! Other than a five minute smoke break at 10.00 hrs, the only proper interruption we marchers enjoyed was for a mid-day meal.

I was having a sense of humour failure by now, my feet were numb from the cold, my toes felt like they'd been bashed by a hammer, and my brain had seized up. What the fuck had Tucker dragged me in to this time? We had only joined up for a laugh, have a break from the wives and kids, get away from the 9 to 5 grind and shift work, let some steam off. I felt like my head was getting crammed with too much bullshit, we weren't investing into the pompous spit & polish wank, surely all that stuff is for guard duties at Buckingham Palace! Unbelievably Tucker was actually enjoying himself, he was totally immersed in the marching manoeuvres and grinning like a village idiot. When at lunchtime I challenged him about his enthusiasm, he told me that prominent in his thoughts during that long cold morning was Granddad Stanley Tucker, who had been in the TA when World War One had broken out in 1914; Granddad had been at the vanguard. Prior to being ferried across the English Channel, him and his mates had been issued with brand new boots, and on landing at Calais had had to march through open countryside to Mons on the French-Belgium border to join the 1st Cheshire Regiment as their back up. Consequently by the time Grandad's mob had gotten to Mons their feet were blistered to buggery, but worse was yet to come. The German 5th Army had forced their way across Belgium into France at an intense pace not expecting any resistance, but they did encounter the 1st Cheshire Regiment near Audregnies, between Mons and Valenciennes. Unfortunately for the 1st Cheshire's, their reinforcements were still hobbling painfully some miles away and had not arrived thus far to provide necessary support. There was nothing for it, the 1st Cheshire regiment had to get stuck in against the Bosh unassisted. Having thought all day against insurmountable odds the brave Cheshire-men were ultimately surrounded, and inevitably owing to a consequent lack of ammunition to sustain an indefinite fire fight, they reluctantly surrendered.

Meanwhile, to avoid walking into an ambush, General Haig's Army top brass decided to implement a tactical withdrawal for Stanley Tucker and his oppo's. They were horrified at not engaging the enemy but withdrawing back to the coast became a battle in itself. The Cheshire Regiment reservists' feet were now in a diabolical condition as they made the slow hard retreat. It was late august, warm and humid as the reservists negotiated crossing the River Somme. Many carried their new boots slung over their shoulders, choosing to wrap their puttees (leggings) around their feet as footwear instead. The men were so desperate from hobbling to hell and back on bleeding blistered feet that they begged their senior officers to let them halt the painful humiliating withdrawal and have a pop at the advancing Germans instead. Fortunately the Germans were as surprised as the British at making contact at Mons and were too tired, after marching across Belgium, to slog it out with the reservists as they painfully escaped to the coast.

Tucker reverentially surmised that marching back-and-fro on a neat little parade square in the middle of Hampshire in no way conveyed any resemblance whatsoever to what our forefathers had endured, but in all modesty, hours of square bashing *can* be equally incessant. Our new boots were blistering our feet to buggery, so much so that one of the blokes in 2 Platoon had thrown his hand in before the drill session was halfway over. The poor chap snapped, he'd simply had enough of the bitter cold and relentless miles of pounding the square and couldn't take it anymore. He stopped dead in his tracks as the ranks of men around him performed an about-turn on the march, and while they manoeuvred towards the other end of the parade ground in unison, the recruit in question ambled off to the edge of the parade square all on his tod.

Sgt McBride was infuriated, he tried to entice the defector back into the ranks but was unsuccessful; maybe the tone of voice the DI utilised was inappropriate! 'YAY DON'T GET

TO EXCUSE YOURSELF ON MY SQUARE LADDY, STAND STILL! DON'T YE DARE SPIT YARE DUMMY OUT, WHAT'S YAY FECKING PROBLEM SUNSHINE?'

'Nothing Sergeant,' replied the protester peevishly. 'I just need some space.'

'SPACE, OH FECK ME, SPACE IS IT? WHAT DO YAY THINK YAY ARE, A FECKIN ROCKET MAN? YOU'RE GONNA GET YAY WEE ARSE FELL IN WITH THE REST OF THE RABBLE NOW SO YAY ARE!'

While this bollocking was going on we reached the opposite end of the Square, and with no letting up of the pace, the Ulster Drill Pig ordered us to about-turn. As we marched back we observed Sgt McBride employing a stony stare to allure the pessimistic renegade back into the ranks. This tactless urging had insufficient effect, so the sergeant erupted once more, only this time he was genuinely upset. 'I'LL GIVE YAY SPACE YA SAD MAN. GET THE FUCK OFF OF MY PARADE SQUARE NOY. GET YA SORRY ARSE OFF MY SQUARE, YE MISSERABLE EXCUSE FOR A HUMAN BEING YEOU. YOU'RE A SHIT BAG LADDY, A COMPLETE WASTE OF FECKING RATIONS!'

The quitter never argued; he didn't even glance back as he extricated himself from the ordeal, he just kept walking towards the guardroom and the ill-perceived notion of liberation from his tormentor.

On recapturing his poise, Sgt McBride performed the perfect about turn, rubbed the toecaps of his boots against the back of his trousers as if decontaminating them, and then resumed instructing the residue of square bashers as if nothing had occurred. We could discern no extra upset or anger in the Drill-Pig's barking voice as he remote controlled us across the tarmac, only his demeanour betrayed any hint of emotion at losing a recruit at this stage of the game. He brought us to a halt and stepped briskly up to Tom the cockney rebel and seethed. 'Everybody is out of step except for yeay!'

Tom waited until the instructor was just out of earshot before mumbling. 'Well you're in charge sunshine, you better sort them out then!'

'WHO WAS THAT?' demanded the Drill-Pig.

For the rest of the Drill period the DI screamed and bawled with his whole body, bending at the waist as his upper torso craned forward with each syllable of every order, as if he was trying to pick a fight with the entire recruit course. Then it happened again, someone cursed aloud!

‘Fucking Hell…’ long and drawn out, exasperated.

‘HALT!’ commanded the Gravel-crusher. He marched briskly to the head of the column, smashing his polished boots into the tarmac with such force that the highly glossed surface on them fractured like broken mirrors. This did not escape his notice as he gave some GBH-of-the-ear-hole to Tish Hewitt, the right-hand-marker. Sgt McBride sounded like he wasn’t having a very good day. ‘GOT SOMETHING TO SAY HAVE YE GOLIATH?’

Tish said nothing; at 6ft & 7 inches tall he towered above the Drill Instructor and was easily able to avoid eye contact. Sgt McBride decided to dominate the giant by bringing him down to size a peg or two. ‘DON’T GET TOO BIG FOR YA FECKING BOOTS LURCH, OR I’LL RAM THIS PACE STICK UP YA HAIRY ARSE AND MARCH YE ROUND LIKE A LOLLYPOP! HAVE YAY GOT THAT, YA GREAT BIG BALOON?’

The Drill Pig’s eyes smouldered with contempt for us; he was still convinced that one of us had tried to kill him with a negligent discharge when returning the rifles to him on the Binner the previous day. ‘YOU ARE SHAGGING IDLE. THIS IS NOT AN ATTENDANCE ONLY COURSE, YOU WILL PUT SOME FECKIN EFFORT IN. THERE IS NO SUCH THING AS CAN’T. CAN’T MEANS WON’T AND WON’T MEANS JAIL. I’LL HAVE YAY ALL MARCHING AROUND LIKE FECKING TICK TOCK BY NEXT WEEK; OTHERWISE YAY WILL NOT BE PASSING OUT ON MY PARADE SQUARE. I DON’T CARE IF YA MUDDER, FADDER OR CRIPPLED AUNT FANNY FROM HIGH WYCOMBE TURNS UP. YAY CUNTS WILL NOT MAKE A SHOW OF ME BY BIMBLING AROUND ALL MAMBY PAMBY LIKE A HERD OF SPASTICATED GIRAFFES. HAVE YOY GOT THAT INTO YA THICK SKULLS YET?’

‘Yes Sergeant,’ we murmured.

‘Pardon me Ladies I can’t feckin hear yay, I make more feckin noise slapping my cock against the urinal!’ he teased. ‘HAVE YAY GOT THAT?’

‘YES SERGEANT!’ We bawled.

‘DEAD RIGHT YAY HAVE. NOW LISTEN IN, BY THE LEFT, WAIT FOR IT, WAIT FOR IT….. KWICKK-MARCH. LEFT RIGHT LEFT IGHT, EFT IGHT, ERFFT.’ He loved us really!

We were knocked off at 14.30hrs and ordered to change into combat fatigues and red PT shirts, then bundled onto the back of the trucks and zoomed away to the assault-course a mile down the road. We were welcomed by a team of muscled PTI's dressed in green light weight trousers, shiny boots, and crisp white vests with red piping around the arm holes and neck line. Stitched onto the chest of their vest was a red badge motif of crossed swords and a crown which they wore with the pride of an Olympic Gold Medallist. The masochistic athletes had been itching to get their hands on us all week and now that they had they were about to flex their muscles. They walked and talked us around the course, explaining our task and the best way to tackle each obstacle; they assured us that helping one another over the difficult bits would mould each platoon into a tighter unit. The course was laid out methodically in two parts. The first leg was downhill starting with six damp parallel telegraph poles which had to be climbed like a staircase, with a 5ft drop at the summit designed to knock the breath out of us. Then it was onto the first of several brick walls which looked daunting; although we did not yet know it, at ten foot in height the first wall was the highest. It could only be breached using teamwork. For obvious reasons, Tish Hewitt and Sooty Corbett were placed at the base because they were easier to haul up after everybody else had trampled across their backs. They supported themselves by holding their arms out in front of them while leaning against the wall like human ramps. The next four lads climbed upon their backs and scrambled up the wall digging the toes of their boots into the mortared crevices to get some purchase. Once atop these four lads then straddled across the course of brickwork and reached down offering helping arms for the rest of us to jump up and grab hold of. When the last men had used the human ramps and heaved themselves up and over, big Tish and Sooty took a run at the wall and grasped hold of the helping hands and were themselves hauled up and over. The top of the wall was worn smooth and easy to slip across, everybody was cautioned by the Sergeant PTI to make sure that they faced the wall as they made the ten foot drop on the other side, so as to avoid stumbling backwards and smashing their skull open against the bricks and spilling brains everywhere!

We thundered away down the assault course, jumping over a series of wooden hurdles like horses at the Grand National. Next was a water jump, which no matter how it was approached, our toes got wet. This was closely followed by a run up a sand embankment with a six foot drop, and then under a heavy rope Cargo-net, which we had to crawl through on all fours, pushing it up out of the way with our backs like Tortoises to make progress. Out on the other side we raced across to a second wall, constructed from old wooden sleepers measuring eight foot in height. I avoided the splinters as I hauled myself over unaided, then scampered up an eighteen foot high climbing frame. Attached between the tops of the frame a couple of twenty four foot long parallel ropes were suspended like electric cables between pylons. This piece of equipment looked to me as if it might have had a Health & Safety prohibition notice slapped upon it sometime in the past to put it out of bounds, but the PTI's looked like the sort of chaps who would disregard such legislation in exceptional circumstances. Those who were scared of heights, or by this point were suffering from the effects of exertion on their limbs, inevitably got wobbly disco legs at the thought of tackling this obstacle.

'Your mission,' the senior PTI briefed us, 'is to edge to the centre of the rope and carefully suspend yourself at arm's length. From that position you will haul yourself up and remount to complete the rest of the traverse.'

Another PTI wearing a blue tracksuit top over his vest climbed up from the opposite side, monkey fashion, and gave a practical demonstration. As he shimmied along the rope he demonstrated that the knack of doing so was to bend one leg and hook the foot onto the rope behind him, while his other leg dangled vertically to balance his body weight. He eased his body sideways and tentatively lowered himself to full arms stretch, and then pulled his torso back up and reached over the rope with his right leg. Hooking the crease of the back of his knee he worked his body up parallel with the rope until he was balanced and then crawled forward pulling with his arms. When the gymnastic instructor had safely reached the other side, he looked down and yelled to us, 'Easy peasy!'

'Whores piss!' replied Martin Flowers sceptically.

Tucker was fearless, I watched in awe as he shimmied across to the centre, his arms pulling him across in a steady rhythm; it looked like a piece of cake once he'd got going! He was as fit as a flea and displayed no problem in lowering himself and remounting.

On my attempt I managed to dangle like a sloth and remount through sheer terror, the rope was difficult to grip; it was damp and stiff from the wintry weather. A lot of blokes came unstuck on this piece of equipment; below us for safety reasons was a four foot deep pool of water to cushion the blow in case anyone should fall in. I estimated that it didn't look deep enough for such a purpose and was proved right when a lad from 2platoon fell in and broke his leg, spilling claret everywhere as he splashed around. While the supervising PT Buster sorrowfully shook his head in disappointment, his merciful PTI team waded in to prevent the victim from drowning. Despite the drama, the recruits behind me were encouraged to continue across the cables, while the casualty, moaning and oozing blood, got stretchered away to the medical facility.

After descending we had to climb up a scaffold contraption and inched towards some swinging ropes. Tucker swung across the Tarzan ropes, let go and dropped onto another Cargo-net. Hanging on for dear life he somehow got his arms and legs into motion, climbed up and flipped his body over the apex before the man following could land on top of him and squash him into the netting like a waffle. I was next and once I'd retrieved the rope I was zealously slapped on the back by an encouraging PT Buster who yelled at me, 'GO!'

Watching where I placed my feet when I landed, I carefully made the descent on the other side - one slip could have ruptured my wedding tackle and turned my twins and sausage into a bag full of boiled cauliflower.

Next up was another brick wall which was only a trifling 4ft, but it might as well have been Mount Kilimanjaro as my stamina started to ebb away with all the exertion. After that wall there was ten car tyres laid out flat in a zigzag line, we had to run through them placing our feet inside, and then it was a fifty metre dash around a bend to start the second leg of the course, uphill all the way.

We were getting a real sweat on as we approached the first obstacle on this stretch, it was a fifteen foot high frame with a thirty foot gap, bridged at ten foot intervals by a series of single planks wrapped in Hessian cloth offering good grip to minimise slip. There was no pool of water to break the fall on this occasion. Tucker let out a nervous laugh as he climbed the framework to the planking at the top; it was the nearest thing to walking a tight rope either of us had ever attempted, I was fired up on a cocktail of adrenalin and fear as I followed him.

'Take your time,' soothed a PTI below us, 'look straight ahead, that's good, you're cooking on four rings now.'

There was no turning back; we were committed, besides there were plenty of other trapeze artists following closely behind us, so we had to get a move on. Once negotiated, we dropped to the ground like alley cats and dashed to another Cargo-net suspended in the middle by a twenty foot high A-frame. We climbed up and over it, then streamed across to another series of slippery telegraph poles. They were slung like jungle ravine bridges between metal suspension chains. Beyond this was a set of man-size Monkey-bars, reminiscent to the ones you see in children's play grounds. Tucker competed with Sooty Corbett to swing hand over hand like an ape, I was back to resembling a dangling sloth by this stage. Regardless I caught up with Tucker as he swayed his way across another Tarzan swing rope which was suspended over a deep pool of muddy water. I was beginning to buckle, I lacked strength in my arms and fell victim to gravitational pull, the icy cesspool below shocked the breath from me. I managed to wade to the edge like a drowned rat and scrambled away dripping wet to my platoon mates who, utilising teamwork, hauled me up and over another five foot brick wall. I dropped to the ground like a sack of potatoes. I felt arms hook me up until I was on my feet, my team mates then literally dragged and pushed me into a run up a sand bank, where oooff, a steep drop knocked the wind out of us all when we landed. One more obstacle remained; we clambered over a five foot vertical frame in the shape of a gymkhana horse jump hurdle, made from more telegraph poles supplemented with slippery moss. Using teamwork we had almost completed the assault course; all that remained was a sprint across a sandy area which sapped our bodies of any remaining energy and left our legs feeling like rubber. We had truly challenged ourselves. I did not feel euphoric, in fact I felt vulnerable as I sat clasping my knees to my chest, dizzily gulping in air, wet, queasy, hot and sweaty, my heart fit to burst, blood singing in my stinging ears. From that moment on, the challenge of the assault course was to get myself fit enough to beat it the next time and still remain standing on my own two feet until the bitter end.

With the combined exertion of throwing ourselves around an obstacle course and hours and hours of square bashing beforehand, teatime couldn't have arrived sooner, especially since we had skipped the previous day's main meal. Me and Tucker piled our plates high with chicken curry, chips and rice, and wasted no time getting stuck in - it was the business. We sat in the tropics with Tom, Robby, Spike and Martin Flowers beside the hot radiator. Stan-the-Cab and Sooty Corbett squeezed in at the ends too.

'Did you see McBride's face when that mad fucker Illingsworth binned the drill session today? Red as beetroot he was. I thought, here we go, this drill instructor's gonna have a Sean Conary, ho ho ho!' Robby exaggerated his elation.

'McBride's only doing a job mate, ain't' he!' proposed Stan-the-Cab, hungrily slapping curry covered chips onto a round of bread & butter.

'Maybe so uncle, but he gets on me tits. Can't stand the geezer can I hey?'

'Here boy,' smiled Martin pointing a finger accusingly, 'it weren't you what tried to ruddy shoot him yeztaday were it? He's right pissed off about that he is!'

'No way mate I wouldn't have missed! I thought it was you, or was it that knob rot Illingsworth?'

Sooty Corbett sighed contemplatively. 'I'm not having any of it. I reckon it was a blank round, you know, meant to spook us up a bit. Come on, those rifles all have numbers painted on'em; they would have known who it was. Surely if someone was dicking them about like that, then the police would have been involved wouldn't they?'

'Oh yeh, what's it to you then?' remarked Spike. 'I thought you were one of the boys!'

'I wish someone *had* shot that porridge wog, I'm not far off breaking point meself!'

'He's not that bad,' reassured Tucker. 'You just need to calm down a bit.'

'Oy, he's a twenty-four carrot bastard that one. If you broke him in half he'd have it stamped right through his centre like a stick of Brighton Rock. B.A.S.T.A.R.D. Bastard!'

'Fuck me, you're going all wrong there mate, he's a geyser just like us with a trouble and strife and a couple of bin lids to feed,' insisted Stan-the-Cab through a mouthful of chip butty.

Spike the biker said, 'I heard that he put his wife on a charge once for burning his dinner!'

We all chuckled at that.

'Listen, don't take it so personal china; he's allwright is McBride trust me, you're just too young to see it is all.'

'Yeh, turn it in,' added Tom, 'I've felt like binning it meself, I bet most of us have if the truth is known. Don't go getting any daft ideas like that Muppet Illingsworth - you're worth two of a tosspot like him. Larry Lightweight's probably at home sucking his thumb and kotching with his mother by now. "How's Mummy's brave little soldier?" she'll be saying. He's history mate.'

We all had a good laugh at the thought of Illingsworth's mum giving him a cuddle and roughing up his hair and telling him how the "Big bad horrible man can't get him anymore!"

Robby looked around at his new mates and took a moment to reflect on our support, then to save Odd-job the chore of washing up, he licked his plate clean and chuckled, 'Nice Ruby this, real pukha, geyser can't half cook!'

'Yeh, triffic!' agreed Stan-the-Cab. 'Pint of Stella would wash it down nicely!'

'You're not wrong there!' I approved with a wink.

Back at the Spider after the meal we burst in on Cpl Hazel rummaging around our accommodation looking for dust. He could sense our animosity at being beasted for the negligent discharge the previous day in addition to losing out on our evening meal. He now wanted to build bridges to get us back on board, so suggested. 'You're making a nice job on this floor lads, I've never seen it looking so good. In fact I'm so pleased with your performance today that I've decided to relent a little. Provided tomorrow goes without any hiccups and you screw the nut, I'll take you all out to a nice little pub I know and you can treat me to a pint. Its only twenty minutes down the road and it'll give me a chance to get to know you better, you know, on a social level. What you reckon, up for it?'

'Top man!' exclaimed Big Tish, warming to the idea.

'Right,' Cpl Hazel reposed himself. 'Tug here tells me you've read Part-One-Orders and are asking what PULHEEMS stands for? Don't worry your tiny little heads unnecessarily ladies, every serving member of the Armed Forces goes through this process. Tomorrow you'll be given, at enormous expense to the tax payer, all the necessary inoculations needed to immunise yourself from all the nastiness in the northern hemisphere; try saying that when you've had a skin full.'

Tug Wilson mouthed the words to himself while Cpl Hazel continued. 'After a short lesson on First-Aid, you will convene at ten hundred hours outside the medical centre. Dress as for a BFT run, i.e. Lightweights, boots and red PE tops; so that you won't have to faff around rolling your bleeding sleeves up. It don't hurt honest, any one scared of needles, see me and I'll hold your fucking hand. Wear a Combat smock to keep you warm, I don't want you faggots having all them inoculations, then go catching a ruddy cold, do I? You'll be there all morning, so take something to read; we've got lots to get through yet so I suggest revision. Any questions? No? Good.'

Having a pint off base in a real pub seemed like a dream come true, the thought of alcohol coursing through our veins momentarily shut out any concerns regarding PULHEEMS.

'Right crack on with your best boots and start revising for the three tests you've got lined up on Friday. First Aid, Weapons test and NBC Theory. OK lads, I'm off home to the wife and kids for an hour, poor sods see so little of me they're starting to ask "Mummy who's that strange man who comes to visit us?", even the dog attacks me when I go home. Any problems see Tug here; he knows how to get hold of me!'

The instructor pulled his DPM Smock taut beneath his Stable-Belt and tweaked his beret tight until it moulded his head, befitting his action man features. The Corporal stared coolly at his mob, putting each of us in our place with a knowing look which said, "Don't mess with me while I'm away or I'll rip your fucking ears off!"

Once the corporal had left the room, big Tish commented. 'We still never found out what that word PULHEEMS means.'

Ronny Churchill was a mild mannered lad who always seemed deep in thought, he suggested. 'Perhaps it means Pox, Ulcers, Lassa fever, Haemorrhoids, Eardrops, Eczema, Mumps and Syphilis!'

'Yeh, sounds good to me,' approved Spike the biker. 'If mister bullshit doesn't wanna let us in on the secret, then fuck him. If it comes up on my First-aid test on Friday, that's what I'm gonna put down for the answer!'

'Don't worry your tiny little heads,' Tug mimicked the NCO. 'How old does he think we are?'

'Yeh, he's a right slippery bastard that one!' concluded Stan-the-Cab.

'I heard that cunty bollocks,' Cpl Hazel, re-entered the room unannounced. 'Make sure that I'm off the premises before you start ripping me to pieces, Rodger that?'

Rodger dodge, conveyed our surprised expressions; the sneaky corporal must have been lurking in the corridor again. 'Right then let's put this to bed shall we? PULHEEMS is the acronym we use for a medical assessment, which grades from one to seven, the individual qualities associated with: Physique, Upper limbs, Lower limbs, Ears, Eyes, Mental capacity and Stability. Got it!'

Without another word he stomped out of the Spider and Yomped across the Square towards the main gate, then out to the Married-Quarters off Base; one of the smartest Soldiers you're ever likely to meet. His children would be overjoyed to see him, but his wife indifferent. She yearned to be back in Germany with her girlfriends at RAF Brüggen, she missed shopping in Düsseldorf too. Their marriage was a test of love; Geoff Hazel was married to his career, he had transferred from the RAF to the Army, and his wife and kids had had to follow him. His weaponry and soldiering skills, honed by years of arduous military training in the Rhineland and some frontline action in Ulster, made him a reliable pair of hands. He could be depended on to watch a brother soldier's back in hostile situations, give cover as they patrolled the mean streets of Belfast, and be prepared to put his life on the line to rescue a mate from danger. His workmates loved him and admired his single mindedness at chasing his dreams no matter what; he was a man's man. But his wife could no doubt tell you a different story, a tale of abandonment in pursuit of the selfish glory and self-gratitude.

After the usual routine of pressing creases into kit, bulling up boots and revising, the lads of 3platoon knocked it in the head and turned in for some zeds. Right on cue, Wingnut started to work on his unfinished symphony "Midnight in Hampshire!"

It was a work in progress. In the first instance it seemed innocuous, merely the clatter of an orchestra warming up on the first night of the Proms, but after half an hour of intermittence, he launched full belt into the evening's main schedule; a variable Smorgasbord of delights such as Elgar's: "Serenade for Snores" in E minor; leading straight into, Puccini's: "Snoring Chorus" from Madam Butterfly; and after a very short interval, he moistened his prominent teeth with his tongue, proudly puckered up his lips, then attempted to wake the dead by exploiting exceptional demands on his adenoid with an extravagant virtuoso of Vaughan Bryant's: Five Variants of "Snore and Lazarus."!

One by one the lads of 3Platoon irritably sat up in bed. We switched on our bedside lamps and stared intently at our torturer. This nightly ritual had become untenable and it was high time for a drastic resolution! We each and all had the same uncanny thought and made a collective unanimous decision to dispose of the problem. Using silent nods and gestures we deftly organised ourselves. Ronny Churchill gingerly opened the fire exit door at the end of the room, while six others, acting as pallbearers, stealthily carried Wingnut's bed outside. The rest of us followed, forming a sombre funeral cortège, hauling his bedside cabinet and wardrobe between us like a line of foraging soldier ants. The only thing missing from this ad hoc ceremony was a Louisiana Blues Band playing a lament in the background, so Spike obligingly hummed the funeral dirge – Dum dum dum dum, dum, dum dum dum dum dum dum!

Martin Flowers' green eyes flitted around merrily in their sockets, the pirate sniggered. 'It wasn't the cough that carried him off; it was the coffin they carried him off in!'

Wingnut was placed in the middle of the parade square, his bedside furniture laid out around him as per army regulations. In the circumstances it was too cold to hang about and hold a minute's silence, so we mourners dismissively saluted the comatose al fresco snoring pig and made our way back to the warmth of the Spider.

Once back in the warmth of our beds, Tish Hewitt fluffed up his pillow and called out the phrase taken from the closing scene of the Walton's T.V. show. 'Goodnight John boy?'

One by one the rest of us responded with a resounding "Goodnight John boy!"

Within five minutes we were all snoring blissfully, up until 01.30hrs that is, when L/Cpl Hughes charged into 3Platoon's dormitory and switched on the main lights.

'Bore da you divvy baztards, manos ariba.' He bawled as he ran around drunkenly tipping us all out of bed.

The spotty Welshman was hysterical. 'Get'im in this Llys right now you soft shites. Ewes could've killed'im boys, it is miners seven by heure tonight, miners' elephan with the chill faxtors, int it see!'

On making his return from a drinking session over at "C" Company, he'd passed young Wingnut, who was by that time covered in an inch of permafrost. 'What was ewes bloddy finkin? Tisn't fuckin funny evfarr. Ewes is lucky I seen'im first see init, be four the sir giant mayja turned up? He'd rip yewer stewpad heads offy wood and piss down yewer necks for chewer see.'

Martin Flowers, Tish Hewitt and Tug Wilson, simultaneously burst out laughing.

'Look Hugh ya mad man,' he pointed at Tug Wilson, 'yewer in charge, get'im in heure right now and take them gormless feckaz wiv'yewes!'

'It wasn't us Corporal, honest,' lied Sooty unconvincingly.

'Ffyc chi, streak lanky o piss!'

'He must have been sleepwalking or something!' big Tish Suggested.

'Sleepwalking is it? Mae'n ddrwg gyda fi glywed so, what a fabewless excuse!'

'Yes corporal, I thought I heard him shuffling around earlier, he does it a lot you know.'

'Do ewes expect me to credyd y llwyth o shit Doctor Hewitt?'

'There's no pulling the wool over your eyes, hey Taff!' laughed Tish Hewitt.

'Fuck you!' the Welshman rounded us up and chased us out into the bitter cold.

Chapter 10

We awoke refreshed to complete the six o'clock run smoothly and quietly. Our platoon was by now getting into the rhythm of army life and no longer needed to be cajoled or beasted every inch of the way; instead, the DS team called out words of praise. "Good lads, good effort, give it stacks!"

Besides sleep apnoea, Wingnut was also developing Tourette's syndrome; he occasionally called out, 'Bastards!'

To warm down and get our breath back once we had completed the BFT we were sedately marched to the Spiders past the Guardroom. We were surprised to see Illingsworth there, the bloke who had spat his dummy out on the Parade Square the previous day, we all thought that he had cleared off home. Apparently one of the DS staff had accidentally given him the wrong directions to get back to civilisation; easy enough error when dealing with a Muppet with his knickers in a twist. Illingsworth stood forlornly to attention, looking tired and humiliatingly defeated.

Martin Flowers tersely condemned the defeatist with a broadside. 'Look at that sad tosser!'

'Quiet in the ranks,' ordered a senior NCO.

I bore the incident no more thought. But later, on the way to the Medical-Centre to receive our PULHEEMS at 09.45, the Bedford RL we were being transported in momentarily halted at the Guardroom. Incomprehensively, Illingsworth was still hanging about like a lame dog. Watching him grovel for new directions was too embarrassing to observe, but our looks of disdain turned to simpering glee when Martin Flowers, in his West Country drawl, began taunting Illingsworth. 'What's up my lover, missed us already have you?'

The majority of lads in 3Platoon condoned the vindictiveness of the Mil Training Staff; this morsel of schadenfreude cheered them up no end. I felt a momentary pang of sadness for Illingsworth, he looked pathetic. Tucker too was more bemused than amused. It hadn't taken long for Illingsworth to become an ostracised interloper and most of the lads felt smug about it. Had Cpl Hazel succeeded in de-sensitising them like he said he would, had they now developed swinging bricks for a hearts, or simply bonded as a platoon and to hell with any quitters?

'I wouldn't have come back,' I shrugged jadedly. 'There's no way I'd have shown my face around here if I'd fucked them off like he has. They must be absolutely pissing themselves now!'

Tucker agreed. 'Robby was right about that Sergeant McBride, he really is a twenty-four carrot bastard, aint he!'

As the truck clunked into gear and lurched off down the road, outrageous Martin Flowers immaturely called out. 'Oy Illingsworth!'

Illingsworth looked frustrated as Flowers dropped his trousers and stuck his backside over the tail board to dangle his cheeks out of the rear of the truck whilst making a childish noise, 'Nar nar nar nar nar!'

Boys will be boys, it was contagious and others followed suit. Not Tucker, Stan-the-Cab, Tug, big Tish or me though, we just laughed apathetically at this lunatic antic and sat it out. I hadn't heard a nar nar naer nar nar since I was a kid; it was such a comic touch!

The warm disinfected medical centre was a sunny respite from all the square bashing and lectures. The morning dragged by at that tranquil pace found in doctor's waiting rooms, country bus stops and public libraries. The lads of 3Platoon relished the sedative fussing attention of a female nurse, she smelt girly. The rustle of starched cotton garment against her soft unexposed flesh was enthralling her sex famished audience. Eyes glazed lustfully as she calculated raised blood pressures, height and weight as a preamble to stabbing our arms full of noxious antibodies and mild strains of exotic diseases.

Tucker flirted with her when it was his turn. 'I love your uniform.'

'It wouldn't fit you sweetheart!' sarcastically replied Florence Nightingale.

'Nurse, is it time for my bed-bath yet?' asked Spike when dismissed by the doctor.

'In your dreams sunbeam,' she winked at him.

Stan-the-Cab was next in line for the treatment. As Stan pulled shut the curtain which screened the doctor's surgery, the quack enquired. 'Have you got any vascular history?'

Quick as a flash Stan replied, 'No doc, I aint got any 'O' levels whatsoever!'

One by one our syndicate were put through the sausage machine until PULHEEMS was complete, then afterwards we were rewarded with a cup of hot sweet tea in the recovery room; Tucker flaked out like a light after drinking his. I succumbed to sleep too after my vaccination; the medicinal interactions left me folded up and drooling amidst the rows of uncomfortable plastic chairs like an itinerant alcoholic. I wasn't sure if the comatose lethargy was induced by the inoculative cocktail of antigenic substances Doctor Singh had dexterously administered, or fatigue from all the physical exertion coaxed from us over the past few days. Whichever was culpable, the anti-sceptic ambience or womb like embrace of weariness, the next hour seemed to float by indistinctly.

We trundled back to the Spiders once recuperated.

Cpl Hazel was in a black mood. 'Listen in you bunch of retards, you do not go around bearing your fucking arses at civilians from the back of army vehicles, do I make myself clear?'

What civilians collectively thought the platoon?

'Illingsworth is now technically a member of the public and that sort of behaviour isn't tolerated.' The instructor enjoyed lambasting us and issued a caveat. 'If you're going to be a bastard, don't be a silly bastard!'

I was taking a shine to Cpl Hazel; that advice was just the sort of counselling grandfather's imparted! Tucker exaggerated a wink at me.

'And above all else, don't be a complete bastard!' Cpl Hazel stared severely at Martin Flowers. 'Because no one likes that sort of bastard!

Martin Flowers had different sentiments. He groaned unguardedly. 'Whores piss.'

'For your information Flowers, it has come to light that a close member of Illingsworth's family has recently passed away and consequently he's still in a bit of a mess.'

Ouch! That was a kick in the stomach.

The instructor continued in a conciliatory tone. 'It can take a year or two for the grieving process to pass. The loss of a loved one is an ever-present shadow on the heart! I'm sure that under different circumstances he'd have soldiered on like the rest of you, and I've no doubt he will be back to try again in a year's time - at least he had the guts to show his face!'

'Yeh, you gotta give him that!' agreed Stan-the-Cab.

Tish Hewitt became tender and weirdly compassionate for a big guy. 'Eyes bathed by tears see life and death more clearly; Gran taught us that!'

'For fucks sake Corporal,' exploded the pirate reproachfully. 'It was you bastards who started it in the first place; we weren't to know were we?'

'Shut the fuck up Flowers and wind your scrawpy neck in,' cautioned Cpl Hazel. 'When I want your opinion you bone head I'll give it to you. Shit rolls downhill, just you remember that!'

Cpl Hazel slinked away like a cat which has deposited a dead bird on a doorstep. Under normal circumstances the recruits might have got to know Illingsworth a little better, but the training staff were adept Time-Bandits who didn't afford us a moment for a group hug!

After lunch 3Platoon was plunged head first into camouflage and concealment. Whilst we concealment trainees distractedly massaged our sore inoculated arms, Sgt Royce from 4pltn demonstrated how to utilise a Poncho, which was worn over Combats and Webbing during inclement weather. According to the British Army there is no such thing as bad weather; you simply have to have the right kit! The armed forces Poncho was a brilliant design concept measuring 80inches in length by 62inches in width. This sheet of green waterproof material had a hole in the middle for sticking your head through, and around the perimeter of the hole was fixed a hood to keep your bonce dry; a green Sombrero hat would set it off nicely but would simply be superfluous. To stop the whole thing flapping away during a storm, there was a length of green para-cord stitched into the front underside which secured the garment around the waist. The length of hem running the 80inches either side was adorned with a series of stud fasteners, which could be used to metamorphose the sides into sleeves. Interspersed with the stud fasteners were six one-and-a-half centimetre metal rings, three each side; one at each corner, and one either side of the centre. These were pressed flush into the fabric during manufacture enabling the Poncho to be stretched taut without tearing it to form a parasol.

He showed us how to knock together a sleeping space known as a Basha (British Army Standard Hotel Accommodation), by imaginatively clipping the Poncho to a sleeping bag (Maggot) to provide protection from the elements during a vacation at the "Star Light Hotel" and more importantly, how to disguise it. Sleeping in a Basha is the army equivalent of camping out. Distinct from other organisations catering for adventure enthusiasts in so much that soldiers are not required to rub two boy scouts together to keep warm at night. Ideally the structure of a Basha should be kept as low to the ground as possible to avoid silhouette. This is achieved by threading lengths of para-cord or elastic bungee's through the loops on the poncho and tying them off to a local tree, bush, or other fixed object, much as you would a tarpaulin. Then all that is required is the application of camouflage and the insertion of a green maggot (sleeping bag) to sleep in, and then Robert's your mother's brother. The Boffin who came up with this unsophisticated creation is a genius of Nobel Prize winning magnitude; it's such a brilliant, uncomplicated, practical piece of design engineering! After demonstrating the flexibility of the humble Poncho and extolling the virtues of its designers, we were led to the fringe of a wood.

'Right,' calmly directed Sgt Royce. 'Take a look at this wooded area and tell me if you notice anything peculiar?'

We scratched our heads, what was he getting at, it looked like any other wood to us, just trees, bushes, and undergrowth. 'Take a good hard look! Come on lads you're not trying, does nobody notice something unusual?'

Eyes were strained intently; everything looked as much as it should. 'Very well you blind bastards, follow me.'

Sgt Royce led us closer to the tree-line, halting at its perimeter. 'Over there we've hidden a Bedford Four-Tonner, can anyone distinguish it now that I've told you what you're looking for?'

Diddy Baxter pointed to a location in the proximity of a fallen tree which was covered in moss; we focused our indecisive attention on the position. Yep, there was something hidden away amongst the trees, however, we merely sensed it rather than distinguished it. Sgt Royce strolled right over to the something and pounded a fist against it, producing a metallic thud.

He tugged, then heaved and pulled away a large Camouflage-net, which was suspended and supported at intervals by branches and pieces of green para-cord. The illusion of a leafy fairy grotto soon transformed itself into a nightmare of military might, as one by one, several Land Rovers, a twelve man tent and an impressive machine-gun position complete with two camouflaged soldiers, was revealed.

'Now it's your turn you numpties. The best place to hide a leaf is in a forest, yeh? so think like a leaf! Remember, the basic rules in the art of concealment are to eliminate shape, shine, shadow, silhouette and movement. Use the Hessian to block off the underside of vehicles to do away with shadows, and drape some of it across the glass of the cabs to eradicate shine. Distort the camouflage netting away from the object to break up its shape by pushing and pulling the whole outline. Use dead branches to obliterate its silhouette; this will blend it into the surrounding canopy of trees nicely. Off you go then, you have forty five minutes to crack on and hide this little lot while I chinf off for a ciggie and a cup of Rosy-lee!'

We were back in the Spiders an hour later to change into PT kit; it seemed to me that we were always shifting out of one set of clothing into another. Protocol demanded that we should be properly dressed for each occasion and all our unused kit smartly squared away into our lockers once we were changed. At 15.00 hours 3Platoon were formed up with the other recruits in front of the Mil-Training-Wing shack. The sky had turned a dusky grey with diaphanous stripes of blue weaving meagrely across the horizon. It didn't seem quite as cold as the past few days but that wasn't a cause to rejoice, I could smell the tang of snow in the air.

L/Cpl Hughes and Cpl Hazel moved amongst us, randomly issuing cardboard numerals to pin to our vest; mine was 88 and Tucker was dealt number 57. Tucker commented that my number represented two fat ladies in a bingo call and his digits were synonymous with beans on toast. Food was always on our mind; we were so hungry from burning off so many calories during the past few days that we felt like we were running on empty most of the time, we simply ate what was given us to fuel our bodies.

At ten past three, a burly PTI escorted us across the parade square and out past the red and white stripy barrier pole at the gatehouse towards the woods on the left. A trail of torn newspaper combined with dead leaves and confetti had been sprinkled upon the compacted pathway. We were plainly tasked with following this confected route through the trees and beyond. We knew not where the trail extended, nor how much time was required to complete the steeple chase, but four miles later, the lad from 2platoon called Pin-head (who had grappled with Stan-the-Cab in the wrestling competition on the Firing-Ranges) romped home in 1st position with the rest of the pack close on his heels.

Once showered and changed, another race ensued to be 1st in line at Odd-Jobs Happy Eater. Always hungry, Tish Hewitt was proving to be a difficult lad to properly feed; he could have munched his way through an entire 24 hour ration pack in thirty minutes if left to it! Whilst in the meal queue I nudged Tucker to listen in when I overheard Tish Hewitt making a requisition to one of the more novice cooks. 'Hey up cocker, you'd better give me some for Ron!'

'Ron who?' The confused cook looked enquiringly up and down the dinner queue.

'Later Ron!' replied Tish cheekily.

'Oh him!' mused the chef, taking a quick peep over his shoulder to see if Odd job was watching - he was. Sgt Ernie Lee stared at Tish in contemplation, and then half-heartedly consented with a slight nod of his head; that was the only criteria needed for audacious Tish to fill his boots for the remainder of the fortnight!

'Here you go big man,' an extra portion was issued with a shoo of the hand, 'bon appetite!'

'Fucking Gannet,' chorused Robby and Tom in unison from the comfort of the tropical dining table. This caused many heads to look up and take an interest in Tish Hewitt's preferential treatment.

'You maggots can eat shit and die.' smirking Tish replied smarmily.

'Yeh, but we don't have to eat as much of it as you do china.'

Back at the Spider, anticipation gripped the members of 3Platoon. Our excitement had been brewing unspoilt throughout the day, and once all the ironing was squared off, Cpl Hazel gave us access to our "Civvy" clothing. The clothes smelt slightly musty from being stored away in a cupboard, but a quick spray of deodorant soon remedied that. Although we had grown accustomed to wearing combats it was comforting to be dressed in our personal apparel; I felt fitter and more confident in my new persona. Tucker and some of the other lads dressed smart casual, I was happy in a clean navy blue T-shirt and jeans, but Tug Wilson had swapped one uniform for another though, he wore grey slacks, white shirt, a stripy school tie and a black Barafia blazer bearing the TA regimental badge which he'd sewn onto the breast pocket; he looked like one of those poppy wearing old soldiers who shimmy along to the British legion for a pint on pension day. Cpl Hazel looked us up and down. Our clothing no doubt gave an insight into our character; his clothing certainly gave an insight into his! He wore a blue waxed Barber jacket over a Fair Isle knitted grey round neck woollen jumper inlaid with traditional purple and black mosaic patterns on the front. The legs of his Levi denim jeans extended down to a pair of Suede Desert boots, typical Mufti for an off duty squaddie.

After looking us up and down he announced. 'Right then, you'll do. Play time, let's go!'

The platoon were loosely organised into groups of four and packed into cars belonging to recruits who had brought their own transport. Some of the larger vehicles squeezed five in. Cpl Hazel encouraged ten bods to cram into the back of an army Sherpa van which he had scrounged; Lance Corporal Hughes sat up front as chauffer.

Tucker squeezed into the front of Tish Hewitt's white Ford Transit van alongside Stan-the-Cab. Martin Flowers, Spike, Wingnut, Diddy Baxter and myself, hunkered down in the back amongst small scaffolding pipes and an arrangement of plastic Lin-bins containing ad-hoc galvanised nuts and bolts, securing collars and the tools used in the roofing trade for erecting it all.

Car doors slammed shut excitedly and engines gunned into life. Tish Hewitt's white van had been stood immobile for days, so the starter motor almost drained the battery when he cranked the idle engine over. Amid puffs of thick grungy diesel smoke, the machine spluttered nervously for a brief moment and then it got some confidence and shamelessly raced into a gnarly Grrrraarrr Grrrraarrr Grrrraarrr, and then into a tap-tap tapping existence as Big Tish relaxed and unburdened the throttle. The poisonous exhaust fumes engulfed the vehicle, from its cheap remoulded rubber tyres right up to its huge rusty roof rack. The brakes squealed as the Transit van pulled forward and merged with the diminutive convoy ahead of us, where, in a semblance of order it was relegated to the back of the queue of vehicles. Once clear of the Guardhouse, the Sherpa van escorting the jumbled procession moved out of the camp and cruised along the A325 in winter darkness, destination unknown; all that we had gleaned from the instructor was that one of his relatives managed a near-by watering hole.

After several miles we passed a road sign at a crossroad indicating directions for the villages of Blacknest, Buckshorn Oak, Batt's Corner and Bird World, we then snaked through the hamlet of Rowledge, turning right just before Wrecclesham Hill into Echo Barn Lane. After a few minutes the Sherpa braked uncertainly, hesitantly indicating to turn right and then it slowly disappeared through what looked like a gap in a hedge. The others followed tentatively, descending down a steep unmade road, either side of which wild overgrown hawthorn hedges scratched and scrubbed away at the peeling paintwork on Tish Hewitt's battered transit van. The vehicles were jostled from side to side as more potholes than was healthy were hit, in fact a Land Rover would have had trouble negotiating this lane. I held on for dear life as nuts and bolts, tools and odd pieces of scaffolding lying unsecured in the back of the Transit van ricocheted and collided against us like bits of shrapnel. Tish Hewitt glanced sceptically at Tucker and Stan-the-Cab, none of them could imagine a Pub being at the end of the track; in fact Stan-the-Cab expressed a crazy notion that this was in some way part of our training and that Cpl Hazel was covertly steering us into an ambush. The steep brow eventually petered out onto more level ground as the track veered right, leading into a car park flanked by an antiquated Pub!

The Bat & Ball Inn owed its origins to Ye merry Olde England, when the lesser well off would vacate the neighbouring towns each September for a hop picking holiday out in the cuds. The hop-pickers' children were left in the relatively safe proximity of the Inn, supplied with a bat and ball to while away the long summer days, pending their parents return from toiling in the fresh countryside air.

3Platoon ambled into the bar, not one of us wanted to look too eager to get at the amber nectar. The Inn-keeper was a very jovial bloke who wore pressed grey slacks and a white open necked blue check patterned shirt, with a snug fitting royal blue wool cardigan over the top of this. His neatly brushed back white hair was thinning at the front while dishevelled grey sideburns grew level with his shirt-collar to emphasise his winter-break bronze suntan. Warm syrupy eyes and a plump putty nose completed his country squire countenance; he seemed very much at home running a pub. The barmaids were very girl next door types and the lads were glad of a bit of female company. Undoubtedly the serving wenches would blossom into beauty queens once the boys had got their beer goggles on. Due to it being midweek the Bar was like a graveyard, there were only two locals present. Tucker confided that he considered it a likely reason people stayed away in their droves was that they didn't wish to put their car suspension through the "Raiders of the lost ark" ordeal which connected this hidey-hole backwater tavern to the real world at the top of the brow outside. I agreed.

Cpl Hazel stipulated that none of us was to have any more than three pints, and the drivers were restricted to one each; but of course we endeavoured to sneak in a few extra, as you do. Every tap had a long handled pump and each tap pumped real ale; each ale was distinguished by an attached oval or round plaque. Being a northerner I didn't recognise any of the brews on offer, the names of which were all new-fangled to me. Included amongst this comprehensive array were: "Bishop's Todger", "Wrecclesham embalming fluid", and one called "Dumpy's rusty nuts".

Cpl Hazel's Brother-in-law Phil welcomed us warmly, I detected a smattering of an undistinguished Northern accent, Scots, Geordie, Merseyside maybe? 'Bet you're glad of a bit of normality aint you lads.'

'Not half fella,' Joked Tish Hewitt lamely. 'Wingnut's worked himself into a tizzy, he's so excited he's just done a little wee in his pants!'

'Has he now?' The barman raised a sceptical eyebrow. 'Right get your wallets out and make yourselves at home.'

Tug Wilson made a fuss of buying Cpl Hazel and L/Cpl Hughes a pint each, setting a precedent the rest of us were reluctant to follow. I settled for something called "E.S.P" or some such, and Tucker experimented with a pint of "Flowers" which he said tasted like homebrew. It was no great surprise to learn that Wingnut didn't drink alcohol; he requested a ginger beer instead.

Tish Hewitt picked up on this straight away and while ordering a pint of Winter Ale could not resist ripping the piss out of the teetotaller. 'Hey up landlord, you better plop a cherry and umbrella in it, she don't want get it mixed up with one of ours does she?'

Wingnut cringed as big Tish continued sarcastically. 'Aint you supping then Wingnut?

'No, I got done by the law!'

'What for, receiving swollen goods?'

Wingnut flinched even more.

'Leave it art you big lump!' scathed Stan-the-Cab.

'Just enquiring Stanley, just enquiring!'

Wingnut, bolstered by Stan's guardianship, guardedly admitted that he'd been banned for two years for drunk driving.

'Hey up, that's nuttier than a squirrels fart.' Big Tish was unabashed. 'So let me get me noggin arand this un, because you've been banned from driving you're not supping? I think you've got that back to flipping front you dizzy kipper!'

'My choice!' Wingnut shrugged it off somewhat embarrassed.

'Right then you flipping pop wallah; if you're not drinking and driving, and not drinking, you can drive because you're not drinking and I can have a drink and you can drive my van back to barracks!'

'Told you, aint got a license!'

'Aint got nothing to lose then have yuz hey? Reet then, I'm getting leathered, I deserve it.'

The landlord soon wiped the smile off Tish Hewitt's face when he announced that the Winter Ale he was supping was rationed to his customers in half pints only, on account of it being a limited brew (when its gone its gone), and being how it was so strong (11%ABV). However, he would make an exception for Tish, if he left poor Wingnut alone to enjoy his soft drink in peace.

Tish Hewitt held his palms up in surrender, then joked to the landlord. 'How do you make any money with being in such an isolated spot like this then?'

Phil assured him that the winter months were a welcome respite from the hordes of summer revellers who crawled out of the urban sprawl of Aldershot to escape soap-opera television sets and noisy Jukebox pubs. Although the Southern beer didn't have a head on it, admittedly it had bite, and a wonderful hoppy flowery aftertaste which was soothing; the ale alone was well worth journeying down the potholed lane outside. Playing at soldiers is thirsty work and after a week of abstinence my first pint of "ESP" slowed me down with a vengeance, and then halfway down my second I felt as if I was beginning to levitate. Tucker asked me if I felt ok? he said my face was flushed! I gripped the bar firmly and contemplated whether ESP was an acronym for Extra Sensory Perception. I double checked the enamelled oval name badge attached to the pump handle, it lavishly read "ESP Directors Vintage 6.5%". I slowed down the intake of my remaining second pint by sipping at it like a fine wine and nonchalantly studying my surroundings, a bit sozzled, while the others caught up with my alcohol ingestion; big Tish was not far behind me in that regard and his brew was nearly double the strength of mine.

The Bat & Ball Inn retained a lot of history; the walls of the bar room were adorned with age old sepia photographs portraying joyful Hop-pickers, happily slogging away in the fresh air, industrious amongst the walls of flowering creepers and horse drawn carts laden with the hops stripped from the vines. Poorly dressed weather tanned mischievous children stared blankly out at you from wobbly wooden frames, posing unenthusiastically, their faces unsure if the camera might steal their souls, it had! In contrast, other photos showed the same children at play, oblivious, laughing and shrieking unconsciously, frozen in time, a time gone by! Relics of hand held implements and small ancient farming apparatus festooned the nooks & crannies of the Inn. Rather at odds with this rustic décor was a blue and white Everton FC supporter's scarf affectionately draped across a poster depicting the current line-up of that Merseyside team? Tucker asked who the Evertonian was? and the Phil, the Landlord, proudly informed him that before moving to Hampshire, he was originally a *sock robber* from Kirkby, before settling in Hoylake on the Wirral in his teens as a trainee manager at the clubhouse of the Royal Liverpool Golf Club. The Landlord enthused that he never missed a game and launched into his football diatribe with relish. Understandably with the room now bursting at the seams with football fans from every corner of the British Isles, a heated debate as to the best team and most talented of players soon got underway. The lads of 3Platoon fanned out around a roaring open log fire, we made ourselves at home; the hospitality and atmosphere was very genial. Tug Wilson, a Norwich City supporter, recounted a joke about the Everton football club Manager who on being phoned up in the middle of the night and informed that his football club was on fire had asked whether the flames had reached the Cups? He was assured that the fire had not damaged the canteen yet! That went down like a lead balloon with Phil, who reciprocated by good humouredly ribbing Tug with a very witty football chant, sang to the tune of The Adams Family - "Your father is your brother; your sister is your mother. You all love one another, the Norwich family!"

The whole pub erupted with laughter at Tug Wilson's humiliation.

'All right, all right, calm down; let's not get into a battle of wits. In days of old,' recounted Cpl Hazel, 'when troops were on the march, they would often make camp close to an Inn like this one. The Commissioned-Officers, no doubt landlords themselves, would commandeer the premises and use it as a billet, taking over the tenant's living room or lounge as paying guests. From the comfort of this carpeted accommodation, the commanding officers would issue their orders across a bar to the senior NCOs - the lower classes were barred from association with the gentry back then. The Bar divided the public house into separate rooms: carpets and comfortable living accommodation for the tenants' family and guests, saw-dust covered floors and wooden benches for NCOs. The senior of the Non-Commissioned-Officers were Sergeants – an old French word, sergent to serve. They customarily received their orders across the bar and served them to the other ranks that would be tented outdoors. Public houses probably get the terms "Bar", "outdoor", and "can I serve you sir", from these turbulent historical times.'

Cpl Hazel was really switched on, he told us that the infantry soldier would purchase his ale from a window at the side of the Inn, or a maid would serve it from a jug at an exit corridor – the outdoor. In the evenings each group would imbibe of their pleasures and gradually descend into bawdry behaviour as they let their hair down. The Corporal (Caporal – leader of a body of troops) was given carte blanche to dish out summary beatings and conduct imaginative methods of screwing a soldier into the ground, by beasting him or detailing anyone unfortunate to have incurred the NCOs' wrath to dig latrines, or clear the mess made by the commissioned and non-commissioned officers at their accommodation – the Officers mess, and the Sergeants mess.

History lesson over, the evening picked up momentum, and just to help things along, Cpl Hazel blithely proposed a toast. 'Fun!'

3Platoon raised their pint glasses and heartily cheered. "Fun!"

'Fun is the challenge of a task and the satisfaction of a job well done. And for you blokes, it's a change from the routine of civilian life. It is the excitement of adventure and a jar of ale in congenial company. What I'm getting at lads is, well, it's vital that you don't neglect the elements of adventure and good company, and always, always endeavour to have fun along the way!'

"Fun!" once more we merrily applauded like musketeers on a works outing.

In his rich tenor voice, L/Cpl Hughes chipped in. 'Let the fleeting hour be drunk with joy!'

As we sipped on our beer no one seemed to know what to talk about, so Martin Flowers asked Cpl Hazel about his spell in the RAF. 'Tucker told us that you were a Bryllcreme boy?'

'RAF Regiment!' replied the instructor.

Tish Hewitt, prompted him. 'Tucker said you're a bit of a mountain goat, said ya were in mountain rescue?'

Cpl Hazel eyed the platoon calmly before reluctantly elaborating. 'Yeh got into it by accident really. A climbing buddy of mine got swept away by an avalanche up in the Cairngorms. I was roped to him and he pulled me along, down the side of a mountain. He disappeared beneath the snow but I managed to cling onto a rock, and when everything had settled I managed to dig him out. Took me near on forty minutes and when I got to him he was nearly dead from suffocation. Changed my whole outlook on life did that, how easily your life can be rubbed out. You've got to make every moment count, live it to the full. That's why I'm off to Alaska next month, golden opportunity!'

Martin Flowers had until then held a dislikeable opinion of Cpl Hazel, but that all changed, Martin was now filling up with admiration for the bloke. 'Bugger me; you're a regular Saint Bernarrrd aren't you!'

That first pint had hit the spot effortlessly, and with little prompting, each member of the platoon told a joke, funny story, or folk tale. Ronny Churchill told us that he'd nearly been killed while having a number two on his toilet at home. While sat on his throne in his bungalow he heard a hissing noise, he thought the cistern was leaky and gave it no more contemplation until he felt something tapping him on his bum. When he stood up to have a look he literally shit himself, there was an eight foot Python slithering around the U-bend! He had to bash the snake over the head with the bog brush to knock it out, then wrap it up in a bath towel and throw it out of the window before it regained consciousness. He said he was so rattled by it that he had to spend the rest of the week getting pissed down at his local pub to build up the courage to go home at night. Ronny narrowly escaped a murder charge a couple of days later when one of his neighbours knocked on his front door enquiringly, "I believe you've found my Cyril?"

Spike the biker chose to entertain the troops with a party trick. He un-wrapped a condom, spooled it out and fed it up one of his nostrils, poked it over his septum with his little finger and teased it through the other nostril; he then pulled the ends back-and-forth, flossing his snout out and thoroughly turning everybody's stomach. Before this exhibitionism became febrile, Stan-the-Cab counteracted it by belting out that old cockney classic "My old man's a dustman".

The lads joined in merrily on the chorus and when finished Tish Hewitt asked. 'Hey up love has thar got any fly roasted peanuts or ewlt to eat I'm famished? Oh and some canapés for Wingnut as well.'

The barmaid laughed awkwardly. 'Canapés, I don't think so mate!'

Big Tish put an arm around Whittling and gave him a friendly hug. 'Come on Dorothy, don't be mawky, can you whistle we're off to see the wizard of Oz for me?'

Stan-the-Cab leapt to Wingnut's defence. 'Leave it out china!'

But it was too late the lads were up for a singsong now, and give him his due, Wingnut willingly joined in as we repeatedly belted out the chorus, 'because, because, because, because, because… because of the wonderful things he does…'

By the time we'd supped up our second pint we were in excellent spirits and started to cluster in little knots around the room. The pub had a dartboard but no pool table. The sidewall flanking the end of the bar was laid over to a game, which up until then I hadn't seen before? It was Bar-Skittles and was very similar to American ten pin bowling, but obviously on a smaller scale. Instead of ten pins to knock down there were three skittles, each with a length of string tied to the top and loosely looped across a beam in the ceiling to righten up the skittles once they'd been knocked over. Phil, the landlord, devised a knockout tournament and in no time at all each man had his name chalked onto a blackboard over the bar, and just to make things more interesting, Sooty Corbett collected 50p from each man and put it into a kitty for the winner. We took three attempts each to roll a gnarled oak ball at the skittles, and during the tournament a barmaid brought out a huge wooden tray laden with hand carved country bloomer doorstep sandwiches. They were generously filled with a choice of Cheddar Cheese and tomatoes, or Roast Beef with Horse radish sauce. There were plenty to go around; the host was very generous so the lads graciously helped themselves to one of each.

Having satisfied his hunger, homophobic Tish Hewitt started necking off his third pint of 11%ABV winter ale and couldn't resist taking the piss out of Wingnut. He uncouthly wiped the froth from his mouth then placed his hand on his hip like a teapot, did a clumsy jig around Wingnut like a Morris dancer and launched into some poetry with an effected lisp. 'I wandered lonely as a cloud that floats on high o'er dales and fells, when all at once I saw a crowd, a host of golden daffodells.'

The lads laughed and jeered as Phil the landlord declared. 'That ale's blown his bloody head off!'

The barmaid distributing the pub grub clutched Wingnut's hand defensively. 'Leave him alone you bully, he's a sensitive soul, aren't you!'

Tish Hewitt slipped a hairy arm around her waist and breathed groggily. 'What's got eighteen inches and speaks French?'

She shrugged and then pulled away blushing as big Tish errantly informed her. 'Moi!'

'Oy Hewitt,' intervened Cpl Hazel, embarrassed. 'Apologise!'

Tish blew the corporal a kiss. 'Sorry gorgeous, didn't see you standing there!'

'Not me you divvy, that's my niece, stop coming on to her!'

Cpl Hazel's niece chortled with a dismissive vulgar laugh.

Tucker joked. 'You're not his type love, you're not inflatable!'

Cpl Hazel fixed big Tish with a steely stare and coughed to clear his throat. 'Right, it's poetry you're fond of is it. Here goes then: To be or not to be – that is the question. Whether it is nobler in the mind to suffer the slings and arrows of outrageous fortune, or to take arms against a sea of troubles and by opposing, end them? To die, to sleep no more: and by a sleep, o say we end the heartache and the thousand natural shocks that flesh is heir to, 'tis a consumption devoutly to be wished. To die, to sleep; perchance to dream. Ah, there's the rub!'

I was unsure if the "ESP" which I'd consumed had heightened my perception, but for the first time in my life I was actually able to understand a piece of Shakespeare. Cpl Hazel had injected such dynamism into every syllable of each word, had phrased and suspended the lines with so much heartfelt empathy that it was difficult for any man standing there not to have been moved by it. The NCO was proving to be a bit of a showman at heart, and for his talent was clapped and whistled at approvingly!

Cpl Hazel's blast at poetry had silenced two loquacious regulars who'd been standing at the end of the bar mumbling to each other, they too clapped their hands appreciatively. They were glad of fresh company and a touch of culture; we new comers were beginning to charm and amuse them, which caused the old boys to be contemplative. The shorter of the two was a dogged character in his late sixties. He owned a lived in face with a stubborn glint in his watery eyes. He smoked a smelly roll-up constructed from a pinch of pipe tobacco that his friend had offered him, a habit picked up during the Second World War at some stage of rationing. The nicotine stains on his fingers and the discolouration of his uneven teeth exposed him as a heavy smoker; even his brushed back thinning hair was yellow tinged from tobacco smoke. The face of the bald headed old boy standing next to him was adorned with white mutton chop side burns. Mutton chops tapped his empty glass on the bar for silence, and then asserted himself. 'My turn!'

He had a glass eye and bulbous red nose, with blue veins streaking across its bridge. His one good eye was commanding and his voice was deep, rich, reflective, and boozy. 'We shall fight in France, we shall fight on the seas and oceans, and we shall fight with growing confidence and growing strength in the air. We shall defend our island whatever the cost may be, we shall fight on the beaches, we shall fight on the landing grounds, we shall fight in the fields and in the streets, we shall fight in the hills: We shall never surrender.'

'Fuck me, what have you been drinking granddad?' Tish Hewitt laughed.

'Ta very much young man, pint of Spitfire for myself and chuck a Boilermaker in there for Gerald!' the old man brazenly slid two empty glasses across the bar to Tish.

'You cheeky fookers!' protested Hewitt at being caught out with such drollness.

That brought the house down, 3platoon were banging on the table tops, clapping, and yahooing like crazy; it was another bonding moment. L/Cpl Taffy Hughes was the only man not cheering. 'Can't abide Churchill see.'

'What's he ever done to you then?' demanded Ronny Churchill, the recruit.

'No offence to yew Bach but that man was responsible for the murder of Welsh miners see. There were pictures in nashnal papers showing him peeping round a corner, watching his gunmen carry it out he was; my Granddad showed me them. It were before he was Prime minister mind, him was Home Secretary back then, said they was the IRA, terrific, he got that wrong did'ne? IRA in Wales, I ask ewes! Can't bloody stomach him in the Valleys, yach.'

Tish Hewitt had deep pockets and short arms and while pocketing his change from reluctantly buying Mutton chops and his nicotine-stained drinking buddy a fresh pint of ale each, he glanced at Taff Hughes scornfully. 'Pure shite is that!'

'Yeh that's gash, no one was killed right,' insisted Cpl Hazel remedially, 'they were only shot at over their heads and I'm not sure whether that's true or not. I think it was all just a story.'

'Just a story is it? There's lovely,' laughed the Welshman. 'You weren't there Bach.'

'Nor were you Viet-Taff!' shrugged Cpl Hazel. 'So put a bloody cork in it.'

The age-old enmity between the Shropshire border townsfolk and the Welsh hill dwellers was apparent when you witnessed these two lads picking at one another, mind you there was a time when they would have been cutting each other's ears off or trying to hang each other for trespassing; the north-Welsh always seem more Celtic than the south-Welsh for some reason!

I was just a kid when Winston Churchill died in 1965; it was one of my earliest enduring memories. I vividly remembered watching the funeral on the television and feeling the pangs of grief when the cortege carrying Churchill's coffin passed through the streets of London, and as young as I was, I knew that it was a very solemn occasion, and like Cpl Hazel and Tish Hewitt, I too felt a bit miffed at L/Cpl Hughes's unpatriotic outburst; but politicians can be duplicitous and Taffy's flare-up had raised questions in my mind?

Arfon Hughes' intelligent blue eyes smouldered; he was clearly not the diffident type. He started to make an objection but Cpl Hazel cut him dead. 'Shut it face ache, you sheep shaggers are always banging on about being true Britons and subjugation and all that, if you were true Britons you'd integrate, but you can't because you're impotent, you're all sick with inbreeding and clinging on to the past.'

'Proud I am!'

'Maybe Taff, but I'd sooner have you inside the tent pissing out, than outside the tent pissing in!'

The room was embarrassingly quiet, there was a gulf as wide as Offa's Dyke between the two NCO's but this was not the occasion to air contretemps.

Tish Hewitt nudged Tucker and wisecracked out of the side of his mouth. 'Wales… the only country where you can get a delicious hotpot, a smashing jumper and a decent shag, all from the same animal!'

Tucker snorted with laughter and nearly choked on his beer as he sneezed some froth from his nostrils. L/Cpl Hughes shot Tucker and Tish Hewitt an indignant look but the old man with the glass-eye made a timely intervention. 'We're all entitled to an opinion and minorities are almost always right. If Taff thinks Sir Winny was a bad'n, then he's perfectly entitled to think like that!'

Mutton chops stuffed his brier pipe full of tobacco and wryly continued. 'Lady Astor, now she was a bad'n lad's! Started off with good intentions – they all do, but she had a sour side to her. She was all for the women's movement – she reckoned women were superior to men but needed the right to vote so as to achieve equality in a male dominated world. Huh, I ask you!'

'Gawd sake, who the Dickens is Lady Astor?' asked Stan-the-Cab.

Old mutton chops took a few puffs on his pipe and filled the air with cocoa scented smoke. 'An American, she married into aristocracy - a bloke called Lord Astor. Lord Astor started off as an MP representing Sutton in Plymouth, but when his father kicked the bucket, he inherited the title and peerage and moved up to the House of Lords leaving his constituency up for grabs. Well, they wanted to keep it in the family, so his missus stood for his empty seat. She was the first woman to get a seat in Parliament, said she wanted more rights for women, but when the women of Plymouth gave her their vote, she went and stabbed them in the back by stopping the allowance they received while their poor husbands were away at sea.'

Mutton chops gave a gravely cough before resuming. 'The Royal Navy had this squad of small inshore boats. They used them for re-supplying ammunition to the fleet what was protecting the Merchant Navy convoys from attack by German U-Boats in the North Atlantic sea-lanes. The Admiralty saved themselves hundreds of man hours by not having to divert the fleet into harbour; the English Channel was crawling with German E Boats which could pick them off too, nasty bastards they were.'

He struck another match and relit his pipe, this time it properly belched into life.

'The trouble with that supply squad was they were only a brown water fleet, not sea going vessels at all, not suitable see, they were only designed for river jobs and maybe a bit of coastal work in light seas. Some bright spark in Whitehall - some say it was Churchill himself - had the daft brainwave of sending them out into the ocean depths; totally inappropriate. No protection from the squall in rough seas, water swamped the small decks and threatened to sink 'em with the weight of all that Ammo they was carrying inside. Took some guts did that!'

I imagined the tiny vessels bobbing up and down over white crested rolling waves, and then sliding perilously through the foaming wake to reach a hindered destiny. Martin Flowers piped up, he was from Plymouth but he'd never heard this tale before. 'Those Janners must have had nerves of steel!'

'Balls of steel more like!' Mutton chops puffed furiously on his pipe and wafted the pall of smoke away from his one good eye then continued. 'Another thing was, they could be away for days at a time and there were no bunks to get their heads down for a sleep in them tugs, so they curled up wherever they could. After a while the RN were finding it harder and harder to get a crew to man them. Your old Matelot thought it was suicidal, and although not exactly going on mutiny, they weren't queuing up to volunteer either - they certainly let them in charge know that they were disgruntled. Because it was over and beyond the call of duty and there were no medals in it, the Admiralty came to a compromise and gave them a small allowance; hardship money they's called it. Them boys were only getting about fourteen shillings a week and with the extra few bob, it boosted it up to a pound, hardly a king's ransom were it? When Lady Astor heard about it she had it stopped, she argued, "Why should they have it and none of the others on the bigger ships?" silly cow!'

Mutton chops story raised a few sceptical eyebrows, and although most of the lads had never heard of the woman before, heads nodded in agreement with his sentiment.

'It was her what said that our boys fighting in Italy in the Eighth Army were D Day dodgers, simply because they weren't fighting in France during the Second World War. That was a load of Tommy rot; they couldn't be in two places at once could they? And when advances to repel the Nazi's in Italy seemed to be taking a long time, she accused them of dossing around getting drunk on cheap Italian wine and shacking up with the local women; "Roman whores" I think she called them. Daft woman didn't have a clue; she was from a privileged background and had no rights to be dabbling in politics, totally ignorant of the war effort. She put a lot of backs up did that one; the Eighth Army was absolutely incensed with her.'

'Yeh, there was a song about her,' joined in his nicotine-stained drinking partner as he helped himself to some more of Mutton chops pipe tobacco. He stretched the dark strands along a vacant cigarette paper, which he screwed up into a roll, then licked from side to side as if he was having a quick blast on a harmonica. 'How did it go? Oh yeh, "The ballad of the D-Day dodger", that were it!'

He lit his roll-up, blew out a stream of smoke, coughed reactively, and then gave a rendition to the tune of Marlene Dietrich's Lily Marlene - an old war time song. The words certainly verified Mutton chops story, something about how hard the boys were having it and how Lady Astor should keep her big mouth shut!

'Most of them boys fighting in Italy had come straight from the campaign in the Western Deserts, they never had any leave or rest,' continued old Mutton chops. 'North Africa had been hot and harsh, but Italy was slow and bloody. I know, I was there lads.'

His drinking partner picked a strand of loose tobacco from his lips, played with it between nicotine stained fingers and expounded. 'Yeh, three hundred thousand European allied forces were killed out there in that Italian campaign, not to mention all those dead yanks from the fifth too! Compare that to the four hundred thousand British that were killed in this country during the entire war and you start to get the picture, and all for two Shillings a day lads, ten bloody pence, and you had to send half of that home to your suffering poor bloody wife!'

The lads sipped silently on their pints while Mutton chops took a few more long draws on his smelly pipe and casually wafted the smoke away with his left hand. 'Winston Churchill couldn't stand her either, he thought she had too much to say for herself; a right gobby bint – you know the sort!'

We all nodded sagely in agreement and Tucker used the diversion to order another two pints by casually winking to the barmaid to re-fill our empty glasses. 'When you've got a minute love, and have one for yourself!'

The glasses were removed and replaced with two fresh ones without any fuss from Cpl Hazel, who was relying on honesty to adhere to his three pints per man ruling. As Tucker sneakily slid one over to me, the barmaid returned his change minus a tip with a wink.

Mutton chops ploughed on with his tale. 'Lady Astor once told him "Sir you're drunk!" and quick as a flash he say's to her "Yes madam I am, but in the morning I will be sober and you will still be ugly!" She didn't like that one bit, so she tell's him, "Sir, if you were my husband I would poison your drink" and he replied, "Madam, if you were my wife I would drink it!" Good old Winny, hey? Bloody good bloke he was!'

3Platoon were all enlightened as to whom Lady Astor was, but the gravity of the yarn had subdued the mood, so the landlord conjured up a guitar and started twanging away on the strings with a rousing tune, and sang. “Oh, one man went to mow went to mow a meadow…” and everybody joined in on the chorus, “Three men, two men, one man and his dog named Butch with his wooden crutch, went to mow a meadow”.

That got everybody buzzing again but sadly the evening was drawing to a premature end, and while the last few inches of rationed ale was reluctantly sipped, L/Cpl Hughes called for order. ‘Listen in boyo’s; before the evening is over we have a presentation to make see. Oy Corbett, put that barmaid down.’

As Sooty folded up a piece of paper with a telephone number scrawled on it and secreted it into the barmaid’s hand, the lance-jack passed a brown paper parcel to Cpl Hazel who announced. ‘Wingnut, step forward please?’

Whittling pushed through the crowd and stood bemused as he clumsily caught the package that was launched at him like a volleyball.

‘What’s this for?’ He lamely asked unaware of what merited a gift.

Cpl Hazel smiled wryly. ‘It’s something to keep you warm at night!’

Wingnut opened the parcel and revealed its contents, a pair of stripy pyjamas with a tennis ball sewn into the back of the jacket like a Camel’s hump.

‘Stops yew sleeping on yewer back and snoring see, rest of yewer platoon can get some decent zeds now. More importantly, them jimjams will prevent yew catching yewer death of cold from exposure; see butty, them really will keep yews warm isn’t it!’

Cpl Hazel smiled and proclaimed. ‘You lot can stop behaving like a bunch of juveniles now and start pulling together, nothing gets past me, nothing. Don’t be freezing Wingnut out,’ he winked conspiringly and drained his glass. ‘There’s always a solution to a problem if you look hard enough! Right you lot, that’s it, end-ex back to base.’

‘What, straight back corporal?’ asked Tish Hewitt? ‘Aint we gonna hit a club first?’

In gratitude for a good night out, Tug Wilson thanked Cpl Hazel’s brother-in-law Phil and his bar staff for their hospitality, and while the barmaids collected up all the empty glasses, 3Platoon reluctantly filed through the door to the car park and squeezed ourselves back into the vehicles.

Tish Hewitt collared Whittling and forced the ignition keys to the Ford Transit into his hand. 'Here you go Wingnut, you aint drank much. You drive, I'm too nazzy.'

With that, Big Tish sprawled out in the back of his white van, utilising his toolbox for a pillow. We scrambled in and sat as best we could either side of him. Wingnut irritably slammed the rear doors shut, then squeezed in behind the steering wheel and wrestled with the steering lock, and then gunned the engine into life. Through bilious exhaust clouds the stricken white van rumbled and inched forward like a locomotive crop sprayer, resolutely following the vehicles in front to make the Everest like ascent back up the wild overgrown track to Echo Barn Lane at its crest. Once the climb had been accomplished, the Transit shunted the rest of the straggling convoy up to the bumper of Cpl Hazel's leading Sherpa van and sandwiched it all in tightly, then the return journey to Martinique Baracks got underway. It had attempted to snow while they had been in the pub, gracious flecks had drifted discreetly in the frigid air before melting away unobtrusively on contact with an inhospitable environment. What started off as scattered seeds had now propagated with fecundity into swelling buds of cotton, freefalling with the vengeance of Icelandic paratroopers tumbling from an unzipped Valhalla? Wingnut squinted as snowflakes the size of dinner plates glided like Frisbee's into his eye line, wreaking havoc with his concentration and obscuring his vision. The flakes burst like mop heads as they splattered against the windscreen to form a scab. We inebriated passengers pissed ourselves laughing at the sight of Wingnut scrabbling around erratically with switches and dials on the dashboard as he attempted to turn on the windscreen wipers. Tish lifted his head and instructed Wingnut to feel for a knob on the steering wheel column.

'It's the only knob thar'll be fooking playing with tonight, I tell thee!'

The large wiper arms swept snow from the screen, fruitlessly clearing the way for yet more accumulation. Panicky Wingnut fumbled to turn on the demisters which eventually roared into life; condensation had collaborated with the snowstorm to doubly frustrate his ability to see through the glass. He had difficulty keeping up with the tail lights in front, but once the van had turned onto the main A325 at Wrecclesham Hill, we knew it was a clear run back to base. The screen wipers diligently cleared away two wedges of snow and the blast from the heater dispersed the mist, but it was insufficient. Stan-the-Cab wound down the passenger door window, enabling him to reach out and clear away some of the build up from the periphery. As he and Tucker helped navigate, the crunch of snow compacted under the tyres and stifled the clamour from the 2 litre diesel engine. The snowflakes swirled in the air obliquely, and save for its tyre tracks; the vehicle in front was almost invisible. By the time our platoon had reached the barracks, the snow had turned into a real blizzard, summoning up visions of the base being cut off from civilisation. The beer must have clouded our minds because we foolishly entertained the thought that a whiteout would force the Mil Training Staff to go easy on us. During the previous winter, when severe snowstorms had swept the North East of the USA and much of Great Britain, it had been declared one of the worst ever winters recorded. The winter of 1979 must have been a close second because Denis Howell MP was duly appointed Minister for Snow?

Chapter 11

The wooden Spider had creaked and groaned throughout the night, agitating 60watt light bulbs to dance lazily in synchronised circles. Through it all 3Platoon had slept oblivious like bugs in a rug; our slumber indisputably ameliorated by Wingnut's magic pyjamas plus the few pints of hop seasoned beer consumed off base, but all too soon it was 0530hrs and time for the morning run. The open countryside encircling the camp had not hindered the crosswinds one iota, consequently more than a fair share of the white stuff had superimposed itself onto buildings and any hard and fast structure remotely barring its way. At best the snow was one to two feet deep, at worst five or six where it had banked itself up against buildings. We had involuntarily vacated our beds and true to form were clad in our meagre all weather gear of red PT cotton tops, green light-weight trousers and shiny black boots. The Mil Training instructors were dressed dichotomously in combats and woolly hats; Cpl Hazel and L/Cpl Hughes wore so many layers that they resembled Tweedle-dee and Tweedle-dum. A full moon bathed the snowscape; I shivered empathetically for weary old Scandinavian depressives who grow suicidal during such conditions. Sgt McBride's hallowed parade square was completely indiscernible. Along the designated car-park anomalous igloo shapes disrupted the surface hither and thither where cars which had been hastily parked the previous evening had all but disappeared. Only two shapes were plausibly recognisable, the forlorn Monkey puzzle tree and the top half of Tish Hewitt's battered Ford Transit van which now supported a loaf of snow on its rusty roof rack comparable to a tier on a wedding cake.

The muffled roar of a Bedford MK four tonner broke the hushed wintry silence. The heavy truck corrupted the virginal mantle as its wheels crunched past the guardroom. Blazing headlight beams momentarily dazzled us as the vehicle tentatively navigated its way around the drill square. Somehow it managed to avoid the indistinct rocky perimeter of white stones enclosing the square before sliding higgledy-piggledy to a compressed halt outside the Mil Training Wing shack. Two animated PTI's jumped athletically from the cab into the axle deep snow, and with that typically British knack for ironically understating the situation, one of them enthused. 'It's a bit wintry today so let's not stand about admiring it!'

'Its bleedin taters mate,' grumbled a cockney voice. 'Absolutely Baltic, I want me mum!'

'Don't worry ladies, soon have you warmed up!'

There is something about a new fall of snow which manages to bring out the child in grownups; overgrown toddlers pining to put footprints into it like the first man to walk on the moon. Martin Flowers fell into the other category of juveniles, more orientated to making snowballs. The childish bastard in him surfaced and stuffed a handful of snow down the back of Tucker's red PT top. Tucker contorted from the shock as the rest of us set off in three ranks laughing at his dilemma. He wriggled to dislodge the snowball before it turned to slush and seeped into the crack of his bum, but it didn't really matter; within minutes the BFT had descended into a time-consuming farce as those at the front struggled to progress through the waist deep drifts. Only big Tish and lanky Sooty Corbett exhibited any freedom of movement, so the rest of us held back a little and urged the two abdominal snowmen to pioneer a route through the mass. In due course the remaining hundred odd men followed lamely in the yeti like giant footsteps. Progress was absolutely knackering and took close on twenty-five minutes to complete the first mile and a half circuit. The PTI's and Mil Training Staff made no attempt to follow us on the opening lap, but compensated for this disinclination by beasting the foot-draggers to near exhaustion on the second mile and a half. I struggled on regardless and scrambled through the thick of it, my aching lungs sucking in cold fresh air as my leg muscles burned with lactic acid from the exertion. Tucker and a handful of other arctic explorers managed to keep up with Tish Hewitt and Sooty Corbett; I scrambled after them uncontrollably on rubbery legs along with the rest of the herd and collapsed into a snotty heap at the finishing line with my heart banging so fiercely that I thought it was going to burst. It was another fifteen minutes before the last of the stragglers struggled in, and incredulously the Sgt PTI lambasted everybody for taking so long. 'You have all failed this morning, rules are rules, I expect much better from you tomorrow!'

After breakfast and the inevitable room inspection, we were loaded onto the backs of a fleet of trucks and ferried to a large hanger on a neighbouring army base. There to welcome us was Sgt McBride, looking as if he'd just escaped from a Burtons shop window.

'Good morning men, this is shed eleven!' the Ulsterman portentously explained. 'During inclement weather yay will carry out all aspects of drill here, unhindered and undisrupted by the elements.'

His voice echoed thunderously within the vast metallic emptiness, causing flakes of rusting paint to peel from the rafters and swirl to ground like sycamore seeds.

'Noy then, I am not going to be lenient with ye today, we simply ain't the time for it. Yay'll all give me an extra fifty per cent in effort so you will, that's an order. Any one of yay ladies cocking things up today will have their ears violently ripped from their head and then yay'll be summarily placed on a charge for insubordination, got it? There's no excuse noy, ye all know the pack drill. Each and every time yay fail to respond to an order, I'll be compelled to put ye on a Fizzer for disobeying me. DO I MAKE MY SELF CLEAR ON THAT?'

Not half mate, clear as daylight! The huge hanger was especially designed for storing 432's – tracked Armoured Personnel Carriers. These APC's used part of shed eleven as a car park when not out on the road teaching regular Squaddies how to drive a tracked vehicle as a precursor to letting them loose in a Main Battle Tank; they were all out on the road so subsequently we had the place all to ourselves. Part of the hanger at the far end was in the process of being prepared to house Chieftain Main Battle Tanks (MBTs), which were due for future arrival. The British Army of the Rhine (BAOR) in the late 1970s and early 1980s included nine tank regiments (or battalions), each being equipped with a total of 74 Chieftain MBTs, with another two regiments expected to be formed in the mid 1980s. In 1983, after extensive trials, the first of two hundred and thirty seven new Challenger MBTs were handed over for service - converting four of the BAORs then current aging Chieftain Tank regiments over to the newer Challenger. The total Chieftain strength was estimated to be around 900 and once they started coming out of service, the Chieftain's would have to be stored in mothballs until the MOD decided what best to do with them. In the interim shed eleven stood idle during daylight hours and Sgt McBride the entrepreneurial Drill-Pig had ardently requisitioned it.

'Listen in yay toe rags. RIGHT HAND MARKER, TO ME!'

Tish Hewitt came to attention and marched Tick-Tock like a toy soldier over to Sgt McBride, where he was put on his spot. The screaming skull then manoeuvred the rest of the marchers. 'PARRAAYDE - FALL IN. DRESSING RIGHT, RIGHT DRESS. EIYYYES FRONT!'

With the absence of hypothermia and frostbite to contend with, we were so much better at handling our weapons and perfecting drill movements. Sgt McBride was elated as he shepherded us around the huge empty hanger like a flock of green sheep; proving Tom the Cockney-rebel right in his speculation that the relentless instructor probably did have the word B.A.S.T.A.R.D stamped right through the middle of his body.

Sgt McBride had an excellent command voice, distinct and loud with loads of inflection, projection and snap! He broke down the complex rifle drill movements into simpler parts and with each part isolated, had us practice them over and over, then put them all back together so that the desired result was achieved. He told us that drilling had been a vital component in fighting battles hundreds of years ago, especially musket drill which was used to maximise the efficiency and deadliness of a combat soldier, and although now largely ceremonial in a modern army, drill was still a good tool in instilling discipline and teaching recruits how to move and work as a cohesive team. Once everything started clicking into place I and my platoon mates experienced a wonderful feeling, a satisfaction reminiscent of having a decent rally in a tennis match, we were really chuffed with ourselves.

At 10.30am we were knocked off for a short NAFFI break on the host base. The barracks was an avant-garde fortification, composed of modern red brick buildings laid out conspicuously in uniform blocks. By comparison these double-glazed structures with all-mod-cons were severely divergent from the austere wooden huts on Martinique Barracks. We lined up in an orderly manner, kicking snow from our boots as we entered the NAFFI building, once inside we bashfully mingled with regular soldiers. The regulars disdainfully looked down their noses at us novices, not with prejudice, more with smug narrow-minded intolerance. The Territorial Army was a seemingly lacklustre arm of the British Armed Forces back in the dark days, frequently nursing the bruises of dark sarcasm and often considered the poor relation to the Regular British Army, and as such habitually marginalized by regular soldiers and indecorously misapprehended by the general public.

We TA lads categorically understood these sentiments, during the mid-1970s the Regulars were keeping the peace between the Greeks and Turkish in Cyprus, and were heavily involved in maintaining the Cold War status-quo along the borderlands of East and West Germany. They also patrolled at the sharp end in Northern Ireland and frequently came under fire and the likelihood of being slotted by a sniper or blown away by a bomb blast. Understandably because of exemption from serving in Ulster, the TA was considered mere hobby soldiers in comparison. Myself, Tucker and our new comrades were to encounter this acrimony routinely over the coming years. The phrase STAB resembled an injurious racial slur and still persists today to some degree; though since serving alongside the Regulars in Iraq and Afghanistan on tours of duty, the term STAB is now used more affectionately for part time soldiering, and conversely TA soldiers seem to have replaced the acronym FART's (Fucking Arrogant Regular Twats) with the more sentimental idiom of ARAB's (Arrogant Regular Army Bastards).

Growingly aware of our second rate status, me and my new pals resolved not to let the sneering attitudes hamper our moral during the recruit course; in effect it only served to spur us on. Once the NAFFI break was over we trudged back to Shed Eleven and formed up inside, eager to get the drill manoeuvres spot on. Melded into a cohesive force by Sgt McBride, we marched solidly for the rest of the morning and the best part of the afternoon, taking pride in all our newly acquired skills and to hell with any detractors.

Back at Martinique Barracks during an hours meal break, Cpl Hazel handed a clutch of letters received via Royal Mail to Tug Wilson to dish out. There was no such thing as email or texting on a mobile phone in the 1970s because such technology had not yet emerged; any message you wished to dispatch was relayed via the G.P.O.

Tug Wilson handed out what little correspondence there was to Diddy Baxter and a lad called Joe Ward from Spalding in Lincolnshire – Joe was a quiet lad with a cheeky grin who kept himself to himself. There were two epistles for Jennings, who had earlier aborted the recruit course for medical reasons, and a bemusing letter for Tucker. He recognised the handwriting and felt discomfited as he ripped open the envelope with his pinkie finger. The scribbly was from his ex-girlfriend Sarah, who was now becoming a fading memory, but she had found him, not that he had ever been lost. She had no doubt gleaned Tuckers temporary address from a family member, probably mother; being maternal she had a fondness for the girl.

Tucker was a bit reserved with his emotions in company; unconsciously he turned his back on his fellow recruits while skimming over the pages, judiciously picking out the bones of it to formulate the crux of the message. I thought, here we go, bad news!

Tucker passed the letter to me to read, I always gave him an unbiased opinion but no advice, and he respected me for that. In the preamble, Sarah asked how he was getting on with his course, was it tough, had he made any new friends etc., and then plunged into a frank admission of how much she missed him and how much she wanted to rekindle the relationship, real full on stuff. Marvellous I thought, when they were together they had almost destroyed each other. Admittedly she made him feel warm and soft when he was with her, but he felt vulnerable too. She was so manipulative and clingy, anxious to know what he was feeling or thinking and wanting to pervade his mind and delve into his soul, but all Tucker wanted to do was reach a climax and ejaculate, not hang about on her arm like some girly handbag accessory.

She was always cleaning up after him and fussing about his appearance which seemed like a contradiction to him because her bedroom was full of girly clutter, like shoes, magazines, make-up and fashion clobber. He felt that they spent too much time together and she complained it was not enough. Tucker had a healthy sense of independence and individuality, not psychotically but manageable, and she liked that about him but didn't appreciate feeling used and abandoned; she wanted to curl up on the couch and cuddle all the time, and when she couldn't get her way she would try to put him on a guilt trip, which confused him, making him feel exposed and susceptible. She wasn't satisfied with his sexual prowess alone; she wanted to be lavished with attention. She would often wait on his door step all dolled up when he came home from work, stalking him around the house expecting to be waltzed off to the cinema when all he wanted to do was get washed and change out of his work clobber and grab a bite to eat! If the attention she craved was in short supply she would throw a flippant remark or have a fit. He'd console her and then she'd pick at a loose thread and begin to unravel his psyche, acting coy, wanting to know all about him, what made him tick, get connected, wanting to know his deepest thoughts. Truth was he had very few deep feelings, his mind was a blank page at various times; like most men he had a manly necessity to switch off once in a while and let it all hang out; he needed to hang out with the lads every now and then to burn off some testosterone and grab some sanity. Sarah didn't get it and often accused him of being immature, well maybe he was, he was in no rush to grow up. Besides having good looks she was clever too, and alarmingly Sarah was the only person who could unnerve him. She had the power to make him do things he wouldn't normally consider doing, sometimes in a fun way, sometimes not, as if testing him, trying him out emotionally to see how far she could push him; afterwards she would scrutinize the corollary, as if studying a butterfly pinned to a card. Tucker was no butterfly, he'd realised that she was always trying to dazzle him and he could see right through her now. Since splitting up he had felt sad and elated both at the same time which was a confusing mix of emotions. I had joked to him that it was probably because of all the bonking he had been doing and he was prematurely going through the male menopause; I suggested HRT and he laughed at his own dismay. The rest of Tucker's mates were not much help; they laughed at his quandary and simply told him to get rid. But here she was raking over the embers.

I could see it in his face; his mind was churning things over. In the letter Sarah wrote that she understood that he needed his space but she needed contact with him. She needed him in her life and if *he* felt the same way then she was offering an olive branch, yada-yada. I knew Tucker all too well. He would have considered reaching out for it but all she wanted to do was to settle down to a life of raising kittens and knitting cakes. That was why their relationship had inevitably gone stale, she'd caged him in. He didn't want suffocating; he wasn't used to it; if she had just given him some space it might have worked.

My girlfriend was bad enough, she was an interfering Earth Mother who thought she knew what was good for everyone, and just like me Tucker managed to duck under her radar unscathed by paying lip service to her excessive practical advice. She thought that Sarah was the one for Tucker, but Tucker couldn't see it, which made him unsure. Eventually Tucker had convinced himself that he was over Sarah, that he was moving on, but I realised that deep down she could still stir his emotions. One way or another it was an unresolved issue, Sarah could still pluck away at his heartstrings.

I playfully punched him in the arm as a gesture of support. Tucker sighed inwardly and in frustration crumpled the letter up, then as an afterthought tenderly unravelled it, smoothed it out and folded the whole thing back into the envelope. What to do about Sarah, he couldn't live with her or without her?

While we'd been pondering this dilemma, a snowplough had cleared a route through the camp leaving the snow banked up even higher around the Spiders so that it partially obliterated window light. Cpl Hazel hounded us all out of our accommodation and assertively organised us into two gangs, issuing shovels to clear away the paths interlinking the Spiders. We scraped and shovelled at the slush like navvies while Sooty Corbett and big Tish Hewitt leant across the bank of snow and vigorously chipped away at window height to allow sunlight into the billet. Predictably, Martin Flowers childishly made a snowman at the base of the steps of the fire escape. When the paths had been scoured clear, we returned to Shed Eleven for the afternoon drill session. The snowman stood guard over the wooden lodgings like a frost bitten arctic monkey replete with Wingnut's shiny best boots and a rifle fashioned from a broom handle.

Chapter 12

09.00hrs on Wednesday of the second weeks' training; out of the initial one hundred and twenty volunteers who had arrived at Martinique Barracks, ninety six now remained. It rubs against the grain to keep that many testosterone fuelled young men too long in close confinement, but at last the moment we had all been anticipating had finally arrived. Days of endless marching back and forth and throwing ourselves over assault courses, polishing, ironing and swotting up by dim bedside lamps had now moulded a degree of unity into each platoon. We never thought we would be grateful to be sat in the backs of the bone shaking Bedford RL 3 tonners, but somewhat galvanised we were. Each man was dressed in CEFO (combat equipment fighting order), decked out like a Christmas tree with all our kit issue hanging from us! We were about to be tested on all the bumph the Military Training Wing had judiciously imparted, enabling the training staff to weigh up our battle skills and combat awareness. Tucker, me and our mates in 3Platoon had gotten a taste for the Field-craft taught to us in classroom and were now chomping on the bit to be deployed out in the open within Battle-formations; Cpl Hazel had primed us well.

The vehicles slipped out of the garrison unceremoniously and left behind the methodical layout of Spartan wooden buildings. All the sterility became absorbed by Hampshire woodland until eventually Martinique Barracks had blended in disregarded. It was not long before we were reacquainted with civilisation. Ten minutes down the road our small procession trundled along a vigilantly gritted snow cleared high street. The recent snowfall had begun thawing at some stage but had then iced up during the cold evenings permitting dissenting slivers of brown slush to cling disconsolately to the concrete kerbside. Our transport whizzed past a line of red brick houses, each abode was covered in trailing two tone green ivy which invaded the gutters and eaves of some buildings. This idyllic mosaic was rudely punctuated by a slab of aged concrete. The mossy rectangle bordered and clutched in chorus a makeshift municipal breeze block evangelical church, the planeness adorned with a white cross painted contritely above a green metal utility door. The gaudy and temporary nature of this minster was capped by a silver grey corrugated tin roof and an unnecessary galvanised spire; Prince Charles would be flabbergasted! As if aware of the insolent structural disharmony, the blemish had a piece of Graffiti scrawled on one of its walls above a blue stained window, a colourful slogan which read “THE TIN TABERNACLE”; whether this had been spray painted by a delinquent or affectionally applied by one of the congregation it leant the building the befitting imagery of a Salvador Dali conception.

We passed a clutch of black and white timber framed cottages, decorative hanging baskets of periwinkle and winter pansies were exhibited in their porch ways. I momentarily discerned how gay and colourful the real world appeared in comparison to the sombre military landscaping of Martinique Barracks, something inside me had stirred, I must have been having a funny turn. I had never felt so alive and as if awaking from a lifelong hibernation I also noticed snowdrops bursting defiantly through well-tended lawns to politely contrast the grimy grey concrete paths which hemmed them in. This observation alarmed me but then I thought of poor old Nelson Mandela, imprisoned on Robben Island since 1964. If Rolihlahla was ever released, would the enigmatic mythical troublemaker notice how much the outside world had changed since his imprisonment, or initially due to deprivation, would he simply drink in the sheer beauty and awe of nature? I snapped out of my musing as the engines spluttered; our fully laden vehicles laboured uphill and the noise rattled the windows of shiny glass fronted shops displaying fancy merchandise at enticing winter sale prices. Martin Flowers wolf-whistled at a tenacious young mother as she shoved a pushchair containing a chocolate eating child along an uneven pavement. Flattered at Martin’s crude amorous behaviour she craned her head and fluttered her heavily made up eyelids in response, and then blushing with embarrassment she clipped the leg of a dog-walking man who had the collar of his tanned sheepskin coat turned up against the bitter cold. The dog owner sneered reactively while his astute Golden Labrador sniffed inquisitively at the pink clothed child in the pram; the toddler’s chocolate smothered smile bubbled excitedly as she reached out a sticky hand to pat the dog. The dog licked her fingers hungrily, but on realising that there was no savoury treat in store it shunned the empty attention in favour of sniffing at the garments of an orderly queue standing patiently outside the post office. Deprived of pension money and in need of stamps, the inactive crocodile of wintery faces frowned grumpily. Other more energetic pedestrians went about their own personal business in oblivion; none of them paid any heed to the rufty-tufty cargo of soldiers in the passing Lorries. The shoppers seemed indifferent to the warriors' mission; military vehicles were common place and no concern of theirs. Tucker clocked me ogling ordinary people going about their everyday lives and smiled, likewise he never paid this much attention to his surroundings, not normally anyway, it felt good to observe. I was contemplating that until we had in fact completed our basic training we were still civilians much like them, or were we? As if reading my mind two old boys simultaneously waved at each other across the road and with knowing winks and nods they shot fond glances in the direction of the military vehicles, saluting us light-heartedly.

As fast as the trucks had entered the small town they petered out the other side, engines revving up through the gears as we departed. The packet of HGVs raced along A-roads, cautiously negotiating winding bends, dipping and weaving through Hampshire forest and out into sparse Surrey heath-land, completely disorientating us passengers. The journey was sedate until ultimately arriving at a clandestine destination. In the shadow of trees by the roadside a sign warned off unsolicited visitors. It was a standard MOD caution, disseminating fear and notifying the penalties imposed in consequence of trespass, archetypal of such secret installations as Menwith Hill or Portland Down, and tempting in enigmatic mystery!

The convoy veered off the main drag at this junction onto a vaporous forest dirt track, where one by one the trucks engaged four-wheel drive and laboriously hauled themselves through tall jungle pine. After a short time the tall verdant trees receded, shimmering in the vehicles wake like an organic emerald curtain drawn across the track to shut the convoy off from prying eyes. The noisy trucks crawled across shallow ditches and frozen peaty ruts, and then growling, ventured out onto an expanse of scrubby weatherworn heath land. The sun had not yet infiltrated the murky slate-coloured sky, but fortunately on preceding days its thermonuclear fusion had created sporadic heat rays strong enough to penetrate the northern hemisphere. The recent snowfall had begun to thaw away and had left the uncultivated landscape relatively hospitable, just a few strips of snow lurked insolently in the creases and shadows. The misty countryside was covered in a complex mosaic of gorse, heather, bracken, scrub and purple moor grass, with odd patches of sphagnum moss and lichens fighting for survival on the nutrient poor acidic soil. Three to four thousand years ago, before Stone-age-man had cleared away trees for grazing and cultivation, this land would have been covered by lush forest. The top-soil of that ancient development had now eroded and the land fallen apart. The only foliage remaining were a scattering of scraggly Silver-Birch and the odd Mountain-Ash, leaving the landscape looking very remote.

The trucks halted unexpectedly and the sound of quarrelling authoritative voices competed with one another above the dull lazy tick-over of the petrol engines. As an accompaniment, a bewildering resonance of hungry dog-barks floated down the line of vehicles too. We were ordered to sit tight and stay alert, but eager to get a glimpse at what was holding us up we scrambled and jostled each other out of the way. Tucker and I pushed at the seams of the canvas sides, exposing cracks to use as covert peep holes. Up ahead a hunt straddled the path, it was the full Monty, blokes on horseback clad in red tunics, black hats, full-length boots and cream riding britches. Riding crops and hunting horns hung loosely by their sides and a pack of braying Beagle-hounds encircled them, yelping, panting and slobbering. The hazy morning sun had stirred up a mist and the movements from the savage dogs caused this vapour to twirl and mingle with their panting exhalations. Dogs' legs and torsos were engulfed in whiffs of steam, lending them the appearance of basking sharks slicing through a whirling pool of smoky acid. Staff Sgt Mackintosh and Sgt McBride were out of the leading Land Rover conducting a heated discussion with the corporate bellied master of the hunt. The barking mayhem which ensued made it difficult to hear precisely what was being said, up until the Huntsman loudly cautioned the two senior NCOs to get back into their vehicle for safety. Apparently the dogs had not been fed for three days and the podgy sixty year old declared that he could not be held accountable for their behaviour. Clearly rattled, the huge Scott's Staff Sergeant demanded of him. 'Are ye threatening me Sir?'

'I'm merely offering you a warning, that's all chummy!' was the flippant reply.

'Sir this is MOD land yous're trespassing on, besides, the Stag-hunting season's concluded now surely?'

'Not quite!' the huntsman's frisky stallion shuffled uneasily, braying with irritation, eager to move on.

'Ach c'mon man. Autumn Stag's early August'til end of October, and Spring Stag's March to April, ye know that indisputably, and fox's are October to November and again March to April, so what are ye hoping to bag in January?'

The chestnut horse whinnied and snorted, and the old man glared indignantly. 'You certainly know your hunts Staff Sergeant, I commend you.'

'Aye, back home I was a Ghillie as a wane, so don't be bamboozling me!'

'Wouldn't dream of it. We're here for Hinds and Roe Bucks, perfectly legal I assure you.'

'Not on MOD property it isn't.'

'So too for that matter are Muntjac and Chinese Water Deer…' old John Peel patted the horses neck consolingly while blathering on regardless, '…neither of which have a statutory close season.'

Apparently when the Army are not playing war games on MOD land, the general public stray onto it and fowl it up with dog pooh and horse droppings. You can't blame them really, the MOD own some spectacular real-estate.

'What part of "you are trespassing" do ye not ken the meaning of?'

'Who's your commanding Officer?' demanded the fractious Hunt Master.

'None of your damn business mister, now clear off before I'm away for the poliss!'

'You have no idea who I am have you?'

'No sir I don't, so if you'll kindly excuse me I have an Exercise to conduct and you're delaying its progress. Will ye please vacate the area?'

'I am Colonel Harris-Tweed retired, and have express permission from my good friend Brigadier Miles-Fortitude to take my hunt across his training area.'

'Whatever Sir, I can't argue with rank, but if Brigadier Miles-Fortitude were here in person, he would relegate your hunt second place to this important Military Exercise. So if ye care to pursue the matter further would ye please contact our Training Major, Major Einstein, at Central Volunteer Head Quarters?'

'Now look here….'

'Sorry sir, orders are orders, rules and regulations, ye understand!'

Flabbergasted and clearly disgruntled, the corporeal posse, trailed by the pack of barking pursuit hounds, feverishly giddy-upped to pastures new for their blood sport.

'Muntjac and Chinese fucking Water Deer, who's he bloody kidding?' muttered the Staff Sergeant to no one in particular.

'Watch your back Mack, that stonner can banjax you,' advised Sgt McBride, nervously tugging at his right ear lobe. 'The big brass will bust yay if that bassa makes it an issue, remember shit rolls down hill so it does!'

'Fuck him paddy; roll your umbilical cord in, he's retired now. If ye let the old boy network ride all over ye, your life's not worth sixpence, besides,' S/Sgt Mackintosh tapped the side of his nose perceptively. 'I've been promised Company Sergeant Major when this wee stig is all over, no worries.'

'Whatever,' sighed Sgt McBride, shrugging his shoulders? He'd obviously seen bigger men than Malcolm Mackintosh given the bullet by the powers that be.

S/Sgt Mackintosh growled in the direction of the recruits' peeping eyes. 'What ye lot bleeding looking at? Get these shagging vehicles moovin.'

The exercise detail entered its final rendezvous and was ordered off the trucks, I was more than grateful; I was beginning to get a Kit-Kat arse from sitting too long on the slatted wooden seats. When formed up into platoons we were given our initial task, the digging of shell scrapes. Although much of the vast area comprised of sand or compact peat, the ground in the location chosen for excavation was adjacent to sand cliffs and much too hard to dig trenches without mechanical assistance, or so we thought!

'Shell scrapes will suffice for today lads but you will work on a trench tomorrow,' confidently assured Cpl Hazel. He was dressed in his combat fatigues and beret and resembled a life-sized Action-Man. 'Now listen in, any fool can be uncomfortable; all it takes to be warm, dry and happy in the field is a correct attitude and the determined application of some acquired knowledge - monkey see, monkey do? Right then, get yourself a hot meal and a brew on the go, and save all your empty cans, you're gonna need them should anyone try to bump us during the night!'

Once we had eaten some scran the perimeter of our position was booby trapped to form an early warning system. We did this by using lengths of green Para-cord with empty tin cans from our ration packs suspended along it in pairs. Cpl Hazel then paired us off and explained the correct way of applying camouflage cream to break up our features. The Al Jolson Kit was passed around and using the "Buddy-Buddy" system each pair applied cam cream to the others face. Unfortunately big Tish Hewitt collared Wingnut. 'Hey up flower, slap some of this muck on me kipper will ya. Don't ponce around ya faffing fairy, what you messing for? Right, my turn, let's show ya how it' s'posed be done!'

Like a face painter at a children's party, big Tish smeared cats' whiskers across Wingnut's cheeks and managed to daub the word "PUSSY" across his forehead without arousing any suspicion! 'Ya look proper animal now, go get'em tiger!'

Tug Wilson was just about to spill the beans but Cpl Hazel restrained him. The NCO rolled his eyes up to the heavens and tutted warily. 'He'll have to get switched on Tug; he's no fucking use to anyone if he doesn't work out what's going on around us for himself, he'll survive!'

Cpl Hazel shoved a box filled with Flash-eliminators at Tug and gestured with a nod and a jerk of his head that he wanted them sharing out; Tug issued each man with a piece of this kit to attach to the end of our SLR's. When firing blank rounds on exercise, this piece of kit eliminates the flash from the muzzle (so often enhanced in gangster movies for dramatic effect) by suppressing the gases in the barrel. The gas is diverted through a gas port below the barrel to the breach-block, simulating the blowback effect of a live round, this enables the chamber mechanism to eject the empty shell case and reload a fresh round of ammunition; hence Self Loading Rifle. The Flash-eliminator was painted bright yellow to assure the DS Staff that it was fitted correctly, if incorrectly fitted these eliminators had a tendency to get detached under the force of the charge and fly off like a self-propelled grenade. Being painted yellow gave the added advantage of spotting and retrieving the device from amidst the flora - Tucker was to lose his Flash-eliminator several times while out on exercise and I blew mine off once or twice too!

'Now a word of warning whilst out here on the training area,' barked Cpl Hazel. 'If you lose any items of kit, especially a magazine or God forbid your personal weapon, you must report it immediately to a member of staff. We don't want the IRA or some duffer from the dog-walking fraternity to find it on our behalf do we?'

The guidance was sound advice. 'Let's face it, we've got enough pony trekking nutters wandering around where they shouldn't be, as doubtless you saw earlier. Equally if you discover a discarded rifle or magazine innocently lying about the place, don't touch it, it might be booby-trapped and BANG there goes your fucking arm or leg!'

The instructor was deadly serious. ‘Remember when you arrived at Martinique barracks last week and the green slime put you in the picture in the classroom, yeh? Well I can tell you now gentlemen, the IRA are a real threat and should be treated as such because blowing peoples arms and legs off is right up their street, it’s what they’re bloody good at! I cannot emphasise this enough, please, please, please, keep your equipment safe and secure at all times; you don’t want to hand your guts to these opportunist bastards on a plate do you? No you fucking don’t!

Once we had secured the area and established 3Platoons’ stand-to positions and arcs of fire we were lead out into the open and given a session on movement in the field. We practiced the Monkey run and the Leopard crawl until we had got it off to a T while all the time looking for places that offered good cover. Once we had grasped movement by stealth, the I.A drills (immediate action) for taking cover were explained: run in a zigzag, drop down, roll away and crawl into cover, observe, set your sights and fire.

“TAKE COVER!” called out the instructor as we practiced the I.A drills over and over again until bruised black and blue and every muscle in our bodies ached. All that running around seemed to toughen us up a bit. There was a perceivable change in Wingnut too; he looked like a real warrior bastard, even with cats whiskers radiating across his cheeks and the word “PUSSY” daubed across his forehead. When we had first arrived at Martinique Barracks we had thought that Cpl Hazel, having just passed his Skill at Arms (SAA) course, was a barking mad knob-head out to impress everyone, but now all of us in the platoon recognised the instructor for the skilled soldier he actually was. The NCO proved to be a genuine bloody good bloke with a fountain of knowledge, it poured out of him effortlessly and the platoon were impressed by the wisdom he patiently passed on to us. We weren’t realistically expected to memorise every aspect at this stage but if something important did not sink in, he’d go over it again. There was no time to waste. When Cpl Hazel was satisfied that his lads were reasonably able to keep their heads down and identify the direction of attack, he moved straight on to the next element. In order to carry out section battle drills our platoon was formed up into eight-man sections, and then each section divided into two smaller four-man fire-teams for section formations. All the stuff which had been covered in theory by chalking it up on blackboards in the warmth of the classrooms was now practiced and honed; the six Battle drills consisting of: battle preparation, reaction to effective fire, location of the enemy, winning the fire-fight, attack, and finally, reorganisation.

‘Listen in, teamwork is essential, it gives the enemy someone else to shoot at besides you yourself! If the enemy is within range, so are you, so be very careful not to draw any enemy fire because if you do it will really irritate the rest of your section wont it?’ The lads laughed at the corporal’s humour.

‘Make the most of available cover,’ advised the instructor, ‘and remember the difference between concealment and cover; if I can get a glimpse of you so can the enemy! So let’s get switched on. The enemy only attacks on two occasions, when he’s ready and when you’re not!’ explained Cpl Hazel. ‘Having said this, the most difficult job during a fire-fight is trying to locate exactly where all the dick shit enemy fire is actually coming from? Once you have cracked that gentlemen, you can start winning the game by giving a fire control order, which should in theory get everyone in your section zapping away at the same piece of countryside – this especially applies to a cockeyed prick like you Mr Churchill, so take note yeh!.....’

Ronny Churchill put his thumb up reassuringly and Cpl Hazel continued, ‘.....this done, you can use every weapon you’ve got in your section to hose the enemy down to stop them putting effective fire down onto you and your mates. But don’t be content with just plugging away lads, it might not be enough in a real gun battle – you must include your lovely, lovely forty millimetre grenades and get on the radio to call in the mortars for back-up and stonk the buggers, yeh?’

‘Yes Staff!’ the platoon agreed in unison, the logic was infallible!

Sweaty and sore we were put through our paces, patrolling in sections and identifying enemy fire and getting into cover to return it; while all the time keeping a tally of how many rounds we had each fired so that once we’d found cover each man knew when to change magazines and not to get compromised by running out of ammo. Cpl Hazel pushed us relentlessly but eventually knocked us off for a brew and a rest. Then barely twenty minutes later had us back on our feet. This time we were merged with the other platoons for a demonstration and collectively introduced to the Shimulees (Whiz-Bangs). Cpl Hazel demonstrated the power that can be unleashed from these Shimulees by priming one for activation. He then placed it on the ground and covered it over with an old army issue combat helmet before retreating to a safe distance. BOOM!

The helmet rocketed a good 50 metres into space from the force.

'Right listen in, you do not want to muck about with one of these buggers, they can take your hand off quite easily! Cpl Hazel rummaged around in the undergrowth and retrieved the helmet. 'Look what it's done to this lid!'

All the recruits were in awe of the persuasive demonstration.

Before the day ended, Cpl Hazel advised us to knock up a hot meal and make the most of it because we were going tactical and it was the last chance of a brew until morning. Dusk tiptoed in, and to allow our eyesight to adjust to the darkness - and it was dark - we were stood-to in our defensive positions. It promised to be a long night as Cpl Hazel staked out two men on stag on the GPMG, rotating the pair for fresh ones every couple of hours. I soon discovered that there wasn't a lot to do other than rest if you were not keeping your eyes and ears peeled while manning the gun. The hours seemed to drag by, each hour the same as the last one, dark, secluded and in your face. I tried to sleep but rigor mortis had set in, the batteries on my insulating mat must have been faulty. I dozed off restlessly and then at 03.00 hours a heavy hand latched onto my shoulder startling me from a half sleep; it was Stan-the-Cab. He whispered gruffly. 'Corporal Hazel wants us; we're going on a night patrol!'

I gave Tucker a shake. Cpl Hazel woke the others up with a light prod from his size ten boot. 'Rise and shine gentlemen, we're going for a romantic moonlight stroll!'

There are no complicated facts or theories involved with movement by night, just stealth and vigilance. Dark landscapes play tricks on the mind and make the sixth sense jittery, especially when the body is working overtime. At 3 o'clock in the morning your brain is telling you to knock off and get some zeds but your section leader is threatening to kick your arse if you do so. To negotiate the open heath land and reach safe cover, Cpl Hazel's patrol used the Catwalk and Kitten crawl, then utilised the Ghost walk to weave our way through woods. The tour crossed icy ditches and rocky outcrops, then lead us diagonally across escalating ground and then up a prominence called "Hill 99". To eliminate any silhouette we skirted around the top and then tentatively felt for footholds in the dark as we traipsed back down the other side. We then scrambled up another hill 136 metres in height to find a trig point. On the next descent the path curved to the right for what seemed ages in the dark and then ascended until the patrol reached another prominence called Kettlebury Hill. From the top of it we could make out a flickering glow in the distance. Twenty five minutes later our route passed the source of the dim illumination where three members of the Directing Staff endeavoured to keep warm around the embers of a fading campfire. You could have heard a pin drop as our patrol crept past, apparently one of the DS Staff members did?

A scowling Scottish voice called out. 'We can hear ye, ya noisy bassa's!'

The next gradient was soft under foot and hindered our up to now splendid progress, but it was not long before we traipsed across another rocky outcrop, where one false step and any one of us could have lost our balance and stumbled, or clumsily kicked a stone and sent it clattering. We reached level ground and Corporal Hazel held up his hand to halt the patrol, the signal was relayed down the line. He then patted his head with his hand to signal the lads to close up on him and then circled his index finger at knee height to indicate we should gather around him. Like ghosts we furtively encircled the patrol leader and crouched down low in a huddle. Cpl Hazel retrieved a flashlight from his webbing which had a green filter fitted across the lens to diffuse the light. Regardless we still closed our good eye to save some night vision in case we were compromised. There was no danger of any of the green light escaping, not with Big Tish eclipsing our cluster like the Incredible Hulk. Cpl Hazel waved the dim beam at ground level and probed around, the luminance exposed some footprints in the loamy sand. The green light enhanced the imprints which were on the edge of the path. A quick glance at his Silva-compass indicated that their trajectory headed eastwards toward a heavily wooded area more or less in the same direction as our platoons' base location.

'Observation and experience lads,' the NCO whispered, 'see that footprint, jump boots, very sloppy!'

The instructor was aroused by the discovery but his dimly lit camouflaged face didn't appear apprehensive by his deduction, in fact his otherwise impassive features betrayed the inkling of a carnivorous smile. As he breathed his next sentence he sounded like he had a hard on. 'Listen in, it's possible the Para's have dropped by for a visit lads, eyes and ears everybody eyes and ears!'

As we slipped away I felt as if our movements were being watched, but if there was someone lurking in the dark our patrol never encountered them. When our platoon eventually returned to our base location we were totally chin strapped from silently creeping about in the dark. Tucker loosened his webbing to make himself more comfortable and eased his booted feet and legs into his maggot, the sleeping bag had his poncho clipped to it to form a basha. He then fished a green package from his rations pack and ripped it open and munched on a hard tack biscuit to replenish his energy levels, he then fully inserted himself into the basha and fell asleep instantaneously. I envied his ability to drop to sleep at the drop of a hat, I eased my cold aching body into my own basha and it was not long before I too was out for the count.

It seemed like no time at all before we were once more dragged from our slumbers.

"STAND-TO!"

I hate being disturbed in my sleep. Begrudgingly I scrambled out of the comparable warmth of my green maggot to help secure the area from a possible dawn raid; it was now half an hour before sunrise and frosty. The advent of daybreak experimented unenthusiastically along the rim of our new environment. The blushing sun emerged shyly, bleeding dim light into the dull grey horizon of the eastern sky; gradually it permitted my inexperienced scratchy eyeballs to focus on that obscure corner of hell. I had woken with a stiff neck. Tucker was hungry and grumpy, and just as we were settling down to keep an eye out for an enemy attack he was rudely jolted into life. He'd been munching on a Mars-Bar for an energy boost and somehow managed to bite the inside of his mouth. Tucker suppressed a yelp and for the next half hour dabbed his tongue at the swelling soreness. Served himself right, greedy bastard, if he'd shared half of his chocolate bar with me perhaps he wouldn't have maimed himself. I sniggered at his discomfort.

The sun eventually ripened on a cold dawn and once it had fully established itself our platoon was stood down. Shivering uncontrollably I half-filled one of my mess-tins with water and plopped an unopened can of bacon slice into it. I unpacked a small fire lighter called a Hexi-block which was used for cooking our scran, and placed it in the centre of a flimsy metal contraption that hinged open to support a mess-tin. My fingers were numb as I struck a wind-proof non-flammable safety match, it fizzled into life and the flare burnt my thumb. Having dropped the match I fumbled to light another to get the Hexi-burner on the go. My hands soon warmed up as the yellow and blue flames licked the sides of the pan; the sooty smoke blackened the metal with smut. As I stared into the flickering flames I went into a trance, I had a vision into the future foretelling me that it was going to take half an hour to clean the sooty grunge from my mess-tin. A slight stream of vapour started to rise into the frosty air and when the boiling bubbles had been winking away for some minutes I emptied half the liquid into my plastic field mug for a brew, saving the remainder for a wash and shave. Tucker and the rest of our platoon were doing exactly the same as me; to an onlooker it would have appeared orchestrated. I sipped at my mug of lukewarm instant and tried to warm my fingers sufficiently to open my breakfast with a tiny tin opener called a P38. This little tool was issued in compo rations along with chewing gum, safety matches and a few sheets of toilet paper which the Regulars fondly referred to as John Wayne, because it's rough, it's tough and takes no shit from nobody. The lads had all been issued with two ration packs each, one to be used on the day of distribution and one for reserve, which was stashed away in our backpacks in case we couldn't be re-supplied from the rear echelon. As it was, my backpack was already bulky enough with all the equipment I had to carry, so one rat-pack was broken up and dispersed amongst the rest of my kit to even it out a bit. Tish Hewitt had less to stash away than the rest of the platoon because he'd been continually munching on one of his rat-packs since leaving Martinique Barracks and was now eagerly eyeing up his reserve. He'd have eaten that one by now too if he hadn't retrieved his Butty-box from his Transit van before leaving the barracks and filling it up with sandwiches made from scraps of meat he'd scrounged at meal times. You burn up a lot of energy on exercise but there's more than enough calories crammed away in the rations to keep you going, however big Tish would no doubt disagree. Once I had gorged on bacon slice and hard tack biscuits I got my shit & shave out of the way as fast as I could, then packed up my equipment into my backpack ready for action. Thankfully my morale picked up immensely as soon as I had completed these few basic tasks and my head began to clear from the lack of sleep. The lads were restless. Each man was involved in his own mini workout, bending to touch their toes and stretching stiff limbs which had seized up after a cold night. It had not been easy sleeping rough. Lying upon cold earth trying to rack up some much needed zeds or standing around manning the GPMG had made it necessary to limb up and get some blood flowing around the body. Thankfully we didn't have to go on a three mile run but my limbs still needed some sort of exertion. Tucker heaved me up to my feet and we had a little wrestle to ease up our stiff joints and stretch our torsos. I sat back down on my backpack once sorted out and casually slurped the remainder of my coffee. I took this moment to look around at the lads in our platoon, their faces appeared tough, intelligent, dignified and slightly apprehensive at the prospect of being bumped by paratroopers. I had noticed a perceivable change in them all during the past ten days, from looking eager but unsure of themselves when they had first arrived, to now being more astute through steady arduous experience. They appeared reflective of what was occurring. Mind you, one or two still looked bewildered by it all.

Tucker must have been contemplating the same thoughts as me, he laughed out loud at their anxiety; he just couldn't help it. 'For fuck's sake, what's the worst that can happen?'

Quizzical smiles erupted in response, relieved that at least one of us was finding the potential raid humorous. We smiled at each other all the more when Wingnut returned from having a number two; he'd been on the bog quite a lot during the night. The boys had scrounged all of his Hard-tack biscuits from him and swapped them for fruit biscuits, similar to Garibaldi's in shape with tiny pieces of desiccated prunes and figs imbedded into them. Hard-tack biscuits or biscuits AB are made from a tasteless compressed cardboard like pastry designed to bung you up whilst out on exercise (AB either stands for alternative bread, annul blockage or arse busters!), and the alternative fruit biscuits are intended to do the complete opposite, loosen you up when you needed a dump.

Wingnut winced as he sat down on his webbing. 'If this keeps up I'll have to wedge a pine-cone up my frigging arse!'

'By heck Wingnut, thar'll absolutely love a treat like that!' laughed big Tish.

Martin Flowers added. 'Anyone want a Walnut-whip?'

The Cray brothers (Tom & Robby) crawled over on all fours, they had sneaked away from their platoon's position on 3Platoon's right flank to have a crafty chinwag with Tucker and Martin Flowers. Big mouth Robby called out. 'Oy oy. Thought we'd nip over for a smoker!'

Tom greeted Stan-the-Cab with a pat on the back. 'All right uncle, how's it going?'

Stan welcomed his fellow Londoners with a wink. 'Watcha.'

'Fuck me, what's that smell?' asked Tom, pinching the nostrils of his broken nose together between his fingers.

'It's Wingnut, he's got a rotty botty, proper gopping aint it?' triumphantly answered big Tish. 'He's just sneezed and farted at the same time and shit his pants!'

'Yeh he blew his brains out too by the look of him!' Stan-the-cab joked.

'Poor bleeder!' sympathised Robby disdainfully.

‘Not to worry, hey Wingnut,’ big Tish teased. ‘Soon have you all nice and clean when we lather you up in that communal shower back at Martinique Barracks, int that right lads!’

‘Ooh lovely,’ minced Martin Flowers. ‘Do you like baby oil?’

Spike the Biker added. ‘Don’t forget your loofer Wingnut!’

‘Fuck off you sad bastards!’ was the tormented reply as Whittling fumbled about in his backpack. ‘Thought I had a spare pair of shreddies in here. Hey Tish, when we get back to barracks, check that I’ve not left my underpants in your bed will you!’

‘Fook off banana dick!’ shuddered big Tish.

Whittling complained. ‘This army toilet paper is rubbish, I can’t get my arse clean with it!’

Stan the Cab asked. ‘What side are you using? The shiny side is for officers and the rough side is for squaddies!’

‘Tried both sides. It just smears shit all over my arse or else my fingers goes right through it like tissue paper!

Spike the biker said. ‘yep, that’s happened to me too. I poked my fingers through some once and they got all shitty and slipped and my hand got all squishy. My knuckles and thumb slid in right up until I was wrist deep with my whole fist inside.’

‘Oh for fuck sake, that’s disgusting.’ Stan the Cab baulked.

‘Suppose so. Anyway I got the sack. They’ve never let me work with kids or old people since!’

‘You’re sick mate!’

‘Here Stan, we’ve got a right pair of narners in our lot, Clive and Kieran, must’a been in the bleedin girl guides together.’ Robby crossed his eyes and wobbled his head from side to side like a lunatic. ‘Doing me crust in they are!’

Tom agreed. ‘Yeh, you wanna hear’ em boys, its all “You don’t wanna do it like that. Do it proper like this!” like we’re all effin useless or sumink.’

‘I tell ya, they’re really tearing the arse out of it. What them two benders don’t know about camping you could write on a mouse turd!’

‘We’ve only bimbled over here to give our lug-holes a rest. What you lot up to?’

‘Not much,’ shrugged Martin, ‘digging holes and playing silly buggers.’

‘We’ve been doing some of that shovel warfare too mate. Bit of a lark init?’

'Yeh init,' chuckled Tucker, mimicking the cockneys. It was a break to see some happy faces and have a grin.

Stan-the-Cab asked. 'Oy, you got the same ration packs we got?'

'Might have, what you got then?'

'All bloody A's aint we. It's unbelievable!'

'We've got B's and D's!'

'So who's got all the C's then?'

'I've heard that the C's are chicken curry?'

'You'd think they'd mix' em up a bit, would'nt'cha? Situation normal all fucked up!'

'Yeh, a proper cluster fuck!'

'I bet the instructors have bleeding nabbed'em all!'

'I heard that the chicken is as tough as old rope and that the curry tastes like baby pooh!'

'Don't care mate, properly out of order, missing me Ruby I am!'

'Pies and mash, Jellied Eels, lovely jublee!' Tucker mocked exaggeratedly in a Dick van Dyke voice.

'Fuck off you northern monkey.'

'Any you lads wanna swap?' asked Stan-the-Cab casually.

'Dunno mate, I bet you do though don'tcha?' replied Robby.

'Does the Pope shit in a wood?'

'Cost ya!'

'You're having a giraffe ain'tcha?'

'Oy, only joking Stan, don't get moody sunshine, me and me china will have a butchers later, see if we can get our Germans on any, OK?'

'Tastick!'

'Hey up lads, if you've got any fruit bickies going spare,' suggested Tish, 'giv'em to Wingnut here, he absolutely loves fruit, don't you cup cake?'

'Yeh, right up his Gary Glitter I bet!'

The joke was wearing a bit thin now but Wingnut's resilience was developing by the hour. His lips parted and his graveyard teeth erupted into a broad Cheshire-cat grin, fittingly enhanced by the cats whiskers daubed across his cheeks. The cartoon cat shook his head despairingly and gave Tish a petulant two finger salute. 'Up yours, bastard!'

Other than 3Platoon's unique repetition of eating an unvaried diet, all of Robby and Tom's experiences were identical. Cpl Hazel showed up to dampen our exuberant mood and chased Tom & Robby away. He then ordered our platoon to pack up our kit and get ready to bug out. We strapped our sleeping bag to the top of the backpack and lashed our Poncho and NBC suit to the bottom, then strapped the whole caboodle to our webbing. Once fully assembled this is known in the trade as Combat Equipment Full Order (CEFO), and since we were on military manoeuvres, we were expected to carry extra ammo too. Anyone unfortunate to be picked out to be part of the two man Gun crew (usually two big guys) was stuck with an LMG or GPMG and even more ammunition. It was beginning to feel that our platoon were no better than pack animals some of the time, but thankfully most of the weight could be discarded once we reached and got settled into a new location.

We Yomped for about half an hour across undulating ground following contours rather than being exposed out in the open, and once bugged in to our new position we set about digging shell scrapes and trenches again. The British Army trench is a pig to dig and requires a lot of effort, especially in winter when the ground is frozen solid. Modern infantry units now employ mechanical diggers to do the job, but on basic training we TA rookies as no doubt regular jar-heads, were expected to use elbow grease. Pick-Axes and folding Combat-Shovels were all we had to chip away at the iron earth, it was hot arduous stuff; we were only knocked off from the task to rotate the gun crew on the Gimpy which constantly guarded our position. This change over was a welcome respite from the laborious toil, it gave the lads a chance to communicate in whispers and compare how we were each holding up on our ordeal, but those periods of inactivity were fraught with the added problem of sweat freezing and chilling our bodies, causing our aching limbs to stiffen up once more.

Cpl Hazel had a remedy for that. For the next three hours our platoon was run ragged. We carried out reconnaissance patrols and flanking assaults to take out enemy positions, then covered the procedures involved in regrouping after a skirmish. Although we were a bit ropy at first it wasn't long before Cpl Hazel noticed natural leadership skills developing amongst some of the lads in his platoon, obviously Stan-the-Cab was a daddy and Big Tish had his weight to throw around too, but the small quiet lad called Diddy Baxter from Derbyshire surprised everybody as he blossomed into a quasi-Field Marshal. Tug Wilson was still piling up points by currying favour with his superior which meant that the likes of Rodger Boileiu

(Balloo) who was keeping his head down and Joe Ward from Spalding in Lincolnshire - the mild mannered lad with a cheeky grin who kept himself to himself - and a few other reclusive volunteers took a back seat. Tucker was willing to be tested by going one up to do some sole surveillance, but I like the others simply followed orders. I was tired; my mind was not working properly. It was far easier to be told what to do under duress than have to think for ourselves and that was precisely what Cpl Hazel was trying to instil at this stage of the game, the ability to carry out orders unquestionably and obediently, but Diddy Baxter and Tug Wilson seemed to be volunteering to lead the charge at every given possibility! Our instructor filed away mental notes of such enthusiasm as he revealed how to choose the best location to set up and carry out an ambush, plus the Immediate-Action drills should the platoon itself become ambushed. We were introduced to the Claymore anti-personnel mine and how best to utilise it - though for training purposes we weren't actually allowed to use a real mine, and ever the clown, Martin Flowers inevitably asked why not? Later on during an hour in the afternoon Cpl Hazel wiped the smile off Martin's face as we squeezed in some mind numbing N.B.C routines. We felt cut off from reality once dressed in our Noddy suits and respirators but were glad of the extra insulation that the Charcoal lined garments offered against the elements.

We were knocked off to get a hot scran on the go about mid-day, I was getting a bit sick of eating reconstituted food; I would have given anything for a pukka curry and a beer. Although they had little nutritional value the biscuits AB did actually bung you up if you ate enough of them, this was value enough since there were no portaloo's on the exercise area. So having no turdies to crap in meant that we had to dig a small hole when we needed to crouch down and clean our shoes. We then covered our Richard the 3rd over with loose soil and camouflaged it with grass and dead leaves so as not to leave a trace, hoping that nobody would be unfortunate enough to have to dig a shell scrape in that location over the coming days! We quickly discovered that the knack to crapping in the field was to squat whilst gripping our rifle, minding we didn't urinate all over our kecks, while somehow maintaining our balance so as not to topple back into our fresh number two's. Tucker was convinced that we should be awarded some sort of a badge for achieving this! Our rifle had to go everywhere that we went; we slept with it, ate with it, washed with it and crapped with it, and woe betides anyone who misplaced it! Sgt McBride's party trick was to roam around the training area looking for unattended weapons, then discretely lifting them and scurrying away to the Directing Staff (DS) Truck and hiding the weapon away. Consequently a few recruits went to pieces on discovering the loss of their rifle. When the poor sods reported it, the DS play-acted it up for all their worth, then made the hapless victim scour the area for half an hour. The threat of a Court Martial was thrown in for good measure, reducing some almost to tears. There was an instance where one rookie from our platoon lost his rifle and unhooked (borrowed) another weapon as replacement, claiming it for his own. Unfortunately for the miscreant, all the serial numbers on the breach mechanisms had been logged prior to the exercise, and for this deception, Staff Sgt Mackintosh gave the soft bugger an all-mighty bollocking for shitting on one of his own platoon comrades.

Subsequently, Cpl Hazel went ballistic too. 'Count yourself lucky the RSM aint here cos he'd tear you into little pieces and use you for toilet paper. I told you if you are going to be a bastard, don't be a silly bastard! What do I have to do, write it on a piece of fucking paper and nail it to your fucking forehead?'

The lad in question was a bit of a weasel, you know the sort, holds themselves back, only joins in if they have to, won't go out of their way to volunteer or help, and if need be, only do enough to look busy, a slack bladder! Cpl Hazel had had this lad in his sights from the beginning though, it was obvious by the way the instructor laid into him.

'Did you perceive that we would not check any genuine loss of weapon or are you so tired of living you don't give a flying fuck? You're a liability, a selfish jack; you're as much use as a snooze button on a smoke alarm!'

All the instructors were firm but fair on matters of discipline and having been truly shamed in front of the entire recruit course for being a cad and bounder, the little shit was ordered to perform fifty Star-bursts in full kit, but collapsed utterly exhausted after doing just twenty three. No cajoling could budge the offender from his flagging prone position, but the shock from the antagonistic DS staff grabbing hold of his webbing and hauling him up to his feet must have revived him. 'Listen in shit for brains; you haven't got time for a kip. On your feet and get fell in.'

After lunch we were shown how to set up a trip flare - potentially dangerous stuff in inexperienced hands. Cpl Hazel lead our platoon along a path and drew our attention to two green metal prongs which were strategically positioned either side of the track. He emphasised that normally the prongs would be camouflaged behind a bush or tree. Having revealed the position of the prongs, he then led us off into another clearing to form up with the other platoons. We all fanned out in a semi-circle and sat on our webbing for a tool-box talk. Two identical prongs had been inserted for demonstration purposes and a flare device secured onto one of the prongs. Cpl Hazel paid out a length of near invisible cord which he attached to the other spike. A bucket of water was on stand-by should the demonstration go askew.

'Remember your First Aid training,' he prompted. 'This flare is filled with phosphorus which burns on exposure to air, so subsequently, if this goes a bit Tango Uniform - tits up - and I get some of it on my hand, I will calmly utter that notorious macho pleasantry "Oops a fucking daisy" then plunge my smouldering limb into the nearest bucket of water where I will remove the offending pieces of phosphorus with a twig. Whatever you do numb nuts; don't use your fucking fingers. Believe me, shit does happen, so hopefully you are beginning to see the importance of all that classroom drill we've been drumming into you. Keep all your shit in one sock and you'll be safe, it's not all tosh; it might save your life one day!'

Carefully he crawled forward on his belly, gripped the safety pin in his left hand, tentatively rolled to his right so that his back was to the device, and then eased the pin out gently. 'Don't on any account throw away this pin; they only do that in American movies to look big and hard, if you do it you'll look stupid. If nobody has set this bitch off while you're bugged into your location at night, some unlucky bar-steward will have to crawl out of his basha the following day and make safe by performing the reverse of this tricky procedure, so you need to retain the fucking pin don't you!'

A look of mild terror was etched on Cpl Hazel's face as he duly re-inserted the pin. The rest of the NCOs had gathered round and looked pensively concerned, but their body language communicated that they were glad it wasn't them undertaking the procedure. If someone was to have shouted "BANG" for a laugh at that moment I can guarantee that Cpl Hazel would have shit a brick. He stood up gingerly and dusted the frozen sand from the front of his tunic, and then took a step forward with his arms outstretched theatrically like an amateur illusionist and made a dramatic "Da-dahr" noise.

Everybody clapped at Cpl Hazel's bravado and he shrugged and smiled inanely and gave the best Tommy Cooper impersonation ever witnessed. 'Haa haa haa, just like that, thank you very much.'

He cut his audience off mid-clap by sliding his right hand palm-down across his throat in a slicing motion. 'For demonstration purposes only, I will now repeat the procedure!'

He returned to the trip flare and furtively inched his body forward to remove the safety pin once more, and in a trembling voice declared. 'This isn't Squaddie-proof yet!'

Once the pin was re-removed Cpl Hazel withdrew to a safe distance using animatedly large strides, while Sgt Royce dramatically stepped forward from some bushes and emulated a patrol as seen in the TV series Dad's Army. He blundered against the tripwire and fell arse over tit, calling out, "OOOOPS!"

WHOOSH! A Rocket flew into the cold grey air and exploded high above, then a bright light slowly drifted back to earth suspended by a parachute; a second demonstration was convened for nightfall to fully illustrate the brilliance of the flair which converts night into day! Things became decidedly interesting when we were taught how to arm, aim, fire, and navigate the Milan anti-Tank missile across undulating ground until it hit its target; beneficial if a tank takes cover behind dead ground.

We had been in the field for roughly thirty six hours when Shaggy and Scooby-Doo put in an appearance. Desperately trying to focus our concentration against the effects of fatigue was a battle in itself, but the arrival of the Training Major and his great big dog, both being chauffeured around by the RSM, had an electrifying jolt on the recruit's morale. However, that enhancement evaporated as soon as Major Einstein engaged in verbal intercourse.

'My training-staff tell me that you are exceeding their expectations. In fact you are showing great promise. First rate, very well done. Now let's look at the bigger picture here.' He pontificated like a Calvinistic Bible basher. 'British soldiers are the most revered throughout the world. Just remember that one day you might be called upon to fight for democracy, and if you carry out your tasks correctly you should be able to overcome any mission undaunted. This can only be achieved by the sheer benefit British Army training instils within you. Hopefully after a battle, a sea of sewage and dead opposition may be against you, and as the intensive establishment of a new tribal group emerges… Blah blah blahdy blah…'

Tucker raised his eyebrows and shrugged. I looked around at my comrades and clocked their dirty disconsolate faces; each of them expressed a look of mild indifference. After running around for 36 hours we were all brain dead, our minds were fogged up, we were past the point of caring. None of us needed the grand speech so the words glided over our heads with the merest comprehension.

'….and a resounding operational success inevitably will be conceded I think you will all agree!'' concluded the overzealous Major.

I thought that the commanding officer talked a good fight but I was beginning to doubt his leadership skills, in my semi-stupor the OC now resembled the Wizard of Oz, all smoke and mirrors. Surely we were being trained up to become hairy arsed soldiers, not combat philosophers! The Major eventually wound up his eloquent tub thumping oratory at which point big Tish made me and Tucker crease up in stitches by quietly asking in a dour voice out of the side of his mouth. 'How was it for you darling?'

On the Training Major's command the platoons were force-marched for half an hour in CEFO (Combat equipment full order). I monged the rest of the day. My mind went into shut down, my body barely going through the motions. The rest of the lads were no better, the instructors had to shout and beast us about to keep us on our toes. We eventually arrived at a prominence on the edges of the Training area called Gold Hill. Once the tor had been secured and lookouts posted all about, we got a hot cuppa-soup on the go and warmed up tins of scran on the Hexi-burners to nourish our flagging spirits.

Big Tish slumped down into a squatting position, pulled out his plastic butty-box and munched on a mottled green stale curly sandwich as a starter while his main meal heated through. 'I'm fooking paggered. I could just polish off a big plate of roast beef and Yorkshire puds right now, with a few crispy fried wantons thrown in as well!'

'A plate of steaming hot new Cheshire potatoes with a knob of best butter!' Tucker licked his dehydrated lips at the thought.

'Grilled cheese on toast with sliced tomatoes!' I salivated.

'How about thee then Wingnut you perverted sod?' Big Tish extracted the piss. 'Chucky eggs and soldiers is it or a mouthful of fat greasy Cumberland sausage?'

Wingnut shook his head good naturedly and replied. 'Yum fucking yum!'

Was big Tish a latent homosexual I wondered? The rest of the group in turn conjured up some tormenting delicious salivating fantasies, each trying to outdo the other.

'Fuck me, my Dannie's are nithered!' Tish Hewitt fumbled with cold fingers to pick at the knots in his boot laces, loosened them, then eased off his soggy right boot and peeled back a steaming smelly sock to examine his bleached white foot; the skin had the consistency of a dried prune. He had the early stages of trench foot which he dried and powdered with talcum, before plunging the pampered foot back into a fresh dry sock and lacing the boot back up.

'My dogs are barking too!' added Stan-the-cab lethargically.

'Flipping heck, I daren't look at other,' Tish was having a right good grumble and didn't want to be out grumbled by Stan; 'cos I know it's got blisters on fettling blisters.'

Tish unwound his left puttee and unsecured the lace of the other boot. 'Just hope I'm all right for work on Monday fookin morning is all!'

By dusk every single one of us was ready to jack it all in but managed to bolster each other up with the knowledge that at best, End-Ex was only fifteen hours away, at worst twenty tops. Tucker had packed up smoking on New-Year's Day and ever since had been full of praise for maintaining self-discipline and improving his fitness. However, Spike the Biker smoked like a chimney and it was to him that Tucker desperately turned to for the scrounging of a roll-up. Tucker screwed up the weed and sheet of gossamer paper between his cold index fingers and thumbs, licked the gummed edge, then ignited the crude cigarette and inhaled intoxicating fumes deep into his lungs; you could see from his expression that the hit from the nicotine was instant. His brain must have felt soothed and his nerves less jangled as he slowly exhaled a long stream of smoke. The satisfaction was slightly marred by loose shreds of tobacco stinging his parched lips, but that didn't particularly bother him, he just spat to dislodge them, in fact from that moment on Tucker couldn't give a damn about anything. Well he wasn't giving a damn up until Cpl Hazel moseyed over and conveyed some grave news. We could expect to be bumped sometime during the night, probably by a squadron of Paratroopers, so we should be extra vigilant. Apparently the Para's had been given orders to capture and interrogate us; ergo 3platoons' counter orders were to repel those forces as diligently as possible and win the fire-fight.

‘Shit, Paratroopers,’ coughed Spike the Biker apprehensively. ‘We’re barely out of short fucking pants?’

‘Complete and utter bleeding animals!’ added Big Tish. He wiped his snotty nose on the sleeve of his mud caked combat jacket. ‘What the fook, I’m up for some of that!’

The rest of us looked at Tish with scepticism. Cpl Hazel studied our downtrodden faces and in a dour voice proclaimed. ‘We aint here to hug trees you know, buck up and switch the fuck on!’

Tucker finished his smoke and flicked the dog-end away dismissively. I knew how he felt, we all knew how he felt, none of us relished the prospect of sitting on our bony-arses all nightlong in the freezing cold just to get caught by those Para’ animals - sod that for a lark! We rotated the watch and those not on stag crawled into our Maggots to catch some zeds. At one point during the night I somehow managed to roll a good ten yards downhill without even waking up. The rest of the platoon slept in fits and starts, but one bloke it never bothered was Wingnut. He could be heard snoring for miles around and was subsequently ordered by Cpl Hazel to wear his NBC respirator to muffle the din; why hadn’t any of us thought of that idea when we were trying to get some kip back at Martinique barracks? Me and Tucker drew the short straw to man the Gimpy at five in the morning, the rest of the section were allowed a lie in until half an hour before first light at which time the jammy sods were quietly roused and ordered to Stand-to!

Right on cue the enemy forces bumped us; it was the day of reckoning. The fire-fight was intense with added oomph from Shimulees, whiz-bangs and lots of smoke grenades - it resembled Beirut out there! Cpl Hazel tried to rally his troops. ‘Cheer up, it could be worse!’

So we cheered up and it did get worse. Our platoon seemed to be over-run, no matter how much we tried to zap our attackers. We were consequently ordered to fall back from our position on the hill to regroup on lower ground, which didn’t make any sense to me, seeing how we held the higher ground! But what was my opinion worth?

The bangs and explosions intensified and smoke drifted across the training area. Having regrouped 3platoon carried out a mock count for dead and wounded to establish our company strength, then executed an ammunition check. Whilst estimating our potency the other platoons appeared from all the mêlée and went to ground on our flanks. They too went to town establishing their own weaknesses and strength. The DS decided that none of the platoons now possessed enough ammunition to carry out another sustained fire-fight, so an order for a tactical withdrawal was issued. The British Army never retreats; it honourably makes a Tactical Withdrawal.

The NCOs divided the platoons into two flanks, spreading us out in an extended line so that we could fire controlled bursts at the pursuing enemy, who incidentally seemed to be advancing like lunatics. Under no circumstance were we to be harpooned (captured) by our adversaries; that option meant that we would likely get roughed up for a bit of fun. Bolocks to that! To harass and disorientate the hunting force smoke grenades were discharged, and then at the blow of a whistle the left hand flank withdrew, whilst the right flank gave covering fire. Once the left flank had withdrawn fifty metres or so they went to ground and opened fire, covering the right flank's extraction. With loud bangs and booms going off all around us this operation was repeated until we had all reached safe cover on the far side of the open heath land. This location was known as Lions Mouth. From there the platoons scarpered down a dirt path and didn't stop until we had all been legging it for a good fifteen minutes. Tucker was still lumbered with the Gimpy while I in his wake struggled with the ammo box, my slur (SLR) and the rest of my bloody kit. I laughed and shrugged when Tucker asked me. 'How the hell did I end up carrying this heavy fucker, do you want a go?'

'Yeh, like fuck I do! I've got this heavy bastard, hang on to it mate you might need it!'

After traipsing across Westbrook Moor we scurried up Yagden Hill and then picked our way down the other side of it until we came to a fork in a path where we were ordered to go to ground in a defensive position. Glad of a rest we fanned out in all round defence under cover of a crop of Silver Birch trees, interlacing our feet like a giant cartwheel for silent communication. My heart banged like a trip hammer in my chest, my breathing was laboured. Tucker to my left and the lads to the right of me had sweaty green & black streaked faces, so I imagined that I must have looked pretty much the same. Everyone was panting uncontrollably, in effect it took a good seven to eight minutes to properly wrestle our breathing under some degree of control, and even then pulses still throbbed from pumping burning lactic acid through to the aching muscles of our legs. I felt physically sick. Cpl Hazel tried raising our spirits by assuring us. 'It's only pain!'

Yeh sure! When it became apparent that we were no longer being pursued by maniacs, the DS staff ordered us to form up onto the right hand track of the forked path and then informed us that we were now on the final stage of the exercise. Yippee! This briefing suggested that what merely remained to be done was reach a pick up point where we would all be extracted from. The six-figure map reference given indicated that the FRV (Final Rendezvous) was a mile away. The troops were advised to reach that location within the next ten minutes otherwise the transport would leave without us and we would therefore have to trudge back to Martinique Barracks in a forced march. Sod that! Tucker slung the Gimpy over his shoulder to balance out the heaviness, but it jarred the side of his head and neck as he loped forward. He had always been able to find a reserve of strength in such situations, he'd learnt the hard way by competing in various track events at school; I remembered his first major test of running, it had been in a fifteen thousand metre race where he had set off ahead of the pack like a hare chased by hounds but was lapped by the other competitors when his strength was spent after one lap around the track. He thought that he had learnt from this, so the next year he had entered for the sprint, but just wasn't fast enough to gain a winning place; so he had gained knowledge of how to pace himself and with practice he won the next year's five thousand metre event! I and our other mates were very proud of his achievement; he could accomplish anything if he set his mind to it. For now, although hampered with the section Gun, he still managed with great effort to keep up with the leading man and reach the extraction point in second place. I loped after him trying to stay on his shirt tails. Nothing else mattered to him, nothing at all, nothing but staying focused and sticking right behind the leader. Disappointingly it was all a ruse when we reached our coordinate. Major Einstein and RSM John Daniels were stood at the mouth of a clearing on the left of the track ready to greet the first of the runners with a clipboard and pen; the Major's great Mastiff roamed about in the background vainly sniffing around for Scooby-snacks.

'Name and number?' casually enquired the Major in his soft Scottish brogue.

'Two double five six,' gasped Martin, 'three eight four nine, Flowers sir.'

Tucker needed a few seconds to breathe before he could reply. 'Two, huh, huh, double, huh, five, huh, six, huh, huh, huh, three six, glug, huh, nine six, Tuckhurrrr sir!'

I could not breathe; what saliva I could produce would not slide down my parched throat, it cloyed and caused me to wretch. I merely pointed at my name on the clip board and the major nodded understandingly. RSM Daniels marked us down in pole position then congratulated and directed us to the back of a truck where a folding table had been set up and laid out with scoff to feed us. A green tea urn and several loaves of sliced white bread were stacked on the trestles alongside a big pan of all in stew. Togged up in a black beret, combat fatigues and an enigmatic smile, head-slop-jockey Odd-job was on hand to dish up the steaming hot grub. Tucker could not stifle a mad chuckle at the sight of him. 'Look at him in his cabbage suit!'

'He'd really suit a Bowler hat much better!' Martin Flowers smirked.

'Go on lads, have a good chuckle, you've earned it!' encouraged the cook, completely misreading Tucker and Martin's mirth as he dislodged a ladle of sticky stew into each of their mess tins; his misinterpretation cracked them up even more.

'Mad men!' the RSM commented to the Major.

Looking around to see what all the commotion was, the commanding officer shook his head lamentably and agreed. 'Aye, where do we get them from these days?'

I was still trying to catch my breath when the rest of the troops hot-footed it in to be marked off on the clipboard. I didn't want to be relegated to the back of the meal queue after making such an effort so I joined Tucker and Flowers. With our mess tins full we quickly set about stuffing our ravenous faces with Odd job's epicure stew. All-in-stew has the consistency of half set concrete and while making it, anything that the cabbage commandos can find hanging around the kitchen which has not been nailed down gets lobbed in too. Besides the intended stewing steak, carrots and spuds, it is surprising what other ingredients can be found: Pork chops, chicken nuggets, beef burgers, even bits of black pudding, sausages and left over beans from breakfast; it all goes into a properly prepared pan of stew to bulk it out a bit - any soldier will tell you, you will eat anything on exercise.

As the incoming troops scoffed on the scran and swilled it all down with hot sweet tea, the sound of running feet thumped into earshot with someone at the rear calling out the timing.

'Eft, ight, eft, ight, eft, ight, eft - LEFT WHEEL!'

A Squadron of Troopers doubled in and came to a halt; I correctly surmised that these lads were the enemy force who'd put in the dawn attack against our defensive position on Gold hill at daybreak. Their average height was five foot five inches and they were mean-looking bastards, every single one of them. They were neither Parachute Regiment, nor Nepalese Ghurkhas - who were this elite band of warriors? No less than the local ACF (Army Cadet Force) and they stood ganged together like a mob of young Gorilla rebels, triumphant at our surprised expressions.

‘Fuck me, they’re only kids!’ croaked tired Tish Hewitt, incredulously.

With a twinkle in his Celtic eyes, Major Einstein bimbled over and addressed us in his sage bagpipe drone. ‘Ah now, you look crestfallen lads, don’t be. Down the ages the British Tom has won many battles against insurmountable odds, using no more than pure nerve and a pinch of cunning guile. We told you to expect the worst and in doing so our deception completely fazed you. Today gentlemen you have learnt a valuable lesson in astuteness, “We don’t need more strength or more ability or greater opportunity. What we need, is to use what we have!” – Basil. S. Walsh.’

Chapter 13

In the sky above the barracks a low slung colossal heavy metal cloud scraped hazardously across the buildings as if attached to the underside of an industrial conveyer belt in a scrap metal merchant's yard. Rude northerly gusts disturbed crumbling leaves from their wintery deathbeds, spitefully sweeping them upwards into the blue grey ice laden firmament. Over on the far side of the parade square, in a bid to get the show on the road and intensify this turbulent scene, a brass band overenthusiastically warmed up their weapons of mass disruption. Vulgar parp parp parps and the odd bump-bump from a big Bass-drum punctured a wail of brassy screeches and rasping squeals. Once the band had become more orchestrated, the dead leaves, twigs and other sullen rusty remnants of a long vanished autumn seemed to dance acrobatically to random military tunes; it was too blowy for sheet music so the instrumentalists simply improvised.

On the last days of any Holiday there is often a reluctance to pack up and go home, and that's just how Tucker felt, now that he had discovered something that he was rather good at; the day before he'd confided in me that he did not want it to end. I myself on the other hand, seeing how I had only tagged along for a bit of a laugh, was relieved that our basic training was nearly over; fifteen days had been more than enough for me. We stood awkwardly at ease watching the assembly, now at long last dressed in the number two's and red & black peaked caps which for the past two weeks had hung enticingly in our lockers. The TA, mores the pity, no longer gets issued with the smart brown uniform worn for parades.

On Cpl Hazel's suggestion, the conniving NCO had taken our tunics into town to get them professionally pressed at a cost of £1.50 per head. Tucker, me and a few other platoon mates had thought that our creases could not be further improved upon, but the corporal insisted that the garments needed a final special tweaking. None of us could discern any significant modification when the instructor returned the costumes; probably another of his NCO money making scams!

We recruits were not the only thing dressed up. The harmonious inversions of the chords the band now played were lovingly clothed in stable consonance and unstable dissonance, the quavers and semi-quavers were designed to both soothe and excite our weary spirits. Bizarrely as the jingles ricocheted and clashed against the surrounding wooden buildings they became haphazard, and the timbre of the brassy resonance curiously developed the impetus of a clapped out fairground Wurlitzer. Having a humungous hangover didn't help matters either!

When we had first arrived at Martinique Barracks, the prospect of two weeks devoid of nipping down the pub for a pint, or placing a bet on a gee-gee, or even watching a bit of TV in the evening had seemed unendurable, but by the morning of the passing out parade we had become inured to all of that culture. In anticipation of an early dispersal, our platoon had already crammed full our long green canvass holdalls. They were stuffed with muddy combats, scratchy woollen shirts, sweaty P.E. kit, minging underwear, smelly socks, and spare hobnail boots. Me and Tucker had worked out how best to pack the rest of our kit away. The 58 pattern webbing was unassembled and crammed into a back-pack which would be carried over the shoulder, and all the other acquired sundry bits and pieces were attentively inserted into our suitcases, leaving just enough space to stash away the uniform we were standing up in on this final parade. How the hell we were eventually going to cart all this kit home would be an ordeal in itself!

Tish Hewitt had scrounged everybody's left over rations during the last few hours on Exercise, even broken biscuits and buckshee boiled sweets (Boilies) were hungrily hoovered up. The stores had already taken back all the kit they had loaned the recruits, and in lieu of soggy bedding, those poor sods unfortunate to have mingled weak bladders with copious jars of ale during the end-of-course piss up were duly taxed for replacement mattresses. As a small farewell gesture, Odd-job had not been parsimonious with the breakfast scran; without doubt that man understood how a well administered greasy fry-up could heal a reveller marinated in alcohol. In a bid to ease a massive hangover we had each wolfed down a mountaineers breakfast and gulped a litre of tonsil varnish too, but seeing how we couldn't chinf off during the imminent ceremony to drain our spuds, we now wished that we hadn't drank quite so much diuretic fluid.

While the band launched into Grieg's Elegiac melody No2, I studied the incredibly burnished toecaps of my footwear; they were the shiniest they had ever been. On more than one occasion Cpl Hazel had resignedly shook his head in woeful disbelief at my efforts at bulling boots. "You shit sucking tool; you must have the wrong sort of spit!"

As he had so often done while we had grown up together Tucker once more bailed me out, he was a wizard with a couple of one-on and one-off bristled shoe shine brushes and a can of Kiwi shoe polish, plus cotton wool, water and a pair of ladies tights; it had merely taken him an hour to turn my heals and toes into something like glass mirrors!

Whittling had had some difficulty with his boots also; some persuasive bastard had assured him that covering his new boots in thick polish and setting light to them would burn all the rough bobbles out of the leather and make them smoother and easier to work on. Consequently poor old Wingnut had had to put twice as much effort into sorting out the aftermath; Tucker had helped *him* too!

Pensively waiting to march onto the parade square in my shiny best boots I entertained a flashback to the previous evening. After returning from exercise all of us cavemen had shaved and washed away the clammy odour of tramp sweat, and then scrubbed our grotty finger nails and brushed our teeth thoroughly before changing into fresh clothing and moseying over to the rugby club. Even though we were all thoroughly knackered from our recent exertions, we were equally excited to be finishing on a high note. Odd-Job had knocked up an exotic curry and there were plenty of pies and sandwiches to munch on too, but more significantly the bar was stocked with gallons of amber refreshment.

As soon as the training staff had polished off a few jars of ale, they had let their hair down and we soon realised what a thoroughly good mob these instructors actually were. The NCO's elaborated on how some regiments of the British Army, traditionally on passing out, presented new soldiers with a pint tankard filled with a cocktail mixture of spirits, urine, beer, and Baileys; this concoction could even include a fresh turd floating around like a Cadbury's flake, to be drunk in one go, pips and all! Providently the TA recruit course initiation ceremony simply entailed getting plastered and under no circumstance leaving the bash until the senior NCO had passed out drunk. We reverently endeavoured to implement the spiking of the senior instructor's drinks, but this must have been another of the NCOs practical jokes because Staff Sergeant Mackintosh seemed blissfully unaware of such a stipulation.

S/Sgt Mackintosh slowly lost the ability to speak, closely followed by the uncoordinated function of his legs, but before collapsing, he prompted each recruit to take a turn on the floor to tell a joke, and it had to be our best joke. There were a few natural comedians who had everybody wetting their pants, but some of the more egotistical performers tried to hog the floor and consequently got booed off for doing so.

Sgt McBride was not customarily a funny man but gave a side-splitting rendition of a selection of servicemen going to the ablutions for a crap. As props, he placed a toilet roll and chair in the centre of the room, he then stepped back waiting for silence. Starting with the RAF, he walked to an imaginary door, quaintly opened it, stepped nimbly in, dropped his trolleys, plopped himself down and proceeded to comb his hair while doing the business. When finished, he took one piece of toilet paper and screwed it around in his backside as if he was cleaning out one of his ear holes, inspected it, then discarded the tissue and flushed it away. Stepping out of the bog, he picked a speck of dust from off the lapel of his tunic and straightened his tie.

The Royal Navy were up next. With bowed knees, reminiscent of pop-eye the sailor man, Sgt McBride swaggered up to the door, kicked it open, strode in, dropped his kecks and began masturbating while he had a crap. He then lit a cigarette, reeled off yards of bog roll, gave his knob a wipe, and with the same bundle of toilet tissue wiped his arse. He then hauled up his pants and smiled inanely as he flicked his fag end into the bowl, then stepped out of the toilet without flushing it.

This comic genius had the entire room pissing ourselves with laughter as finally it was the turn of the British Squaddie. Sgt McBride, enacted something along the lines of Changing the Guard at Buckingham Palace, by marching smartly up to the door and shouting "Halt", then raising his right leg to chest height he slammed his foot to the floor while screaming like a banshee, '123 - 1.' He opened the door, stepped smartly into the lavatory and closed it briskly behind him calling out the timing '123–1', and then did an about turn, dropped his kecks and sat down on the lavatory '123-1.' He went red in the face and his eyes bulged out of their sockets as he squeezed the cheeks of his backside together and bawled out the timing, '123 – 123 – 123 – 1.'

He reached around and snapped off an imaginary turd, measured it with his pace stick, measured one arm's length of toilet paper, tore it off precisely, wrapped the turd up and placed it with fussy precision into the bowl, '123', '123,' with another precise length of toilet paper he wiped his backside up and down, side to side, and round and round, '123 – 123 – 123 – 1.'

After discarding the tissue, he stood up, '123,' pulled up his trolleys, '123,' came to attention, '123', and about turned, '123-1', saluted and flushed the toilet, '123 –1,' then did an exaggerated about turn, opened the door, stepped out and checked himself. 'Steady now. Quick march, eft, rye, eft, rye, eft, rye, efttt!"

There wasn't a dry eye in the house and after more beers the Mil Training Staff mercilessly took the piss out of everybody on the course, exposing individuals who had been responsible for giant fuck ups and mimicking quirky character traits and shortcomings with nefarious precision. So as not to feel hard done by, the recruits were cordially invited to return the gesture and each member of the training staff was impersonated, one by one, with such exactitude that some instructors got the hump! However this teasing was short-lived, the training staff reaped more revenge by dishing out character assessments - or more implicitly, character assassinations in the way that only British NCOs can do!

As I braced myself against the bitter cold breeze shrieking across the parade ground, I had difficulty recalling all of them, after all I'd been tired and more than slightly drunk towards the end of the evening, but the gist of it went something like this: -

As reported. - The truth.

Single minded and uncompromising. - Pig-headed and obstinate.

Capable of very original thought. - Crackpot – Should be locked up!

Resourceful. - Ignores all procedures and rules.

Dynamic. - Uncontrollable.

Does well in view of his poor health. - A natural malingerer.

A born leader. - Can't keep his nose out of everybody else's business.

Keen awareness of modern military problems. - A stirrer & barrack room lawyer.

Rarely makes mistakes. - Rarely does anything!

Has a relaxed non-flappable attitude. - Lazy & half asleep.

Keeps me personally up to date with his progress. - A born creeper.

A perfectionist who attends to detail. - A nit-picking idiot.

Forthright. - Bloody rude.

Delegates well. - Passes the buck – will go far!

Is developing combat awareness. - I have at last got this through his thick skull.

Needs the minimum of supervision. - Resents all NCOs and has put 3 in hospital.

Is now ready for promotion. - Somebody please take him off my hands.

For all that I could remember it had been a bloody good night; but pulling me out of my reverie and back to the cuds of Hampshire, the RSM's bark brought me and the entire parade to order. The Regimental Sergeant Major called for Tish Hewitt to take up the position of right hand marker for the passing out parade, and Tish duly obliged.

At top centre of the square, a visiting officer and his entourage were seated on a dais in preparation to receiving the recruit courses' first salute on the march. The officer was a Staff Officer, often referred to as a Geranium by regular soldiers because of the red band around his cap and the red tabs on his collars. The families and friends of those recruits who were fortunate to live within travelling distance of Martinique barracks sat on either side of this party of officials. My thoughts turned to my own family and friends, I wouldn't have bothered any of them to come and see me. I turned my attention to Tucker standing shoulder to shoulder by my side; this had been one of many adventures we had shared growing up together. We were both young and free for the moment with nothing but dreams to fulfil. He had always agreed not to get married until we were old and good for nothing; we saw it as a noble pursuit. Looking at him now I could see the light in his eyes was fading, he looked detached, preoccupied, no doubt he was thinking about his ex-girlfriend Sarah again; he had talked quite a bit about her during lulls in training. He'd have been more than glad to see her face in the crowd over by the dignitaries as he passed by swanking in a formation with his new mates. There was so much he wanted to tell her; he missed her and knew in his heart that he wanted to patch their relationship up and make a new start. In joining the TA he had created an escape, but for all the space he'd acquired by creating it he now felt strangely empty without her, she made him feel whole. Sarah knew him better than any other girl, he was certain of that. I didn't like to meddle in other people's personal relationships but knowing the situation between them both I simply advised that it could work if they tried, they just had to get it right, let each other breathe. And judging by the letter Sarah had sent him the previous week, she'd realised the exact same thing, but then again she *had* been preparing him for a shock?

On return to barracks from the exercise, Cpl Hazel had dished out mail delivered since the recruits had been away. There was another letter for Tucker. He had read it with foreboding, then remorse and disparagement, and then guilt, happiness and hope in that order; Oops, Sarah was pregnant!

It had knocked the wind right out of his sails; he thought that she had been on the pill, what was she playing at? Was it just a mind game; she was good at that sort of thing but surely not so cruel. Was he really going to be a father? I know that he now regretted not wearing a condom, but he hated them, too clinical. He did however regret not responding to Sarah's earlier letter the week before, he had invented the justification that he was too busy with all the running around he was doing. That was a load of old tosh, Jennings had managed to scribble a few lines to his lover hadn't he? Tucker had stubbornly dismissed writing a reply; he had thought it was too late for atonement, and shrugged as he told me that you win some you lose some, there were plenty more fish in the sea, not worth crying over spilt milk. I said yeh ok then, don't be a soppy sod, let it go, it's her loss not yours, get over it!

But for all the bravado he had mustered, I could see that Tucker had learnt a valuable lesson from all of this. He'd said that deep down it had dawned on him that for all the space he needed he shouldn't ostracise himself. I agreed and to bolster him up a little I muttered some rubbish about building walls and how when walls collapse they crush you, proper country & western bollocks! I should have said something funnier or took the piss out of him to make him bounce back, but I knew better, he wanted to be alone with his thoughts on this one. Sarah's pregnancy news had sent his head reeling, but at least being away from the situation had given him a new bearing on life. Joining this recruit course had regenerated him morally and he now felt like he could overcome any challenge, even the arrival of a child (he did not yet know it but he and Sarah would go on to have another four children together). Recently up until this moment his world had begun to expand but it was now in danger of shrivelling up! Tucker's luck had always been that way, waxing and waning; his whole life was one big challenge, why was there so much yin & yang in it?

I'd often told him that life is just like that, don't let any of the shit define who you are!

A large Union flag flapped lively in the stiff cold breeze out on the parade square, its lanyard relentlessly twanging like a huge rubber band against the flagpole. "Ching ching ching ching… yin, yang yin."

While we had been playing soldiers in the wilds of Surrey cut off from the real world, China had invaded North Vietnam, and Ayatollah Khomeini, overthrowing Mohammad Reza Shah Pahlavi, had seized power in Iran. Also whilst we had been jostled around insecurely in the backs of ancient army trucks, the compulsory wearing of seatbelts had been debated in parliament and would become law in one week's time; seatbelts were to be obligatorily fitted to all British cars by 1983. When 3Platoon had been out under the stars on night manoeuvres it had snowed in the Sahara Desert for the first time in thirty years, and the planet Pluto had moved inside Neptune's orbit for the first time since either sphere had been known to science. Being unable to pick up Radio One on the army radio frequency the recruits were unaware that Meatloaf's Bat out of hell, and Queen's Don't stop me now, were trailing in the charts to Blondie, who were at number one with Heart of glass. The lads were not in a state of total ignorance though, the buzz around barracks concerned the biggest news event of that week, Britain's first £1m football transfer deal had taken place; England forward, Trevor Francis, had signed up for Brian Clough's Nottingham Forest side!

Big Tish Hewitt took up position on the right hand marker spot; he looked forlorn as he waited for the rest of the recruits to join him out on the bracing blustery Square. This parade was the culmination of our training and I couldn't help reflecting upon the tremendous pace of life the last two weeks had fostered upon us. The one single element of the course which none of the lads had enjoyed was the CS-Gas chamber, where prior to being released we had each had to remove respirators and call out our name, rank and number, then escape the cloying choking teargas, eyes burning and nose streaming with snot, throat scorched and lungs coughing, to retch our guts up outside. As recruits we had had our identities broken down, almost to the point where nothing remained but individual character and resolve. We had been pushed to our physical limits and overloaded with technical jargon and practical information, in the hope that some of it would seep through and carry forward into our forthcoming military future. The regular soldier at that time received six months basic training, which only went to show the skill of the Military Training Wing in comprehensively indoctrinating TA recruits in just fifteen days. I and my platoon mates had behaved like vulnerable small boys at times, not knowing what to do until we were put under pressure, and subsequently releasing some of that pent up stress with childish pranks during what little free time we had. But looking back now it had been cobs of fun, there had been moments during the fortnight when Tucker and I had thought we would not make it, but our new comrades had bolstered us up, as indeed we in turn had likewise done for them. We were now young men bristling with pride at this achievement; we had given it a damn good go and succeeded. Not for the first time I realised that these lads were some of the best I had ever met and eagerly anticipated further encounters on upcoming fortnight's away. We were like brothers. Tucker felt the same way. Corporal Hazel had grown on both of us, and the rest of the lads of 3Platoon too; he'd treated us all as incompetent two-hats on arrival but as soon as he had taken us under his wing, as *his* platoon, he had changed. He knew that if he continued to treat us like incompetent two-hats we would just switch off and behave like incompetent two-hats, he hadn't done that, he'd treated us like adults and we had behaved like adults. Ultimately he knew that we were volunteers, and inevitably that some of us had seen a bit more of life than him and that we could very quickly spot a bull shitter. Even when we had occasionally messed up he did not lose his cool, he kept it professional; he had been gruff but concerned, like a reluctant older brother left in charge of siblings during school holidays!

'LISTEN IN,' demanded the RSM. 'RECRUIT COURSE, NUMBER ONE THREE FIVE, HAT TEN SHUNN. RECRUIT COURSE, ONE THREE FIVE, GET ON PARRAYYYDE!'

Bearing our gleaming rifles at shoulder arms, the platoons moved forward in unison and took up position on the square. The Razzman did his stuff. 'IN OPEN ORDER, RIGHT DRESS.'

The front rank moved two paces forward and the rear rank two paces backwards, leaving the centre rank to stay put. The platoon instructors straightened the ranks out with miniscule commands such as, 'Number two, move forward, STOP. Number four, move back, STOP. STAND STILL THE FRONT RANK.'

The centre rank was quicker to sort out. 'STAND STILL THE CENTRE RANK.'

Similar directions were repeated at the rear rank, there was a bit of shuffling around, then the order. 'STAND STILL THE REAR RANK.'

RSM Daniels saluted the senior officer and then bawled into his face. 'PARADE READY FOR YOUR INSPECTION SIR!'

The pompous flag waving theatrics got underway and in the background the armed forces band played Rondo from Mozart's Horn Concerto No4. Brigadier Miles-Fortitude, paced up and down the assembled ranks accompanied by Bert Einstein the training Major. In the course of this ceremonial trumpet blowing and bashing of drums, the pair of officers finally approached our platoon. Cpl Hazel introduced the head honcho to each of his recruits individually and in return we responded by calling out our name, rank and number. When the Brigadier had completed his inspection of the entire parade he courteously saluted, tweaked his silver senior officer's moustache and waffled delightedly to the RSM. 'Good turnout J.D. - absolutely spot on, very well done!'

The band reached a crescendo with a crash of symbols as the Brigadier bimbled back to the dais whilst securing his hat in place with his left hand to stop it blowing away. During the ensuing lull the Badge (RSM) closed the ranks up into platoon formation, and then from a standing position put the platoons through their paces by having us demonstrate to the audience the entire British Army Rifle Drill. I felt very much like a member of the New

Zealand All-Blacks rugby team when they do the Hokey-Cokey thing before a Rugger match. "Shoulder arms… port arms… order arms… slope arms…"

Marching skills were next; the band struck up once more and the parade was handed back to Major Einstein. He clutched a Wilkinson military sword in front of him at chest height as he lead the parade back and forth across God's acre to the tune of, March from Le Coq de Or by Rimsky Korsakov. We gave it bags of swank, pounding the Parade Square like a highly polished machine. The visitors were greatly impressed. Photographic flashbulbs burst excitedly while we manoeuvred to Rimsky's good old marching tune. The formation executed all the movements laid out in the drill manual and we pneumatically bashed our lovingly polished boots upon the tarmac. Absurdly the reflective surfaces of our toecaps cracked like vermicelli; all that hard work spent bulling them up night after night was woeful.

When the platoons were eventually brought to a halt, each and every rank was evenly spaced - all that hard work at perfecting symmetry had paid off nicely! Over the Tannoy system, Brigadier Miles-Fortitude gave us all an effective speech regarding human adaptability and endeavour, some of the verbiage was snatched away by gusts of wind before reaching our ears. The Brigadier then called forward certain individuals whose exemplifying performance during the course of the fortnight had merited acclaim, such as winner of the Steeple chase, and best Marks-man on the ranges. Each frontrunner in turn was ceremoniously presented with an award, then photographed for the annuals of regimental posterity and amply applauded by all in attendance. Wingnut who had been so self-centred at the beginning of the course was now congratulated for emerging from his egotistical shell and becoming more gregarious, and in recognition of being the most improved recruit he was presented with a pewter letter opener in the shape of a miniature sword. Tom Lloyd, one of the Cockney rebels who were chummy with Tucker, looked shocked to hear his name called out, he was presented with a Stable-belt for being runner up best recruit on the course. As luck would have it Tucker was called out next to be awarded with a miniature pewter figurine of a soldier for being the best course recruit. He also accepted a silver trophy on behalf of us all in 3platoon for winning the recruit course competition! I was really chuffed for him. There were three cheers of hip-hip hooray, and then sour faced Staff Sergeant Mackintosh passed an envelope to Cpl Hazel containing the winnings from a wager (£10 each) set up between the

NCOs. The instructor's face lit up and a smile cracked his features as he winked at us; up until that point we had thought that Corporal Hazel was incapable of smiling.

For the grand finale the platoons were marched past the visitors and dignitaries to the tune of Lilly Bolero, a tune dating from the English civil war and later appropriated by Henry Purcell.

The RSM called out the order, "SALUTING ON THE MARCH – EYES RIGHT!"

Brigadier Miles-Fortitude acknowledged the grand gesture and returned the salutation. We were left-wheeled and returned to our original positions and given our final order. "Officer on parade; FALL OUT!"

That was it, Cpl Hazel had had his pound of flesh and in doing so won a wager, making him a very happy man and enabling him to spoil his wife & kids before he set off on his intrepid adventure to Alaska. He'd done his best; his lads had duly passed basic training as fully paid up members of HRH Queen Elizabeth the 2nd's fighting forces - God save her majesty. And as for me and Tucker, best mates and nonidentical twin brothers, we were now brothers-in-arms too!

Made in the USA
Monee, IL
18 August 2020

37879488R00132